PRETENDERS TO THE THRONE

PRETENDERS TO THE THRONE

A Cautionary Tale

To the folks @ Westminster Winter Park

Bill Amend
February, 2015

A Novel by

William J C Amend, Jr.

To order additional copies of this book, contact:
Xlibris LLC
1-888-795-4274
www.Xlibris.com
Orders@Xlibris.com
636710

DEDICATION

Pretenders to the Throne is dedicated to my dear wife, Connie, who has been lovingly instrumental and helpful during the writing process, as well as tremendously encouraging toward 'our' project. I also would like to thank the near-decade long support of our four children, Bill, Rich, Nicole and Mark and their families.

ACKNOWLEDGEMENTS

I relied heavily on the expertise and editing skill of Mr. Peter Stine, an Amherst College classmate. Peter gave the original text much more clarity and style. I would also like to thank Richard and Priscilla Roberts for their careful reading and suggestions, and to Madeline Amend for her cover design.

For historical references, I was pleased to primarily use these books (authors).

Founding Brothers, The Revolutionary Generation (Joseph Ellis)
Setting the World Ablaze (John Ferling)
1775, A Good Year for Revolution (Kevin Phillips)
Washington, A Life (Ron Chernow)
Washington Walked Here (Mollie Somerville)
Cincinnatus, George Washington & The Enlightenment, Images of Power in Early America (Garry Wills)
George Washington's Mount Vernon (Official Guidebook, Mount Vernon Ladies' Association of the Union)
Alexander Hamilton (Ron Chernow)
John Adams (David McCullough)
Decision in Philadelphia, The Constitutional Convention of 1787 (Christopher Collier and James Lincoln Collier)
The Summer of 1787, The Men Who Invented The Constitution (David O. Stewart)
We The People, Great Documents of the American Nation (Jerome B. Agel, ed.)
Roads from Gettysburg (John W. Schildt)

Frontispiece

When I pen fact – it often seems fiction

When I compose fiction – it may become fact

Chinese Proverb
8th Century
Author Unknown

Note to the Reader:

Many of the historical characters in Part 1 were, in-fact, real persons but are placed in fictional contexts and circumstances within the novel. The other characters throughout the book are purely fictional and can be found in the *List of Fictional Characters*.

Any references to actual people or events are intended to be read as fiction.

Some of the various documents, maps, and genealogies described in the text have additionally been placed at the end of the book in a section titled: "Information Booklet."

List of Fictional Characters – The Beginnings, Part 1 (1755 – 1968)

Sarah Washington – Lawrence and Anne Washington's last surviving child. When she is two years old, she seemingly dies from an attempt on her life but miraculously recovers.

Priscilla Farris-Fairfax – Sarah Washington's assumed name after being secretly adopted by her true-life mother, Anne Fairfax.

    ---- *Jonathan Winfield* – Priscilla's husband; former manager of Colonel Fairfax's estate of Belvoir. The couple was gifted Woodlawn, later renamed Woodlawn Mills.

    ---- *Polly, Charlotte* and *Franklin* – their children. *Aubrey* Winfield – their fourth child; died mysteriously.

    ---- *Colonel Eugene Winfield* – fourth generation descendant of Lawrence Washington and third generation of Priscilla Winfield. Civil War casualty; died at Manassas, Virginia, 1861.

        ---- *Richard Winfield* – his son. Takes his mother and the remaining Winfield family to Maryland for the duration of the Civil War.

Seamus McIntyre – Irish-American overseer at the Belvoir estate for Colonel Fairfax.

8th Lord of Aplington – member of King George III of England's Privy Council.

Alfred Adams – professor; second-generation descendant of John Adams.

Later in 1968:

Robert Hamilton – descendant of Alexander Hamilton

Langdon Eccles – descendant of John Adams

Sir Edmund Farrington (13th Lord of Aplington) – descendant of the 8th Lord of Aplington

Patrice du Motier – descendant of Marquis de Lafayette

List of Fictional Characters – The Eagle Flies, Part 2 (2004-2019)

The Ascension, Part 3 (2019-2021)

David Winfield – CEO Eurit, military defense contractor, lives at Woodlawn
Mills. Scion of the House of Washington, direct descendant of Lawrence
Washington.
  ---- *Suzanne Winfield* – his wife, Associate Professor of Political Science at
  Georgetown. Docent at Mount Vernon.
    ---- *Caroline, Jeffrey, Bobby* – their children.
  ---- *Admiral Thomas Winfield (Ret.) and Nancy Winfield* – David's parents.
  ---- *Marilyn Ashford* – David's sister, lives in Connecticut.
  ---- *Sara Claridge* – Suzanne's mother afflicted with cancer.
  ---- *Harrison Claridge*, playwright, and *Lisa Sargent* – Suzanne's siblings.
Anthony Drumin – President of the United States (2004).
Richard (Dick) Buchanan – Vice-President of the United States (2004).

In 2018-2021, the leaders of PATRI (name of each person's ancestor):

Evan Hamilton* (Alexander Hamilton) CEO First Federal Bank, NYC; lives in
Westchester County, NY.
  * designated as PATRI's concierge, the holder of the keys.
  ---- *Robert Hamilton* – his father (noted in Part 1), now deceased.
  ---- *Francesca Hamilton* – his wife.
    ---- *Everett Hamilton* – his son.
Philip Lee Mason* (Henry Lee, later Robert Lee) – Army General in charge of the
defense of the District of Columbia with a special strike-force known as
DOSECOF; stationed at Fort Marshall, Maryland.
  * designated as PATRI's guardian of the House of Washington-Winfield.
  ---- *Betsy Mason* – his wife. They are longtime social friends of the
  Winfields.

Gayle Eccles* (John Adams) – Dean of Faculty at Bowdoin College; a widow.
 *designated as PATRI's organizer and administrator.
 ---- *Langdon Eccles* – her father (noted in Part 1), now deceased.

Other PATRI members in 2018-2021:

Ed Finch (Henry Knox) – civil service worker at the Department of Navy, has multiple contacts at the Pentagon, an Annapolis graduate.
 ---- *Bill Finch* – his son, graduate student in computer engineering at MIT.
Leone Gutierrez (Gouverneur Morris) – housewife in Bronx; 3 children.
Karen York (John Jay) – businesswoman in Chicago. Divorced; now lesbian with one child.
Maureen Nightbird-Reynolds (Benjamin Franklin; Frederick Reynolds) – biologist with NOAA in Alaska; single 26 year-old. Her father died while on an expedition. Her mother is a member of the Yakahima tribe.
Connie Marshall-Rubin (John Marshall) – married lawyer. Has an MBA; a renowned merger analyst from Cleveland.
Katherine (Katy) Blitz (Pierre L'Enfant) – Associate Curator in charge of Art Procurement, National Gallery, Washington, D.C.
Ronald Putney Greene (Nathanial Greene) – General in Air Force; NSA Director.
Nicholas Shippen (William Shippen) – lives in Kansas City. CEO of his family's agricultural conglomerate.
Diane Fleming-James (Robert Morris) – Federal Reserve Governor in Denver.
 ---- *Dr. Avery James* – her husband; an Afro-American plastic surgeon.
Robert Laurens (John Laurens) – CEO of Energy Resources; Houston
Denise Donasti (Philip Schuyler) – former Broadway actress; now managing her large family property in upstate New York along the Hudson River.
Gerald Schubert (William North for Baron von Steuben) – young boy being raised by his mother's family. His father died in an accident, but had left a trust in a designated safe deposit box. In it, he stipulated that there was 'a special inheritance' of membership in a society, for his son.

The leaders of the Europe League in 2018-2021:

Francis du Motier* (Lafayette) Lives in France; has various industrial interests; is the French liaison to the World Bank.

*designated as concierge of the Europe League.

---- *Patrice du Motier* – his father (noted in Part 1), now deceased.

Hugh Rochan (Colonel George Fairfax) – Single; handsome 69 year-old Global media mogul, owner of Manor Media. Residences in London, Dubai, and Newport Beach. Two ex-wives and his children work in his various entertainment enterprises.

Philippe Rouen (House of Rouen; M. Talleyrand) – works in a financial netherworld. His family lives in a chateau near Lausanne, Switzerland. He has many multinational companies; developed the Twin Oaks Mall in Northern Virginia.

Sir Ronald Farrington* – the 14th Lord of Aplington (the 8th Lord of Aplington) – member of the House of Lords and Privy Council. Preserves the connection to the English throne and the other European royal families to ensure support for the PACT signed in 1795.

* designated as the organizer and administrator of the Europe League.

---- *Sir Edmund Farrington* – his father (noted in Part 1), now deceased.

Other Europe League members and their former Royal Houses:

Maria dela Caves – newly married with 1 small child. Spanish royalty of Navarre from the House of Bourbon. Dauphine Louis Charles signed the PACT in 1795 representing her family.

Elina Romanov-Pederson –ex-model who is the illegitimate daughter of a prince, mother of three from St. Petersburg. Descendant of Catherine the Great, Catherine II of the House of the Romanovs.

Olga Frederickson –current Queen of Sweden descendant of King Gustav III of the House of Holstein-Gottorp.

Eric Stahlen –member of the Reichstag with interest in foreign affairs. He is a descendant of the Prussian House of Hohenzollern, King Frederick William II.

Marcello Bonapiento – Italian playboy descended from King Charles Emmanuel of the House of Bourbon.

Catherine Bonard – a sculptor. She and her author husband live near Versailles. She is a seventh generation descendant of King Louis XVI and the House of Bourbon.

Other Important Characters:

John Madison — 44 year-old columnist, blogger and Associate Editor for the *Washington Post*. Divorcee with no children. He is a direct descendant of James Madison; owns the longtime family property of Montpelier in western Virginia.

Patrick Jefferson — 35 year-old, single; professor of agricultural sciences at Southern Illinois University. On academic leave as a first term Democratic Congressman, 12th district, Illinois. A tall, auburn-haired descendant of Thomas Jefferson.

Holly Rhyne — 26 year-old administrative assistant to US Senator from Kentucky. Girlfriend of Patrick Jefferson.

Cary McAllister — co-owner of Holly's condominium. Virgin Airline flight attendant.

Fred Breining — lobbyist and tavern buddy of Madison's at the Fox's Glen.

---- *Georgianne Breining* — his wife. Docent with Suzanne Winfield at Mount Vernon.

Janet Melone — 28 year-old attractive TV newscaster who becomes Manor Media's prime news anchor in New York.

Fred Rodgers — Investigative reporter for Manor Media.

Bryan Schupak — Investigative reporter for Manor Media.

Judy McIntyre — PBS news anchor in Washington, "The McIntyre Report."

Roland Peters — Political Consultant (ex-Republican), Washington, D.C.

Sheila Linden — Political Consultant (ex-Democrat), Washington, D.C.

Sidney Rosenthal — Political Consultant (Independent), New York City.

Victor Marino and Hildy Baker — day-to-day campaign managers for the American Federalist Party.

Senator Doren Winchester — Republican candidate for President (2020)-Texas.

Governor Joseph Martinez — Democratic candidate for President (2020)-California.

Judge Wier — retired judge acting as Pro Tem president of Pennsylvania's Electoral College election in December 2020.

Julia Minor — Democratic Speaker of the House (2021) from California.

William Snyder — outgoing Vice-President; the Pro Tem President of the Senate/House for the Special Legislative Election (January 2021)

Mrs. Walters — longstanding clerk of the House of Representatives.

President Foster Henson — outgoing President (2021). He is a one-term Republican; diagnosed in early 2020 with ALS, "Lou Gehrig's Disease"; did not seek reelection.

Tom ("Buckeye") Moore — Republican House Minority Leader (2020) from Ohio.

Gina Pinelli — Woman in an illicit relationship with Representative Tom Moore.

Richard Thompson — Republican wins the Senate election making him the new Vice-President in January 2021.

Ellie Rosenfeld — Democrat VP Candidate (2020) who loses Senate VP-election.

PROLOGUE

Woodlawn Mills

2021

"Gee Suze', I didn't realize when I was growing up and studying American history that we would end up being such a part of that history."

"It's pretty obvious that we both didn't have a clue, love, but I always knew that you were more than special, Davey – it's in your nature. I suspect that many Americans will now be better off knowing who you are, as well."

David Winfield suggested to his wife, Suzanne, "Let's take a walk over there." He pointed to the cupola of the neighboring home of Mount Vernon and squeezed her hand. "After all, that's where it started. It will be good to visit it again."

PART 1

The Beginnings

The wolf shall live with the lamb,
The leopard shall lie down with the kid,
The calf and the lion and
*   The fatling together*
And a little child shall lead them.

Isaiah 11:6

1

Mount Vernon along the Patowmack

September 1752

"Aieee . . . ow yee! Momma . . . help!"

The little girl curled up into a tight ball and clutched her stomach. Soon, she began to foam at the mouth. The frightened two-year-old stared wide-eyed at her mother. Spasms contorted her drenched body until at last she tossed about like a rag doll and mercifully sank into a coma.

George Washington, Anne Washington and her own Fairfax family from neighboring Belvoir took turns keeping vigil in a first-floor bedroom of Mount Vernon. Washington remembered that he had promised his older half-brother Lawrence, as he lay dying only months before, that he would be a surrogate father for his and Anne's surviving child, their daughter. And now it had come to this. Sarah seemingly going, too – before her life had a chance to take much hold.

After watching for any signs of improvement, the family gathered two nights later at her bedside. They and the house servants were distressed that her frail body had become inexorably weaker since the past day. The child's pale face seemed finally at rest as flickering shadows danced on her cold, moist brow. Little Sarah appeared to take a last shallow breath and slumped deeper into the bed's thick linens. Standing in the shadows behind her mother and family, Washington was thankful that at least his brother had been spared the agony of seeing his remaining child's death.

Dr. Caldwell, the Fairfax family's doctor, had administered different cathartics and strong purgatives in a vain attempt to alter the unusual illness that racked Sarah's body. As the child grew weaker in spite of his various remedies, the physician of physick concluded that it was likely not a case of contagion. After all, he could note that the little girl had had no fevers or rash, nor had any other house contacts become ill. The signs he had observed seemed to suggest a chance of her being poisoned. On the possibility that there might be additional plots against others on their plantations, Dr. Caldwell kept his suspicions known only to Washington, his sister-in-law, her father Colonel Fairfax, and their closest friends, George William Fairfax and his wife, Sally Cary Fairfax.

As the little girl lay dying that night, the five anguished relatives faced the eventuality and made necessary burial plans. The good Scottish doctor proposed that after the child died, the Fairfax and Washington families would need to develop some sort of counter-strategy to ensure their own safety. The others agreed. They had already suffered the deaths of three Washington children over the previous four years, and now were facing another . . . the last of Lawrence Washington's children.

George Washington admonished everyone as they stood silently in the candlelit room, "I do not want to know who among us is to be next."

The day after Sarah's apparent death, the five stood alone with the child's body wrapped within an open crypt in the family burial vault. The monument nestled along a sloping trail leading down from Anne's Mount Vernon home. On that unseasonably chilly September day, fog rising off the nearby Patowmack partly obscured the near bank of the river.

Earlier, Reuben and another slave had carefully fashioned a small stone crypt placed on a rise along the Old Tomb's dank inner walls. The family physician told the workers to take special caution in case the small body was contaminated. Her burial site was set down next to a larger one, that of Lawrence Washington. Three smaller aboveground crypts lay in a row opposite. On a shelf above, George Washington saw Anne's porcelain memory box next to his brother's favorite saddle.

Softly nodding in anguish, the elder Colonel Fairfax leaned against the heavy oaken door and silently held his daughter's hand as she wept, burrowing her face in her other hand.

During the interment ritual, Washington hesitated as he looked down at his tiny niece. "Was that not a flicker of her eyelids?" he thought aloud. "It could not be! There are no exhaled mists in the air above her as there are in the breaths of the rest of us." Taking a metallic mirror from his coat, he held it to the little child's pale lips. In so doing, he thought he could barely discern faint smudges on the piece but he could not be sure.

He whispered, "Did the rest of you see?"

The other three men in the tomb spoke out:

"Was it possible?"

"I say – oh my! While we stand here, let's figure out what we should do now."

"Hold on, now, she might . . . might still be barely alive. Perhaps, Dr. Caldwell, I do not know . . ."

His weeping sister-in-law half-collapsed onto the mossy gravel and said in a gravelly voice, "I have had so much . . . let me be!"

Washington and Anne's father, Colonel Fairfax, were barely able to calm her. Her little Sarah continued to lie unmoving in the open, lined casket.

With a firmness that surprised even him, George Washington said from the shadows, "Let us not be so sure that the little one here has quite given up the ghost until three days have passed. The worst horror to be imagined would be too hasty a burial! If Sarah is dead, as she by most measures appears to be, please allow me the next few days to settle my own concerns. Maybe they are my own fears and no one else's, but . . ."

There was only an awkward silence. The women were so emotionally paralyzed that he had to physically arouse them so that they could hear his sketchy proposal.

"I favor, Anne and you others, that we first take Sarah to a place of safety and treat her much as we have been doing for the past days – as if she were alive." Washington mopped his brow. "If she has no hunger or thirst, and if she is indeed quiet from death and at eternal rest, then we will only have had the burden of prolonging our own grief. Then, I suppose, it will be an even sadder day for us all to return here and bury the child a second time But how much sadder, indeed tragic, if we take no hesitation and instead, in our despair, err and bury her alive."

George Washington read the awkward silence as a sort of numbed acceptance by the others. "We should remain quite circumspect in all matters," he continued. "If by some aid of providence, she is still alive and this fact was known, there is likely a real chance of a second, more determined assault on the child. Perhaps this is the concern Dr. Caldwell expressed when he brought up his suspicion of poisoning. He said, did he not, that we should all 'make a counterplot.' "

After two in the party barely nodded their assents, Washington abruptly encouraged the others, saying, "Come now then, let us carefully secret her away."

Several Fairfax house servants accompanied by Colonel Fairfax carried Sarah's body out of the vault. It was wrapped in a thick cotton sheet and they made their way quietly through the backwoods along Dogue Creek. Upon arriving at Fairfax's Belvoir mansion, they carefully laid her in a private room where trusted servant women attended her.

Meanwhile, difficult as it had been, George Washington took charge and encouraged the three others to stay in place. He and Reuben wrapped some straw in linen and placed the fabricated shroud in the emptied casket. They then earnestly made ready for a faux funeral. Shortly thereafter, the saddened family and a scattering of estate workers stood about as Reverend McAndrews of Christ Church gave a brief prayer outside the family tomb before the casket was sealed and put in place.

Following the cleric's litany, the grieving family somberly returned to the mansion's main sitting room where they talked quietly together. To all else at Mount Vernon, it appeared that lil' Miss Sarah had been given a proper burial.

Throughout the day, Anne Washington was overwhelmed. Although she had acceded to Washington's advice and plan, she was distraught at not being permitted to follow along with her father and escort Sarah's body to Belvoir. Her bitter words cut Washington to the bone. "This is a sham, George . . . just sham!"

To their dismay, Anne and Sally Cary Fairfax were made to sit, exactly as they were told to do, in the formal reception room at Mount Vernon. There they received families from the nearby villages who had ridden over in the midday to give their sympathies. In looking on, neither Washington nor his best friend, George William Fairfax, could sense that any of the consolers had behaved suspiciously.

Later that evening, Anne Washington could not believe her eyes when she finally arrived at Belvoir and saw that her young daughter was showing small but definite signs of life. Over the next days, she and Sally Fairfax worked feverishly to best promote Sarah's recovery.

By October, it was determined that the two-year-old had not suffered a random illness but instead had been the victim of a near-fatal poisoning. Dr. Caldwell reported that a distillation of Sarah's urine, using a technique he had learned from some Scottish practitioners, yielded small quantities of white crystals. When these salts were dissolved in vinegar and diluted by water, the resulting mixture had killed three of four field mice caged in his laboratory.

Beside Dr. Caldwell, the child's whereabouts remained known only to the immediate family and a few trusted Belvoir servants. After grudgingly admitting that there could be a plot against Sarah's life, Anne agreed to continue the ruse. Accordingly, she changed her daughter's name. Sarah Washington would be known as Priscilla Farris, instead.

The two-year-old made a miraculous recovery but despite the return of her full physical strength, she continued to have lingering amnesia. This profoundly affected the girl's recall of her earlier childhood. Dr. Caldwell said that this state of 'distal amnesia' was common after prolonged illness and would likely be permanent. Other than that, he was delighted that she had the usual developmental skills of a two-year-old child with no serious signs of damage.

As a result, over the following year the girl had no problems describing current events and could clearly focus on her new life at the Belvoir estate. Most importantly, Priscilla came to fully believe what she was told about her earlier childhood. Whatever she was told was 'just so.' Hence, the girl came to understand that her whole Farris family had been tragically killed in a house fire, and as a result, she had been taken in at Belvoir. Anne Washington had soon adopted her and renamed her Priscilla Farris-Fairfax. In young Priscilla's eyes, the Fairfaxes and George Washington were more than just friends of her deceased parents – they had become her family.

2

Mount Vernon

October 1755

Three years later, George Washington and his former sister-in-law, now Anne Fairfax Lee, marveled at her energetic adopted daughter Priscilla. The spirited girl skipped ahead of them through the northeast stands of towering oak, sycamore and scattered locust trees on the Belvoir estate. The two could see that her physical strength had fully returned as she played among the fallen leaves and bits of wild mushrooms along the trail. She seemed as sound as any other five-year-old.

Priscilla Farris-Fairfax enjoyed these walks with her mother's neighbor, a handsome young outdoorsman and estate farmer well known in the rolling country of the Northern Neck of Virginia. The imposing colonel had just returned from the western territories and she had not seen him since spring.

Washington leaned down and swooped the girl up in his arms. "The lead bullets flew by from all directions, Priscilla. Oh how you could almost feel the heat of the shot."

"Hear that, Mother? Did you hear? I wish they would let me join the Virginia militia too. It sounds like great fun!"

"I do not think Governor Dinwiddie would allow a girl to serve with his Virginia troops no matter what her age might be, little one." Washington laughed at this bundle of energy before letting her down. "Besides, you have to help your mother right here."

"Were you afraid, George?" Anne Lee asked. "Were you outnumbered?"

"Not by too much, but the French and Mohawks had an unusual pell-mell strategy and employed a thing they called 'camouflage' as well. During the main engagement, General Braddock was mortally wounded and we took on many other casualties. A bad start on my part, I might say, for any military career."

Anne Lee shook her head, raised her eyebrows and observed, "You are so much like your brother, George." She frequently noticed how much he resembled her Lawrence and what she recalled of their father, Augustine. "Strong, opinionated, resolute – no wonder people around here respect you."

"I only wish Governor Dinwiddie could see what you see, dear Anne. I heard a fortnight ago that he is breaking up my Virginia regiment. What is more, the dastardly man refuses to give me a royal commission for the British Army. He and Lord Loudon say that such a privilege does not fall to any colonial soldier."

"Where does that leave you, George?"

"I'll not soon forget their slight, those bastards," he replied. "Because of their blatant capriciousness, I have decided to resign my commission. At least with that, Anne, I would have more time here with you both."

The summer rainfall had been minimal and the normally plentiful corn and wheat yields were noticeably diminished in the northernmost farmlands. Sharp scents of dry decay drifted from the fields on either side.

Anne Lee looked searchingly into his gray eyes. "What will you first do at Mount Vernon, any idea? The lease should work well for both of us. Once my smaller Woodlawn residence is constructed, it will give me a much more manageable property."

George Washington looked down at Anne. As he did, he could not help but note her pert lips and bright brown eyes. He marveled at how she had been able to regain her bright nature despite suffering successive tragedies over the past nine years: three children dying and then her husband, his brother.

Taking her arm and leading her down the road, Washington paused before saying, "To your question, Anne, the financials for the lease-arrangement for Mount Vernon appear quite sound. I will gladly use the same overseers and all current slaves – there will be no changes in personnel whatsoever. In fact, I plan to go over the winter plans tomorrow with Mr. Roberts."

Washington glanced over her shoulder and saw that Priscilla had veered off to pull pinecones from a nearby spruce tree. "I am so happy seeing how wonderfully radiant you are again, Anne." Then he asked, "Does Mr. Lee guess about Sarah and you? We both must be careful. After all, your little one does resemble you. I suppose that I must get reacquainted with calling her 'Priscilla' now that I'm back."

Anne Lee smiled. "You are so right, George, but no, oh no – my husband George and his Lee family know nothing about her true background at all. I dare not share anything and I intend to keep it that way. Only the same few of us know and that is for her necessary protection.

"Of continuing concern, while you were in the western territories, there were even many more strange sicknesses and accidents at Belvoir and hereabouts. The assessment by Dr. Caldwell - you remember him – is that there have been other poisonings. The sheriff suspects certain ne'er-do-wells that he has run up against."

Washington frowned as they resumed walking and responded, "The damned rabble – they have always been around. They make it bad for the good common folk. These rascals must be dealt with harshly."

"George, that is certainly a main reason we are glad to have you back. Oft times it has seemed that our estates are being cruelly singled out. "

When he heard her words, the imposing figure was deeply bothered but nonetheless gathered himself together before calling out, "Priscilla, please mind to fetch me some hickory sticks and some chestnuts – there, over there!" The pair strolled behind as the darting five-year-old nearly tripped over some gnarly roots as she scurried off.

When the little girl ran out of earshot, Washington gently asked, "Well, then, tell me more about your new husband, this Mr. Lee. Not at all like Lawrence, I presume."

Anne Lee moved to straighten her skirt and smiled broadly up at her former brother in-law. "You know what's funny? I just realized how many 'Georges' I have in my life. There's my brother George William, then you, and oh yes - my present husband George and infant son, George Jr. And to think . . . even the King, too!"

She brightly related how fond George Lee had become of her young daughter Priscilla Farris-Fairfax. "He even mentioned the possibility of also adopting Priscilla soon after our marriage, but I insisted that that would not be necessary. In fact, I told him that it might prove confusing to the little girl."

Listening to her, it was clear to Washington that she was rejuvenated by a romantic, fresh love. He was delightfully surprised by his own contented reaction on hearing the details of her new life.

She colorfully described how for the past summer they, their own newborn son, and her adopted Priscilla had moved together into a cottage on Colonel Fairfax's Belvoir estate. They were starting to build a home on an adjoining 800 acres, on a farm named "Woodlawn" that her father had given the couple soon after their wedding.

Anne looked over at Washington and quietly asked, "Do you think your brother, Lawrence, would have minded what I am doing . . . how I am doing it?"

Reassuringly, he took her hand. "I do not think Lawrence would feel any differently about the matter . . . especially since we have to keep what has happened such a secret. Anne, I totally agree with what you said earlier. Given all the danger around here, you and I must be sure that your and Lawrence's one surviving offspring remains protected and well-supported. It is fortunate that no one has recognized her these years later."

"George . . . another thing," Anne said as she folded her other hand warmly around his own. "I do know our mutual friend, Sally, will be so delighted that you have returned after these past months." Anne inwardly smiled as she sensed that her comment had found a certain mark. But seeing that Priscilla was having difficulties, she quickly broke away to help her daughter get untangled from some thick briars.

As she left, George Washington felt strangely rejuvenated. He felt sure that Anne Lee had noticed his flush. He knew that Sally Cary continued to provoke certain latent emotions in him.

Six years earlier, the Fairfaxes had introduced him to one of their high-country Virginia acquaintances, an attractive blue-eyed, raven-haired young woman. Washington along with others became charmed by Sally's seemingly innocent wiles. She laughed flirtatiously as a gamboling teacher might whenever she led him and the colonel's son, George William Fairfax, through intricate dance steps of minuets and reels. Although he knew that the Fairfaxes enjoyed a higher social status than he and therefore that George William was probably more suitable, it had still been wrenching when Sally decided to marry his closest friend.

Hearing some childish laughter up ahead, Washington picked up his pace and caught up to the aimlessly twirling fairy-of-the-forest. The little girl clambered up the trunk of a nearby fallen oak. "This came down a month ago when we had a big rainy wind storm, Mr. Washington. I thought my windows would blow away!"

Imagining what that hurricane coming up from the Carolinas had been like for Priscilla, Washington thought back to the howling tropical cyclone he had lived through on Barbados. He and his half-brother were there in 1751, only months before Lawrence died of consumption. The two men had traveled to the island hoping that the Caribbean air would assist the critically ill man's lung congestion and the frightening hemorrhages brought on by his coughing paroxysms. They were living as guests on a sugar plantation, the Bush Hill House, in the middle of the island near Bridgetown and never fully felt the fury of the rains from the fierce autumnal storm that day. But what they had experienced was bad enough.

"I could tell you about a time I had in the Caribbean with your . . ." Washington stopped short, realizing with a fright that he had nearly named her true father.

"Was your storm as bad as the one we had here?"

"It was different . . . very different."

Priscilla climbed off the tree trunk and came down and squeezed Anne Lee's hand. "Oh Mommy . . . I am always so happy all over that you are my mother! Walks like this are so much fun!" She jumped up and down, lightly wrenching the woman's shoulder. "Besides little George, did you ever have any children, Mother? Where did they go? . . . Did they die? Oh that's right, you told me already. At least you have little Georgie and me now."

Anne swallowed hard when she heard 'Mother,' knowing that the orphan girl must surely feel abandoned at times. She hugged her daughter into her skirt, "I am so grateful to have you. You came into my life at just the right time, little one. Thankfully, Mr. Washington has now come back and will manage Mount Vernon for both of us."

"Was it ever called anything else, Mother?"

"Yes, dear, Epsewasson. That is an Indian saying for 'big view.' "

The girl rubbed her nose and giggled when she tried to say the word herself. "Epsewasson, that's a funny name!"

"The first Washington that settled here many years ago greatly enjoyed the sight from the rise over the river. Even more so after they cleared some land." Anne Lee leaned over and tousled her daughter's hair. Then turning about, the three headed west through deep stands of rough scrub oaks in the direction of Belvoir.

Priscilla walked round in circles and led the way. "These leaves feel so crinkly. Listen to them swishing about . . . Come on, let's all go through them."

Washington smiled and soon was also making crackly, whooshing noises in the undergrowth, trying to keep up with her. Priscilla's energy reminded him of his own childhood when he, Lawrence and several cousins had hiked these same woods. He made a cup with his hands and called ahead, "Mind you, little Priscilla, Mrs. Turner said there would be salt pork for supper."

Before going further, George and Anne turned and saw the outlines of Mount Vernon's degenerating rooflines and rundown garden sheds. The low autumnal morning sun partly affected their view, but Washington could clearly make out the exuberant shrubbery and bunched up plantings that had grown so wild in the past year.

Anne Lee came to his side and tenderly touched his sleeve. "It is up to you, now George, to make this the place like it was when Lawrence was here with me . . . with us. We will be all right. Yes, Priscilla and I will be alright."

Moving on, the three continued their way back to Belvoir.

3

Mount Vernon

February 1761

"It won't be long before the sun burns this moisture off," George Washington remarked as his muscular gray gelding charted a winding way through the woodlands.

A curly haired eleven-year-old rode expertly behind on a smaller chestnut horse. Washington smiled to himself as he reflected on the girl's burgeoning pubescence. She had thick wavy hair like her mother, Anne, and the sturdy carriage of his brother, Lawrence. She was fast becoming much more than the thin little Priscilla that he had known.

His mount slowed and the two rode side-by-side as their horses moved ahead. Washington was pleased that she was tall for her age, like all Washingtons seemed to be. She eagerly took in their surroundings and as she did, he sensed that she, and eventually her own family, would someday be able to successfully handle this Woodlawn property.

When Washington married the widow Mrs. Martha Custis two years before, she had brought a large dowry to his estate. With these added resources, the couple more than tripled his total Mount Vernon farmland and leased holdings to 9000 acres. Although it was not immense by some persons' standards, it was more than adequate for spurring his own interests in agriculture, husbandry and developing a unique fish and oyster industry along the Patowmack.

Washington had consulted Dr. Caldwell regarding his inability to produce an offspring after two years of marriage. "Since Martha has produced two children from her first marriage, obviously the fault is mine," he concluded. After his review, the doctor expressed his suspicion that the severe camp dysentery that Washington had suffered while serving as a colonel fighting the French in 1757 had made him infertile.

Now that he knew that Priscilla would be the most direct inheritor of the Washington-bloodline, George Washington concluded that he had to secretly give even more material support to his older brother's daughter. He asked loudly, "Did you bring the drop line and silk cord, Priscilla?"

"They are in my sack here, sir," she replied, but the spirited girl slapped her shoulder bag nonetheless in order to reassure herself. "What are we going to do with those things, Mr. Washington?" She pointed behind his saddle.

"They are my surveying equipment. Some are newly purchased and just arrived from Scotland. This coming month, I hope to complete an open traverse plot over the property there." He pointed towards the northwest through the barren trees. "And you are here for their first use . . . starting today."

The two riders dismounted and tied their horses to a pair of tulip poplars. From this vantage, the main buildings on the three estates were hidden from view. Belvoir was to the southwest, Woodlawn to the north, and Mount Vernon to the east. In the morning's chill, they could smell the fragrance of cooking meat drifting down from Mount Vernon's adjoining smokehouse.

"Good thing we had a hearty breakfast, Miss Priscilla. Otherwise, I'd surely be starved by now." Washington laughed and started to untie his equipment.

"Do you want me to carry the other end?" she asked and motioned to the long three-legged wooden stand.

"No, thank you very much. It is rather heavy. I have learnt how to balance the tripod quite well over my shoulders, but it does get a bit clumsy at times."

His horse startled when he strained to remove the remaining surveying pieces tied on the gelding's back. "Whoa, boy. Quiet now – take it easy." He calmed the skittish horse with a reassuring pat.

"Tell me how you learned to survey?" Priscilla enjoyed learning from him like this compared to the reading and writing exercises that she was forced to endure at her mother's prodding. His lessons seemed much more interesting.

"When I first met Colonel Fairfax years ago, Priscilla, he could see that I was more interested in land management than were either of his children. That was about the time that I met your mother – just before she married my eldest brother, Lawrence . . ."

Washington nearly choked on his words, suddenly afraid that he might have said too much already. He seemingly forgot something from his saddlebag, so turning away he mumbled, "I was living here with my brother at the time."

Hardly listening to him, Priscilla impatiently moved off into the brush and busied herself chasing a tree toad around a stump.

Thankful for the distraction, Washington nervously exhaled into his hands as he adjusted his surveyor's equipment into the soil. Once the telescope was upright, he called, "Come back, Priscilla, we're going to get going. We have to start from a reference point. See that granite stone across the ravine?"

She looked in the direction and saw what looked like a flat rock some hundred yards away. "There? Next to the holly tree? It looks like there are some letters or numbers chiseled on a plaque."

"Yes, that is the one. It is called the 'Benchmark for Mount Vernon.' It gives the precise elevation from the Patowmack. You may already know that the Patowmack itself is at an elevation that is called 'sea level.'

"My brother Lawrence and Colonel Fairfax had that special boulder marked many years ago. It had to be professionally done since that spot is so critical to the accuracy of every other map that is made in these parts. Colonel Fairfax hired a master surveyor from Williamsburg to take its measurements. See there – it is thirty yards, some 92 feet above the river at low tide. All the other measurements in these parts and about refer then to this Benchmark, this Reference Stone. Let us be off now."

During the morning the two traipsed over the terrain together. At each consecutive measure-point Washington first unloaded his surveying tools, took some measurements and, after penciling in the site on his rough drawing, reloaded the heavy equipment onto his big gray. As they moved from place to place, each took fuller measure of the other. While the young girl learned surveying from him, Washington had the chance to understand even more about Priscilla Farris-Fairfax. It pleased him.

Near noon, they gathered their equipment and led their horses back onto the path leading to Woodlawn. Unbeknownst to her, the white fabric ties that they had placed on trees that morning would mark new boundaries between Woodlawn and Mount Vernon. Finally they reached a lee-place and Washington allowed their horses to freely graze in a neighboring field.

As the two sat in a patch of long brown grass, they snacked on their bread, salted pork and cheese. The estatesman gazed fondly at the hardy eleven-year-old and thought that she could never possibly imagine that someday this property would be hers. Using this new survey, he would surreptitiously transfer these land-holdings to Woodlawn by modifying Mount Vernon's original estate map. Washington surmised that given the extent of their complicated holdings, his wife Martha would hardly notice. He rationalized that both of these particular parcels actually still belonged to Anne Lee and that he was merely reallocating a small bit from one to the other.

Sitting with Priscilla while they ate, Washington was nearly persuaded to tell her all the facts regarding her true identity and future inheritance. But then if he did, he realized there might be little to gain, so he stopped himself short. He decided that at least for the moment her history needed to remain secure as fiction.

That evening, in his study at Mount Vernon, Washington pored over his hastily scratched notes and rough drafts by candlelight. His stepchildren, young Patsy and Jacky Custis, could be heard playing in the distant parlor with their mother. Ice had formed against the fogged windowpanes of the darkened room. The snapping sound of burning aged oak came from the fireplace. A house servant walking by the office saw a brief brightening of the flames as Washington tossed an old survey map into the fire. Satisfied, Washington sat back in his favorite Chippendale chair. The twenty-nine-year-old master of the home sighed, took a sip of heated cherry brandy, and said in a barely audible voice, "It is done . . . well done."

A month later, Anne Fairfax Washington Lee unexpectedly died from variola. After some nettlesome disputes with George Lee's solicitors, it was determined that George Washington was the closest direct blood relative to Lawrence Washington and their father, Augustine. Following this decision, George and Martha Washington would fully inherit Mount Vernon.

The following fall, Mr. Lamb, the senior overseer, and two of his most trusted workers cut-axed a path and affixed metal markers onto stones running between Woodlawn and Mount Vernon. Woodlawn estate had become a 1500-acre property.

Despite again finding herself an orphan at age eleven, Priscilla Farris-Fairfax was able to stay at Woodlawn and Belvoir when George William and Sally Cary Fairfax formally adopted her. Childless themselves, the young Fairfax couple raised the girl as if she were their own. Priscilla was delighted that she was able to remain close to the Washingtons of Mount Vernon as well.

4

New York City

December 4, 1783

"Who does he think he is . . . the King?"

Two scrawny boys barely got out of the way as a careening carriage lurched past. A moment later, an elderly woman screamed as she was struck by one of its wheels and fell to the snowy ground. One of her legs seemed to snap with a sickening sound. Four stallions pulled the fancy white carriage passing through lower New York, snorting frosted exhalations into the cold winter's air. Oblivious to her cries, the driver and his lone passenger rounded a corner and carried on towards the Whitehall Dock. A small crowd of bystanders quickly came to assist the gray-haired woman as her high-pitched moans echoed off the nearby brick buildings.

Joshua and Ethan Downey had been walking from an alley on the opposite side and were now thoroughly splattered by pungent mud. At least they were not hurt, and after recovering from their start, the pair crossed the street to look upon the woman, fearing that she was seriously hurt.

As she was being helped in the street, the old lady shook her head and remarked, "I think that I am more frightened than hurt . . . but now look at me, my clothes and leggings are so filthy." The elderly woman gradually stood up, bent over, and rubbed her scraped bloody hands against her soiled wraps. She glanced wearily down at scattered, broken pieces of maple wood. "'Tis lucky for me that I was carr'in' a bundell o' firewood from the market. Too bad they all took such a blow, breakin' and such, but it must'a protected me someway."

Seeing that her physical condition was better than first imagined, several townspeople started helping her pick up the larger of the wood bits and fragments from the mud and pavement.

"This is the third time I've nearly been hit since I come from Dublin jus' last year," she remarked with a dry voice. "I've got me some kind of luck, we sorts usu'ly do. That's all . . . all, I suppose, 'cause I do'n have much else." Hoisting her rebundled load and flinging a string of spittle in the direction that the carriage had gone, the elderly woman moved on up towards Wall Street. Her woolen wraps dragged in the puddles behind her but she took no notice.

Joshua and Ethan, knowing their mother would soon be looking for them, started up a side street towards their home along the East River.

Joshua hissed, "That Washington . . . he and his driver have such an air. Do you remember that big parade they had this week down Broadway Street, Ethan, and how preening he looked?"

The parade had indeed been an amazing sight. The remaining British regulars and thousands of American loyalists, the hated Tories, had finally evacuated New York City on the 25th of November. Governor Henry Clinton and state assemblymen had come down from the capitol in Poughkeepsie to organize a patriot's reception. Several thousand had enthusiastically turned out to greet the victorious Continentals and their own New York militia. The two brothers had stood on a curbside log that day and celebrated along with everyone else.

"Everyone thought that he was an emperor or something riding in that big, fancy carriage. It's a good thing that they let the soldiers march, too. The way he acted, you'd think he beat the Brits alone." Joshua was still unsettled by remembering how the General's carriage had nearly killed the Irish woman just a few minutes ago. "Washington must think he rules even us New Yorkers, especially now that he's not chasing any more Johnny Bulls. You know, Ethan, we're not his soldier-boys. He can't boss us around."

"Doggone it . . . you're right," Ethan said with the lisp of a boy missing two front teeth. He looked up at his older brother. "He don't haf to have his driver pull him around like some fancy doodle dandy . . . sort of like some Lord or Duke Washington. Why can't he act like the rest of us?"

"Whether he could ever be like us or not, who knows," Joshua countered. "I'm glad he's gonna be leaving New York. It's about time. But why does he have to hurry so? At the speed his carriage was going, he'll probably make it to Morristown by nightfall."

The two boys looked behind them and heard an approaching group of men with their voices carrying in the frigid, dry air. They were surprised to see that General Washington was walking amidst them going westward to the wharves along the half-frozen Hudson River. The bitter wind coming from the New Jersey shore burned the men's faces. Distant bells of St. Paul's rang a noontime Anglican hymn that sounded down the Broadway. Nearby, sounds from the workers on the scaffolds of the older Trinity Church reached the curving alleyways below.

"Golly days, Ethan, that must have been his carriage going along ahead of him with an aide or someone else. The General wasn't even in it!" As he realized his mistake, Joshua's anger deflated like a punctured balloon.

The group with Washington was comprised of both military men and civilians. They were careful to pick their way around Water Street's deep crisscrossing mud-ruts in the midway. Joshua and Ethan could barely make out some of the deep-voiced conversations as the huddled men moved away from them. The two were impressed at how tall and stately the General appeared in his heavy blue overcoat with a matching peaked hat. He seemed not to say much but instead listened intently to his companions as he led them down to a waiting barge.

Ethan turned to look back as the pack rounded the corner and disappeared from sight. "What is he going to do now, Josh? Some say that he's leaving New York and New England for good."

His older brother had heard from one of their relatives that General Washington was going to Virginia and would be meeting with the Continental Congress in Annapolis, Maryland on the way. "I hear he's finally going to his great home along the Potomac after being gone for nearly eight years . . . Mother says that the Washington family farm is one of the biggest in Virginia."

Ethan broke in, "I can't believe the rumors that he's goin' to retire his commission . . . he's too much of a big shot."

The boys' father, a clockmaker, had joined the Sons of Liberty before the War and had barely escaped when Howe and his troops occupied New York City. Mr. Downey had often spoken glowingly to Joshua and Ethan about General Washington and the other revolutionary officers that he had met. Only months before, however, their father had been killed in the concluding Southern campaign.

Owing to the celebrations in the city, Joshua had been let off from work as a printer's apprentice. He asked his younger brother, "Ethan, wasn't that great yesterday?"

"You mean being outside the Fraunces Tavern?"

"Yes, that too. We did get to see a lot of the officers there that father used to mention. Colonel Hamilton was shorter than I expected. He seemed almost pretty for a man, but I know that is mean for me to say given all that he's done and been through. And then there was General Schuyler. I hear he has a big place up near Albany. He was the oldest one there. Good thing that Benedict Arnold's in London, what a scoundrel! He and his lot will never dare come back again, that's certain. They wouldn't dare!"

"Too bad we couldn't get closer, though. I wanted to see father's regiment officer, Colonel Browning."

Joshua walked a little farther down the muddy roadway, then added, "I heard from Uncle Aaron that that lunch meeting lasted all afternoon . . . there were a lot of huzzahs and such. I suppose that since it's December, it's probably safe and sure that the English are gone from hereabout. You've gotta wonder, though, if they'll be back next spring . . . that is, if they do decide to ever come back."

"Who's goin' to take General Washington's place if he does retire?"

"They don't need anybody now . . . everyone's gone home for the winter. But if they did next year, my guess would be either General Gates or Greene."

Ethan wondered, "What do you think they did at the Tavern yesterday besides eat and have a good time?"

"I don't know, for sure." Joshua looked down at his brother. "But maybe they formed an association or something. I hear old soldiers miss their camaraderie and stuff and like to get together when they can to go over the good old days, especially the officers. I hear they like to talk over old battles, camp headquarters and other stuff."

"What's 'camaraderie,' Josh?"

"Well, it's like when a bunch of people are together and feel good about being together. They have something in common and instead of being like we are, born brothers, they choose to be brothers with each other."

Pulling on his older brother's sleeve, Ethan fretfully interrupted. "Come on . . . I'm getting hungry for lunch . . . let's go home, we have to clean up this mud or mother will get really pissey-angry."

Annapolis, Maryland
Continental Congress, Thomas Mifflin, Presiding
December 23, 1783

General George Washington shuffled nervously in the rear of the hall as he waited to be introduced. He distinctly recalled the day eight years ago when an earlier Congress meeting in Philadelphia had granted his commission in the newly formed Continental Army. Some of the delegates to that previous Congress were present here in Annapolis as observers. Everyone was looking forward to his remarks. As he stood alone, he thought to himself how arduous a campaign it had been, but thankfully, by all appearances, it seemed to be over now that Franklin and the others had forged an agreement in Paris. At last, they had rid themselves of King George's pressing tyranny.

The preliminary speeches continued in the background as Washington reflected on how wonderfully prescient General Greene was when he said that as long as the Continental Army could fight another day, the British would be sure to retire. And he was right after all.

Washington smiled contentedly and thought that although our victories in the field were few and far between, his army was able to escape time and again . . . and just outlasted them.

He suddenly felt years older. The assembly had become hushed and he felt their attention focused on him. Walking with determination to the front, he bowed slightly toward Mr. Mifflin's desk and spoke briefly, concluding, "Having now finished the work assigned to me, I now retire from the great theater of action . . . " [1]

Annotation:

[1]   James McHenry to Margaret Caldwell, Dec. 23, 1783 in Paul H. Smith, *Letters of Delegates to Congress, 1774-1789*, 21: 221, Washington, D.C., 1976.

5

Mount Vernon

June 1785

Two men were having a warm animated conversation on the portico as they enjoyed the fresh morning breeze coming off the river. As George Washington sipped his tea, his longtime neighbor Jonathan Winfield looked out over the Potomac. The bright reflections seemed to dance across the uneven waves in the middle channel.

Although Winfield had spent a short time with the Virginia militia during the siege at Newport and Yorktown, he had not had much chance to be with the General during the war. Shortly after Yorktown, Washington's stepson, Jacky Custis serving with the Continentals had suddenly died of the dreaded camp fever. His sister Patsy Custis had died some years earlier. Now childless, Martha had been left alone at Mount Vernon, and Major Winfield was ordered by a deeply grieving General to return immediately to Woodlawn and Mount Vernon late in 1781. He never forgot the General's parting words as he tearfully bade him farewell. "All the Washingtons need you more than ever, myself most of all."

Settling back in his chair, George Washington stared steadily at Winfield. "I have been meaning to talk to you about our properties, Jonathan. I am going to concentrate more on my crab and oyster-farming businesses instead of pushing ahead with more land development here on the five farms of Mount Vernon."

"What are you suggesting, Mr. Washington?" Winfield sensed that his older neighbor had something important on his mind.

"Martha and I feel so close to you and your family – almost a certain kinship. You and Priscilla have such great children."

"Pardon me," Winfield interrupted, "but you ought to see Franklin now, sir – what a little guy!"

"I can believe that – he's always been so full of energy," Washington remarked. "We haven't seen him or his sisters in a fortnight. I'll have to have Martha arrange a visit. Let me preface my further discussion, Jonathan, by first saying how much we have enjoyed seeing you and Priscilla get your Woodlawn on a much better footing. What's more, Martha greatly appreciated your aid during my frequent absences in the recent conflict. You are dear friends."

"We owe thanks to you, as well, sir," the former chief overseer at Belvoir said. "You gave us such good advice over the years, especially early on after our marriage when Colonel Fairfax fully deeded our present farm to Priscilla. We have always felt quite indebted to you both."

"Yes, yes, I understand." Washington laughed at a passing thought. "I suppose we could sit around and endlessly thank each other all morning but let me get more to the point – Martha and I want to do something else for you and Priscilla." He glanced sideways in Winfield's direction. "She and I are increasingly aware that, as it now stands, Mount Vernon has gotten to be too much for us. For instance, my Grist Mill down near Dogue Creek desperately needs repair."

"What does that have to do with us – our Woodlawn?"

"We have been thinking of parceling out some of the western lands of our Mount Vernon and offering it to you, Jonathan. To you and Priscilla . . . to your family."

"How much are you considering?"

Washington got up and went into his study. Shortly, he returned to the porch and unrolled a topographic surveyor's chart. "Let us get it oriented – here, that is it. I have to position the northlands there at the top. All told, Jonathan, we were thinking about twenty-two hundred acres, from beyond the point there." Washington turned and gestured first to the southwest before sweeping his arm. "And around to Dogue Creek."

Winfield frowned and rubbed his nose in disbelief.

His older neighbor fingered the map. "I have done some preliminary measurements. Martha and I would include land on the northwest, from the stand of hickory and juniper trees bordering the wheat fields east to Little Hunting Creek. Mount Vernon would still be plenty large for us, more than six thousand acres."

Winfield felt confused, uncertain. Somehow, the proposal seemed to be much more than a gift. He was unsure about Washington's stated motivation – or were there others? Finally, he asked, "What would be your asking price, sir? . . . Lately, land around here has been valued at some twenty

Virginia Commonwealth dollars per acre. I suppose the total would come to near forty thousand VCD."

"Let me simply put it that Mrs. Washington and I would sell it to you, our friends, by this arrangement. 10% down of twenty thousand VCD amortized at 3% over twenty years. Since we do not have a direct heir, this property would fully cede to you on our deaths. If there is any remaining debt on this transferred property, it would be fully canceled."

"But why me? . . . Why us? The price is well below market value."

"Look at it from our perspective. We did not want to risk having a new neighbor, a new estate owner, when we disposed of this piece of property. Instead, we want to first grant you and your family the opportunity . . ."

Washington paused, and then went on. "I can understand that you are more than a bit stupefied, Jonathan. You certainly do not have to decide today. In the meantime, talk it over with Priscilla. When and if it is agreeable to you both, I will have a Mr. Randolph, a respected lawyer of Williamsburg, draw up the papers. Just now, though, you seem to have hesitated. Do you have the capital? So far, how does it sound?"

"On the face of it, more than fine, but . . . let me see, I have to think. Besides what I consider are extremely liberal terms, are there any pre-conditions?"

"There would not be any other contingencies on paper, but one. The new lands, which would be applied to your current Woodlawn holdings, must be passed to your descendants in perpetuity. If they are not, these twenty-two hundred acres must be sold off and all the proceeds applied to the poor peoples of Fairfax County."

"But so long as it passes through the family?"

"Yes, it would remain as your and your family's Woodlawn. And my mill, the Grist Mill, is part of this transferred property since it lies within these boundaries. See here?" Washington pointed to the western corner of Mount Vernon on the map. "Priscilla must remember that stone mill when it was first being built. She was near twelve-years-old at the time, I believe. She helped me do the initial survey."

Jonathan Winfield was always amazed at how many details Mr. Washington could clearly recount about his wife's childhood.

For his part that morning, Washington was inwardly grateful that he had recently divulged Priscilla Winfield's true identity to Martha. He treasured what she had said at the time, "I was always puzzled, my dear George, where certain acres of ours had gone – but I dared not ask. Besides, since Priscilla does look a bit like Lawrence and Anne's portraits hanging in our west parlor, I always wondered. Trust me, her inheritance will be as close to my heart as it is to yours and I promise to hold it in equal confidence."

At this moment, Martha came out on the portico as if on cue saying, "Did you both have time to go over the proposition that we talked about, George? Or at least, start to go over it?"

"Yes, we did, my dear. Jonathan has at least a general idea."

"That is wonderful." Martha appeared to be quite satisfied, softly adding, "I do hope that you and Priscilla decide to take this opportunity . . . You are the right people for us in so many ways."

Shortly later, as Jonathan Winfield rode off, Martha Washington held her husband's hand and gently smiled. "I am glad that it is to be settled. The Winfield family will be able to enjoy much better prospects at Woodlawn with this arrangement."

"All this – yet Jonathan and Priscilla do not even know the full truth," Washington said wistfully.

"Yes," she said while securing his gaze, "and given the history of this place, best that they never know."

"Martha, it has been a long morning for me. I think I need to take a walk about our place – do you want to come along?"

"No. You should be with yourself awhile – on these hills by the river. I will remain here waiting to hear your thoughts later, though oft times, my dear General, I have sensed that some of your thoughts have not always been shared."

He looked down lovingly into her twinkling, hazel eyes set off by a few gathering wrinkles. "You can rest assured, my dearest Martha, that any thoughts that I deem noteworthy will be shared firstly with you."

George Washington sat down on the porch's edge and slipped on his tall hiking boots. He carefully got up, grumbled aloud about his rheumatism, and slowly began to stroll down the gravel path towards the wharf.

6

Mount Vernon

Early Afternoon, June 1785

Once he made his way down to the wharf, George Washington reflected on the days he had enjoyed boating and fishing with Lawrence. His half-brother had inherited Epsewasson from their father and renamed it Mount Vernon to honor Admiral Vernon, under whom he had served in the British Navy.

Years before, as Lawrence weakened from his consumption, the middle-aged scion of the Washington family understood that his end might be near. In his written testament of May 1752, he directed his younger brother to care for his young wife and their only living child, Sarah, with a last wish: *"When my time comes, Sarah's inheritance will be sure of this place – Mount Vernon. She is a Washington too."*

Sitting on the dock that day, Washington remembered how things had happened so suddenly only months after Lawrence died. Their lives turned upside down, young Sarah Washington's close call with death and soon thereafter four slaves had become ill with similar maladies, two of them dying. Besides these strange illnesses, several barns at nearby estates were torched. Two suspected arsonists were discovered in a shed but were released without evidence of malfeasance. Dr. Caldwell concluded there had now been five cases of poisonings. He sternly warned that other people on the two estates might also be in danger.

Washington silently nodded to himself as he thought of those dark days. Given the circumstances, it was decided that Sarah Washington must remain known as 'Priscilla' for the foreseeable future. Picking up his tan sack, he got up and moved along a path that skirted the shoreline. Before all the turmoil, he recalled, they did have many wonderful times around these parts.

For instance, there was the time he and Sally Cary Fairfax got lost playing a hiding game in the boxwood maze at Belvoir. The young Washington cleverly hid away but as he backed around a curving hedge, he accidentally ran into her nearly toppling them both over. He turned and wrapped his arms about her thin waist to keep her upright. As he struggled to keep his feet, Washington laughed and Sally put her fingers to his lips in order to still him. Softly whispering in his ear, his beautiful raven-haired neighbor had innocently aroused him. Their moment passed soon enough.

"Caught you!" a bratty Fairfax cousin yelled.

"Yes, caught indeed," Sally countered, "You caught two of us at the same time – what a catch!"

As he sat down on the creek bank, Washington bit into an apple from his sack. He frowned and looked about blankly as if he were trying to make some sense. He was wrestling with another bitter memory.

'The TIME,' as it was named back in 1770, had been the time of so much revolution in these parts. It started slowly enough. The English Parliament had again approved another series of harsh levies on the peoples of their American colonies. A number of new taxes were to be imposed and, worst of all, the judges and all the representatives of the colonial governments were to be appointed solely by the Crown.

Popular opposition, centered in Williamsburg, spread like a brush fire as Patrick Henry, Thomas Jefferson, and their mentor George Wythe openly planned their responses. An active correspondence soon developed with like-minded men in Massachusetts and New York. Rebellious citizens formed groups known as Patriot Clubs or the Sons of Liberty throughout the Colonies. The most fearsome club in the middle colonies was labeled 'The New World Patriots.'

The tall, red-haired Thomas Jefferson and Wythe visited George Washington at his vast Mount Vernon estate. They thought that in light of his prior military experience, it was essential to personally enlist his support early on for their cause since the protests might likely provoke an armed response.

George Wythe presented the issue, saying, "You've always understood where we're coming from, George. We are approaching you first since we know you to be very influential. It's in your blood and what's more – you know it."

"Mr. Wythe is quite correct," Jefferson added. "You are a natural leader, George. People will follow your example and, even more, your commands."

"That is flattering for you to say but let me hear of your current concerns in detail," Washington responded.

As he conversed further with them, Washington agreed most strongly with the arguments against having the courts of the Colonies replaced by courts of the Crown. He and Martha Washington had already been victimized more than once by the graft of English-appointed barristers and English-based creditors. Washington agreed that establishing these sorts of courts was a dangerous matter and declared, "That is only what a tyrant would demand.".

After long discussions at Mount Vernon, he concurred with the aims of the visiting legation. He confided to them how much he had enjoyed the heady experience of previously being an elected delegate to the House of Burgesses and was humbled that they considered him to still be influential.

Washington summarized his opinions. "The people of Virginia have to have their own independent legislative body and courts. Virginia should not remain beholden to a king an ocean away, though we shouldn't have our own one here either." Saying that, George Washington secretly gave them his full pledge of support.

Shortly thereafter, the TIME, comprised of increasingly violent protests for American liberty, arrived throughout the Northern Neck of Virginia.

On a subsequent Sunday at Christ Church in Alexandria, the Episcopal priest compared the British monarch to King David of ancient Israel, imploring the congregation that "just as David, kings only do what they must!" Even though he was in the middle of his homily, a few congregants stood and angrily bolted from the worship service.

Later, as the Washingtons departed church, they noticed many of these same people lingering nearby. One mocked, "King George must think he owns the pearly gate! I wonder what the king himself puts in the offering plate – not much of his own, I suspect!"

What shocked them was that these unruly townsfolk were persons that they had always known to be reputable neighbors. On their route home, their lacquered carriage passed two shops that had been pillaged. "If this is the road to Independence," Washington brooded aloud, "this sort of unrest might be seen to be justifiable by some, but it is hard for me to stomach."

The TIME had come to Alexandria.

Over the next several fortnights, he discussed the various arguments in favor of independence with Sally and George William Fairfax whenever visiting Belvoir. George William's first cousin, Lord Fairfax, a prominent member of the House of Lords, had encouraged them in correspondences to support these new measures of British rule. Washington's two close friends had come to believe that any opposition to the king's wishes essentially amounted to treason.

"What you and others call 'independence' is just a silly term, George," Sally Fairfax said. "How can you possibly think yourself to be independent when our very way of life depends so fully on our dear England? If the current system has worked here in America for the past hundred and fifty years, what is the reason to rush out and turn against our king?"

Washington countered, "Most of my former legislative colleagues see these intrusions into our lives as nothing less than the first steps of a despot. The pamphlets that are currently being circulated – they say much more nasty things about King George."

"Well, you can see that Sally and I stand in complete opposition to you, George," George William concluded. "The Crown gave our family, as he did yours, these lands as a trust. None of us should break that trust. We are obliged to continue our fidelity to King George. There are many, many others in the colonies, my friend, who feel the same way."

"It looks like all of us are going to be forced to make a choice, sooner rather than later," Washington reasoned. "The question will be put to each of us. Are you for or against the king?"

He flushed as he warned, "If the Parliament does not rescind these measures, which amount to taxation without representation, we could be in for some nasty upheavals hereabout."

Many testy days followed. A so-called 'friendly delegation of leading patriots' visited Belvoir. Before hearing them out, George William Fairfax reminded them of the Fairfax family's long and loyal relationship with the British Crown.

The well-dressed delegation from Williamsburg quickly got to the true purpose of their call. They earnestly focused on the certitude of the arguments against King George and suggested that Virginia would be better off without him. The smooth-talking Thomas Jefferson, Patrick Henry, and Fairfax's other neighbor to the south, George Mason, pressed their case.

In his typically unctuous manner, Jefferson beseeched George William and Sally to join his movement. Fairfax had never thought much of the red-haired lawyer – he thought him to be ill mannered and too easy with his words. Fairfax was most offended by Jefferson's use of the phrase 'his movement,' as if he owned it in the first place. The three gentlemen concluded their visit by darkly hinting that the Fairfaxes might experience unexpected hardships in the near future if they held their positions.

"It's all rubbish and . . . none of your business, you damned fools. Get out!" In his rage, George William nearly cuffed Mr. Henry after the known firebrand spewed out another vitriolic comment. A moment later, Fairfax had the delegation forcibly removed from the grounds.

Soon thereafter, the TIME would come to Belvoir.

It started with a grisly attack on some fine imported Highland steers. Several were found castrated – the bloody testicles hung on nearby pitchforks.

When a shipment of china from Liverpool came to the mansion, it contained shards of broken ceramic covered with decaying hens, barnyard excrement, and maggots. A scrawled note inside read: "For ideas so foul, we give you these – your fowls." It was signed – "The New World Patriots."

Several weeks later, a more horrific attack occurred which was haltingly recounted to George William and Washington by two slaves of Belvoir. One of the Irish overseers of the Fairfax plantation, Mr. Seamus McIntyre, went to market at Groveton one Saturday with several of his best Negro fieldworkers and the cook. Once recognized as being from Belvoir, their wagon was surrounded by an angry mob. Mr. McIntyre desperately resisted, and was pummeled by three loud-mouthed ruffians. The ruddy-faced overseer was then dragged away from his Negro workers and securely tied to a wooden chair.

Elijah and the other Belvoir slaves were forced to stand at a distance, but saw and heard all that transpired. Their tightly bound overseer screamed as the villagers hemmed him in. A profusely sweating townsman stuffed Seamus's bloody mouth with a cloth wetted with cheap whiskey. A table was carried out from the inn through a side door and placed on the uneven ground in front of him. Someone in the chanting mob brought a piece of paper along with a quill dipped in cow's blood in front of the gagged Irishman. "Sign, sign it," they warned. "Take your pledge!" . . . "If the damn Fairfaxes won't be like the rest of us, hell, Seamus, it's not your problem . . . Don't kiss the king's arse, like they do!"

The Negroes were held back and could only watch helplessly as a heavily perspiring McIntyre strained against his bonds, unable to holler out. Defiantly, he looked about, wildly shaking his head in disbelief. When his chair tipped over into the dust, the mob grabbed a rope and roughly hoisted the dazed foreman aloft, leaving him suspended from the village chestnut tree.

A pox-scarred vagrant yelled at McIntyre, "There's no liberty pole in Groveton, so's we use what we's got." In the back of the crowd, a disheveled, cross-eyed drunkard shouted in a slur, "You just stay there, you pit-hole . . . we's gun to coke youse goose! We's gut ways to handle prissy trayters, ain't I right, boys?"

The slaves saw Mr. McIntyre weaken in the oppressive heat, his head drooping against his chest.

"Let's make 'im hotter," someone screamed into the heavy air. "He'll be a cooked bird 'fore long, eh?"

Several stronger men in the crowd carefully lifted a bulky iron kettle onto some bricks within a flaming fire pit. Some of the villagers suggested aloud that the roofer's tar in the kettle would soon enough make a pleasing patriot brew. As it was stirred, an acrid odor permeated the air.

The strong-armed farmers lowered Mr. McIntyre jerkily into the bed of a wagon that had been drawn up. Two plump women clambered over the sides and started to dance lewdly around Seamus.

"Make 'im ready, Bess."

"Is 'e tender, yet? . . . Not yet, ya say?"

"How 'bout gittin' his skin ready for the oven . . . try 'is foreskin first."

"Are ya wantin' a taste, are ya' now?"

"'Don' takes 'im for a husbin', Mary, yuv' got me already – hah!"

Hearing that, one of the women paused before forcing her hand deep into the front of his freshly soiled britches. "Bess, I wonder if he? . . ." Her next words were lost in the crowd as men jostled the wagon toward the makeshift fire pit. The two village hussies were suddenly toppled from their perches as McIntyre was dragged backwards in the carriage. He was to be the day's roast.

"He was weak, real weak by then, sirs . . .," Elijah tearfully reported, "and then, it came . . . de tar, wit' a pole wrap at one en' wit' de stickum on de cloth . . . gobs oaf it, jus' so much . . . dat smellin', sicken' tar . . . Oh my, Masser Fairfax, oh lord my . . . de tar ana' 'is singein' flesh . . . oh, de tar. I's can still hear 'is muffli' wit' dat rag in 'is mout' . . . oh, de horror, de horror."

The slaves were forced to watch as several down pillows were brought from the inn. A short balding man made vicious, ripping cuts and tossed the headrests into the air. The man cackled as the white feathers rained down on the tar-blackened overseer. "Like a real goose," the villager yelled loudly, "and fit for our market, too!"

McIntyre seemed not to hear the screams that cascaded around him. "Not only you . . . you and your friggin' family, you and your stinking Fairfaxes . . . Belvoir terd!"

A little while later, a troublemaker suggested "a ride to market." When the wagon slowed to a stop, a short, curly-haired merchant stretched Seamus's head back and viciously yanked the kerchief from his mouth. He nearly choked on his spittle and caked blood. The act was especially shocking in that this particular person had always been thought to be mild-mannered. Instead, he had yelled, "That'll let 'im breathe better – we don't want to have 'im die now, do we?"

The two glum estatesmen sitting in Belvoir's drawing room could hardly believe the tale of the two slaves. "Go on. I have long suspected that man, Mr. Walker I believe, of being a scoundrel." Fairfax waved his workers to continue. "You must go on, nonetheless . . . What else?"

Elijah looked down before continuing. "And den, day suspicion dat he was all dun' . . . all gone. 'Dings got real quiet all sudden. 'Day brought de' wagon 'round to da' 'smittie's shop . . . cut him down off de chair . . . told us to get 'im laid down, told us he wuz all right . . . take 'im back to Belvoir. Dat's what 'day dun say, he'l be all right . . . but, he didn' muve, no sir. Smelled so an' broke' all up wit' da' fedders all over 'im. He wa' a good man. He dun die."

"And that is all Jonas? . . . Elijah?"

"Yes, suh' . . . But no . . . der's one 'nother thing . . . someun' mentioned 'bout a pled' or somepin' . . . as we were leavin' with poo' master McIntyre, someun say day' wished he'da sig' da pledge."

Fairfax turned beet red. "Murder has just happened in a nearby village, terrorists are about, and violent mobs are revolting against the Crown's law. And McIntyre . . . my best. All for a piece of paper!"

After they had dismissed the two Negroes, George William muttered, "And you call these 'patriots,' George? What are you thinking?" His disgust hit Washington in the gut. Fairfax and his wife were his two best friends.

Fairfax suddenly became subdued. "All this is closing in on us . . . what are we to do?" His question hung in the air. Washington could hear the anguish in George William's voice – there were to be no easy choices.

Over the next several months, Fairfax and his people at Belvoir were even more openly denounced as traitors to the so-called 'patriot cause.' In contrast, the residents of Mount Vernon were left alone.

Shortly after McIntyre's murder at Groveton, Martha and Sally Fairfax sat with their husbands sipping sherry. George William told them that if it were only up to him, he would stay and physically fight these criminals – whom he called 'hooligans' – but he had his family and their safety to consider. A visit to their relatives in central England seemed the best choice for now and at the same time would lighten Sally's ailing father's spirits.

Now, some twenty years later, Washington leaned over and took a drink from the stream. He threw away some small bits of leftover ham and resumed his walk along Dogue Creek heading west away from the Potomac. He sighed, knowing that so many Tories had been and still were good people. In the end, they had simply made bad choices.

Again Washington remembered back to the TIME and how poignant had been George William and Sally's leave-taking. The Fairfaxes assured the Washingtons that their absence would only be for a short while. They promised their neighbors that they would be back for the fall harvest after things settled a bit. Before leaving Virginia a month later, they argued their Loyalist cause one last time, hoping that others would adopt their way of thinking.

Priscilla and Jonathan Winfield, however, did not agree with the Fairfaxes and elected to stay on their gifted Woodlawn estate. They sided with the Washingtons, Lees, Randolphs, Byrds, Jeffersons and many other families of Virginia. Priscilla spoke for them all. "When all else is said, we are Americans not English subjects. Besides, Jonathan and I have no family to stay with in England or for that matter anywhere else. Our roots are here."

Washington was relieved that he had not been forced to influence their decision, or to reveal Priscilla's true identity. Instead, she and Jonathan had chosen on their own to stay in Virginia and join Martha and him in the growing struggle for American independence.

As George Washington strode up a slight incline, he felt out of breath as his thoughts returned to the struggles that had wrenched them all. Over the next several years, Belvoir was utterly destroyed as a result of its fragmentation into many small farms. The large estate's ruination had begun as a so-called 'patriotic opportunity' that soon seemed motivated more by land-grabbing opportunism than by benevolent idealism.

After the Fairfaxes sailed to England, the Sons of Liberty and certain unsavory groups began to divide up the estate's holdings by denying the authenticity of the original deed. They stated that it was nothing more than an undeserved 'King's Gift.' These rabid revolutionaries rationalized that since they did not believe in the King, they did not believe in his Gift either. Thereafter, the reapportionment of Belvoir took hold after scurrilous documents legitimized these pseudo transactions. Thus, without even purchasing them, the usurpers made haste to assume the tracts of small properties cut from the formerly extensive Belvoir plantation.

As a consequence, many of the estate's valuable English-influenced gardens and greenhouses were dug up and destroyed. Only a few sparsely planted cornfields and scattered vegetable plots took hold in their place. Now that there were so many fields left fallow, weeds and dense undergrowth quickly obliterated most of the once-grand landscape. Most needlessly of all, the Washingtons thought, the lovely sixty-year growth of the labyrinthine bowers was cut and burnt during a 'freedom picnic.'

Any last vestiges suggesting privilege and the attendant aristocratic grace of the estate were utterly destroyed. These ravaging republicans had completely consumed Belvoir's domestic order and tranquility in their drift toward insurrection.

After a time, Belvoir was no more.

7

Mount Vernon

Late Afternoon, June 1785

George Washington eventually made his way to the Grist Mill that he hoped would soon be a part of the Winfield's enlarged estate. As he walked, he remembered that he had been fortunate to discover the plot against Jonathan Winfield that had come to light shortly after the Yorktown campaign of '81. It appeared that a few self-styled patriots did not wish to stop after first destroying Belvoir – the crass profiteers wanted Woodlawn next.

Jonathan Winfield had been in the militia serving alongside the Continental Army and their French allies. While he was away, certain of these scoundrels who had long coveted his Woodlawn property began to compete for the attentions of his young wife. A plot soon took root.

After the decisive battle at Yorktown, one of Washington's senior intelligence officers had given him an intercepted message, a note that was intended for Major Winfield. It appeared that Winfield was secretly working as an agent on behalf of local Tories – specifically for the Fairfax family still self-exiled in England. Background intelligence reports corroborated that were it not for some good fortune, Cornwallis would have escaped the trap on the peninsula.

General Washington had gone over what was termed the "Winfield-affair" with his immediate staff. Unlikely as it seemed, he decided that if Jonathan was indeed proved a traitor, the matter must be dealt with severely. After all, it was Priscilla and her three children who were his true blood relatives, not her husband.

While Washington was debating his course of action, reports came from Martha of recent mysterious happenings. The Winfields' eldest son Aubrey, a six-year-old, had died without any forewarning. Her other news concerned many instances of property desecrations in Alexandria. Martha's letters served to remind him of earlier days during the TIME in the Northern Neck.

A month after receiving the apparently damning intelligence report about Major Winfield, Washington attended a memorial service at Mount Vernon for his stepson, Jacky, who had also unexpectedly died.

While standing in the parlor of his home, the General overheard some delicately spoken conversation coming from an adjoining hallway. Two of the gentlemen of Alexandria, too fine to serve in his Army he thought, were sourly wondering whether their false message implicating Major Winfield had "found its mark." Both were shadowy members of a nearly defunct remnant of the New World Patriots. Not noticing Washington, the two agreed that when the young major was found out and convicted of treason, "he would likely be summarily hung like that André chap."

One demonically gaggled, "When that happens, we can surely take over the full Woodlawn farm. It would be a snap."

"Besides that," the other snorted, "Major Winfield's pretty little wife will not have much of a chance with one or the other of us."

"Certainly not with both of us at once . . . though that prospect might be more interesting, eh Mr. White?"

Washington came around the doorway and pleasantly enough, confronted the two. Acting on impulse, he concocted a shrewd plan then and there. He took them aside to the privacy of his study and had each write a condolence note to Mrs. Washington concerning the untimely death of her dear son, Jacky. Unsuspecting, each of the men penned words of sympathy to the grieving woman.

Several days later, expert analysts and epigraphists from General Washington's intelligence service reported that there was nearly complete handwriting similarity between a certain Mr. White's condolence message to Mrs. Washington and the intercepted note that had imputed Major Winfield's treachery.

Washington recalled how relieved he had been to know the identity of his true enemies – two evildoers plotting under the guise of the New World Patriots:

There was not enough additional evidence for definitive proof, but no matter, Jonathan's exoneration had been of much more importance. The General realized that now he also needed to be wary of a new reptilian-like foe – he could see that these damned opportunistic libertarians were as dangerous, perhaps even more so, as were the outright loyalists. Accordingly, for reasons that only Washington could understand, he hastily reassigned

Major Winfield and a detachment of Virginia militia to protect Mount Vernon, Woodlawn, and most importantly – Priscilla.

Noting the position of the sun, Washington decided to head back to the main house. Along the way, he was able to check on his sheep herd and some newborn calves. Nearing the livestock corrals, the retired general looked back over his shoulders toward the Winfield property to the west. "Yes," he thought, "we have made it through those tough times and now we are heading to new ones. Thankfully, Priscilla and her family are again under my own watch."

Washington straightened up and gazed off to his right, down a curving gravel path toward the Family Vault. As he did, he spoke aloud, "We are still here and she is well, Lawrence. As I promised . . . still here."

Toward the end of June, the Washingtons and the Winfields signed an agreement at Mount Vernon. It was added to the bottom of the estate's original deed.

1746 Deed of Mount Vernon

(Originally known as Epsewasson)
This renamed home and lands about belong to
Lawrence Washington, his wife Anne,
and their future survivors (sic).
This new deed shall supersede all others.
May Providence continue to bless this house.

Lawrence Washington

July 1, 1746
1785 Agreement at Mount Vernon

The Woodlawn Mills – Subdivision
As of this date, 22 hectares will be transferred from
Mount Vernon to the adjoining Woodlawn estate,
henceforth to be known as Woodlawn Mills

George Washington Jonathan Winfield
Martha Washington Priscilla Winfield

Signed at Mount Vernon, June 30, 1785

8

Mount Vernon

Later June 1785

"I have never understood what you and the Adamses see in a college education, Alex. And then you have Mr. James Madison at the College of New Jersey and Mr. Jefferson, he a graduate of William and Mary." George Washington paused in reflection. "Benjamin Franklin never had a formal education, nor did I, yet we both know how erudite he is. As for me, I liked my outdoor schoolroom just fine, thank you."

Alexander Hamilton, one of Washington's most valuable aides during the Revolutionary War, was visiting while on his way to see James Madison. "As long as one is a student of life I suppose, sir," he conceded without argument, "but no, I mostly wish to speak today about our new Society of the Cincinnati."

"And the issues are? I thought we had almost settled the membership question."

"More or less, but frankly, General, the primary concern that our Society will discuss this year is the back pay and pensions due our Continental Army veterans. To settle this obligation, we desperately need to encourage a common currency – America needs a 'coin of the realm,' so to speak." Hamilton's tone was serious. "Only by this, can we address the sizeable debt due from each of the thirteen colonies."

"Why not address your idea to the current Continental Congress, Alexander? You've been a member."

"No luck there, sir – none at all! In a word, your former Continental Army still needs saving, General. Our Society compatriots certainly know it – they need your help and leadership. Even non-combatants like Adams,

---

John Jay, Mr. Madison and others are in agreement in this regard. Only a new centralized monetary system can fix it."

Hamilton squirmed as he added, "On the other hand, there is another group of people like Samuel Adams, Thomas Jefferson and Patrick Henry who prefer that any confederation between the states should be very loose – each state barely interacting with the others. Virginia or Delaware, for instance, would be beholden only to themselves. Please note, General, that none of these pricky-headed bastards ever faced a bullet in battle."

Washington was taken aback by his former aide's outburst, yet found that in the main he had to agree. "You're right, Alexander. I've never much liked Mr. Jefferson's fancy words ever since he claimed all the credit for writing what he called 'his Declaration.' It would be ironic, no tragic, if we won our independence but developed no systematic way to address the kinds of problems that you have referred to. It strikes me that you and men like James Madison will have to provide the solutions. For my part, I will gladly do what I can."

"Since James and I currently agree on many ideas, my visit to Montpelier will give us ample time to go over some options. Frankly, though, this nation-building often seems to go at a snail's pace. Whenever the deliberations in our current Congress get tedious, I think, but only to myself mind you, that maybe we would be better off with a king." Hamilton's bitterness was evident. "Distasteful as it sounds, it would be a distinct improvement over Congress's blustering aimlessness."

Washington leaned forward and haltingly placed his hand on Hamilton. "Well, in any case, we do not want to replace one tyrant-king with another now . . . do we, Alex? That is, if we can help it. You have so easily forgotten that we all, including the two of us, have our idiosyncrasies, our own jealousies, weaknesses, and failures. No one of us is perfect, nor are kings."

"Deep down, I know you are right, sir, but some of my fellow contrarians in New York are already espousing such views. Speaking about having different opinions, Baron von Steuben, General Schuyler and I still feel that the Society of the Cincinnati membership should be passed on in an hereditary fashion."

Washington put his hand up. "Alexander, do realize that if the Society adopts your proposal, people would be even more suspicious of the organization? As you are no doubt aware, folks already talk openly about your well-known love of all things British. We should not, I believe, grant membership out of hand to any bloodline descendant of my Continental Army officer corps. Nonetheless, you are correct in asserting that there should be some sort of mechanism for enlisting future members . . . that is, if we want the Society to survive at all."

As the conversation continued, a short young man came up alongside of the porch. "Pardon and good day, sires." It was John Quincy Adams, who introduced himself to Washington. "I was sent 'round to join you by your housemaid, sir." The eighteen-year-old had sailed from England and was on his way to matriculate at Harvard. "I have letters for you and perhaps you, sir . . . if you are Mr. Hamilton, that is. My mother expressly told me to deliver them, sires."

Looking at Sally Fairfax's familiar handwriting on the envelope, George Washington resolved to privately read her letter later and unobtrusively put the note in a pocket of his waiscoat. "This is indeed Mr. Hamilton, Master Adams, and I'm sure he'll be pleased with his own mail as well." Washington laughter put the young Adams at ease.

"Tell me, John Quincy, have your parents heard any news regarding our esteemed friend, M. Gilbert du Motier, the Marquis de Lafayette?"

"Yes, sir, they said that General Lafayette told them that since he so fondly treasured the time with you and Mrs. Washington here at Mount Vernon, he will soon be sending a gift of special basset hounds as a token of his esteem."

"Did he mention how things have been going for him at his family estate?"

"Yes, sir. Monsieur du Motier, as he is known over there, related that some political groups calling themselves 'democratists,' or some such thing, had recently sprouted up in some provinces of France. These clubs are starting to have, as he put it, 'people's discussions' to provoke limited turmoil."

"Yes, I heard the same," Hamilton interjected. "Mr. Jefferson wrote to my friend, James Madison, just two months ago. In the note, he mentioned that it appeared that the French people, encouraged by our own American experience, are now taking serious issue with their king, Louis the XVI, and are striking out for various liberties of their own. Jefferson's account praised the 'republican experiment that we have started in America' and was 'thankful that it is now beginning to also be keenly felt in Paris.' "

He shook his head and continued, "I hardly believed hearing Jefferson's words until Madison let me see the letter for myself. James and I had a good laugh about Jefferson's epistle. Despite his knack for feathery phrases, we imagined that our erstwhile American in Paris must have been enjoying the fine wines a bit too much, probably even more than his best Monticello grapes."

As Washington laughed at this, a house servant appeared at the open door, "The noon meal will be served shortly, gentlemen. Are you staying, Mr. Hamilton, sir?"

"Yes, that would be lovely, though I must leave by early afternoon."

That evening, Alexander Hamilton sat in his room in the Little Lion Inn of Culpepper where he stayed overnight on his journey to Montpelier. He carefully read the Marquis de Lafayette's note by the light of the room's flickering candle. Since he was fluent in French, he was easily able to review the letter.

April 1785

My dearest friend and warm companion,

Closer now I feel to you than in many years. Our winter has left a month past, yet the air in my countryside has a lingering chill.

My dearest wife, Adrienne, although she has never met you, sends her best. She has heard so much about you, about our late dearest Laurens, and about so many others from my lips. She sometimes wonders if my mind is at most times still there in America or with her here at La Grange.

Other than the nice weather, the atmosphere around here is bad. Just a month ago, a strange fire burnt down Count Levere's barn nearby. It was a clear case of arson, my friend. Last week, some farmers rioted in Auvergne province. I hear that things grow worse, especially with university students in Paris and Lyon.

I am afraid, dear Alex, when I see what people can and will do with too many ideas in their heads. Civil law and order is a most necessary condition. Political change should have a rational basis or it should not happen . . . Do you not agree?

I will try to encourage my fellow noblemen, in the meantime, to review with King Louis what are his wishes. We will tell his Court and ministers to look at America.

Write me soon, my friend, and do keep an eye on our General for me.

Your dear friend,
Gilbert du Motier
Your Lafayette

That same evening, George Washington sat alone in his study and adjusted two large hurricane lamps. He ruminated on the past ten years as he pulled the large chair near his desk. His vision was failing and given his chronic rheumatism, what new malady would visit him next? He morosely wondered if it could be his death.

Putting his brooding aside, Washington nervously opened Sally Cary's letter. He skimmed over the page, again feeling that he had never known such a woman. Taking out some wire-framed glasses from a desk drawer, he began reading.

March 1785

My Dearest George,

Share this note if you must with Martha but know that I mean it for you alone. She might see my letter as intrusive in many ways and have an unwarranted jealousy. It is better that personal letters between the two of us remain confidential.

Sadly, we are required to stay here in Leeds because of our well-known loyalties to the King. With the resulting loss of our beloved Belvoir, it appears less likely that we will ever, how hard is it for me to write this, ever return to Virginia. As well, my dear husband George's health seems to weaken daily despite the ministrations of fine physicians.

As an aside, you will be interested to know that King George has oft asked my husband's brother, Lord Fairfax, if we think that America can stand on its own. His Royal Highness is of the private opinion that he hopes that it might – particularly given the current unrest growing at his backdoor in France.

My dear George, it saddens me to know that not only is our Belvoir gone, but as well the dances with you at Mt. Vernon, my childhood at my father's home on the James, et cetera. These and so many more . . . the times that we all shared seem remote now, forever untouchable.

Please know that I*/we love you, miss you and pray for you daily. Do give my love to Priscilla and her Jonathan. I think of them often– all of our futures are with them and their children.

Your dear affectionate one,
Sally Cary F

The General's eyes misted as he put the note on his desk and wiped his eyelids with the back of his cuffs. "Where is Sally now, how is Sally?" he had to wonder. He tapped his thumbs and hummed the words of a popular madrigal song:

How would you see me these many years gone –
A web spun in mystery, a song never sung . . .

He reread her letter, hoping to find some nuanced word, a phrase –
anything at all that he might have overlooked. Squinting in the poor light, he
stared intently at the last paragraph. There it was – a clue to her heart's true
intent. Sitting above the written 'we' was a correction. He made out her edited
touch on the elegant linen paper. Sally's smudged 'I*' was unmistakable, like a
coded message. He reread the note. After so many years apart, the realization
hit him like a thunderclap. Once again, she was there for him.

George Washington got up and went by himself to the Mansion House's
paper-brocaded reception hall. He recalled meeting the charming Miss
Sally Cary there at many cotillions. The reverie was so vivid that if she
somehow had walked in, George Washington would not have been surprised
in the least. As he quietly danced a few steps by himself in the shadows, the
handsome gentleman farmer of Mount Vernon smiled as he thought about
all the Winfields of Woodlawn:

"Yes, Sally, yes. Priscilla and Jonathan," he thought, "our futures are
limited but not yours."

How would you see me these many years gone,
A web spun in mystery, a song never sung.
   Too much never spoken, too much never heard,
A life missed in walk-with
A life never known.

We once had a start, yes, a bell to be rung,
A chord of endearment, our hearts played as one.
   That love all appealing ourselves to enfold,
Now turned and unreeling
The embers turn cold.

I would be with you if I had the chance,
A time lived forever, a tune we could dance.
    Though true we're apart now yet soon here will be,
I still would romance
And be always with thee.

Madrigal song; composer unknown; 1745

9

Philadelphia, Pennsylvania
July 1787

"Proportional representation as determined by each state's population best fits the aims of our Declaration of Independence. Alex, it seems the right action for us to take . . . this is how we see it in Richmond."

Alexander Hamilton walked over the cobblestones with Edmund Randolph, governor of Virginia. It promised to be another sweltering day in Philadelphia. "I fully agree with you, Edmund. Allotting the same number of delegates for each state is a major flaw of our current Confederation of States. One small state can effectively block the wishes of a larger and more powerful one."

Randolph and his fellow Virginian, James Madison, were the chief proponents of the titled "Virginia Plan" modeled on the House of Burgesses. They favored having a powerful unicameral legislature, a chief executive administrator and lastly, a supreme judiciary court in the new American government.

Hamilton recalled that John Adams had also stressed having a strong executive as head of state. "I know that James Madison," Hamilton said, "frequently cites such ideas from Adams's 'A Defence of the Constitutions of the United States.'"

"Alex, I must say that you most thoroughly argued such an opinion yourself a month ago. Some of us in the room thought that you would even go so far as to call for an American king . . . But instead, you ended arguing the case for having an executive or president receive a lifetime appointment."

"It is amazing to me that some fail to see Adams's big picture for having a robust central government," Hamilton said. "Many men like Messers Henry and Jefferson in your Virginia and Governor George Clinton in my New York are so small-minded and selfish. There is nothing beyond their own state borders – likely even nothing, I imagine, past their own wood-rail fences." He shook his head in frustration and heatedly went on, "I sometimes think that they believe that it was their own, and only *their* own, state militias that won General Washington's war."

The Pennsylvania State House loomed before them in the morning haze like an imposing fortress. The Pennsylvania Keystone militia had cordoned off an area around the plaza to keep away any curious or unruly on-lookers. This helped guarantee the implementation of the first two orders of business that the convening delegates had agreed on months ago – that their sessions be kept absolutely secret and undisturbed.

Once inside, the two men quietly took their seats. Seeing the assembly's president, George Washington, sitting silently at the front desk, Hamilton whispered across the aisle to Randolph, "Edmund, Washington must wonder what he got himself into with all of us. Truly, this is not his cup of tea, eh? He was so much more relaxed in the presence of his officers. He now looks a bit off put, I think."

That morning, Luther Martin, a lawyer from Maryland and William Paterson of New Jersey were once again arguing against the recently approved Virginia Plan and its requirement of proportional representation. They detailed their own "New Jersey Plan." Under the Martin-Paterson scheme, each state, no matter its size, would have the same number of legislators, much like the present Confederation.

A fortnight previously, Alexander Hamilton foresaw that this impasse would be forthcoming. Fortunately, an unexpected opportunity presented itself.

During the previous weekend, Hamilton had secretly met with William Paterson and Luther Martin at the Owl's Nest Tavern in western Conshohocken. The three men were there to discuss the possibility that Hamilton from New York and, with his encouragement, Gouverneur Morris and his fellow Pennsylvania delegates would help their New Jersey motion to pass.

Hamilton spoke in a hushed tone as a conspirator might. He knew better than to be overheard. "Gouverneur Morris, Thomas Mifflin and others can bring Pennsylvania's delegates along with me, Mr. Martin. We will support your concept of a Senate. So construed, each state would have the same number of senators."

Luther Martin took a deep draught from his tankard. He knew that without Mr. Hamilton's and the Pennsylvania delegation's support for his concept of a Senate, there was little chance of its passage, but he was deeply curious about Hamilton's motivation.

As it was presently, Martin was afraid that with a House of Representatives already set in stone, small states such as Maryland and New Jersey would have little political leverage in any national government. If there was not a second chamber, it was likely that the federal legislators selected from Massachusetts, New York, Pennsylvania and the four populous southern states would be free to enact each and every law of the new Union. Given this, Martin was more than perplexed about Hamilton's offer of support since it seemed to go against the self-interest of his own New York.

After a barmaid brought fresh pitchers of ale, Hamilton leaned forward and said, "Gentlemen, let me get to the crux of the matter, as I see it. It is of utmost importance that these so-called Senators of yours are very carefully selected – particularly if there are going to be only two or three from each state, as you propose. My own concept for you both to consider is simply this: if we back your so-called Senate, the original Senators selected in each state would be the initiators of a heredity-based succession. Now listen closely. I will try to explain my reasoning."

"What the hell are you talking about, Mr. Hamilton?" William Paterson asked. "You seem to favor having a rather exclusive club, call it an 'old boy's club,' rather than a legitimately elected body. It's preposterous!"

"Hold off a minute, sir – hear me out. Since this august body – your Senate – would deal with important issues like treaties and foreign relations, as well as judicial and executive appointments, the men selected to it should be removed from the vagaries of popular pressure, in contrast to those serving as Representatives. It would be best if they are men of necessary breeding." Hamilton darkly summarized, "I insist that Senators not be elected – this is my demand, my sole bargaining chip."

Luther Martin tried to reason with the New Yorker, "How firm are you on this, Alexander, this inheritance notion? You know that some here in Philadelphia suspect your, what can I say, Anglophile tendencies . . . Or are you only interested in your own son's inheritance?"

"No, not at all," Hamilton insisted. "But I strongly feel that European parliaments, such as the English with its House of Lords, are good models for us."

Hamilton smugly raised his eyebrows, provoking Paterson to break in. "Are you suggesting that the popular interest is best voiced by the opinions of a few American families? That is the back-end of a bull, sir!"

Luther Martin glanced warily at his associate from New Jersey. It was widely known that Hamilton had a reputation of being violently short-tempered and he feared that he might respond to Paterson in kind. If this discussion kept up, he thought, Paterson would certainly ruin the chance for him to get Hamilton's support for his Senate proposal. Martin was crafty enough to sense that they must lead the New Yorker into believing that he would be getting something in return.

Hamilton shrugged off Paterson's slur. "I personally have no intention of returning to some royalty scheme but if we have a Senate, it must provide a certain amount of worthwhile inertia. I am not much encouraged by turnover and frequent changes in any body politic. Important decisions cannot be made in a forum prone to the whims of short term, popular interests, Mr. Paterson."

"Wait right there, sir." Paterson raised a finger. "Again, tell me – what is wrong with the concept of voting for Senators? Certainly, the citizens have the right . . ."

Hamilton waved him off testily. "It's not their right at all! It is incumbent that we make sure that the office of Senator is passed down within the same family according to the principle of primogeniture. This solution is paramount, I believe, to having a fixed, permanent and effective federal government."

Paterson was annoyed at once again being put down, and sputtered, "Luther, speak to this lunacy – don't just sit there!"

Martin reassured his ally with a pat and whispered under his breath, "Shush, William. I think I can hook him, so mind yourself." Straightening up, the Marylander asked, "Seems quite enough, Mr. Hamilton. Are you nearly done?"

Alexander Hamilton stood and leaned forcefully against the table. "I think you have both clearly heard me out. Put bluntly – if the Pennsylvanians and I *do* decide to give you our support, I would demand that you will then support this, my own proposal in return." Hamilton stared directly into the bulbous eyes of Luther Martin before petulantly turning to Paterson for effect.

"Hold on, Mr. Hamilton, take it slow. One thing at a time." Martin replied unsteadily. His slimy hands made it difficult to grasp his tankard. He realized that if he gave his agreement that evening, Hamilton's critical political support was about to be his and Paterson's. He thought the timing to be fortuitous – a compromise written by Roger Sherman was to be discussed within the week by Eldridge Gerry and their Grand Committee of the Convention. "Mr. Hamilton, hear me out, please. I could never pass my own motion of having a separate Senate if I attached your suggestion for senatorial selection to the proposal."

"Why not, Mr. Martin? Our Philadelphia Convention can approve the whole matter at the same time."

"I can tell you why not, Mr. Hamilton. As of now, the delegates would frankly see your idea as a duplication of the House of Lords – a return to aristocracy. For that reason, and that reason only, they would likely vote our New Jersey Plan down." Martin wondered if the New Yorker could detect the tremor in his voice. "If, on the other hand, my resolution is first passed with your and the Pennsylvanians' support, we could then see what could be done. Let me tell you what I have in mind – it should interest you."

William Paterson rubbed his chin. "Make it short, Luther. All this chatting is getting to be too much – simply give Mr. Hamilton your strategy of steering both proposals through the Convention's rules of order."

Martin smiled with his familiar tic and spoke in a hushed tone. "After the first vote, and with your help its approval, Mr. Paterson and I would bring our support to bear for your brilliant suggestion. It should be an easy matter. With all free men being allowed to vote in elections for members in the so-called House of Representatives, no one should see any harm in having the Senators in this second chamber chosen by the guidelines you have outlined this evening."

Martin leaned forward, turned his tankard and rested his distended belly against the heavy plank table. He wondered if Hamilton could sense his duplicity. The rotund Marylander slurred, "So, as a matter of fact, I agree with you, Mr. Hamilton. This second plan of yours regarding the new Senate will be vital to ensuring a fitting degree of long-term political stability. But, and this is an important 'but,' first things first. We should delay my and Mr. Paterson's support until after the first vote and the decision is finalized. Then, you will get our votes thereafter. After all, we owe so much to all the men and their families who threw off the yoke of the British Lion."

"I'll drink to that," Hamilton said loudly as he raised his ale. "Here's to those families you salute – my own is one of them."

Two weeks later, the practiced lawyer Luther Martin concluded presenting the arguments of the six smaller states while standing at his desk. He used the example of the Roman Republic. "The second legislative body, the Senate, would not be charged with duties of taxation, revenue management and budgets – the ways and means. These would be the function of the people's Representatives. On the other hand, issues such as dealing with judicial appointments or approving foreign treaties do require a different approach. These latter kinds of deliberation would be best held in a second chamber wherein each state has an equitable representation. With this, I rest our case."

After being recognized, Mr. Roger Sherman added, "We have also discussed this scheme thoroughly in Mr. Elbridge Gerry's Grand Committee and I now formally propose this compromise. The new Congress will consist of two chambers – a lower body constituted of Representatives, the proportional number of which would be by state population, and an upper body constituted of two Senators from each of the various states."

It seemed like minutes passed before Luther Martin stood again, looked around at his fellow members, and petitioned the chair. "Sir, I appreciate the amendment of the honorable Mr. Roger Sherman from Connecticut to my motion. At this time, I would also wish to express that Mr. Paterson and I are most grateful for the newly granted support of the distinguished delegate from New York, Mr. Alexander Hamilton."

Gasps of disbelief filled the room.

As Hamilton addressed the others, his arguments sounded strangely ill conceived. The perplexed delegates imagined that he must have either given in to some secret accommodation or else was just completely out-of-sorts.

Randolph whispered an aside to James Madison. "And here we have it, this elfish urbane elitist – do I dare still call him a friend?" His comment was loud enough to be overheard. "Here this Hamilton, a delegate from a large state such as our own, James. He stands to lose so much for New York with Martin's cockeymaney idea and all for what?"

After several hours of contentious discussion, the question was finally called. Washington summarized the voice vote, which completed the Grand Convention's morning business. "The votes in favor of the amended motion of Messer Sherman to the original proposal of Messers Paterson and Martin win – a total of thirty versus twenty five, with two abstentions, my own included."

Even without there being any representative present from the state of Rhode Island, some sarcastically labeled the approval the 'Rhode Island Compromise,' since everyone in the Gunmetal Room that sweltering morning knew that without such a compromise, Rhode Island would in no way join their new Union.

The New York lawyer was aware that he had provoked a bitter reaction with his turnabout. Hamilton felt ostracized to the point of nausea as he and James Madison hurriedly left the session by a side door. Thankfully, they had been invited to the nearby home of Dr. Benjamin Rush for the noon repast, and he could avoid the ire of the other delegates. Despite his discomfort, he looked forward to the break and to meeting Dr. Rush's guest from England, Mrs. Abigail Adams.

After they arrived, they sipped sherry in the parlor. Abigail Adams remarked to the others that she and her husband had just dined with the recently widowed Sally Fairfax and later with John and Angelique Church in London. She laughed at herself and described how much wicked fun the others had had calling themselves 'expatriates' while at the same time speaking fondly of 'our dears – Washington and Hamilton.' Hamilton was momentarily startled to hear his name being suggestively linked with his wife's older sister, Angelique, and could only trust that his emotions did not show.

Hamilton imagined that if John Adams were here, he would have understood and fully supported his point of view and his strategy at the Philadelphia Convention. Each man had always favored traditional English ways of doing things – properly and in order. For both men, the recent peasant uprisings in France served to reinforce their fear of espousing full-blown republicanism in America.

On the other hand, he had heard rumors that Thomas Jefferson, then posted in Paris, continued to exult in all things French –even celebrating their recent riots. It was similar to what Jefferson had so cavalierly said about the recent Shay's rebellion, that "even a bloody revolution is good now and then." Hamilton realized that his negative opinion of Jefferson always came back to this: the man of Monticello could not possibly know the gruesome deprivations that he, Washington, and Lafayette had endured during the War. Hamilton often fumed that this self-centered Virginian allowed himself to voice such grandiose ideas only because of his dastardly libertine nature.

After the meal, he and James Madison excused themselves, stating they had to go over some committee drafts before the afternoon session. On their way to the front door, Abigail Adams intercepted them. "Wait just a moment, Mr. Hamilton; I nearly forgot. My husband gave me a parcel and correspondence to give you. I will fetch them both from my room – please pardon me for a moment."

She shortly returned and gave both packages to him, laughing lightly. "You can see they are still sealed, so you know that I did not peek."

Hamilton bowed formally. "Your service is very much appreciated, Mrs. Adams."

When the Convention reconvened that afternoon, Mr. James Wilson of Pennsylvania, a member of the Committee of Detail, took the floor and introduced an additional consideration regarding the Senate. "I move that selections to the Senate be carried out less frequently than for the Representatives – every six years. After first voting on this, we must then determine the method by which these Senators are to be selected – whether by popular vote or otherwise."

Matters will quickly change later this afternoon, Hamilton felt, when the Convention got to the second issue that Mr. Wilson mentioned. He knew that once he obtained the promised support of Martin and his Marylanders, the membership of the Senate would form up along his wishes. The outcome would prove to be worth his effort, he thought sardonically – the Convention delegates will go ahead and approve his plan of Senatorial selection – succession by birthright.

John Dickinson stood on the other side of the room in order to make a few other points. "May I not amend your motion now, Mr. Wilson? I propose that each Senator should be selected by each state as each state decides. We should not demand that each state use the same formula."

While a heated discussion ensued about Wilson's amended motion, Hamilton sat sullenly as he observed that Luther Martin, the taciturn Maryland lawyer, must have had his usual heavy dose of ale during the lunch break. Hamilton twisted in his chair. He wanted to go over and rouse the fellow, make him get up and declare that these Senators should in no fashion be voted into office. Hamilton felt that Martin should do exactly as he agreed to do the previous weekend at the Owl's Nest when they had cut their deal – he should recommend that the Senators be appointed on a hereditary basis.

"Dammit, Martin," Hamilton thought, "speak out against the question!" Hamilton's icy glare at Luther Martin cut through the hot, late afternoon air, but the Marylander looked away.

Hamilton fumed to himself. He knew that it was only because of his and allied Pennsylvania support earlier that day that Martin and his associates had their Senate at all. He began to suspect that he had been taken for a fool.

In the midst of the rancorous debate, Hamilton's ally, Gouverneur Morris, a respected Pennsylvanian with well-known aristocratic leanings, had the effrontery to blandly suggest that perhaps Senators should be granted their office by some standard means of succession and not be elected as John Dickinson and James Wilson had proposed. He said, "With this important issue of the selection and succession of Senators, it seems quite imperative that we of this Convention devise a more proper roadmap for future generations. What better than to have proper men successively inherit their own family's permanent Senate seat? Good governance cannot arise from the streets, gentlemen, but must be imposed from above from people like us. What do we want with this?"

In mid-sentence, streams of rebuke rang out and Morris's face turned pale.

"Mr. Luther Martin, you have been noticeably silent through this afternoon," George Washington noted as he gaveled the room to order. "Since you and Mr. Paterson introduced the original concept of the Senate to which the Convention finally agreed, do you not have something to say about the members' selection process to this very same Senate?"

Luther Martin stood. His thick knuckles blanched as he gripped the chair's wing top. Despite the room's heat or perhaps because of it, the Marylander spoke out with surprising forcefulness, while not daring to look in Hamilton's direction. "Mr. President and fellow members . . . I find Messers Wilson and Dickinson's motions regarding the selection of Senate members to be entirely satisfactory. A free election by each state – done as they themselves decide – is necessary to keep each state independent in our envisioned Republic. As Jefferson and his committee said eleven years ago in this very room, "All men are created equal." With this proposal, I might add that all states are created equal – they should decide how they choose."

Sitting stone still, Alexander Hamilton couldn't believe what he was hearing. "What a piss-hole," he thought, "Martin is worse than a whoring Jezebel. The ass!"

"This amendment of Mr. Dickinson's best guarantees State's rights, rights which we all hold precious." Martin stole a glance at a frowning Gouverneur Morris. "I support this motion. I have nothing else to say. I move to call the question."

The final draft of the Constitution, signed September 17, 1787.

Article I;   *Section 3 –*

The Senate of the United States shall be composed of two Senators from each State (chosen by the Legislature thereof) for six Years; and each Senator shall have one Vote.

Years later, *Amendment XVII* approved in 1913.

The Senate of the United States shall be composed of two Senators from each State, elected by the people thereof, for six years; and each Senator shall have one Vote.

As Benjamin Franklin, the current President of Pennsylvania, left the State House, a young boy of the city asked, "Do we have a republic or monarchy, sir?"

His response was soft, yet terse. "It is a republic, my lad, as long as you keep it." The elderly statesman limped down the street toward the river (1).

"Alex," Washington asked affectionately as they walked along, "do you honestly think it will all work out? With all the differences found throughout America – large/small states, freemen/indentured slaves, coastal cities/inland farms – do you really think we can work something out? Take Mr. Madison or Patrick Henry. Though they are both from Virginia, look how different they are. You can certainly see that an abolitionist like Mr. Franklin, and Mr. Blount, a plantation owner of North Carolina, do not agree with each other on the issue of slavery. Great as might be the prospect of a united republic, I just wonder how this proposed federation of yours and Mr. Madison's can last for twenty years at the most!"

George Washington was silent for a moment, then added, "The legitimate and sure inheritance of our founding ideas will be an inherent problem – but I think it is important that they are carried on. As my mother's cook used to say, 'You need to keep the soup stock going so that new ingredients will inherit the original flavor.' "

"That is why, sir, I was arguing behind the scenes over the past week for an inheritance-based mechanism for the selection of the so-called Senators. At least with that scheme, founding families like yours, General, would be linked by a chain of patriotic heirs who could govern into the future. Your mother's cook was right, sir. It is indeed the stock that makes the soup."

"But you are no doubt aware, Alex, that you had entrenched resentment to that scheme of yours. Perhaps, though, it will take hold sometime in years to come."

Taking leave of Washington and walking a short way further, Hamilton absently felt the bulge in his inner vest pocket. He reached in and paused to open the courier's letter from John Adams. Before he did, he examined the wrapping on the thick second document, the flat parcel that Abigail Adams had also given to him at lunch. A fancy red wax seal with lion figures bore the recognizable imprint of the British king's family, the House of Hanover. He suspected what this closed document might be about since his wife's sister, Mrs. Angelique Schuyler Church, had mentioned something to him on her recent visit to New York. "King George continues to be most interested in the success of America. He wants to assist in any way possible and may soon send a 'King's Promise' or some other such thing."

As he read the short letter from Adams, Hamilton pondered the message.

> *Mr. Alexander Hamilton:*
>
> *Be sure to place the sealed package, which my wife will give to you, in its designated and secure site. There are, in fact, two missives in the package — one within the other and both should remain so sealed. This is a request from your sister-in-law Mrs. Angelica Church, Mrs. Sally Fairfax, and the other Fairfaxes of Kent and myself, acting as an intermediary here in England. All of us, as you know, are George and Martha Washington's dear friends.*
>
> *Mrs. Sally Fairfax informs me that her dearest acquaintance, General Washington, will know the location of the assigned place at his Mount Vernon. She tells me that she has confidentially corresponded with him about these matters.*
>
> *Besides this directive, we are all praying for the right kind of required success for your Grand Convention there in Philadelphia. London seems so wonderfully civil compared to what Mr. Jefferson reports to me from Paris. Times certainly have changed all through France since I was there four years ago.*
>
> *I presume that your upcoming dinner with the Cincinnatus Order goes well, Alexander. It is not that Mrs. Adams and I adamantly oppose your idea of a hereditary and military basis for your Society's membership, but it is just that . . . oh, I do wish that I had somehow served as well and could be included in your club!*
>
> *John Adams   London, six June 1787*

Alexander Hamilton now wondered what he must do with the sealed packet from the King's Court. He could not give it to Washington right then since the General was presently far from home. He would have to temporarily place the sealed message in a safe location and calculated that such a place would be the new bank of his confidant, Robert Morris, here in Philadelphia. After the Convention's work was complete, he would take the packet to Virginia and, at the direction of Adams's letter, place it in its designated and secure site. Hamilton felt reassured that General Washington could successfully lead them there.

Hamilton went directly back to the City Tavern and continued brooding in the solitude of his stuffy third-floor lodging room.

(1) Attributed to Benjamin Franklin at the close of the Convention of 1787.

10

Philadelphia

September 1787

Two months later, James Madison and other members of his Committee of Style completed drafting the Constitution of the United States in the first-floor East Room of the Pennsylvania State House. Thirty-nine of the remaining delegates, the president, and the secretary signed the final four-page document on the seventeenth of September. It was then ready to be sent to each state convention for ratification. The signators realized that it would still take the approval of nine states, three-fourths of the twelve states on the document, before the United States of America could be formed.

The night the Constitution was signed, Hamilton told his friend Madison that the two should plan to meet in November with a learned friend, Mr. John Jay of New York, in order to spur on the ratification process. Since Madison and Hamilton had developed a like-mindedness over the past four years, the young Virginian responded agreeably. "We certainly need to be clear in our arguments for a Federal cause, Alex. There are so many men that do not see our point of view."

The two colleagues planned to write what became known as 'The Federalist Papers.'

A few weeks earlier, Hamilton had surreptitiously met Benjamin Franklin on Race Street. He told him that he "needed a favor for our General." That same evening, he watched with fascination as Franklin, now in a white smock, carefully placed the still-sealed document into a thick glass cylinder. Hamilton had carefully obscured the packet's seal with an outside wrapping. After the scientist worked the ends of his cylinder by serial firings and cooling, he hooked up some tubing at small openings at both ends. Hamilton smiled as the older man worked with an air of devilish enthusiasm placing a canister holding what he called 'inert gases' next to him on the floor. "Yes, that is it! I will attach the tube to the canister . . . I cannot afford to lose any of the helium specially shipped from the Priestley laboratory."

Mount Vernon
Late September 1787

Before returning to New York, Alexander Hamilton joined George Washington and a slave at Mount Vernon to place the Franklin-modified cylinder in the Washington family's old Burial Vault. They lay it on a lower shelf inside an open wooden box next to a long brass tube. Both men understood that the cylinder contained 'The King's Promise' which was to be opened only at Washington's discretion. Hamilton stood there thinking that it was remarkable that over the years, Washington had given him so much intimate knowledge – and, as Hamilton realized, knowledge is power.

"That brass metal tube there contains my brother's last words to me, Alexander," Washington said. "I hold them close to my heart. You can see both my brother's and his three children's crypts there . . . nearby."

A decorated white porcelain object rested next to a large leather saddle on a second shelf jutting out from the Vault's upper wall. "That is my deceased sister-in-law's memory box," Washington explained. "It is a piece dated from the Ming Dynasty." A small key with an octagonal head lay against the saddle on the wooden platform. "The other is what you might guess," he said with a sigh. ". . . Lawrence Washington's last saddle."

After backing out and closing the Tomb's door, Washington quietly addressed the two other men. "Set in place, I trust. Let it be so for all time." The three men turned and silently returned up the hill to his large Mount Vernon Mansion House.

Sequelae: New York
1788-1789

Six months after Delaware became the first state to ratify the Constitution, the state convention of New Hampshire did likewise on June 20, 1788. It was the ninth state to ratify the submitted Constitution and the new United States of America became a reality.

Not wanting to be geopolitically separated by the other states, Virginia and New York finally voted to join the new Republic later that summer. The Rhode Island and North Carolina state assemblies continued to abstain from joining the new union until certain conditions could be met.

In the fall of 1788, the first national Representatives were elected and Senators chosen. They abolished the Confederation Congress and called for the general election of the chief executive, the first President of the United States. It was determined that each state would appoint a number of Electors proportionate to each state's total number of Senators and Representatives. In February 1789, each Elector met within their respective states and cast a vote for two persons. After the local elections were conducted, the state votes were sent via courier to the capital, New York City.

Frederick Muhlenberg, the first elected Speaker of the House, called a quorum on April 1, 1789 urging the "need to put the Government into immediate operation." On April 6, another quorum was met in the Senate as well. Their first order of official business was to count the votes of the Electors for President. The final tally, as transmitted by James Madison and read by the President of the Senate, Mr. John Langdon, was unanimous. All the 69 Electors voted for George Washington. Mr. John Adams had the second most, 34 votes.

Charles Thompson, Esq, thereafter transmitted a letter to George Washington.

> *Sir, I have the honor to transmit to your Excellency the information of your unanimous election to the Office of President of the United States of America. Suffer me, Sir, to indulge the hope, that so auspicious a mark of public confidence will meet your approbation, and be considered as a sure pledge of the affection and support you are to expect from a free and enlightened people.*

> *I am, Sir, with sentiments of respect,*
> *Your obedient, humble servant.*
> *John Langdon   April 6th* [1]

On April 30, George Washington began his Presidency after an Inauguration on the steps of New York City's Federal Hall, overlooking Wall Street.

The second order of business for the elected Representatives and Senators was that of addressing the contentious debates during the separate state-ratification conventions. Ten amendments were written that some felt were absolutely critical to ensure certain rights for citizens in the various states. These included clauses for the freedom of the press, the separation of state and church that George Mason and Thomas Jefferson had made a centerpiece of the 1776 Virginia Declaration of Rights, and the right of state militias and free citizens to bear arms. This last amendment was nonnegotiable for the legislators from Virginia, New York and Massachusetts. Their states, they argued, had an entrenched fear that any federal army might become the tool of an American despot. Vigilance and arms might be necessary to protect their states from any tyranny imposed by a national military. The Congress, after approving the measures, followed the rules set forth in the freshly approved Constitution and submitted these ten amendments to the eleven states, as well as to the still unassuaged representatives of North Carolina and Rhode Island, for their separate approval. Once the necessary three-fourth of the states had also signed these ten amendments, they were added to the Constitution and became known as the Bill of Rights.

For several years, it appeared that the most fractious issues had been settled. Many of the founding fathers, however, sensed that government building would be a work-in-progress for many more years. In fact, George Washington himself was sure that at this rate and with so many lingering disagreements, the Constitution would probably need to be wholly rewritten by each future generation of Americans.

Annotation:

[1] Documentary History of the First Federal Congress (1789-1791), Volume III; Linda Grant DePauw (ed.); Johns Hopkins Press, Baltimore and London, 1977, p.10.

11

New York City
July 4, 1790

A long column of men in military uniform paraded into the Fraunces Tavern's second-floor reception room for the annual dinner of the Society of the Cincinnati. General Washington realized this cadre of fellow Revolutionary military officers represented his truest friends. He wished that his executive duties gave him half as much pleasure as spending time with them.

As President, it humored him that people now called him "your grace." John Adams had even suggested "Your Highness" or "Your Excellency." Instead, he was heartened that night to once again hear "General Washington, sir." He enthusiastically hailed each passing officer as "major," "colonel," and "Sir." These were the only titles that mattered to him.

Washington towered stiffly over John Adams. The President looked resplendent in his pressed Continental Army uniform and remarked, "You would have been an interesting soldier, John. Goodness me, you are looking fine tonight. Glad to have you join us."

Adams's well-known criticism of the Society had been offsetting to many of its members. He frequently questioned whether it might be a secret aristocratic and militaristic organization. After suggesting his Vice President as an honorary member, Washington took it upon himself to describe the purpose of the Society to Adams. It allowed for the perpetuation of his former officers' camaraderie and goodwill. The only requirement was that each member had been an officer in the Continental Army. He was delighted that both Adams and John Jay would be given honorary memberships for their invaluable ambassadorships in lieu of military service during the recent War of Independence – Adams in Paris and Jay in Spain and France.

On the other side of the dining hall, Alexander Hamilton and Henry Knox were complaining of recent difficulties in establishing both a national treasury and standing army. Jay overheard them and came over. The chief judge of the national Supreme Court agreed, commenting, "Besides those, the legal system is such a mess! There are absolutely zero precedents and no proven jurists."

Knox frowned and voiced his own frustration. "We're all stuck in molasses – only a few in the new Congress see the need for a federal army that our General, our President favors."

"For me, my wish seems so simple. Would that it were," Hamilton sighed. "Any central government worth its salt needs to establish a single currency. Right now, we desperately need a strong national monetary system to standardize banking practices. How else can we expect to run national affairs?"

"It seems evident to me," Jay remarked, "that many Virginians don't believe in a federal government at all, so good luck with that, Alex. And going forward, Mr. Knox, I am not so sure many states will support the national army that you say is so necessary, much less pay for the one that they supposedly supported a decade ago."

Hamilton slammed his fist on the table. "Why the hell can't certain people see it my way! This is sheer . . ." In the middle of his rant, he noticed that a late arrival was moving to find a seat in the rear of the banquet hall and recognized the handsome Henry Lee, nicknamed "Lighthorse Harry Lee" during the Revolution. No one could ride a horse better than the dashing colonel from Alexandria, not even General Washington himself.

"Excuse me, gentlemen." Hamilton pardoned himself and went to the newcomer's side, giving him a hearty greeting. "So glad you could make it, Henry. Oh, by the way, I have some interesting news for you, and I would love to share it later. Come stay with me over at my place. No one is home."

As the two friends embraced, Washington tapped his glass goblet near the lectern to bring about order. "Well done, General Knox, a nice affair but everyone's attention to commands seems a bit lacking."

Henry Knox hardly shared Washington's light mood. "No matter, sir, but it is a whole lot easier than trying to tell Congressman Madison and those of his ilk what to do. Freedoms are all they speak of. I would prefer no free will at all – just obey!"

"I know what you mean, Henry," Washington said. "I have the same feelings about Mr. Jefferson – a fellow Virginian, besides. As far as most things go, Jefferson and I are far apart. You would think that identical plants would sprout if two seeds from the same genus were grown in the same soil of Virginia, but if Thomas Jefferson and I are any example, it doesn't always turn out that way."

"You know, General . . .," Knox commented, "we certainly need to remind people like him about all sorts of things before they go and advocate a bloomin' civil revolution."

"Yes, Henry, I hear you say, but who will be the 'we' and who besides Mr. Jefferson are the 'they?' Oh my," he sighed, stealing a cucumber from a nearby plate, "the two of us are getting too serious. Instead, let's have fun this evening."

Knox agreed and boomed, "Gentlemen, take your places!"

"Is this the extent of the meeting?" John Adams asked Hamilton as they sat down at the front table. "It does not seem like the members have anything more to do than have a good time, though I suppose that can be a worthwhile end in itself."

"You're right, John. We enjoy socializing first but then the Society does get around to an annual business meeting after the meal. You and Mr. Jay will, of course, be excused from that part of the dinner. You know, full members only and all that."

Hearing this, John Adams reached into a satchel resting near his chair and retrieved a wrapped, rectangular package. He said in an aside to Hamilton, "If that is the case, Alexander, now seems like a good time for this."

The Vice President got up and walked over to the head of the table where he interrupted General Knox. "Sir, I have a gift of sorts recently arrived from Paris. It comes from one of your beloved members, Monsieur du Motier, the Marquis de Lafayette. In an accompanying letter, he wished that I present it at your Society's dinner meeting."

"Of course, Mr. Adams, now might be . . ." The evening's presiding officer hastily chewed his large bite and washed it down with water. "Stay still. I will introduce you myself." Knox nearly toppled over – his immense girth caused an awkward stir.

"Here, sir . . . Let me help instead of you trying so hard. General Knox, please sit." Washington stood in his stead. "Mr. Adams, I will be glad to introduce you, but for what I am not sure." He turned and announced with his high-pitched voice, "The Vice President now has the floor."

"Quiet from the front!!" Knox bellowed from his seat as he mopped his perspiring forehead and bald pate.

John Adams was impressed by the rapt attention that Knox had been able to command. "Thank you, Mr. President, General Knox – I have a small announcement. I will be brief." Like Hamilton, the Vice President was prone to run at the mouth but he was quick to remember that military men were typically men of few words.

Adams reached beneath his seat and laid a package on the head table. "General and your fellow officers. Mr. Thomas Paine, now visiting in England, knew that I would be attending this dinner. He sent this package to me and told me to deliver this to you and your Society. It is a personal gift with a letter from one of your original honorary members who could not attend."

Washington opened the envelope but gave it back, "Please read it, Mr. Adams."

"Let me get my glasses, sir. Yes, here they are. The message says,

> "To my dear General G W.
>
> "I remain highly honored to be part of our brothers who now sit with you on July 4th. On occasion of the first meeting of our 1789 Society here in France, a Society that was formed in likeness to your Society of the Cincinnati, we elected to send you one of the treasured keys to our hated Bastille.
>
> "This black iron key represents a token signifying that we hold you in special honor for stirring our own imaginations. We feel a special debt and bond to you, my General.
>
> "I have always treasured being with you. You allowed me to learn so much, my dear friend, like the father that I never got to know.
>
> "Most Affectionately, G. du Motier, Marquis de Lafayette."

George Washington stood and unwrapped the package, lifting out a thick, seven-inch key that he held up to his former officers in the crowded tavern. He noticed there was a second correspondence, which he decided to read later in private.

When he sat back down and resumed his dining, President Washington sadly reflected that now his dear friend was embroiled in his own country's turmoil. He knew that there was little, if anything, his cabinet or he could do about such struggles in Europe. Washington thought it best that their very young country not risk foreign entanglements at this time. It had made for a hard personal decision, given his abiding love and concern for Lafayette and many other former comrades in France.

After the dinner at the tavern concluded, President Washington returned alone to his nearby lodgings and privately read the second letter from Lafayette.

> *My dearest General,*
>
> *This is a review, a resumé of how things truly are with my family and me. You may share this with my brother-in-arms, Alexander H as you might wish.*
>
> *I have recently been appointed the commander of the French National Guard in Paris. We have so many troubles at this time – I could not quite imagine. The King, Louis, and his family are presently under house arrest at the Palais des Tuileries. The situation worsens day-by-day, chaque jour. I am not sure whether the Republican- principles of our revolution will long survive – I trust they will.*
>
> *In my official duty, I traveled to England last month to learn about their constitutional monarchy and see whether it could be done in France. While there, I met with King George and his Privy Council at the suggestion of a John Church and Lord Fairfax. The latter said that he had relatives who once were your neighbors. The head of the Privy Council was somewhat bombastic, a Lord Aplington, but he seemed receptive, as well.*
>
> *During the course of our secret conversations, the King mentioned that he had sent what he called "The King's Promise" to you several years ago. He told me that he had a continuing interest in providing any support in his power that you might require in keeping America at peace.*
>
> *I trust that you and Alexander H will use this Bastille Key to better secure this previous communiqué from King George at Mount Vernon.*
>
> *Your affectionate comrade,*
> *Lafayette   Paris May 25, 1790*

Washington placed the letter in his desk drawer, blew out the candles, and went towards his bedroom. He surmised that he would show this note to Hamilton and have him help honor Lafayette's request regarding the real purpose of the Bastille key at Mount Vernon. Before he fell asleep, he touched the iron object in the drawer of his bedside table to reassure himself that it was still there.

The next day, Alexander Hamilton and his close friend Henry Lee enjoyed having breakfast in the sunroom of the Hamilton home several blocks from the Fraunces Tavern on Wall Street. Moira O'Shea, a young housemaid, served the men strong fragrant coffee, apple slices, eggs and large strips of well-cooked bacon.

After the serving girl left, Lee said, "You look like you have been thinking of something, Alexander – or is it that you had a bit too much wine last night?"

"You know me well. Maybe you can give me a clue, Henry. I need a little insight into James Madison. What he is thinking about? What makes him do certain things? I used to think I knew him well and very much enjoyed his company. Beginning with the Annapolis Convention in '86, we have agreed on so much . . . until lately."

He frowned and asked, "Is there something physically wrong with Madison? If so, it would make it far easier for me to understand his changed attitude. So much has happened lately, my dear Henry. Maybe Mr. Jefferson has him under some spell."

"Could be . . . their homes are pretty close to each other," Lee replied. "I have been to both places. We have an expression in Virginia, my friend, 'neighbors eat from the same soil.' No doubt, the two men may end up lying in the same political bed, so to speak . . . as long as they take their own women to different beds!"

Lee chuckled but Hamilton earnestly continued. "Be serious, now, Henry. Mr. Washington wants to know for himself what it is that is going on between these two."

"Why is that?"

"I will give you some background now so you can appreciate the news that I promised to tell you last night," Hamilton moved his chair back. "Let me recount a recent experience I had, but given that you know everyone involved, I must ask you to pledge that the facts of the matter not leave this room."

"You have my honor as a friend. You know that, Alex."

Over the next half hour, Alexander Hamilton described the recent private dinner that Thomas Jefferson, Washington's Secretary of State, had hosted. "George Washington had suggested that Mr. Jefferson host a meeting-of-the-minds, so to speak, between James Madison and me. As you are aware, Madison has become the leading opponent in Congress to my scheme of retiring the national debt, a plan that I, as the Secretary of Treasury, had devised after many weeks of work."

Lee interrupted him with a laugh. "Oh, how like the young Colonel Hamilton at our camp headquarters, holding your nose to the grindstone and all that! Poor, poor Alex, I am so, so sorry. Still the long-suffering servant. Please excuse my flippancy, but I couldn't resist. Go on, you have the floor."

"Well, I suppose you're right, Henry. Work has always been my middle name. In any case, President Washington supported my idea in full. My proposal also included paying reparations for the seized properties of former Tory citizens. The mechanism for sharing our past conflict's costly burden would require payments from all thirteen states proportional to each state's population based on 1790 census numbers."

"As you can imagine, Alex, rumors of these ideas have already spoiled a lot of men's nights in Richmond and Charlestown."

"I can't control anyone's sleeping habits, you know. But mercy, my train of thought has gotten way off course. Let me get back to the point of my story. I was frankly surprised to be invited by Jefferson to dine with him and Madison. Madison and I had come to loggerheads over this issue. He and other legislators from Virginia and South Carolina bitterly opposed settling the national debt in the manner that I had proposed – they felt that their states would have a resulting inordinate debt payment. Given their vast numbers of slaves, the two states are two of the most populous states."

"Seems reasonable that Jefferson would want to host this discussion – he has his own self-interest to look after. So what happened?" Lee gulped more coffee.

"At the dinner, they both vehemently argued that resolving this sort of debt meant that they would be settling a past national 'need' that was no longer of concern. They angrily mentioned that they did not need to pay for any past, present or future national army when their states' citizens had already paid and were still paying for their own state militias in South Carolina and Virginia."

"Alex, I must say that your and Mr. Washington's request sounds pretty reasonable to me, but did either of the men give an alternative solution for your conundrum?"

Hamilton rolled his eyes. "You won't believe it. Jefferson said something like, 'Goodness me, Mr. Hamilton, I would simply suggest that you forget this national debt which you find so bothersome – merely write it off.' He said that it was an accounting technique that he had often used successfully at Monticello."

Lee rubbed the nape of his neck, "This could seriously impact the central national government, correct? You can't do anything without money."

"You're right, Henry. Before I left, Mr. Jefferson neatly summarized his position. He said that he was convinced that we have too much, much too much government."

Hamilton stood up to stretch. When he came back from the window, he continued, "When I told President Washington about the dinner, he became quite exercised. Our General was truly impressive, Henry. You would have liked seeing him in all his majesty. He immediately met with me, Mr. Jay, Adams and Knox – deciding that the handling of the debt was at a critical impasse and threatened the short-term future of America. He implored us to get this issue resolved as a first priority. He stressed that we must reconstruct ties to England by cleaning the slate of our own national encumbrance, even including reparations to former Tories. Only by doing this, he said, could we assure America's trustworthiness."

"That's the General that we've always known – decisive. Sounds like he hasn't lost his touch."

"Within the week, Washington again pressured Jefferson to intercede with James Madison, the leader of the growing Congressional opposition, and me. During a second clandestine dinner of the three of us, I told them that if they gave their support or, at the very least, took away their opposition to my national debt repayment scheme, Washington and I would give a tit for tat and push ahead with their newly proposed relocation of the nation's capital."

Henry Lee was curious and asked, "Why did these two see this as an attractive offer – what's the catch?"

"Both Jefferson and Madison have intensely disliked the fact that the nation's capital is in teeming, dirty New York City – far from their rural estates in Virginia and the western territories. As our dinner continued, thankfully I was able to get a concession that at least the national banking headquarters would stay here in New York should the plan for a new Federal District be approved."

Sitting upright, Lee was amazed at what Hamilton had just revealed. "Does this mean that the national capital will be relocated to Virginia?"

"Probably so, but the Congress has to pass on it. But remember, Henry, the President wants this to be confidential. As his part of the compromise, Mr. Madison said he would not oppose or favor either proposition but allowed that without his active participation both proposals had fairly good chances of passage."

"And getting back to the details, Alex, the capital . . .?"

"The capital will eventually be moved to a new city constructed on a plot of land shared between Maryland and your Virginia on the Potomac. Near where you live, Henry. It would be located in a more rural setting central to all our thirteen states. Mr. Washington told me later that he figured he needed to give these shrewd operators something special if he was to get anything important in return."

"I can see why you called that an interesting dinner, Alex. What did you eat?"

"I can't remember at all, but getting back to my first concern, Henry, I still can't understand why James Madison has become so distant from me these past months."

"Frankly, I think that he is simply being pragmatic, Alex. No one can be agreeable about everything and, of course, he has to first look out for his and Virginia's own self-interests."

Hamilton pushed himself out of his chair. "Yes, I suppose you are right. There are so many deals being made with so little overall direction – just talk, talk, talk. People act as if only they and they alone know what is best for everyone else. Oft times, I think it would be better if we only listened to a single voice – one leader – like a king, Henry. It would be far easier than dealing with all the confusion we create for ourselves."

As he turned slightly in his chair, Lee could see Alexander Hamilton's firm, chiseled face, bright eyes and practiced mannerisms. He suspected that his friend was very aware of who he had become – a new breed of American aristocrat, entitled not by blood but by his own merit and ambition. Lee had always felt that his good friend might assume the mantle of leadership someday, but for some reason Hamilton's last comment unsettled him.

"Having an American monarch is an interesting concept, Alex, but," Lee said after a pause, "only General Washington could be . . . People would only listen to his voice and no one else. Maybe that prospect is at the core of what bothers Mr. Madison and Mr. Jefferson . . . and all those blasted republicans of theirs."

Moira O'Shea came through the double doors and announced, "Gentlemen, I have drawn your baths. Mr. Lee, you are in the west corner, first floor here. Mr. Hamilton, you are upstairs."

A half hour later, Hamilton lay back in his oval enameled tub. The warm water, spiked with fragrant neroli oils from Barbados, steadily drew out his grime and relieved his tension. He closed his eyes and reminisced about the sweetly perfumed streets bordered with Bougainvilleas, the tinkling metal sounds of wind chimes, and the gulls' pitched calls over Christiansted harbor in St. Croix.

As he settled down in the warm water of the tub, he felt a faint draft and looking back, he glimpsed up at the raven-haired girl. She lifted off her worker's blouse, tugged at an apron string and slowly, wordlessly, loosed her skirt, letting it fall to the floor. Jumbled reveries of the aqua-green Caribbean swept though him.

Moira moved to his side.

12

Carlisle, Pennsylvania
October 1794

Midday sun effected sharp contrasts of light and shade on azaleas scattered amongst the pinewoods along the winding York Pike. Two men in a carriage looked about as they entered the newly incorporated village of Heidlersburg. The town seemed more a collection of family farms than a village, much like other clusters of the rural Amish settlements in nearby Lancaster County. Scattered autumn colors in stands of oak and maple glimmered amongst the surrounding hills and the more distant range of the Allegheny to the west. They were headed northwestward from Hanover to Carlisle, the gathering place of a military, expeditionary force. The President of the United States, opting to wear civilian clothes, sat on the left passenger side and waved to a few residents busily repairing a plow near a dilapidated farm building. A fading hex sign hung over an ill-fitting barn door in the yard.

From the other side of the road, a disgruntled Pennsylvania farmer yelled out with a thick German accent, "Getzen sie back zu your grot fancy city, you vig headed dummerhans. Ve like der wey vi habst it hier . . . ve guvs usselves already."

The driver pulled hard on the reins and brought the carriage to a halt, sending up dust all about. "Sires, that man there is insulting us. What would you have me do?"

Nearby, another farmer's longhaired daughter raised her small fist. Despite her youthfulness, she jeered, "Why should people here have to live like Marylanders? . . . My mother says that they worship the Pope down there. We're not like them at all. In fact, here about we hate those fish-eaters and their evil ways!"

An older man came sluggishly alongside and hoarsely spat out a stream of invectives with a thick, guttural accent. As he did, the two passengers rocked sideways in their coach seats to avoid the stench of his soiled work clothes. He cried out, "Vi dunn likes the likes of you tellin' uz vas habst do. Gehen sie nach hause! Go home, gitzen sie von hier!"

"Mr. Franklin was absolutely right," Treasury Secretary Hamilton noted as he huffed and turned away. "So correct when he told me years ago that these stupid folk here in this lush Pennsylvania farmland do not even try to learn our English language. How can these rascals ever hope to get ahead?" In a squeaky condescending voice, he went on, "And then there's the Frenchmen . . . the Irish . . . Spanish, too . . . so many misfits fleeing their homelands and arriving on our shore. I truly have a most difficult time with all these foreigners, these riff-raffs, sir . . . they truly get beneath my hide." Hamilton continued to fume, "So much for Jefferson's ideas about free speech . . . These people don't care a penny's worth."

Washington covered his nose with a silk cloth and shouted, "Let's be on, Geoffrey. Not to waste time on these rascals. We've got to get on and do our business with Messers Gallatin and William Findley and all their motley rebels and whiskey-makers out in the west state. They are our true enemies – not this rabble."

Hamilton settled back as the carriage lurched. "At least being together for these five days on the road has given us the chance to go over many important matters."

The President nodded affirmatively. Loyal men like Hamilton and Henry Lee had always been there for him. Lee, now the governor of Virginia, would be meeting them in Carlisle and was bringing a near 10,000 strong state militia. Washington supposed that local Pennsylvania regiments might not be trusted in any engagements near Pittsburgh.

Hamilton muttered, "I still cannot believe these Pennsylvanians. They have known about the need for a duty on whiskey for the past year or two. I am appalled that their protests out west are getting so violent."

"We can easily remember, Alexander, that several federal agents charged with collecting these taxes have already been severely injured, nearly killed. The rebellious farmers have certainly stirred the pot. Their provocations mock us."

"There is another thing that bothers me, sir," Hamilton continued. "Mr. Jefferson and Madison don't even have a personal stake in whiskey manufacturing and are not even affected in the least by any tax but here they are fomenting this rebellion." Hamilton was clearly aroused. "These two, they are the worst of false patriots!"

"Now, Alexander, don't get too exercised. This Indian summer day is proving warm enough."

Although Washington seemed calm, his clenched jaw betrayed his inner emotions. The President had reason to be particularly upset. James Madison and others in Congress had even suggested that his present action might be an impeachable act. It was highly insulting when Madison had insisted that it was solely the role of "his Congress" to declare war. The leader of the House of Representatives had argued that this current military action should not proceed – Washington had usurped authority.

Hamilton recalled that he, President Washington, and Attorney General Edmund Randolph had cleverly side-stepped the issue by labeling this so-named 'whiskey tax insurrection' an 'act of anarchy' not an 'act of war.' In so doing, they had taken the thunder out of Madison's argument. Washington was not making a war but fulfilling the essential duty of a President – keeping the domestic peace.

"Yes, Alexander, I agree that your anger this morning seems justified. It is one thing for Jefferson to write the flowery phrases of the Declaration of Independence or for Mr. Madison to write most of the Constitution, but it is a much more difficult task to actually run a government and have citizens live under it. There is a big difference between being a dreamer like Jefferson and being an executive like we both must be."

Washington interrupted himself and motioned out the window. "Just a minute, look ahead over there, Mr. Hamilton far off. There is dust rising in the air."

As the carriage continued to make its way closer to Carlisle, it caught up to two lines of militia. Their kicked-up dust was so thick they could taste it. The marching troops resembled a ragtag group of volunteers rather than a disciplined regiment.

Washington became agitated when he saw their condition. He harrumphed loudly, "And these are the considered soldiers of Knox's national army?" As they passed, he gestured at a wagon and called out, "What have you got in there, soldier?"

"The uniforms that Mr. Hamilton has ordered, sir. Thick blue ones so that the musket balls of those whiskey boys don't cut through."

"Can I see one?" Washington asked the unshaven youth.

"Yes, sir . . . and we have more than enough. See here?" The supply wagon's driver reached around and lifted up a deep, navy blue woolen jacket and matching trousers. Two white sashes lay across the jacket resembling a St. Andrew's cross.

The President finally smiled, wiped sweat from his brow with a kerchief, and sat back in relief. "Well, Mr. Hamilton, again I note that whenever I am with you that things are timely, proper and in order. I could call you 'Colonel' but I am afraid that Mr. Madison and a few others back in Philadelphia might object to you taking a rank."

"And I could call you 'General,' but . . ." The two laughed together at their familiar banter. Hamilton sat back and enjoyed the feeling of once again being Washington's aide-de-camp. "Things should work out fine, sir. I am glad that we chose Carlisle for our staging area. Governor Lee and his Virginians should be here in a few days."

That evening, feeling exhausted from the day's forty-mile trip to Mrs. Vawter's Blue Bird Inn in Carlisle, the two men retired earlier than usual.

Hamilton sleepily lay back on his down pillow and reread the letter he had received a week previously from Angelica Church, his wife's sister. In an earlier letter written some years past, she had detailed some of her dalliances and court intrigues. With these divulgences, she had asked for his understanding, writing *Please, dear Alex, it is something that is always in my nature.* Added to Hamilton's frustration, she had described an enjoyable liaison with Thomas Jefferson during his posting in Paris.

In the present letter, Angelica now wrote that she had renewed a correspondence with the imposing red-haired Virginian during the past summer.

> *By this, let me be your ear, sweet Alex, as you might allow. Jefferson, several other American republicans and a group named the New Patriots are planning to spread rumors in American newspapers that you and George Washington are plotting a return to monarchy. I coyly wrote my former amour if he knew who would be such an American monarch? Mr. Jefferson could not or would not tell me but clearly, he wrote, if such a person were identified – that very person and his family would be at great peril.*
>
> *By this, do take care of all sorts of things, my dearest one.*

His sister-in-law also corresponded that she was most relieved to know that their own special relationship would not be compromised by either her own romantic affairs in England or by Hamilton's relationship with a certain Mrs. Maria Reynolds of Philadelphia. Angelica closed by expressing the hope that Alex would somehow stay faithful to her sister, Elizabeth, as well as to herself, asking him to remember *how many times . . . the two . . . then the three of us walked . . . on the green Hudson Valley hills of Albany.*

Her allusions stirred his imagination. Hamilton inhaled the lingering lilac fragrance of the linen notepaper. He lay on his back, aroused by her perfumed oils of essence, and after blowing out the bedside candle, turned hard into the pillow.

Rain later that night caused rills to run down the thick windowpanes of the inn's rooms facing west. Alone, George Washington finally opened a package that had been delivered several days earlier. His hands trembled as he unwrapped the laced silk ties. He had not heard from Sally Fairfax for nearly six months. He sensed his growing excitement as he scanned the contents.

There was a small silk infant's cap inside the package. He retrieved a tiny locket held within the cap's folds. Turning it in his palm, he noticed an inscription etched on the silver: 'AF' and '1750 – PFF - 1752.' There was also a short notation written by Sally in the infant headpiece, *always a Washington.*

In an accompanying letter for both Martha and George, Sally Cary Fairfax wrote that despite being widowed, her life was as good as could be expected. In concluding, she inquired about Priscilla Winfield and her family at Woodlawn Mills. Her style was characteristically resolute.

> *. . . How especially important it is to guard the Winfields' present and future welfare . . . and at all costs. The support for the Washington legacy will always be forthcoming from the Crown as well as many of my own family resources. Be assured that his Highness, King George, remains among your greatest admirers. Needless to say, this note is to be destroyed after you both have read it, yet the infant cap and its contents are not to be destroyed. They are for the Tomb, the special place at your home of Mount Vernon.*

He turned slightly in his chair in order to more comfortably read Sally's second letter, a note meant only for him. Some of the phrases seemed to leap off the pages. As he read, Washington found it hard to control the emotions her message provoked.

> *. . . How many times . . . the two . . . then, the three of us walked . . . there by your blue Potomac. And now just the two of us . . . and we walk not together . . . but as necessarily apart.*

Sally Cary Fairfax again expressed her sadness that, like Washington, she too was childless. As a consequence of her emptiness, she urged,

> *Do what you must, my dear one . . . but above all, ensure that all of our love and feelings are forever carried on . . . Priscilla is so dear. She represents the child that all of us can share, even though it is only our unspoken love encompassing her . . . With this as her legacy, only with this, is my heart truly at peace . . .*
>
> *Oh . . . George, my dear, how I wish I could see you, hold you again. Since I cannot bring myself to be with you, I must close my eyes and . . .*

Washington folded the letter, looked out the window at the dripping branches of a willow tree draped next to the sill. He closed his eyes in reverie, thinking about his Sally – his dear friend's widow, Sally. "No, rather in sorrow," he thought, ". . . 'til death do we part."

He leaned back and hummed to himself:

'I would be with you if I had the chance,
A time lived forever, a tune we would dance . . . .'

The next morning, the men met in the front reception room of the inn.

"Sometimes, you just do not know . . . Getting old is no fun, Alex. I want, no I need to tell you some important things before Governor Lee gets to Carlisle. It will be only between the two of us, at least for now. Is this a good time?"

"Of course, Mr. President. Any time that you want me for whatever."

"Sit down there, Alex." Washington pointed to a sofa. "I want to see your reactions to what I'll be saying." After a pause, the President spoke in a deliberate manner. "Five years ago, we seemed to be all in it together. By that, I mean we were all mutually involved in the formulation of our new government. Surely we had our differences, but in the main we mostly agreed."

"Yes, you are correct, sir. The ideas that provided the framework for the written Constitution seemed to flow easily for James Madison and me. Perhaps this was because the two of us had already developed a close working partnership."

"Yet we all soon enough discovered that nothing is cast in stone," Washington remarked dourly. "Things seem to be unraveling these days."

Washington leaned back in his chair. "For instance, we have more difficulties with England all over again despite our Proclamation of Neutrality published last year. Because of the French influence on certain of us, namely Mr. Jefferson, the English naturally feel threatened by our country's inclinations. I am glad that I took your advice, Alex, and have assigned Mr. Jay to go and sort things out. Our United States simply cannot afford another war at this time, especially one over trade. Our nation is not ready for it."

Sitting directly across, Hamilton nodded in agreement.

Washington sighed. "Now this, Alex, this rebellion in the West." Suddenly he leaned forward and pounded the table, nearly upsetting his steaming mug of coffee. "We cannot, must not allow for people like these ill-mannered farmers to get away with their crazy insubordinate ideas! They seem drunk on Albert Gallatin's rye whiskey!"

"I agree wholeheartedly with you General . . . Mr. President." Hamilton was startled by the older man's outburst.

"I will . . .," Washington sputtered, "I will not let such ruffians and other scoundrels throughout our new nation threaten to undermine the liberties that we fought for, Alex. The most important prerequisite of any body politic is civil order. First, we addressed our desire for basic freedoms in our Declaration of Independence and overthrew a tyrant. But now to balance any resulting over-zealousness, we need to preserve our democracy as a nation under rule of law – that's your Constitution, Alex."

Washington took a deep breath as he settled back into his chair. "Let me wholly change the course of my current ruminations if I might. Mind this is in strictest confidence, Alex. Two years ago, I enlisted James Madison's aid to write a farewell address. He seemed to me to be the best choice since he has a respected writing style, and at the time, saw many things my way. With my own health getting steadily worse, I was feeling my own mortality and decided that I had to think about the future in a different way – our country's future and mine. In a word, I needed to plan for my succession."

"Why did you call it a 'farewell address,' sir? You are very much still with us."

Washington looked out the six-paneled sash window and sighed. "I told Mr. Madison that this would not be a speech per se but rather a written piece distributed to a few supportive newspapers. I planned to offer my most deeply held thoughts and convictions before I left the presidency – especially my insistence on having a strong federal government."

"At the time," he continued, "I had concluded that one four-year term as President was quite sufficient, but after you and others persuaded me to run for a second term, I volunteered to carry on. The farewell article that Mr. Madison and I crafted has as yet never been published."

Hamilton finished his coffee. He wanted to review what the President had just shared. "And what about this matter? Why talk about it now?"

"The reason for mentioning this article to you at this time, Alex, is that besides the circumstances surrounding our present expedition, I have again become deeply concerned about issues regarding the presidency. My interests include not only describing the function of the office but also, importantly, how it will be subsequently transferred to someone else. We need a high-minded, nonpartisan man – a true patriot as President."

Hamilton leaned forward. "So is that why Mr. Madison has seemed so silent, so cold to me? He probably senses that you might offer me the chance to revise his prior writings. Madison has always seemed a bit jealous of our close friendship, General."

"No, that is not the point. I surmise that both you and I have greatly fallen in his estimation, and now, he in mine. Mr. Madison, in a word, sees himself as no longer in our camp, Alex. He is unlikely to be persuaded by any of our arguments in the future."

"Permit me to directly ask you then, if I might. Do you have another treatise presently in mind?"

"You are quite right, Alexander, to be curious about the status of my farewell testament to America. You see, you are presently my closest confidant."

"Only closest after Mrs. Washington, sir."

"Of course, of course." Washington smiled. "I have held the rough draft of the original farewell address in reserve. This first version that Madison helped me write is presently stored in my library at Mount Vernon. No one has seen it."

"Will the rest of us ever see it? . . . read it?"

The President looked Hamilton in the eye. "I certainly hope so. I had hoped that such a document expressing my sincerest hopes for America might serve as a roadmap of sorts for our countrymen. After all, I am a surveyor at heart. When I eventually take leave as President, I hope we avoid all manner of crass and unseemly contentiousness. I have come to see that it is a most honorable office."

"You, sir, have thus far been the cement for our nation. I ofttimes worry what will become of us all when you leave . . ."

Washington warmly shook his aide's hand. "So given what I have said, what I would like to request, my dear Alex, is that you assist me in the drafting of a completely new farewell message. It should be published prior to my taking leave of the executive office. I now realize that you are the single person who best mirrors my inmost thoughts."

Hamilton was humbled by the prospect of collaborating and quietly replied, "I would greatly honor your request and gladly do what I can."

As they collected themselves, Hamilton nervously shifted in his seat. "Pardon me, General. Going along with what you have been saying, do you remember that yesterday I mentioned having what I called a redundancy scheme for our government?"

George Washington shook his head. "I wasn't quite sure where you were going with that, Alex. Were you suggesting that America needs a shadow cabinet similar to what a minority party has in the House of Commons?"

"To restate the context of my thinking, Mr. President, you have often said you would be surprised to see our fledging United States last another fifty years, especially if the issue of slavery tears us apart. Many of the compromises at the Grand Convention of '87, which were necessary to form our present Union, were barely agreed upon. Given the trajectories of our present crisis as well as other mounting turmoil, your previous statements may not be too far off the mark. By having a backup organization of reliable patriots, there would be an assurance for America's survival in case our current federal system should falter. As well, I think my proposition ties in nicely with your just-stated desire to promote an orderly line of succession for future American leaders."

Hamilton waited to be sure he would be understood. "But dare I go a bit farther, sir? Distasteful as it might seem, if matters completely collapse, America may in fact need its own king – but only as a matter of last resort."

George Washington frowned as he tried to digest his aide's words. "What? So soon?" he thought. "Only a few years ago, the two of them fought to defeat King George III's tyranny – and now this? Hamilton's suggestion? No. Never, never. Americans would never accept this even if it were the only option. But then . . ."

Washington remembered when he took the oath of office that he had pledged to preserve, protect and defend the Constitution. It was now readily apparent that he had to establish domestic order first and foremost. Once again, he was facing dire and unusual circumstances. "It had been good in the past to trust a handful of men like Hamilton, Lee and the late General Nathaniel Greene to develop all sorts of contingencies during the War. It might be good for times like these, too," he thought.

Hamilton interrupted the President's musings. "Excuse me, sir, I might have missed it, but you haven't yet stated your reaction to my idea."

Washington replied, "Trust me, on first hearing your proposal yesterday I did not know what to say. Your concept at first seemed far-fetched, but after sleeping on it and conversing with you this morning, I admit I'm intrigued. Given that the King's Promise lies unopened at Mount Vernon, persons in England may have thoughts similar to our own about the future of our fragile Republic.

"Somehow, though, I sense we can weather the current difficulty near Pittsburgh and move on, at least for the moment. Frankly, though, I do not know for sure. To help me sort out options, when I return to Philadelphia I will instruct John Jay whilst he is in London settling the present trade difficulties to confidentially explore exactly what is meant by possible assistance to America by the British Crown."

Encouraged by Washington's interest, Hamilton pressed the issue. "That is fine as a start, sir, but at least tell me. Do you not agree that some form of a shadow government might be useful?"

Washington hesitated before answering. "No matter what I think, Alex, I pray that the failure of our nation's government will never happen."

"As do I, sir. No well-meaning American could wish it."

President Washington stood up and slowly walked to a window. Looking out, he said, "Tell you what – let's leave off on our conversation for a moment. After Henry Lee arrives, the three of us will have ample opportunity to discuss this and many other issues – he is a staunch friend and advisor. You and I know that he can keep a strict confidence." He turned and nodded in Hamilton's direction. "As to your idea, Alex, frankly I can't give you my opinion yet, but I am sure that the three of us will have the time to fully explore your concept over the coming days."

Mrs. Vawter and a young kitchen lad entered from the hallway and announced, "A rider just arrived to the rear of our inn, sires. He says that Governor Lee and his forward detachment will be here by evening. The remainder of his regiments will arrive over the next two days. I plan to keep the back bedroom on the ground floor open for him and prepare some extra portions for the dinner meal."

"Thank you very much, Mrs.Vawter. If it is the same Mr. Lee that we know, he might be here sooner as long as his long blonde locks do not slow him!"

"The rumors say that he's a strong man in the saddle and then some." She shook her skirt and rested her hands suggestively on her ample hips. "The men in the village say that the rebels out near Pittsburgh are a wee bit frightened by his cavalry troops, but they tell me that those farmers still intend a fight."

Hamilton sat up stiffly, squared his shoulders and sniffed. "We will see how ready they are, Mrs. Vawter, when we are all formed up in front of them."

"Yes indeed, ma'm," Washington said with confidence. "We know that those rebels have a large number of irregulars, some six thousand men scattered about, but we have the full authority of the United States behind us."

While clearing the men's dishes, a cook's helper overheard them and said, "That is not what some of Muhlenberg's people and others say up near 'bouts Kutztown. Pennsylvania is, after all, where we live and Mr. Klemmer, our Dutchman preacher, tells us that we are not under any other authority but God's and our own!"

Washington shooed him away as he would a fly. "Mind your manners, young man. Just you see, after all . . . You'll see!"

Later that fall, Washington's militia-conscripts arrived in the countryside west of the Alleghenies. As they approached a knoll near Pittsburgh, the thirteen thousand conscripted federal forces faced down a motley group of some thousand farmers and villagers armed only with pitchforks and shovels.

Racing directly into the unkempt rebels, Washington's troops bloodied the protestors on both sides like a honed scythe clearing a hayfield. Many of the strongest, most aggressive rebels were restrained and placed under guard in a commandeered barn. Alexander Hamilton and Governor Lee rode over to the Methodist church and had the movement's organizers placed under house arrest, along with a number of vociferous troublemakers loitering near the village tavern. In a matter of days, the Whiskey Insurrection had been put down without a shot being fired.

When George Washington returned to Philadelphia, he ordered presidential pardons for the leaders of the failed insurgency. Despite the farmers' crushing defeat and Washington's conciliatory gesture, many settlers and residents of the western territories and southern states became even more determined to pursue individual liberties and states' rights.

Hamilton and Lee remained with a squadron of Virginia militia near Pittsburgh. The troops finally settled the conflict before the winter snows deepened.

During their encampment, the two men had many chances to have deep conversations while relaxing in their quarters. Turning in his bunk one night, Lee broke the silence. "I will say this about our General Washington. You have to wonder who could ever possibly succeed him as our president – or even as a king. If that were your new order, Alex, it would have to be a Washington, no other. He was always first in war . . . and now, he's first in peace."

"Let me tell you, Harry, what our General said to me before you came to Carlisle. It is only for the three of us and two other living family members to know . . ."

As the candles burnt low, Hamilton told Lee all about Priscilla, the Winfields, the Fairfaxes and the Washington legacy.

Mount Vernon
December 1794

When George Washington returned to Mount Vernon for Christmas, he and the elderly William Lee, his favorite long-time slave, went to the Washington family Burial Vault. After using the iron Bastille Key on the grotto's sturdy lock (a lock he had custom-fashioned for the key), the President was heartened despite the gloom to see the glass cylinder and brass tube still intact after seven years. They were both resting in place in the wooden storage container on the lower shelf next to his brother's crypt. His brother's saddle and Anne Washington Lee's memory-box repository lay on an upper shelf. Washington opened the porcelain Chinese urn by using its uniquely shaped key and placed the baby skullcap with the locket into the satin-lined container. Before leaving the Vault, he took the small octagonal-headed key and reminded himself that he should save it in his study. He dared not lose it in the dank tomb.

Afterwards, as they walked up the incline, Washington quietly remarked, "Thank you, William, Miss Martha and I are so grateful . . . No one else here about knows what we are doing."

13

Philadelphia

March 1795

"Here it is, sir, the first draft of what the English and I have titled 'The Treaty of London.' It will no doubt face stiff opposition in the Senate during the ratification hearings – but I feel it is the best agreement that we could get given the circumstances."

President Washington looked over the papers that his emissary John Jay had hand-delivered. "You're spot on – the numerous Francophiles in America will surely argue against it. The so-called 'glorious' French Revolution has enamored weasels like Jefferson and Mr. Madison. Do these vermin not feel for our friend Lafayette sitting in a dank prison? But tell me this, John, when you were in England, did you get a chance to meet with Lord Fairfax as I hoped?"

"I did, sir. Lord Fairfax was in fact quite direct. He introduced me to the head of the Privy Council, a Lord Aplington, and thereafter we three had fruitful discussions."

Jay reviewed what had transpired.

The higher-ranked Lord Aplington led most of the conversation. "I have been looking forward to your visit, Mr. Jay. We believe that the issue which the two of us will discuss is critically important to America . . . perhaps, even more so than are your current trade negotiations. My Royal Highness, King George, has an abiding, long-term interest in his former colonies in America. Presently, he and many other royals in Europe realize that they cannot afford to have the winds from the French Revolution, particularly the example of the vile Jacobins, take hold in your United States. Such chaos, such civil unrest and pointless murder – it cannot be allowed!"

I replied, "President Washington has directed me to sort out England's intentions, Sir. He mentioned receiving a note sometime ago from your King George seeming to offer some sort of assistance. As of now, he has not read it."

Lord Fairfax drummed his fingers on the table and said, "That was nearly a decade ago. It was entitled 'The King's Promise.' "

Lord Aplington added condescendingly, "He doesn't need it anymore. It is outdated, Mr. Jay. King George and a number of other royalties have recently allied themselves as what they call the Europe League. This secret alliance pledges to stand down any more revolutionary upheavals on the European continent; a threat to one monarchy is a threat to all! Tell Mr. Washington about this consortium."

I paused for only a moment before asking, "How does this alliance affect us in America?"

"Ah yes, not currently but . . . if your country is engulfed by civil disorders, they might spread across the Atlantic to our own shores. England will not tolerate that! Nor, sir, will the other Houses of Royalty."

"So . . .?"

Lord Fairfax interrupted in a clipped manner. "Let us set you straight, Mr. Jay. Besides your well-publicized trade negotiations with our foreign office, the Court of my Royal Highness has another treaty for you to take back to your President Washington."

I sat there trying to fathom his words before asking, "Who are the signatories to this present treaty?"

"That is not for us to presently reveal," Lord Aplington replied as he opened a desk drawer and retrieved a sealed package. "This second treaty is not to be presented to your Senate as I understand the other one must. It is meant only for the benefit of a cadre of well-meaning Americans."

Having thus reported to the president, John Jay pulled that same package from his leather courier's case and laid it on the desk. "This is for you, sir. The pictured eagles with the words 'Republica regni fit,' which mean 'out of a Republic comes a Kingdom' on the cover, puzzle me. I have never encountered any similar motifs in my other trips to Europe."

After Washington dismissed John Jay, he remained alone in his office. He carefully opened the parchment in order to avoid damaging the seal, and then pondered the contents of the confidential transmittal that the Chief Justice had given him.

PAN ATLANTIC COMMUNITY TREATY

Wherein there is a natural and common bond of our peoples across the Atlantic waters and whereas there are clear and present internal dangers roiling all of our Nations positioned along both shores and whereas there is a recognized need for a common, civilized approach to quell those insurrections in any or all of our sovereign States and Kingdoms, we hereby make this treaty of Alliance and mutual Assistance.

The peace and tranquility of America now and in future years is necessary for the Welfare of the entire Atlantic Community.

Should this experiment politic of the new American Confederation fail, now or at any time in the future, we of the Europe League pledge to fully assist in the formation of a new Government, a legitimate Monarchy in America.

This PACT thereby will ensure future order in America — order that is so necessary for all of our civilized Nations.

Europe League   January 1795
Attested hereby   Lord Aplington

George III of England	House of Hanover
Louis Charles, dauphin of France and Navarre represented with M. Jean Laurent	the House of Bourbon
Catherine of Russia	the family Romanov
Francis II of Austria and Tuscany	the House of Habsburg
Gustav IV Adolph of Sweden	House of Holstein-Gottorp
represented with Regent Charles, duke of Sodermanland	
Frederick William II of Prussia	House of Hohenzollern

Philadelphia
Early April 1795

As Alexander Hamilton scrutinized the PACT, George Washington sat across from him, and soon impatiently asked, "What do you think, Alex? Is this of use to us?" He adjusted his chair. "I first thought that it might be like the unopened, presumed pledge that the two of us received from King George in 1787, but I was surprised to see that this document is signed by certain other Houses of Royalty in Europe."

Hamilton looked over. "I agree. This is probably quite different from 'The King's Promise.'"

Washington leaned back. "Alex, seriously now. Let me tell you what I have been thinking – what you must do for me now that we have both read this PACT. First, keep it secret – with the exception of our close compatriot, Henry Lee. Ride within the fortnight and tell him. He is the only person who already knows everything that the two of us know. Suggest to him, as well, that in the meantime he should be even more vigilant about guarding the Winfields. He has told me about all sorts of ill-defined threats hovering about the Northern Neck of Virginia. As you can imagine, it is vital that Mrs. Winfield and her children's identities and direct connection to my bloodline not be found out.

"Second, this PACT document must remain locked up in your family's bank in New York for safekeeping. I want you and your family to be, so to speak, the 'keeper of the keys.'"

President Washington took a deep breath and looked at the bright morning sky. "Even though there is this guarantee of assistance from certain European royals," he thought, "I still have serious misgivings about Hamilton's scheme. For all I know, it might lead to an American empire of sorts. But despite my reservations, I suppose that I should at least test the waters for now."

With that, Washington leaned toward Hamilton and said, "One last thing. Perhaps with this PACT in hand, it might be best for us to at least start thinking of men who could constitute your so-called 'shadow cabinet.' The final arrangement would probably be similar to what you have suggested. It is conceivable, at least to me, that such a group would be charged to decide whether to ever utilize the PACT, now or in the future." He added softly as an after-thought, "But only, mind you, for America's preservation."

Hamilton frowned and sat motionless, trying to measure the other man. The President's words felt like a drumbeat.

"Well, what do you say, Alex?"

"My thoughts exactly, sir – exactly."

Washington stood and waved him off with the PACT still in hand. "Then good day. When you get to Richmond, give my regards to our friend Henry and his wonderful wife."

Hamilton stiffly rose and found himself nearly bowing as he backed away. "Good day to you, General – Mr. President. Good day."

"Thank you for your wishes, Alex. I may finally have one."

14

Watkins House, Philadelphia

February 22, 1797

During a bitterly cold winter evening, a group of men met in an imposing brick home. Alexander Hamilton and his father-in-law, Philip Schuyler, had issued confidential invitations to a handful of patriots. The surrounding farm with its outbuildings sat atop a ridge overlooking the half-frozen Schuylkill River.

The evening's host was Mr. William Shippen, a wealthy merchant of Philadelphia and Norristown. He had been instrumental in keeping Washington's Continental Army fed and clothed during the dark days of the Valley Forge encampment. As a consequence, he had suffered profound losses – many of his factories closed, his home destroyed and his other properties seized. Worst of all, his young wife had died as a result of their impoverished condition. It had taken Shippen more than a decade to reestablish his profitable commerce, and during those years he had remarried and purchased this farmstead. The Watkins House was the former residence of a Tory sympathizer now self-exiled to Canada. Shippen had felt strangely honored when George Washington requested that he host what the President called 'a most important function.'

The President-elect, John Adams, stood next to John Marshall in the home's reception room. He had been worried over the past month with nagging doubts. Would he be accepted as much as Washington had been? Who would he select for his Cabinet? How could he work with men like Madison or Jefferson? Adams was somewhat surprised to see, on the other hand, how unusually relaxed America's first President seemed as he conversed with several others near the crackling fireplace. Adams surmised that his behavior was owing to Washington's relief that his term of office was ending.

Philip Schulyer scanned the shadowy room and tersely announced, "It seems it is time to begin our meeting. First, though, Mr. Hamilton and I insist on having an agreement of confidentiality from all present. If you cannot give it, please leave now."

The invitees looked at each other uncomfortably as they tried to understand the old man's words. John Adams's stomach became unsettled as he too was left to wonder what was going on. He could see that the meeting likely did not concern the Society of the Cincinnati – several present in the room were not Society members. Nevertheless, it appeared to be some sort of handpicked group. Adams suddenly realized that there were two notable absentees that night – Thomas Jefferson and James Madison. It was known that these two Virginians were leading a growing movement of republicans who met in democratic clubs. Adams came to the conclusion that everyone at William Shippen's dinner might have something in common after all – each was a committed Federalist.

William North walked slowly from his chair to Schuyler's side with a rolled piece of parchment. Getting attention, he said sternly, "As General Schuyler requested, we must all sign this agreement before proceeding on with our agenda. It will be placed in Mr. Hamilton's Bank of New York for safekeeping."

The guests stirred but before any man rose, Mrs. Shippen entered from a side door. "Sires, excuse me – let me bring in the latecomers. They have finally arrived."

John Adams felt even more awkward as he saw a youth and two young men enter the drawing room and wondered what they were doing there. Once again, he felt more than a step removed from some new sort of inner sanctum – a feeling that he had already experienced many times as Vice President.

George Washington moved forward and grasped the arm of a good-looking lad who appeared to be ten or twelve years old. "This young man, my friends, is the Marquis de Lafayette's oldest son, George-Washington du Motier. The lad has been staying with the Hamiltons in New York these past two years and is now visiting Philadelphia."

He looked down. "Your father was like a son to me." Washington's jaw allowed for only the barest hint of a grin. "Since that is so, consider that you are also family. Mr. Hamilton told me that you are my petit-fils."

Hamilton came over and held the shy French boy's hand. "Master du Motier was sent to America when the wretched Reign of Terror caused all sorts of dreadful consequences for his family." He stayed by his side. "I thought the young du Motier should come tonight along with the sons of some of his father's friends. The Marquis wrote from Austria that he hoped his son would be able to meet the late John Lauren and Nathaniel Greene's sons when he visited America. These two other young men are they – Justin Laurens and Nathan Greene. The President and I greatly miss your fathers."

Hamilton added as an aside, "We can clearly see that these two lads, along with Frederick Reynolds of the Franklin family, represent links joining our country's past to its future."

Washington reflected to himself that Priscilla Winfield's son back at Woodlawn Mills was nearly the same age. The President sensed that Franklin Winfield and these two young men from the Carolinas had all been born with the right qualities to take up the mantle in their own time.

After Schuyler excused Mrs. Shippen and Lafayette's son, he redirected the men's' attention. "Gentlemen, as Mr. North and I mentioned before the interruption, you must now each sign a pledge of confidentiality. We intend to have serious deliberations tonight so this is necessarily our first order of business. So far, we have simply been celebrating the President's birthday, the occasion noted on everyone's invitation."

Washington broke in, "I presume that none of you will consider this requirement of General Schuyler's to be too objectionable. After all, gentlemen, many of us freely signed a similar pledge of silence as the first order of business at the Constitutional Convention here in Philadelphia some ten years ago."

Schuyler continued on somberly. "There is a difference, though. In contrast to that agreement, once this present parchment is signed and sealed, any leak of confidence will bring a painful retribution. I hesitate to fully detail the penalty but it is thus. Any such traitor will be forced to witness the torture and slow deaths of his family before his own execution, and his complete bloodline will perish on the same day. Secrecy and denial is demanded, gentlemen. Is this understood?"

John Adams raised his hand and, despite knowing that many were glaring at him suspiciously, voiced a personal concern. "As most of you know, Mr. Hamilton and I have had significant disputes lately. I do not feel that it is right for me to blindly sign a confidentiality agreement or anything else to which he is a partner. As for the rest of you, I have no objections."

As he spoke, the diminutive man's face reddened. Hamilton shot to his feet and cried out, "Are you imputing anything about my person . . .my honor? If you are, we must settle . . ."

The Vice President took a napkin and tremulously wiped his brow. "No, not in the least . . . but I always prefer not to enter into any association blindly."

President Washington knew that since Adams's election, enmity had burgeoned between the two. As he sat firmly in his winged chair, he was annoyed that his dinner meeting had started out so acrimoniously. "Trust me, John, we are here not for or against one another but for the good of our country. You and Mr. Hamilton must try to settle your differences at another time and place – although I don't know half of what they are . . . nor do I care to!"

Maintaining his austerity, Washington continued, "Honestly, you are like squabbling children. Sometimes, I think you both need to listen to a voice of respected authority . . . take General Schuyler's here, or my own. I intend to give my written agreement to keep our meeting confidential."

Despite Adams's and Hamilton's ongoing personal feud, Washington was convinced that they would join the others, and in the end give him their assent and fealty. Schuyler, Lee and he had carefully selected these particular men mostly because of their abiding affection for him. The three all agreed that well-placed personal loyalty was the highest mark of a true patriot.

With this, the President pulled on his wire glasses, looked up and announced, "Phil, I will ratify your pledge first. Where do I sign? Give me the quill and ink if you please."

One by one, the others followed in silence to the table where Philip Schuyler carefully scrutinized each signature. After a while, William Shippen slipped out of the room and rang a hand-held glass bell. He swung open a French door and announced, "Dinner is served, gentlemen."

After a sumptuous meal, shortened by everyone's impatience to get on with the meeting, the men retired to the larger sitting room and settled into Heppelwhite and Chippendale chairs. Some of the guests sipped small glasses of port while a few smoked on Meerschaum pipes. Several lustrous oil paintings by Charles and James Peale depicting hunting scenes and still-life renditions of killed game hung on the textured walls.

George Washington walked in and said, "Please let me take the floor. I hope that what has thus far been seen as a celebration of my sixty-fifth birthday will prove to be more than that. Tonight, gentlemen, I plan to share my hopes for our United States."

His words were met with silence. As everyone was wondering what would come next, a voice sounded out in the hallway. "Mr. Shippen, sir, a Mr. L'Enfant has just arrived. He has been detained by the storm. Is he to come in?"

After motioning for L'Enfant to enter, Washington told the group to stay settled in their seats – he knew he had much to discuss. The guests were aware that at most times, Washington was content to sit back and stoically absorb people's counsels. That evening he seemed to be quite different. Their President projected an aura of spontaneity and openness – no one could recall ever seeing him behave in such high spirits.

Alexander Hamilton felt smug knowing that he was the only one that had a clue as to what was prompting Washington to meet with them.

Several weeks earlier, he had visited President Washington in his executive office in Philadelphia. Noticing some of the newspapers lying about, newsprints that he knew Washington read closely, he remarked that the President's loyal friends and inner circle needed to hear from him directly, even more dramatically and fully than ever.

"About what, Alex?"

"You owe it to these, your special friends that we have selected to let them know how you really think. Face the matter, sir. You are being personally attacked daily by a number of pamphlets and correspondences.

"At first, I thought it was good for America that you allowed me to mute what were your true, albeit bitter feelings about certain people and their politics in your published Farewell Address. It had seemed good at the time, but then came the recent, divisive election and now these scathing partisan criticisms."

He had not needed to point out to President Washington that during the five months since the Farewell Address was published in Dunlap and Claypoole's American *Daily Advertiser*, many other Philadelphia newspapers such as Bache's *Aurora* had circulated outrageously critical articles.

"Besides those righteous editors, what are Jefferson and his minions thinking?" Hamilton asked the President.

Listening to his longtime former aide, Washington slammed his fist on the large walnut desk in his office. "You're right. Damn it, damn them, Alexander . . . damn the whole, worthless mess. We did not win our so-called Revolution to be defeated by another revolution. In fact, what we won was our Independence." His distress was as if he had been pricked by a bothersome nettle.

"As only one example," he went on, "we have their reactions to Jay's Treaty for the past year. Even from the standpoint of their own self-interest, do not they see it as best for America? Did we not write about avoiding foreign problems and entanglements? And besides, it gives us a brilliant trade agreement with England. Alex, we need to first settle our young nation down. It must develop peacefully rather than getting embroiled in all sorts of European affairs.

"We have problems enough of our own. Henry Lee has recently told me of even more instances of barn burnings and thievery on properties contiguous to Mount Vernon. Thankfully, he remains near-at-hand to quell such civil disturbances."

Washington jumped up and marched around his office with clenched fists. "Jefferson, Freneau, Citizen Genet! Damn them! I frankly characterize their actions as seditious and plan to mention them to John Adams. Let him forcefully deal with them after he becomes President."

With that, Washington threw a book down on his desk. "I think it is due time to act on your shadow government idea, Alexander. Get the members together. We must hold our first meeting."

George Washington, despite his bothersome rheumatism, stood and turned to William North. "Please, Captain, read the roll so that I can be assured of the concurrence of everyone present." He looked at the gathering with his familiar steely stare and ordered, "As your name is called please affirm your presence."

North strode to the fireplace. "I would be honored, sir. Sounding out roll calls has been my specialty these many years gone."

North read loudly – each man responded in kind: "Aye." The roll included:

George Washington	Philip Schuyler
John Marshall	John Jay
Frederick Reynolds – of Franklin Family	
John Adams	Justin Laurens – of Laurens Family
Nathan Greene – of Greene Family	Alexander Hamilton
William Shippen	Robert Morris
Gouverneur Morris	Governor Harry Lee
Henry Knox	

"And oh, yes, I cannot overlook myself." William North straightened and said, "Mr. William North . . . Aye."

"Captain North," Washington interrupted, "you forgot our late arrival. Monsieur L'Enfant's signature needs to be added to the roll – Pierre?"

After he heard and also accepted the conditions, L'Enfant added his elegant signature to the bottom of the deerskin parchment.

Philip Schuyler had been monitoring the room and said aloud, "Now, at last, all present are accounted for, sir. Whilst looking over our document and listening to the Messer North's call-outs, I can assure that no more nor less are present, sir."

Leaning heavily against his chair, President Washington began, "This pledge of confidentiality will also serve as the roster for a new organization that I have in mind. First, let me say with that being the case, it is my honor to welcome each of you to my association. I appreciate your willingness, ahead of time, to join me . . . and one another." After a minute of silence, he went on. "May we, with the Almighty's help, serve together to preserve our United States!"

Hearing this, Hamilton bristled and leapt up before Washington said another word. "Hold it right there, sir! Don't make it sound like some social club. Gentlemen, you should consider this the point of no return. If any of you are *not* intent on joining the President's new organization, he and I request that you leave immediately. Your signature will be deleted, as you would wish. Remember, though," he warned, "what Philip Schuyler said earlier. If any man elects to withdraw, he must not divulge anything that has happened thus far."

None of the men in the Watkins House moved towards the door.

"After getting each man's voiced assent, Captain North will seal that man's signature up here. As President Washington stated, our signed confidentiality agreement will thereafter serve as our membership roll." Hamilton pointed to the document on a side table and explained, "This will certify that you are a founding member of Mr. Washington's patriotic association and are present at its first meeting. Once this notarization is complete, Mr. Washington and I will fully explain our new polity."

As he heard each man's response, North tipped a candle and dripped large spots of wax over the guest's signature. He firmly pressed a newly fashioned pestle onto each spilled dollop of the hot beeswax. The men moved about the table and as they did, they could see the commissioned seal that Pierre L' Enfant had fashioned. There were words beneath a relief of two facing eagles that read:

Ex Regnum

PATRI

E Pluribus Unum

Earlier, while the others had been finishing their desserts and liqueurs, Alexander Hamilton had added some sentences to the bottom of the parchment.

> . . . We the above constitute a new order necessary for the continuance of our dear United States of America.
>
> Let all fellow countrymen stand to follow the tenets and governance of PATRI – now and in the future – spoken and unspoken.
>
> By our hands at the Watkins House, Philadelphia
>
> February 22
> Year of our Lord, 1797
>
> Signed   Alexander Hamilton

The date and his signature were then covered by a generous portion of the candle wax and also impressed with L'Enfant's designed seal. Captain North moved to the side and left the notarized parchment on the cherry wood side table for all to see.

15

Watkins House, Philadelphia

Later Evening

After putting the membership roster aside, Washington turned to address the group. "Gentleman, I wish to make some background comments. I must admit that lately I have been under considerable strain. It seems to me that there is a group of sunshine patriots who are more interested in enjoying their liberties than in supporting our new Republic. Such men are full of arrogance and slander, wishing to change the rules once the game has started. It has not gotten to the point of frank treachery, my friends, but we all can see their telltale activities. Heaven only knows where it will lead."

Hamilton stood next to him and added, "They call themselves citizens but look at how they behave. Hardly 'civil,' I would say. Jefferson and Madison's ideals for a citizenry take their lesson from the mobs of Paris. Let them test the streets if they wish, but first they should take note of what has happened in France. Once loose, the Big Blade became too unwieldy for evil men of Paris to control. If our own scoundrels keep insulting law and order here in America, then a blade fashioned of American steel could just as easily catch them up as well."

Washington put his hands on his hips and spoke in a more measured manner. "We all know that our friend, Alexander, is outspoken at times but I'm sure, just as he intimates, that the horrors of past and present conflicts have made everyone in this room wary of any sort of unrest or disorder. Gentlemen, it is this concern of mine that prompted me to call you together tonight."

The others were not too surprised when Hamilton barged in. "Civil peace and order trumps freedom anytime!" he shouted. "Who better to determine when such force is necessary and timely but a single strong and moral leader . . .?" Almost as an afterthought, he added, "Honestly men, sometimes I wonder if America would be better off with a king."

Henry Knox couldn't suppress quipping, "Well, Alex, it's certain that Mr. Washington's successor, Mr. Adams, will never start any sort of dynasty. After all, who could ever mistake him for a Washington when our General's stature, hair and handsome looks have completely eluded the native of Massachusetts."

After a few muffled snickers, Washington spoke out loudly to regain everyone's attention. "Hold it down, I think we are getting a bit off center. Returning to what I said a moment ago, being thus motivated I asked General Schuyler to assemble this evening's gathering that I might present a freshly conceived idea. If you bear with me, I will first give a little background.

"Three years ago, Mr. Hamilton, Henry Lee and I discussed the concept of having a shadow government much as is found in the English Parliament. Such a constituted group would have as its purpose the preservation of a strong federal government for the good of America. PATRI represents the beginnings of that shadow government."

His words stunned the men, especially Shippen, Frederick Reynolds and others who had had no governmental experience; Washington knew that he would have a challenge to reassure them. "You have been selected to join PATRI not only because of your various merits, but most importantly for your proven loyalty to our country."

Alexander Hamilton moved to the middle of the room. "You are getting ahead of yourself, sir. Let me go back to the roots of our thinking if I might." The men knew that this New Yorker had a well-worn habit of interrupting and speaking for people. "Our ideas began to coalesce shortly after President Washington, Henry Lee and I spent time together in Carlisle two years ago. During those days of meddlesome pointless rebellion, the three of us saw firsthand the inherent dangers of unharnessed democracy."

"We all remember that time well, do we not?" Robert Morris asked the assembled men. "It terribly affected all sorts of business in the Middle States, nearly brought us to a standstill. And now Philadelphia and other teeming cities seem at times to be run over by as many vagrants and miscreants as there are sewer rats."

Hamilton was heartened that Morris had appeared to reaffirm his observations. He nodded his thanks and said, "As Messers Washington and Morris mentioned, we can easily see disorder all around us. In '94, not knowing if the United States would last much longer, the three of us discussed having a number of options if the civil disturbances became more widespread – in essence, developing a contingency plan. Having some form of shadow government topped the list."

"Thankfully, gentlemen, the Whiskey Revolt quickly subsided but on my return to Philadelphia," Washington explained, "I felt the need to further assess Alexander's notion. Years before, the Marquis de Lafayette had offhandedly written me about certain European royals having an interest in preserving stability in America. Knowing that, I decided to discretely determine for myself whether, indeed, there was any sort of potential English support for a contingency shadow government. To that end, I enlisted Mr. Jay to feel things out. Right John?"

Chief Justice John Jay smiled like a Cheshire cat and replied, "I remember it well, sir. I admit I was a bit mystified about the purpose of my assignment."

President Washington laughed. "That was my intent, John, to keep it a mystery. But seriously, the entreaty seemed appropriate at the time since America was already based so much on British law and governance. Its educational system, its religions, its values . . . have we not made these our own? Need I say more? I think it best if John now speaks to the events that occurred during his special trade mission two years ago."

John Jay of New York began, "Following President Washington's request, I had an initial meeting with Lord Fairfax and Lord Aplington in London. Lord Aplington, the head of the Privy Council, said that he also represented several other houses of European royalty. Evidently, many of these had voiced concern that, as a matter of course, the boiling civil revolts in France might spread unwanted turmoil and violence to their own countries, and to America as well. Lord Aplington divulged that if the American system were perceived to be failing in the future with, as he put it, 'the wheels falling off the wagon,' these royals were committed to support the formation of a new form of stable government in the New World."

"Please note, Mr. Jay mentioned a 'perceived failure' – what would any such failure look like?" Washington asked. "Here are some of the signs. *Lawless behavior* of all kinds in the name of individual liberty. *Minority opinions* snuffing out the wishes of the majority. And most importantly, the absence of *communal enterprises* vital for a free, prosperous society. In this scenario, gentlemen, America would be frankly descending into anarchy. Our country would be totally unhinged and totter toward collapse.

"If there was the sense of any such failure in America, the English lords told Mr. Jay that their cross-Atlantic community would offer to intercede based on their own self-interest of preserving stability for their own countries."

Jay nodded in agreement. "I transmitted a sealed copy describing their alliance from Lord Aplington to President Washington as proof of their intent. Since this first contact, these houses of royalty have assured us that they have met together on subsequent occasions to further develop their plans. "

"For everyone's review,' Hamilton said standing next to Washington, "I have brought what is called the PACT that Mr. Jay just mentioned from my Bank of New York. Let me read it." He unfolded a packet and read the Europe League's treaty aloud. The recital was met by suspended disbelief.

"PAN ATLANTIC COMMUNITY TREATY

Wherein there is a natural and common bond of our peoples across the Atlantic waters . . . . .

. . . we of the Europe League additionally pledge to fully assist in the formation of a new Government, a legitimate Monarchy in America . . .

"And it is signed . . ."

Hamilton read the signatories of the six European Houses of Royalty. When he finished, he placed the treaty on a side table, next to the PATRI roster.

Henry Knox abruptly stood and scowled. "A friggin' king? Who in blazes, Alex? What are you talking about?"

Washington raised his hand and commanded, "Sit back down, Henry. Sorry that you're so stirred up. We will answer that question shortly."

"Perhaps, but how does this scheme work Alex?" John Marshall demanded testily. "Go on, tell us." Before Hamilton could even answer, Marshall continued, "But John Jay intimated in his well-publicized Treaty of London that there were to be no alignments between America and other countries. Why would we choose to take this just-mentioned course that you and the President recommend? On the contrary, such an arrangement like this seems rather well-aligned."

Hamilton rubbed his hands together as a practiced barrister might. "Not at all . . . In the future, if the members of PATRI felt prompted to do something drastic like this, it would only be as a last resort. Take it from General Washington and me. Such a decision would only be made if it was absolutely necessary and in America's best interest. It would be a crossing-the-Rubicon moment; PATRI would then be making a decision to become what you call 'well-aligned' with these foreign countries."

Hamilton's expression looked haughty and menacing in the light of a nearby stand of candles. He sensed that his arguments were starting to sink in. He sounded as if he, and not George Washington, knew all the answers and he realized why not? Hadn't he been the one to write the General's orders during his campaigns? Alexander Hamilton knew that he could detail the logistics of the plan far better than Washington and loudly demanded, "Pay attention, Mr. Marshall, I'll explain. At such a time of crisis, our PATRI members would readily see that something had to be done in order to preserve America. Gentlemen, it would be an ugly time. America's degenerating society will be perversely accepted as a new norm – uncivil behavior tolerated without consequence, open licentiousness allowed to flourish in the name of liberty and freedom, irresolution strangling our government – with its elected leaders cowed into inaction by special interests. Having some form of a limited monarchy, friends, might prove to be the best option for our nation's survival."

"Forget all your fancy words, Alex!" Knox rebutted. "Even if it was necessary in your wildest dreams, who the hell could possibly be an American king? We all have seen that European kings and queens are worthless. These degenerates are not worth a horse's arse! Whatever they want, they feel it's their God-given right to get . . . and that includes anything!"

He took a swig of wine and scowled. "Look where that got 'em? These fancy people with their crowns don't even know how to command a commander. Well, we had our Washington for them, yes indeed. Nothin' beat his army . . . and nothin' ever will!"

President Washington, now standing to one side, nodded in agreement. "I can imagine how you feel, Henry. I too recall how we threw off the royal tyrant and his dastardly colonial system. But now that I've been President for eight years, I've come to realize there are always a slew of different possibilities of . . ."

President-elect Adams impatiently interjected, "I'm still not understanding. Even granted a possible benefit, and at the moment I'm not sure of that. Will you clarify something? You both have been talking much too rapidly. Suppose they, this Europe League wants us to have an American king and we do not want one, or vice versa. Are there checks and balances?"

Hamilton suspected that a shrewd lawyer might ask this kind of question. The two had their differences, to be sure, but Hamilton always admired this skilled Harvard-trained barrister for his style, using what Adams himself called his 'consequential thinking.' The feisty attorney had a clever courtroom demeanor honed by his law practice in Boston. With his short stature and erratic behavior, he scurried about like some brown squirrel of autumn. Despite the enmity of the recent election, Hamilton had grudgingly conceded that John Adams might not be a bad second President after all.

"Thank you for asking, Mr. Adams. We have finally arrived at the point of discussing certain practical matters such as your important question of how this alliance would formally be put into place. First, gentlemen, what President Washington and I call PACT's plans are born starting with this very meeting. In future years, our full PATRI would meet together with the Europe League when, and only when, there is a mutual agreement that the time had come to enact the PACT and carry out its directive."

"Still it seems to me," John Marshall opined, "as Mr. Adams has implied, we're giving up control."

"No, no." George Washington emphatically held his hands out. He knew this was an important objection that both Marshall and Adams were pressing. They wanted to ensure America's hard-won sovereignty. "You haven't been listening, John. Let Alexander continue to further detail my contingency plans to address your legitimate concern."

Hamilton walked over and rested his hand on the PACT. "Thank you, sir, for your confidence. I'll try to be as direct as possible. The decision whether we even have such a joint meeting with these Europeans, much less whether to enact the PACT, represents the ultimate check and balance that Mr. Adams favors. If we do not feel it necessary to meet the Europe League, then we simply don't meet. But if both parties chose to convene, then at such a time we would join them and discuss the need to mutually take the second step: using the PACT and activating the Plan to establish an American king. As you can plainly see, PATRI will separately make its own decision on both matters."

As he spoke, Washington sat to the side not hearing his words, but thinking, "My heart is heavy – but there may not be any other choice. Still, I wish it hadn't come to this. But, and I must remember that this is an IF, if events demand desperate actions then PATRI would be forced to proceed. It is good that every man here espouses one thing above all else, unconditional loyalty to his country. Our system of government, whatever it is or becomes, must always serve to preserve America."

Across the room, Hamilton temporarily stopped his exhortations and laid out a map on a heavy table. Everyone looked on as he tapped his index finger on the multicolored cartograph as if wanting to drill his message home.

He glared at the others. "If either our PATRI or the Europe League deems that the question of having an American monarch has serious merit, a message will be sent either to or from the European League . . . these six members here." Hamilton traced a finger across the Atlantic Ocean and circled the countries throughout Europe pictured on the map.

"Oh Alexander," Frederick Reynolds called out, "this is really too much. It sounds like fiction."

"Fiction or not, Mr. Reynolds, let's be polite and hear Mr. Hamilton out," Shippen advised. "We should give him his due since Mr. Hamilton's ideas have generally yielded good results for President Washington and our Republic."

Unperturbed, Hamilton said, "Thank you, Mr. Shippen. Now – perhaps I can be better understood if I describe a potential scenario. For instance, suppose our shadow society (or theirs) decides that mutual discussions should take place. Then, the requesting organization would notify the other by code: *'the Eagle must fly.'* The second party then has a chance to agree to fly or not. If it does, then this meeting between the two parties will take place . . . here . . ." Hamilton pointed to Lake Leman's eastern shore where lay the secluded Chateau de Chillon near Montreux, Switzerland.

"I will now give an idea of how it might play out. After such an arranged meeting," he speculated, "should both parties agree to fully cooperate, a second code-phrase will be given: *'the Eagle has landed.'* Thus, the PLAN will be activated – allowing for the eventual establishment of an American monarchy."

Hamilton lifted the two documents from the side table and put them next to each other. "Now please, closely look once more at the seal of our PATRI that Monsieur L'Enfant has made, my friends. Notice that there are two eagles. The seal reads: *Ex Regnum – PATRI – E Pluribus Unum.* This stands for *Out of a Kingdom, Patriots make One Nation from Many.*"

"That is correct, Mr. Hamilton," L'Enfant confirmed.

Hamilton went on, "Pierre created another design – the Europe League's royal purple seal, that is placed on this PACT of theirs. Likewise, it has these same two eagles, though theirs has a distinctly different motto: *Republica regni fit.* The phrase, gentlemen, roughly translates *The Republic Becomes a Kingdom.*"

A rush of voices flooded the room as Hamilton ended his presentation. Henry Knox bluntly asked, "Address my original question, Alex. Please! You always talk too much. Who would be such a king?"

Reynolds added skeptically, "Why would anyone in the United States support this one person? Who would believe him . . . and why would they?"

Even young Justin Laurens felt emboldened to ask, "Who is legitimate? Is it by honor? . . . By power? . . . By what?"

Hamilton put his wine glass down while Washington remained seated at his side. "We can all see that putting a non-republican form of government in place would run against the grain of many of our American ideals. Widespread popular opposition would be fierce and expected. Even President Washington has expressed grave concerns about there being unforeseen consequences. Nevertheless, he told me that if there is a looming threat to America, the ends might justify the means.

"For these reasons, it is obvious that if we do so, we must install as king only a man who is seen to be justified to be one." As Hamilton's passions mounted, everyone strained to hear what he might say.

"In Carlisle, General Washington and I suggested to our friend Henry Lee that he and his family were the ideal choice for such an American royal family – if we indeed ever needed to name a king. I presume that you all know there are important English royal bloodlines on both his and his wife Anne Carter Lee's side. In fact, she is a direct descendent of the second King Robert of Scotland. Since Henry and Anne Carter Lee have the prospect of having many children, any of whom would be proper royal heirs, Governor Lee seemed a natural choice.

"Mr. Lee sitting here tonight stubbornly declined. He said something then that I want you all to hear. Would that we could all be so humble as Henry Lee. He told us both that neither he nor his descendants could ever agree to mount an American throne under any circumstance. He said something like this: 'Only your blood and issue, Mr. Washington, would be truly legitimate in the eyes of Americans.' "

Lee called out from the back of the room, "I would say it again, Alexander, anytime. Only our General Washington." The men sitting nearby gave murmurs of approval.

Hamilton concluded, "Well then, I want to direct your attention back to this last crucial piece. In the event that our society ever decides it necessary to install an American monarch, you should be aware that a bloodline descendant of George Washington is actually living. Such a person of the Washington lineage or one of their heirs is the only legitimate person who could ever be this American king."

George Washington sat stone-faced as he listened. A longcase clock nearby with its tick-tock seemed to measure the room's suspense.

"When and if the tipping point should ever come," Hamilton added, "you or your heirs, our nation and the rest of the world will know the identity of that person as well."

If a pin had dropped onto the room's oak floor, it would have sounded like a twenty-penny nail. As he sat back down, Hamilton said, "Mr. Adams, we will meet about these issues again, I trust. By the way, Mr. Washington will present 'A Note of Action' to you after we adjourn."

Wedged against the bookcase, Philip Schuyler hesitated to speak but finally cleared his throat and broke the silence. "I, I do not know what to say . . . so much to think over . . . for all of us to digest. Please get your glasses ready, sires, and hold them high. Now . . . then: To our country, our country, always our country – may we pledge our liege through PATRI to our country! "

"Here, here! To our country!"

"To America!"

"To Washington!"

All the men raised their glasses to each other, to their President, and to President-elect Adams. Washington nodded in silent affirmation.

With some help, he slowly stood and with tears of gratitude, said, "God willing, PATRI will never need to call or answer the Europe League." He coughed and shook his head. In a barely audible voice he added, "But just in case . . . only in case. So be it."

The carriages standing in the swirling snow outside the Watkins House were made ready for their trips back to Philadelphia's center city. As the men reached for their wraps and said farewells, Alexander Hamilton briefly spoke to John Jay and Gouverneur Morris regarding their given assignment.

"Let us go back to the city in my carriage," Morris offered. "Then we can schedule some time for our writing project. You two are old hands at this!"

"Yes, Gouverneur, you are right," Hamilton agreed. "John and I have had a extensive history of writing together going some years back. But while we are so engaged, Messers Madison, Jefferson and Monroe and others of their ilk must not know that I am in Philadelphia. As far as they are concerned, I have no reason to be here at all."

"Then let's check with Robert, there. His summer home is 15 miles north from here and might be safer. I'll ask," Gouverneur Morris suggested.

16

East Newtown, Pennsylvania
February 28, 1797

Thick morning fog gathered over the river and muffled the sounds made by three oarsmen in a flat boat. They had just pushed off toward the unseen New Jersey bank. Woolen rags covered the oar blades in order to blunt the telltale lapping sounds. Squinting as he looked back toward the receding shore, Alexander Hamilton could barely discern his friend Gouverneur Morris silently waving to him. As the bow abruptly lurched and the boatmen struggled to realign the dory in the turbulent waters, he recalled the events of the past week.

After the Watkins House meeting, John Jay and Gouverneur Morris suggested to Hamilton that the three of them go to the nearby summer home of their fellow PATRI member, Robert Morris. As the three worked together, Hamilton unrolled a faded newspaper. "Let us start here . . . and work from there," he suggested as he pointed to the large print. "It is the portion that we have to revise first; everything else will follow."

> . . . .No Title of Nobility shall be granted by the United States: And no Person holding any Office of Profit or Trust under them, shall, without the Consent of the Congress, accept of any present, Emolument, Office, or Title, of any kind whatever, from any King, Prince, or foreign State' . . . . .

> Article. I Section. 9 The Constitution of the United States.

When the document was finished, each of the men of PATRI came to Robert Morris's country house in Newtown and penned their agreement to the newly written Second Constitution.

Thereafter, Alexander Hamilton and Gouverneur Morris watched Frederick Reynolds in his laboratory enclose the fully signed parchment pages within a glass cylinder. The scientist then used one of his grandfather's devices to fill the cylinder with an inert gas and finished the task by flaming the ends shut.

Hamilton was sure that none of their political adversaries had recognized him in Philadelphia. Peering ahead, he saw that the river's current ran faster on the opposite shore. It would make for a treacherous docking.

Soon an unseen figure hailed tentatively, "Alex. Shssh, we are here."

"Are you clear all around?"

"Yes, no one hereabouts. The closest village is some two miles distant."

The wooden ferry roughly banged into a crudely fashioned quay and came along side. Hamilton recognized his father-in-law General Philip Schulyer and William North. The others had crossed the Delaware River two days earlier in order to prepare for the clandestine trip across New Jersey's plains to New York. They stood beside a husky liveryman, their boots slopped and soiled from half-frozen mud. A nondescript carriage rested in a clump of nearby pines, its pair of horses creating a stir as they huffed into leather feeding bags full of oats.

"Watch it, sir . . . We'll get your things."

"Be careful with the trunks, especially that brown and green one. I will get out of the skiff only when you tell me."

"Hold it, hold it a moment, sir. I need to bring it about," the ferry's pilot cautioned.

Once the bow was headed into the current, it was finally possible to fasten it to a decaying post at the end of the dock. A nimble oarsman jumped out and moved sideways like a crab onto the boat's stern to secure a second tie.

Hamilton carefully lifted himself out of the skiff and clambered up the slippery bank. The strong liveryman carried his two trunks across the clearing and lifted them to the roof of his passenger carriage.

Hamilton looked around nervously, "So far, so good, it appears. William, where did you stay last night?"

North pointed up the river past a tree line. "Just south of Trenton. Mr. Schulyer remembered a fine inn near 'bouts Princeton, but as you cautioned, we decided against it – it was too public. Instead, we drove a distance away and found a very fine Quaker farm."

"They did not even care to pry about our business," Schuyler added. "Instead, this Jones family was pleased only to hear about our own families. If our personal business was a family matter, they said, then it was to be blessed and not any of their concern. Can you imagine that, Alexander? 'Our family,' they said."

The three smiled at their good luck, at least thus far.

"We still possess PATRI's signed roster as well as the PACT from Mr. Shippen's dinner in your leather folder, Alex. And you have brought the other?"

"Yes, indeed. Our Second Constitution is so well contained that it would probably float in the Delaware River here."

"Sires, we are ready to go." The driver walked around his carriage and gave firm pats to his horses as he checked the harness lines.

Hamilton reached into his waist pouch in order to pay for the ferry passage.

"Let me handle that for you, Alex. You have been quite busy over this past week for all of us." Philip Schulyer gave two dollar gold coins to the ferry's chief mate. "Thank you my fine fellows, all . . . .we appreciate your work, especially at this early hour."

"And thanks be to you and yours, kind sir." The pilot looked on in amazement – they had never received such a generous token.

As they drove off, Hamilton gazed at the wintry cornfields. This was familiar country for him, the Brandywine battle, Valley Forge, Monmouth, the Pennsylvania State House, the Convention of '87. Then there was Maria Reynolds. He realized that it might be a long time until he would be back to these parts, if ever.

He settled deeper into his seat and closed his eyes in relief. His fatigue was catching up to him. He was thankful that the radically revised Constitution, the notarized PATRI roster, and the copy of the PACT were all secure in the carriage, soon to be placed in a hidden vault at his Bank of New York.

The carriage swayed to a jerky halt several miles to the east after it had broken free from the fog. The burly driver got down to remove the hoof-cloths and give his horses two buckets of water from a nearby spring. "It is safe now. From here on, we can make better time," he explained to his passengers.

Restarting their journey, the horseman drove directly into the glaring winter sun of the New Jersey countryside as the day took hold. The three passengers rested fitfully in their compartment as the carriage noisily lurched toward Morristown.

17

Mount Vernon

April 1797

The recently retired George Washington sat alone in his office and penned a correspondence to President John Adams, Esq., at the Executive Office in the national capital of Philadelphia.

My Esteemed Mr. Adams,

By this hand, Mrs. Washington and I sincerely wish you well and trust that your Executive Years will be most enjoyable – as much as they might be. Give our greetings to your own dear wife, Mrs. Adams, as well as to your family. Martha and I understand that many of your large family have arrived from Massachusetts to join you.

There is one most important point, which I overlooked before Mrs. Washington and I departed the Executive Office more than a month ago. Please allow me to convey my thoughts presently.

Given the 'agreement' to which you and I and certain others are now privy to after our recent social event, I strongly recommend that, as a first order, you should reassign your son Master John Quincy, now the American envoy in Portugal, and make him the first United States ambassador to Prussia. This will allow a more direct access to the halls of a more respectable European power.

I have long admired your son John Quincy's industry and integrity – he is truly 'a shoot from the same tree.'

I do thank you ahead of your decision and for your consideration of my urging, Mr. President. You deeply know that you and I, and now your son, hold these matters to be most important.

America is now yours, Mr. Adams – be a good and faithful steward.

I have the honor to be Sir Your Most Obedt & Hble Servt,
G Washington

Later that day, George and Martha Washington sat with company on the portico of their newly remodeled Main House. Henry Lee and his wife had not visited the Washingtons since Christmas. Since Henry's second wife was only twenty-five years old, the Washingtons often had parental feelings towards the couple. Although Mrs. Lee occasionally had coquettish mannerisms, Martha knew better than to be judgmental. Anne Lee was, after all, a member of the respected Carter family of Virginia.

"It was such a shame, Anne," Martha said finally bringing up the subject, "that you and Henry suffered such a loss last fall."

The younger woman sighed. "Thank you, Mrs. Washington. He was such a sweet boy, too . . . and then to die so suddenly. In fact, there was nothing to be done. Doctor Walker of Great Falls said that it was likely some sort of contagion, though he was not sure. I guess we will never know . . ." Her voice drifted off.

Martha Washington asked as an aside, "I understand – now will you . . .?"

"No need to be so discreet. Please Mrs. Washington. We are close friends and our husbands are grown men." She leaned over and whispered, "But of course. We are already addressing your question – naturally."

The two women laughed together at Anne's witty rejoinder. Martha could only think that the young woman was good for all of them, and by the looks of it, especially for her husband. She had recently recognized that Priscilla Winfield's two daughters were closer in age to Anne Carter Lee than they were to their own mother. It struck her that life really does move on – she had come to the realization that it was time for the next generation to take over.

Washington leaned back and remarked pleasantly, "Mrs. Washington and I are most grateful that you two looked out for our neighbors, the Winfields, whilst we were gone. They are a most lovely family as are you and yours."

Anne smiled demurely and seemingly agreed. "Indeed, the Winfields have a practiced and fine manner, Mr. Washington. However," she continued, "I estimate that their origins are what I would call 'rather suspicious.' When all is said and done, sometimes one can notice a certain vestige of their past lives."

Lee bit his cheek – his wife seemed abrupt and out of sorts. He glanced at the Washingtons before he deflected her cynical repartee. "Anne, dear, if it is merely a matter of springing out of the ground when we are born, I am sure that the Winfields would be no different than the rest of us, but clearly they are. Thankfully, each of us is given chances to refine our character later in life. Remember, sweet, what the priest said last Sunday. 'He, even out of the depths . . . he will redeem you.' "

"Good point, Henry. The School of Enlightenment would salute you. What you say clearly refers to the notion that anyone of us has an innate possibility of rebirth. I imagine that our neighbor, Mrs. Winfield, has already experienced more than a bit of that when my brother's wife took her in and adopted her years back."

Anne Carter Lee suddenly felt a wave of nausea and needed to get air. She inhaled deeply as she got up, saying, "Oh bosh, I didn't mean to get so serious. Now, I confess that I must take a relief and have a stroll. Mrs. Washington, do you mind coming with me? I would love to see your dogwoods. If the men do not care to join us, we can let them go on and discuss their matters." She took another slow breath and added, "Whatever . . . life goes on and I do not care to miss it."

As the two women walked away on the gravel path towards the north gardens, Lee chewed on a fresh date and asked, "Do you have any plans, General, now that you have extra sand in your hourglass?"

"That is a good one, my friend. Martha and the overseers have so much planned for me. By the way, what are you doing early next month? Our good friend, Alexander Hamilton, will be here in a fortnight."

"Sorry, sir. I have already promised my bride a trip to the western state. She desires to see the rhododendrons in bloom near Front Royal. Surely you and Mrs. Washington can understand that a promise to my sweet Annie must be kept."

George Washington took Lee's forearm. "Not to worry, Henry. I will be sure to catch you up about Alex when you return from your holiday."

"Thank you, General. I will be most interested. Today, though, let us simply relax and go see your gardens. I am sure that you love to see how your perennials give witness to what we were talking about earlier – that is, rebirth."

"Something you just said, Henry, strikes me as being rather appropriate in light of the recent dinner at William Shippen's place. In a sense, PATRI is perennial, too. It will be there and allow a fresh beginning whenever the time is right for America."

Lee stretched out his hand and exclaimed, "Well put, sir. With that said, let's be on our way and join the ladies. Permit me to give you a hand, General."

18

Mount Vernon

Late April 1797

George Washington, Martha and their long time neighbors, Jonathan and Priscilla Winfield socialized together as they looked out over the Potomac. Martha offered tea and sweets. "It is really quite remarkable how many things we have accumulated for ourselves in Philadelphia. I am so glad that trade with England has returned to its former levels – the port there along the Delaware is so busy. We can soon hang the silk draperies that I purchased for our Green Room and add some of the new furniture to the dining room."

"I have heard about the wonderful boutiques there, Mrs. Washington. When we visited London a year back, I did not think that I . . ."

The former President was thoroughly relaxed as he listened to the women's voices. He was relieved to know that he would not need to return to Philadelphia any time soon. He was able to revel in the familiar earthy fragrances of springtime Virginia.

On their way south, the Washingtons had passed through the recently made clearings of the new Federal District. While sitting on the porch, he joined the conversation and shared some impressions of the project with the Winfields. He was bemused that his surname 'Washington' had been selected to be the designated title of Pierre L'Enfant's carefully designed capital city. "Better that I suppose," he laughed, "than the present village of George-town. People might instead confuse that with the name of the British royal. Hopefully, Mr. L'Enfant will not construct too many buildings that resemble palaces and Roman temples. If he does, people will no doubt be suspicious of his or my intent. I have no interest in being remembered as some sort of emperor."

Jonathan Winfield agreed and added, "I heard that this idea of moving the capital was motivated by Messers Madison and Jefferson's self-interests. Nonetheless, geographically it appears to be a decent site and closer to Richmond, besides."

"Well, Jonathan, you will be happy to know that after agreeing with their primary proposal, I was able to make provisions to prevent any future incursions onto our lands. During my last week in office, I signed what I termed a Presidential 'land directive' to set aside much of the nearby acreage to our properties."

Winfield was puzzled and wanted to hear more details. "What do you hope to accomplish?"

"It affects us both, Jonathan. Importantly, the scheme should curb development here and about. With the recent surge of land speculation on the frontier, I decided it was necessary to set off a number of land protection sites around America. The first will be right across the river . . . there." As he spoke, Washington pointed to Maryland and some undeveloped woodlands on the shore opposite.

"Five thousand acres over there and a second piece on this side to the south, land where Priscilla's Fairfax family had their former estate of Belvoir. The government decreed these acquisitions by eminent domain and I have authorized a generous settlement paid by the federal government for the purchase. The deeds will be held in the name of the national Treasury Department."

Overhearing his remarks, Priscilla Winfield brightly smiled and inquired, "That sounds like very good news for us, indeed, but beside being beneficial for our privacy, is there some other reason for this arrangement?"

"The main purpose, and I might add that Mrs. Washington is also hearing about this for the first time, is to give our estates of Mount Vernon and Woodlawn Mills what an old soldier like me would call 'a line of defense.' Besides, those Maryland lands are sandy and untillable."

Washington turned toward her and explained, "Several men at a recent dinner meeting suggested that I set aside lands around Mount Vernon for my family's comfort and protection. Mr. Hamilton, the principle spokesman, and Henry Lee thought it best to include your neighboring lands as well, Priscilla."

"Is this not favoritism at its worst, sir?" Winfield asked. He knew that Washington had always been wary of any outward appearance of privilege.

"No, no – I forgot to mention that I also agreed to have land-use directives in several other states. President Adams will soon designate several federal reservations, as well. Some of these, no doubt, will be used for military purposes – the first being for Henry Knox's new military college at West Point along the Hudson River."

Martha got up, adjusted her dress and moved to the edge of the wooden steps that led down to the back lawn. She smiled before suggesting, "Enough of this sitting and chatting. After being away so much, George and I are most delighted to be back – not for days but for years to come. How wonderful!" She motioned with her hand. "Let us all take a walk down to the wharf. It is such a lovely afternoon. Mr. Washington, come on now, you too. We need to enjoy some good country living with the Winfields once again."

As the four meandered down the southern path by the pungent stables and compost bins, they passed near the Washington family tomb, The Burial Vault. The retired President made a mental note that he would be returning to this hallowed place with Hamilton sometime in the coming week.

"Dear Lawrence . . . dear Anne," he reflected as the two couples strolled along, "we are home at last. Thank heavens."

Many of the slaves working in the fields and animal enclosures greeted the Washingtons and Winfields as they walked past.

"Iz good to has' yous back, Misser Washin' tun."

"Welcome hum', suh."

"Louk to see ya suun in yer field, Mista' Wash'."

Wanting to hasten Washington's pace, Priscilla took his arm while doing a half-spinning reel on the gravel walkway. Her spontaneity lifted his spirits, causing him to laugh out loud. Despite his rheumatism, he picked up his gait and gallantly tried to follow her dancing feet.

Here they were – the four of them together again. He started to hum a favorite ditty, a tune from long ago. As they walked together, Washington thought he remembered the lyrics asking something about *'How he'd be seen these many years gone?'*

"Yes," he thought, "I'm most delighted to be home."

19

Mount Vernon

May 1797

Alexander Hamilton had arrived in mid-morning with George-Washington du Motier, Lafayette's twelve-year-old son. Walking into the Main House, he first inquired, "Where are the others, Mr. Washington?"

"Martha has gone to town with Mrs. Winfield. Nearly all the help is out in the western fields today with clearing to be done. You did bring it, Alex, did you not? We should be alone for the next several hours."

After the founding meeting of PATRI earlier that year, George Washington had communicated with Lafayette who was still being held as a prisoner of war in Austria. His words were carefully chosen in case his missive was intercepted.

> *My Dear Friend,*
> *I trust you will be released soon — the rumor is that Napoleon himself will be of assistance.*
> *We had an interesting meeting of my American patriots last week. These men now understand the intents of your own European confrères.*
> *With that, what I need from you now is a safe repository for certain of my personal possessions. These include items detailing my own lineage.*
> *I certainly hope that you can fill my request.*
>
> *As always,   G Wash'   March 3, 1797*

Lafayette replied with a similarly obtuse message.

Dearest General,

I will do my best to design a clever device for you. Already, I have the piece in mind . . . my very own storage case. I will make modifications and send it along with instructions to my son at Alexander Hamilton's residence. Yes, the word for me is good . . . I may be released the end of May.

Most fondly yours,

M. de Lafayette   *March 25, 1797*

George-Washington du Motier excused himself in order to fetch the storage trunk his father had sent to him. Returning with a house servant, the lad awkwardly carried a two-foot-long ebony box into Washington's office. The two placed the case down on the floor before the servant was dismissed.

The box had bronzed carvings of what appeared to be Roman scenes — one of a pastoral scene and another of an assembly of toga-clad senators. With the lid ajar, Hamilton and Washington could see that rich purple velvet lined the inside.

"My father said that renowned metalwork artisans of Holland produced the designs. He calls this his 'Caesar Box.' Let me show you what is truly special."

The boy ran his fingers over the lining and suggested that the two men do the same. "Can you feel it? . . . just beneath? Part of the reason this Caesar Box is so heavy is that steel girding-sheets are attached to the inner sides and then overlaid with royal velvet. The engineering gives the container added strength, sirs." As he described the workmanship, the young du Motier made sure that a muslin cloth stayed in place so that the lid did not inadvertently snap shut.

Hamilton observed to Washington, "I'm amazed how mature this lad is at his age."

His friend replied, "It's probably just the way such European boys develop. You remember, Alex, that his father was only nineteen himself when he was commissioned a major general before the battle at the Brandywine."

Washington looked over at Lafayette's son and asked, "When you first arrived, didn't you ask me whether I had the Bastille Key handy, the one that your father gifted me years ago? Why was that?"

"Oui, monsieur, let me explain. Following your recent request to my father, he had master craftsmen from Salzburg forge an additional lock onto the ebony wood of his own storage box and attach inner steel grates. When he shipped this to me, he enclosed a set of instructions and told me to demonstrate that this case has two separate keyholes and latches — an original one in the middle and a newly fashioned one on the right. Each lock is separately opened by one of two different Bastille Keys. He said you already had one of the keys, Mr. Washington."

"Keys?" Hamilton was puzzled. "Not *the* Bastille Key?"

"There is more than one Bastille Key, sir. In fact, there are more than ten different keys and corresponding locks located throughout France and Europe. Members of my father's National Guard took them from the Prison as souvenirs.

"In order to see if your own one fits, might I see your Bastille Key now, Mr. Washington? My father assured me that you would be keeping it safe – it should work the lock on the right side. If it's available, I should be better able to demonstrate the Box."

"Yes, yes, of course. It is here at Mount Vernon held in a prominent case in the front passageway – near where we passed into the study. The key is displayed on the main floor, below the room where your father slept when he stayed here years ago."

George-Washington du Motier ran his hand along the smooth edge of the wood and his fingers traced the steel outlines of the wrought-iron lock. "I am to show you and Mr. Hamilton how at least one of these locks works using your own key. I have seen other Bastille Keys – they are usually quite large."

Hamilton motioned Washington to remain seated. "Both of you stay where you are. I know where it is . . ." As he left, he said as an afterthought, "By the way, sir, I like the upgrade of the passageway that you are presently doing. The faux bois technique gives a fine similitude of mahogany paneling." He departed and wended his way through the adjoining canary yellow pantry.

After Hamilton returned with Washington's Bastille Key and settled into his chair, Lafayette's son took it and knelt next to the box.

Young du Motier felt honored to be presenting his father's container to these important Americans, and nervously said, "I must be careful not to accidentally move the cloth while I show you more of the Caesar Box. Yes, there. It is still tied down.

"Now then, according to my father's letter, your Bastille Key should operate the latch on the box's right side. Let me try." When he did, sounds of gear movements came from the latch deep within the wood.

"But father wrote that your key does not work in the middle keyhole, sirs, so let's see what happens there." George-Washington du Motier jiggled the key – no similar noises were heard when the Mount Vernon key was placed in the second lock.

"My father said that his lock came from the Prison's north brick tower whereas the second one, which he had mounted to make this Caesar Box, was removed from a south Prison door and subsequently stored in his barn. Each requires a different Bastille Key.

"The second key for this Caesar Box was formerly displayed at our home of LaGrange just as yours is at Mount Vernon. When my father was forced to escape the Terror, though, he took a precaution and placed it in a Swiss bank. It's still there."

"But why two separate keys, young master George?"

"In response to your request, Mr. Washington, my father designed this custom case to best hold *'your interests.'* That is how he put it. In his letter to me that accompanied the Box, though, he wrote something that I didn't quite understand."

"What was that?" Hamilton asked.

"He said that two associations might gather together in the future if an agreed-upon matter of extreme importance would arise. If and when that happened, he said, these two groups would decide whether it was necessary to explore the contents that you elect to place in this container."

The young du Motier continued. "Father added that in order to see your stored-items, both parties must bring their separate Bastille Keys to a subsequent meeting and use them simultaneously in order to open this Box of Caesar. He mentioned that requiring two keys created a desirable check and balance."

Washington and Alexander Hamilton understood what the young du Motier boy apparently did not – the two parties of whom he spoke were PATRI and the Europe League. The Caesar Box would next be opened only after *'the Eagle had landed.'*

George du Motier remained hunched over the opened box. "You must be very careful not to accidentally snap-close the box until all your items are in it." He ran two fingers gently over the top of the container and added, "When you are ready, the muslin along the edges slides off easily. I had a hard enough time keeping it in place, but it has done the job of keeping the latches apart, at least so far. Remember this, sirs. Once the lid is shut, the Caesar Box will remain closed tight until both keys are used simultaneously."

The two Americans silently looked at each other as George-Washington du Motier again demonstrated that George Washington's Bastille Key worked only one of the box's locks. Hamilton could only wonder what, besides this box, the lad knew – especially about the PACT or PATRI. Even though the French boy had not been in the drawing room with the others at the Watkins House in Philadelphia, he fretted that somehow he had been told of their plans.

The young du Motier quickly put him at ease. "My father did not write much else, just the things that I have told you. He said that you would know for what purpose to use the Caesar Box. I was only to deliver this and show you how to use it."

The two men smiled and Hamilton spoke with evident relief, "You did your assignment well, young man. We appreciate all your energy, Master Lafayette-to-be."

"Stand aside a moment, if you please. I am interested in examining this box more closely if I might." Washington bent over and carefully tilted the box to more carefully inspect the ornate decoration. "Look at the fine workmanship – the figures here that these Dutch craftsmen placed." He discerned the pastoral scene of a farmer standing behind a plow with his family and slave-workers working in the fields. He was sure it was a representation of Cincinnatus, and thought it a nice touch by Lafayette, an honorary member of his Order of the Cincinnati.

Washington carefully turned the ebony box and resting it on the bench, he eyed the bronzed panel on the opposite side. This one depicted Julius Caesar in the Roman Senate with Marc Anthony and some others. On the top of the ornate box, the artists had crafted a splendid rendering of Romulus and Remus along the Tigris River.

"George, I will correspond with your father and tell him how much we appreciate receiving his, how can I say, 'wonderful instrument.' This is a remarkable piece." As he spoke, Washington ran his hand over the decorations trying to gauge the Box's size. "My, this must weigh near a good stone's worth, I imagine."

He warmly placed his hand on the lad's shoulders and fondly looked into his blue eyes. "You have earned my gratitude, young man, for doing your father's business in all of this. We must prove your efforts to be worthwhile – your family and many such families in Europe are so like ourselves in very many ways."

"Anything else that you can think we should understand, Master du Motier?" Hamilton asked. "Mr. Washington and I most sincerely appreciate your efforts."

George-Washington du Motier answered, "No, nothing at all." The youth politely left the two men alone – to use his father's gifted Box for whatever purpose they wished.

Alexander Hamilton remained in Mount Vernon's study while George Washington quietly arranged some papers on his desk. Late morning sun pierced the thick lead-glass windowpanes behind the General.

Washington hesitated for a moment and stared into the air as he tried to recall something. He opened a desk drawer, peered in and retrieved several oil-skinned Egyptian papyri. After pushing his chair back, he got up and went over to a bookcase where he lifted a brass cylinder off the upper shelf.

Washington turned it in his hands before saying, "Finally, Alex, we can get started with the business at hand. Firstly, I have to roll up these three scripted pages more tightly."

Once he was satisfied, Washington opened the brass cylinder and slid the papers inside a rolled-up scroll already lying in the tube. As he screwed the end cap back in place, he said, "This brass piece was custom-made here in Alexandria years back. Thus far, it has seemed to work well in keeping some of my records safe."

As he sat back down and pushed his chair back, he touched a hidden catch beneath the desk with his knee. A tiny compartment concealed within the stained wood opened next to his shin. Washington marveled aloud, "Well, like him or not, Mr. Jefferson's ingenuity with these kinds of furniture gadgets is certainly noteworthy. I do believe, though, that he borrowed this particular idea from Peter Waxman, a well-known furniture maker over in Cornwall. But as you and I well know, Jefferson and his ilk are not often inclined to give others credit."

Still at his desk, he adjusted his seat and asked no one in particular, "Where is it? Oh, yes, there it is I think . . ." He reached deeper into the drawer and withdrew a short brass key with an unusual octagonal head. After turning it over in his hand, he carefully placed it in his waistcoat pocket.

Without further discussion, Hamilton and Washington placed the brass cylinder into Lafayette's Caesar Box. As they did, Hamilton remembered what the young du Motier had warned and carefully left the muslin in place. For the moment, the lid had to remain ajar.

The two men knew that they would add several more items of interest to the repository before finally locking it shut.

20

Mount Vernon

May 1797

Following the noon meal, George-Washington du Motier took a walk north along the Potomac. While he was gone, George Washington asked his most trusted valet, William 'Billy' Lee, to join Hamilton and him for a special task.

Hamilton picked his way down a path with Washington, gingerly carrying the ebony container. Since he knew that the Caesar Box was kept open only by a cloth along its edges, he felt as if he was carrying a fragile baby.

William Lee cautiously walked down a side trail above the Potomac with an axe and shovel from the tool shed. Over the years, he and his owner had developed a special bond, familiar and content in each other's company. Worsening hand tremors had begun to severely cripple the silver-haired, seventy-year-old Negro.

The three men arrived at a weathered brick vault built into an ivy-covered hillside. Hamilton placed the Caesar Box to the side on a patch of moss. Rustling willows and stands of towering oaks surrounded the site. When Washington and his nephew, George Augustine Washington, had replaced the door years before in 1790, they judged that Lafayette's gifted Bastille Key would draw little attention. Using it as the key for a new specially made lock assured the family Tomb's privacy. Hamilton turned the Bastille Key in the door lock easily, but when he tried to open the door of the Burial Vault, the thick wooden portal stayed shut. A mass of prickly juniper bushes stood along the sill.

"Les me hilp, sirrh." The elderly slave had brought a sharp shovel. Moving past Hamilton, he used it with good effect to cut through the dense undergrowth and brambles wrapped against the heavy iron-studded door. Despite the cool afternoon, sweat soon covered the old Negro's face. "Massah Wash', no 'un wans to com'in here, no suh . . . I jes glad you both here . . . jes like de las' time, yes suh! De las' time."

After some heaped up soil and roots were cleared away, he and Hamilton were able to swing open the door on its rusting hinges. Peering into the entranceway, they could barely discern the crypts and semi-rotten shelves in the darkness. Rivulets from nearby springs made the chilly stonewall and dirt-brick floor streaked with mud.

Fearful, Billy Lee stepped back and nearly fell against the Caesar Box positioned on the ground. Hamilton quickly braced him by the shoulder and warned, "Careful there, William. Don't go and upset the box!"

As their eyes grew accustomed to the darkness, they could see George Washington's brother's crypt and three smaller ones nearby. Lawrence Washington's saddle lay crusted with mildew on a wooden ledge above his headstone. A ceramic urn-like object, a memory coffer that Anne Fairfax Washington Lee had placed years before, was positioned next to it on the partially decomposed shelf.

"Let us see, Alexander," Washington said as he ducked to enter the Tomb. "Be careful to bring Lafayette's Caesar Box in and put it down against the wall on the left. It is relatively dry over there. So far, only the brass tube that we took from my study should be in Lafayette's box."

After Hamilton carefully slid the Caesar Box over, Washington kneeled to recheck that the metal cylinder was in it before asking, "Help get Anne's porcelain urn from the upper shelf, Alex. Do you remember seeing it that other time when you were here with me in the Vault?"

"I certainly do, sir, even though it has been years. The piece is memorably distinctive with its exotic designs. I remember first thinking that it was a receptacle for ashes."

"Ah – but you and I know better, Alex."

After gently placing the hand-decorated Chinese ware on the Tomb's uneven stone floor, Washington took the small octagonal-headed key out of his pocket. He fitted it into the urn's small keyhole and the lid sprung open with a barely audible click. Washington picked up the exquisitely designed piece to get a better view of its contents. Just as he hoped, an intertwined hair necklace, a symbolic token of his brother and wife Anne's marriage, lay in a middle compartment. Nestled against the coffer's sides were three lockets containing the hair of their children and a fourth locket resting in a baby's linen skullcap.

A small note lay in the cap and George Washington recognized Sally Fairfax's handwriting. He held it up close, barely able to see the words, *'always a Washington.'* Then he tucked the note back into the skullcap and put them back inside Anne's urn.

"As I can recall, Billy, the coffer's contents are the same as the last time we came to the Tomb," Washington said over his shoulder.

"Yes, massah . . . looks dat way," William Lee replied from the door. "Ev'n da baby Sarah's cap and her Momma's locktit insize da cap. Day' bot' sitten right der un de ting."

Washington carefully reached back into the urn. "I must take this one locket out now, though. Sally would want Priscilla to have her mother's keepsake. I will leave the fading skullcap in the porcelain container along with the three other lockets and this wreath of hair. It is what Anne called her 'marriage circle,' Alexander."

The stooping estatesman fingered with sentiment the silver and enameled locket, which was attached to a silver chain. "Yes, she and her own family must have it," he whispered, remembering something else Sally Fairfax had written several years ago, *'Priscilla is so dear.'*

Turning it over in his large hands, Washington could barely make out the engravings on the frontispiece. *AF* for Anne Fairfax was above and below, *PFF* for Priscilla Farris Fairfax was nestled between the year of her birth, *1750,* the year of her adoption: *1752.* On the back of the neckpiece, placed in decorative bowers of ivy and flowers, were the barely legible letters *lw &* *aw,* worn down by years of Anne's and then Sally's anxious rubbing. With the poor light, he could not quite make out the faint *sw 1750* underneath the initials, but he was sure that it was there, hidden in the etched vines.

His eyes grew moist as he imagined Anne wearing this locket containing a snippet of hair from her 'adopted daughter Priscilla.' Washington gently teased the locket open and was relieved to see that wisps of infant-hair were still there. He remembered that as Anne Fairfax Lee lay dying, she had given the locket to Sally Cary Fairfax, asking her closest friend to continue to hold Priscilla in her own heart.

With a start, he suddenly had a fresh idea. Washington closed the porcelain coffer with the octagonal key and placed Anne's heirloom locket in his coat pocket. In his rush, he put the eight-sided double flute key aside.

"Thank heavens, sir, the other items there in Mrs. Lee's memory container look to be in fine shape. I never have completely understood, though, why baby hair and christening caps are so important for a mother's memory." Hamilton looked perplexed. "Seems a bit sentimental."

"Yes, Alexander, I agree, women are that way, but it is a common tradition down here in the South. My dear Martha has lockets of her own children, Jacky and Patsy, on her bedside stand." He sadly shook his head in puzzlement and wondered aloud, "Where have all the children gone? If not for Priscilla, there would be none left."

Hamilton came over and touched Washington on the shoulder. After a brief moment he suggested, "We must carry on, sir, the day is moving along."

"I know, I know. You're right to keep us focused on the tasks at hand. Hold on now, let me check – Oh first, Billy, is there anyone about?" The elderly slave was still posted outside the Burial Vault's entrance.

"No suh, massah Wash'n; dis alls set – iz now real quie'."

"Well, let me get to it, then, Mr. Hamilton. I want to tuck this memory coffer of Anne's right next to the brass cylinder in our friend Lafayette's Caesar Box . . . I think it can fit somewhere . . . That's it, just so." First, he squeezed the porcelain urn against the velvet material at one end and then he rearranged the brass container from his study against the other side.

"Do we have it all now, sir? The things that we talked about?"

"Yes, so far, we seem to be getting well enough along, but I am sure we are not finished loading it yet." Washington groaned as he crouched down against a timber. ". . . There, Alexander, look there behind you. I thought that you would have remembered. When we came here in '87 after the Constitutional Convention, we hid an important item in a wooden flat under Lawrence's saddle on the bottom shelf. There . . . there. Go further back on the lower shelf. Actually, if I'm not mistaken I believe you'll find two things of importance there."

Hamilton got down on his knees on the damp stones and found a weathered brass tube with a corroded metal screwtop sitting in a narrow storage bin. Next to it lay the contraption that he recalled from years before. It held the 'King's Promise.'

"I recall that this glass cylinder is of Mr. Franklin's making, General, but what is in this other tube? There is quite a bit of wear and tear on the metal. I think that you told me of its contents previously, but I have since forgotten . . . or perhaps, I never knew. The etching here on the surface looks like your family's coat of arms with the words *'Exitus Acta Probat'*, 'The End Proves the Deed.' "

"Yes, that motto captures the essence of my Washington family through the centuries. Inside that second brass tube, Alex, is my brother's personal message to me when he was terminally ill. I have kept it all these years as his last testament. It is his written admonishment to me to provide care for his family and his Mount Vernon."

Washington thought for a moment before saying, "I favor that we place it in this Caesar Box. It is important to me. We might also consider putting this King's Promise in the box as well . . . That is, if there is any room."

Washington bent over and, given his practiced eye for surveying, estimated the cylinder's dimensions. "We've never mentioned this sealed package from King George to anyone, Alex. I have often wondered why I never found any need to open it. Now I will never have the occasion – and, with the PACT, probably don't need to. But nonetheless, if it fits in this Caesar Box, it might be of some historic interest someday. There should be space for all three receptacles, I wager."

Since he didn't want to risk breaking the glass cylinder, Hamilton thought it best to first position the tube containing Lawrence Washington's testament in the bottom of the box alongside George Washington's own brass tube that was already in place. Estimating the remaining space, Hamilton figured that he would have to devise some sort of makeshift cradle.

"It is a good thing that our friend Lafayette had thick velvet placed to line his customized box. It will better serve to protect the contents." Hamilton continued to fuss in the cramped vault. He fashioned a crude sling from two silk handkerchiefs and then gently laid the Franklin-modified tube onto the fabric. "But then, again, Lafayette already knew that we had this glass cylinder and he might have supposed that there might be other fragile items that we might store."

"Right. Now let's see . . . let me be sure." Washington imagined that all the contents would be snug and secure, but as he moved the lid down to test the fit, he caught himself nearly displacing the muslin along the container's front edge. "My misstep, sorry!" he mumbled. "I must watch it."

"Take care there, General," Hamilton cautioned. "Be doubly sure that we have put in all the items that you planned to store. For my vantage point, the container is quite full as it now stands. Have one last look even though the light in here is poor."

Hamilton stared into the dark recesses. "Remember that the young du Motier boy warned that when the lid shuts and the catches close, that will be it. Sounds like Shakespeare's Macbeth, 'What's done cannot be undone.' It's nearly the same. When we close the Caesar Box, we can't undo that act either . . . it will remain closed. Thereafter, two separate keys from the Bastille will be required at the same time to undo the locks. We have but one."

"Oh my, Alexander, you are so full of literary allusions as usual." Washington laughed. "Thinking about it, we have got everything *in,* but . . . I forgot to take something *out* . . . the other key, the small octagonal-headed one. Here it is, nearly hidden beneath the fabric. I forgot to put it in my pocket along with Priscilla's locket a while back. Thank heavens, good notice, old man." He was speaking to himself. "I'll keep it for now . . . Let me see, is there anything else? Billy still has the Mount Vernon Bastille Key with him, but beside that, can you think of anything else, Alex?"

The men kneeled in silence and pondered their task. Finally, Hamilton said, "No, I think not. The three items we need to secure plus your own brass tube are presently inside the box. It doesn't seem that there's anything else that needs to go in or to come out. It seems to me that our job is done."

Hamilton untied and removed the muslin cloth as he carefully held the box open. He then glanced up and directed, "Mr. Washington, when you are ready please close this Caesar Box."

After Washington agreed that everything seemed in order, he took full charge and slowly lowered the heavy lid into place. Two high-pitched, snapping clicks echoed in the damp Vault. The two locks, purloined from the doors of the Bastille, held fast. As a test, Washington tried to reopen the Caesar Box using only his Bastille Key — the lid remained tightly shut.

"Two different keys from the French prison will be needed indeed," Hamilton said. "This is but one –."

The men had to yell out for William Lee several times before the slave reluctantly agreed to reenter the Tomb, with his longtime fear of gloomy places. The three men then struggled to lift the loaded Caesar Box off the damp floor and somehow manage to work it into a narrow rock niche between the crypts of Lawrence Washington and his children.

Without delay, the three men lowered their heads and backed out of the Vault. Billy Lee was finally able to feel relief after he swung the hinged door shut and secured it once again. Washington took hold of the large key and said that he planned to return it to its usual display case in the public passageway of Mount Vernon. "No one will even suspect."

Hamilton raised a question as they walked back up the path. "What about that small octagonal-headed key? Are you going to return it to your desk? It cannot be of much use since the Chinese memory vessel of Anne Washington is put away within the Caesar Box."

"Oh no, Alexander, I have already thought about it. Mrs. Jonathan Winfield, just next door, will soon be getting a lovely keepsake – a lacquered jewelry box with ivory inlay from Martha and me. She celebrates her wedding anniversary next month."

Stopping on the path, he retrieved the two objects from his pocket. "For the occasion, we will also be gifting this silver locket which Sally Fairfax sent to me several years back. Martha and I are sure that Priscilla will be most thrilled to receive both presents. We trust that the neckpiece will bring back fond memories of her childhood. She saw both her mother and Sally Fairfax wear it."

"My goodness, I didn't know you to be such a schemer, sir."

"Yes, but hardly as good as you, John Laurens, and your friend Lafayette were in the old days. The lacquer box, which she will use to hold her locket and other jewelry, will have a keyhole tooled for this same key – the one that also opened Anne's memory coffer back there." Washington pointed back to the Burial Vault, now nearly hidden along the steep slope. "Mrs. Washington assures me that Priscilla will keep both gifts as part of her own Winfield family heirlooms. Women like Priscilla, Martha and your Eliza are wonderful with the way they treasure their families. And I'd say, good for them. When you think about it, Alex, without them there would be no history for any of us at all."

Before reaching the back portico, Billy Lee limped off to return the shovel and axe to the stable's tool shed. Washington gazed over the wide Potomac. Its usual outgoing current was caught in a stall – stopped by an incoming tide. He grasped Hamilton by the shoulder. "Being down there," he said gesturing back over his shoulder, "reminds me of something that I have always told my family and all my people here at Mount Vernon. I should tell you, too, Alexander. When my time comes, I insist on not being buried for three days. They can lay me out on my bed as if I am asleep and just wait a while."

"Why is that, Mr. Washington?"

"I am fearfully afraid of being buried whilst I am still alive. Remember I told you, Alex, I saw it almost happen around here once, with my niece no less. Thankfully, with a stroke of good fate, everything came out all right."

As they walked farther up the hill and neared the mansion's piazza, George Washington felt deeply satisfied. He looked back in the direction of the Vault and said, "Things are finally in place, Alex. I am glad it is done, finally done."

21

Woodlawn Mills

November 1799

Martha Washington was finally able to leave Mount Vernon for the first time in nearly two months. Dr. James Craik had been treating her for debilitating bilious fevers. Despite her weakened condition, she was delighted to go to Woodlawn Mills and celebrate the birthday of the oldest Winfield daughter, Polly. In addition, Martha was looking forward to again seeing Polly Winfield's fiancé James Mason, a student of law at William and Mary. Franklin Winfield, a strapping fifteen-year-old, met George and Martha at the front door as a domestic took their coats.

"It is so nice of you to greet us, young man," Martha said, "I trust your family is well."

"Yes ma'm," the boy answered. "Can either of you quite believe that Polly is twenty-two? I can't."

"I can hardly believe it myself, though I clearly remember when you were each born," Washington replied. "But to be absolutely truthful, I was here only for your brother Aubrey's birth. As for you others, I was north on campaigns when you and your sisters showed up, Franklin."

Franklin Winfield laughed. "I am sure that my mother would say that it was a lot more than us just 'showing up,' Mr. Washington."

Martha smiled at his repartee. "No matter, all of you young folks are worth her effort." She paused and took Franklin's arm saying, "I believe I can hear some voices coming from the Great Room. Let us join them."

Priscilla Winfield greeted them as they entered the home's Great Room. A fire crackled in the wide hearth opposite. After reintroducing James Mason who was standing in the background, she pleaded, "Please do sit down here next to Polly and me, Mrs. Washington. We are so glad that you are recovering from your infirmity."

"Yes," Martha replied, joining them on the sofa. "It's been a struggle, but each day I feel a little stronger. I do thank you for your concern."

Priscilla turned in George Washington's direction and lightly added, "And you, sir, you must sit on your favorite, time-worn cushioned chair – I insist on it."

Washington settled into it and then boomed, "Priscilla, dear, you and the others must speak more clearly. My hearing is fading as much as the rest of me."

Jonathan Winfield and his other daughter, Charlotte, came in from the hallway to join them. Washington frequently thought that Charlotte looked just as beautiful as her grandmother, Anne Fairfax, had at her age.

"Welcome, friends," Winfield said boisterously as he motioned to a servant. "Permit me to have our dining steward pour us a bit of sherry for Polly's celebration."

"Even me?" a voice asked. A young cousin excitedly bounded in from an adjoining room. He halted in his tracks when he realized that their afternoon's two important guests were already in the Great Room. "I'm sorry sir, Mr. Washington and I mean . . . and, you Mrs. Washington," he mumbled in apology. "I only asked . . ."

"Of course, master Andrew." Winfield tousled his nephew's hair. "I am sure Polly would want her mother to allow it."

The house-steward formally gave the first glasses to the visitors from Mount Vernon. Washington contentedly observed Priscilla with her four healthy children, knowing that each of them was a Washington too.

Winfield proposed a toast once everyone had been served. "Let us take a sip to our Polly on her birthday and also as importantly, if not more, to her mother my sweet Priscilla. After all, Polly's life is grounded in her mother's roots . . . and soon will be grafted to James as well." He lifted his small crystal goblet. "We wish you both years of happiness."

Given their infirmities, the Washingtons remained seated as the others made their way around the room and clinked their glasses in celebration. "This is so grand that you have included us. Thank you, Priscilla and Jonathan." Martha said with warmth.

Priscilla's eyes twinkled as she leaned over. "Mrs. Washington, as you know, little of this could have happened without both of you." In a quiet voice, she added, "You are like life-long grandparents for our Winfield family."

Following a five-course supper, Washington and Winfield conversed in the library, while the others socialized with a game of whist in the parlor. Jonathan leisurely smoked a pipe. "It was an exceedingly troublesome year, sir," he confided, "for both plantations. The drought deeply cut into our yields."

"So much of a failure, Jonathan. In fact, Martha and I with the aid of Mr. Tobias Lear, my secretary, have assessed how to keep solvent in such times as these. Because of my many years of public service, my absences from Mount Vernon have certainly not helped. It seems like some new problem arises to take the place of another."

"Pardon me for saying so, sir, but this evening you appear more morose than I can ever recall. These problems or difficulties must be wearing you down . . . Are you all right?"

Washington knew that in fact he wasn't, but nonetheless wanted to seem hale and hearty for the party. He had already concluded that he would simply, as always, have to work his own way out of his current circumstances.

"I suppose that overall I feel well enough, but there has been a lot going on, Jonathan. I am almost leery to tell you. At times, it is so oppressive. Would that it was only a matter at Mount Vernon."

He went on to explain. "Some men up in Philadelphia want me to come out of retirement – yet once again! These so-called friends of mine use the argument that President Adams and now his rival Thomas Jefferson are causing our new republic to fail. America must be saved, they keep telling me . . . and incessantly demand that I be some sort of savior. No matter what they say, I just cannot do this. My health simply won't allow it."

"Is there something going on, Mr. Washington? I mean physically? You have my confidence should you wish to tell me."

"Nothing like that to speak of, Jonathan. It's probably a state of mind." Washington sighed. "After my last surviving brother recently died, I took notice that there is but one living family member left in Martha's and my whole generation. It is down to the two of us. Literally, we are the last leaves on the tree."

"Come now, Mr. Washington, cheer up a bit. See yourself as being a vital part of our children's lives as well as our own. You've got so much to add – you might feel younger and more like your former self come Christmas. Remember how much you and Mrs. Washington were gaily laughing during Polly's celebration just an hour ago? A few moments like that will assuredly brighten you up."

Washington agreed but only in part. "Yes, we may be vital enough persons for a few occasions, perhaps. But Jonathan, in the end we cannot be a full part of your lives, nor for any others of your generation, for that matter. The author of the Old Testament Book of Ecclesiastes was quite correct. *'There is a time for everything and a season for every matter under heaven . . .'* Mrs.Washington and I very well know – we have had our season, my friend."

After a brief time, Washington rose slowly from his hard-backed chair. "Perhaps now that you have allowed me to express a poor man's homespun philosophy, we should rejoin the others. It's near time to get my Martha back home. Do you mind helping me stand, Jonathan?"

When they were both upright, the men warmly shook hands and George Washington remarked, "Thank you for everything you have done over the years. The future certainly seems bright for you and your family. Before I forget, one more thing Jonathan. Be sure to continue to stay in close contact with my close friend Henry Lee of Alexandria. A fortnight ago, Mr. Lee told me to deliver his fondest greetings. His interest in you is much as my own."

The two men made their way arm in arm back to the Great Room.

Subsequent Events

- After George Washington died in December 1799, Martha Washington moved to one of her other properties and stayed there with her married granddaughter, Eleanor Parke Custis Lewis, the daughter of Jacky Custis.
- In 1802, monies were transferred from George Washington's estate to Woodlawn Mills for the purpose of maintaining this large, neighboring estate and freeing their slaves, as well. The remaining mortgage debt of Jonathan and Priscilla Winfield, from their 1785 land purchase contract, was retired.
- One of George Washington's relatives, his nephew Bushrod Washington, assumed ownership of Mount Vernon in the years that followed. The estate was subsequently transferred through that branch of the family for the next several generations.
- As specified in George Washington's will, a new Burial Vault was constructed at Mount Vernon several decades after his and his wife's deaths. The family caskets were reinterred at the new site two hundred yards to the west. By the will's request, several 'items of interest' were retained in the original family Vault.
- In the mid-nineteenth century, when the Bushrod Washington descendants could no longer manage the extensive property, Mount Vernon entered a period of irreversible decline and disrepair.

- In 1858, Miss Cunningham of South Carolina and her Mount Vernon Ladies' Association purchased the Washington mansion and some two hundred surrounding acres. Over many years, the Association eventually restored the estate much as it had been in George Washington's lifetime.

22

New York City
July 4, 1804

Alexander Hamilton appeared even more lively than usual during the annual Society of the Cincinnati dinner at the Fraunces Tavern. With his combed-back hair, the respected attorney reveled in the camaraderie. "How fortunate that we have all aged so well," he jested, "but at the least, I suppose, we should consider ourselves fortunate to be aging at all!" He had already consumed two pints of ale and was speaking out loudly and without reserve.

"Any plans this summer, Alex?" asked another former officer of the Continentals.

"No, not really. I have to stay in the city and continue my law work in order to pay off a pile of debts. I did not fully realize that our new house would cost so much. Eliza, the children and I love the garden, though, so the extravagance seems worth it. We named the home 'The Grange' after our friend Lafayette's residence near Paris."

"But is there any chance that you will be coming up river anytime soon?"

"Not until next month at the earliest. I have some affairs to settle. Perhaps I'll take a short holiday then. Indeed, the waters above Newburgh are pleasantly clear."

Hamilton saw Vice President Aaron Burr sulking alone in a corner and thought that the dim lighting accentuated a foreboding expression on his high forehead and fancied that he looked like a weasel. Although Burr was also a former Continental Army officer, he had joined the Society of the Cincinnati during the past year, doing so only because of his well-known political ambitions. Hamilton felt that the Vice President's tepid interest in the Society gave proof of his craven opportunism. This rival's attendance that night seemed egregious – the last straw. The annual dinner of the Society was meant solely to provide the former officers a yearly chance to kick back and celebrate old times together. Politics was to be left at the door.

Shaking his head, Hamilton slurred drunkenly to several companions, "That inveterate philanderer sitting over there reminds me of a ripe story, men."

"I don't know whether to believe you or not, Alex." A colleague moved over, almost tipping his ale, and asked, "What's the story?"

"Shssh, you know – let's see if I remember it. Why was the fox able to stay in the hen's shed? No? Hah, it's a laugh. The hens preferred the sly rascal to their old cock."

"Come now, Colonel. I don't get how that applies to Burr, but I have heard many tales about problems with him keeping his breeches on."

"Well, however he does it, it's funny that the sly fox seems to get away with it," Hamilton said, belching. He saw that Burr still sat sullenly twirling his own half-empty glass.

"Alex, are you and Mr. Burr on speaking terms yet?" another diner asked.

The lawyer turned and stroked some of the curls on the nape of his neck. "I suppose so, as long as I'm the one doing the talking and he the listening."

Later that night, Hamilton returned to his newly constructed home in the northern section of Manhattan Island. Thankfully, Eliza and their children were staying with her sister, Mrs. Angelica Church, during the month of July at their father's estate in Saratoga. Fully dressed, Hamilton staggered in the dark towards his bed. In the midst of a drunken haze, he tried to recall if he had left a freshly written note and other assorted messages back on his law office desk that afternoon.

His mind swirled as he lurched about trying to get ready for bed. The room turned despite his grip on a bedpost. He managed to sit on the edge of his mattress and stared blankly for a while at images rising up from nowhere – insects, spiders, wormlike creatures danced in the air. Tugging his boots and ill-fitting uniform off, Hamilton was haunted by specters of grotesquely injured faces, victims of the many bloody duels that he had seen during his youth. Ever since his early childhood in the Caribbean, he had always considered duels to be a respected way to settle affairs. He knew this to be a long-used method whereby two gentlemen might end a disagreement – by engaging in a necessary action of honor.

Moving restlessly onto his bed, he sensed that three figures were present in his bedchamber. His father, a man he had never known, his mother, a woman of St. Nevis, and his deceased eldest son, Philip. Strangely, Hamilton was not afraid of the specters. "Why are they in my room?" he wondered. "Why now?"

In his drunkenness, his father James Hamilton seemed to be saying, "I am here finally . . . Here . . . Here with you."

His beautiful mother wept and tearfully pleaded, "Come . . . Come to me."

And then, his dear son Philip, cruelly murdered in a duel of his own, hovered at the foot of the large bed. "Oh Father . . . Father – why?"

Weehawken, New Jersey

July 11, 1804

Alexander Hamilton's dream of ensuring his own American family legacy nearly died along with him one week later.

On an early morning above the rolling Hudson River, Aaron Burr mortally wounded him with a single shot after his pistol misfired seconds before. As Hamilton's life ebbed, his second, Mr. Pendleton, and others carried him down from the grassy knoll. They struggled to get him into a small boat and then rowed him back across the river to Manhattan.

Despite the attentions of Dr. Hosack and his assistants, Hamilton died the next day surrounded by his family at the home of a close friend, William Bayard, Jr.

A week after Hamilton's funeral, his friend Gouverneur Morris, who had come from Pennsylvania, gave the grieving sixteen-year-old James Alexander Hamilton, his father's written testament kept in a desk drawer at his law office.

"It was fortunate that your father was prescient to do this, but it is so like the Hamilton that we knew," Morris told the oldest surviving son. "He admits to being an original member of a secret group of patriots. I am also a founding member, James. Please read what he wrote.

The young Hamilton read in silence.

> *This is the most important part of your inheritance – this obligation as my eldest heir. Mr. Gouverneur Morris and others will give you more details, in time. In a word, PATRI is about ensuring that there is a proper succession of leaders for the preservation of America's future. Our society's purpose is to insure that important, nay vital principles for America are passed on, my dearest James, over succeeding generations.*
>
> *The full membership roll in a leather packet must be kept in my, now your, Hamilton bank vault. It is there along with two other very important documents, one of which is sealed in a thick, glass cylinder. As the years pass, you and the later Hamilton family scions must keep current the membership rolls with new names added to the roster – the future-surviving descendants of the original PATRI families. I have directed my dear friend, Mr. Gouverneur Morris, to show you where the keys for the vault are located. James, you and future Hamilton heirs need to keep them well!*

Gouverneur Morris touched a trick panel under Hamilton's desk and lifted out an item from a shallow drawer. "These are the keys to your father's special repository deep in the Bank of New York, James. He told me where he stored them. From what I understand, you Hamiltons are meant to be the concierges of PATRI, the 'holders of the keys.' You and I should go directly to the vault. I know of the pieces about which your father wrote – I have not seen them myself for some time."

Before they went down to the basement, the young Hamilton looked at his father's familiar writing and read the conclusion of Alexander Hamilton's testament.

> *. . . You James, and the heirs of the other families named in the originally signed agreement of February 1797, must assure that PATRI will go on.*
>
> *Alexander Hamilton, esq. 16 June 1802*

Once he was in the Hamilton bank vault, James Alexander could see a silken scroll on a rickety table. It was addressed "for the Hamilton family alone," and was labeled 'A Note of Action.' He removed the tie and privately read the small print.

In the future, when our PATRI, along with their allies from the Europe League, mutually agree that the PACT must be enacted, a legitimate monarch must necessarily ascend to an American throne. A Second American Constitution to ratify this new government is hereby signed by all original PATRI patriots and is hermetically sealed in a Franklin-Glass. It should remain somewhere in the secure possession of the society's concierge until the due time.

I charge the House of Hamilton to be the concierge of PATRI — the holders-of-the-keys — and responsible with secretly possessing the society's documents and other necessary evidence in the New York City and Mount Vernon vaults. Your Hamilton family key opens your bank vault; my Bastille Key opens my vault at Mount Vernon.

I also charge that only the Houses of Hamilton & Lee should know the true identity of my rightful heir — Priscilla Winfield of Woodlawn Mills.

When PATRI and the Europe League agree to activate the PACT, the first step of the PLAN will be the divulgence of a legitimate American king to the assembled members.

Signed this day of our Lord, 27 February, 1797
Geo Wash'

23

Woodlawn Mills, Virginia

Fort Marshall, Maryland

Civil War Years

In April 1861, the Civil War, or to many the 'War Between the States,' began following the bombardment of Fort Sumter in South Carolina.

One month later, General Robert E. Lee of Arlington, the son of Henry Lee, met with Colonel Eugene Winfield at Woodlawn Mills. At the time, Robert Lee was actively considering resigning from the United States Army in order to take a general's commission in the Northern Army of Virginia.

That day he told Colonel Winfield that all his family must move to a sanctuary, a designated Federal Site across the Potomac in Maryland, for the duration of the conflict. His order to the colonel was absolute – nonnegotiable. Robert Lee said that his directive was motivated by what he called 'certain interests which affect us all.' He stated that after the Winfield family was evacuated and had settled at Fort Marshall, he would station a special regiment of his Virginia militia to ensure the protection of both their estate of Woodlawn Mills and George Washington's former Mount Vernon. Lee additionally mentioned that if the properties were overrun in the coming months by federal troops, he had already entrusted guardian duty to a certain officer of the Army of the Potomac.

When Colonel Winfield objected, the silver-haired Lee said curtly, "You cannot ask . . . You must not. See it as an order that must be obeyed, Colonel!"

General Robert Lee had long possessed 'A Note to Action' given to him by his father, Henry (Lighthorse Harry) Lee. It read,

In the future, when our PATRI, along with their allies from the Europe League, mutually agree that the PACT must be enacted, a legitimate monarch must necessarily ascend to an American throne. A Second American Constitution to ratify this new government is hereby signed by all original PATRI patriots and is hermetically sealed in a Franklin-Glass. It should remain somewhere in the secure possession of the society's concierge until the due time.

I charge the House of Lee to be the loyal guardian of PATRI – responsible for the protection of the Winfield family for all time.

I also charge that only the Houses of Lee & Hamilton know the true identity of my rightful heir – Priscilla Winfield of Woodlawn Mills.

When PATRI and the Europe League agree to activate the PACT, the first step of the PLAN will be the divulgence of a legitimate American king to the assembled members.

Signed this day of our Lord, 27 February, 1797
Geo Wash'

In July 1861, Colonel Eugene Winfield was among the first casualties of the war at the Battle of Bull Run, the Battle of Manassas, when a Confederate sharpshooter shot him in the head.

From 1861-1865, his son, Richard Winfield, managed the family affairs while he and the other Winfields lived along the Piscataway Creek in Maryland. In the late spring of 1865, after the truce was signed at Appomattox, the Winfields finally moved back to their home of Woodlawn Mills. They were relieved that Union soldiers and their camp followers had not damaged the estate during the conflict.

Mount Vernon survived the Civil War as well. The dilapidated Mansion House and surrounding grasslands returned to the benevolent care of the Mount Vernon Ladies' Association.

24

Gettysburg, Pennsylvania
July 4, 1863

The small group of men rode in single file through the deep woods of Pennsylvania. The muggy noonday heat caused their sweat to thoroughly stain their gray uniforms. The sky turned ominous – far off rumbles of thunder presaged an oncoming storm. General Robert Lee cautiously rode Lucy Long, a well-behaved mare, down a steep path leading to the Fairfield Road.

Lee, Jeb Stuart and several other Confederate officers had just attended an abbreviated Society of the Cincinnati dinner at the Cashtown Inn. Confederate Army doctors had been using the tavern as a field hospital.

Throughout the previous night, Lee and his general staff had met to argue battle strategy for that day, Saturday the fourth of July. Two of his senior generals, John Bell Hood from Texas and James 'Pete' Longstreet of South Carolina, had encouraged him to regroup and make a further offensive strike. "One more try, sir, if we could just . . . Pickett's men came so close. We dare not forget them."

Robert Lee determined otherwise. The evacuation of the Northern Army of Virginia must begin at once, even before daybreak, in order to preserve what remained of his battered army. After making the decision, General Lee had thought it necessary for the sake of tradition to gather that day with a select cadre of Confederates who were direct descendants of Revolutionary War officers. He realized that some traditions were important, no matter what the circumstance. As he rode up to the Inn from his headquarters on Seminary Hill, Lee somberly told General Stuart, "Despite the horrors all around us, we must somehow find the heart to celebrate our traditional July 4th event for my officers, Jeb. For their spirits as well as our own!"

Now, as Lee rode back down from Cashtown, he and the others heard anguished cries of men and dying horses all around them. The color of the clouds turned an ominous gray-green over the surrounding ridge to their rear, and the riders were soon drenched in a sudden torrent pitched from the west. Their horses turned skittish, frightened by sharp forks of lightening and cymbal-like peals of thunder. Within minutes, the downpour turned the trail into sloppy treacherous rills. The officers on horseback finally came to the main road and encountered the scattered, disheveled remnants of the once-proud Army of Northern Virginia.

Two English military observers traveling with the Confederate troops, an Adjutant Colonel Arthur Fremantle and a Mr. Lawley rode up. One called out through the downpour, "Even though the rain is harsh, sir, those rolls of thunder seem even louder and more constant."

General Lee sadly shook his head. "No, sir. Those you hear are not of heaven's making but of our own. General Imboden's medical carriages are back up there on the Chambersburg Road heading west. They are just starting out and in this weather! So many injured loaded onto his wagons . . . ours and theirs . . . so many . . ."

The three carried on together through the driving rainstorm. During a momentary lull in the rain, the Confederate officers and the two observers stopped and saw dead and gravely injured horses still strapped to their overturned caissons in wildly unnatural poses. Farther off, they saw massive numbers of casualties strewn over a shattered, noiseless cornfield. That morning, the two armies had mercifully agreed to a temporary cease-fire. Clusters of unarmed blue- and butternut-uniformed patrols now made their ways through the mud patches trying to remove the dead and wounded. They had been instructed to look for any useable scraps of war as they combed the field.

Appearing to come out of nowhere, an odd mix of scavengers called 'devil-helpers' aggressively competed with both the Union and Confederate patrols. These civilians hellishly pushed their rickety carts over the killing fields, collecting the clothes, canteens, and other spoils of the dead. They combed large swaths of the battlefield like crabs obscenely fighting over a beached whale carcass.

Looking out, Lee's entourage witnessed another sickening sight. Vermin, screaming carrion, clouds of flies and bloated maggots competed over unrecognizable bits of stinking human flesh in the torn-up pasture. Off in the distance, a half-dead soldier groaned loudly – forecasting his ultimate fate. Corpsmen, wearing bandanas to ward off the stench, threw the dead and stricken together on the muddy ground, making for some of the soldiers a morgue, for the others – worse. Thick cakes of purplish coagulum washed off the mounting pile and turned the trampled loam black as rain puddled nearby.

The ruddy-faced military attaché from Her Majesty's Highlanders admiringly looked over at the white-haired Virginian. The General's bearing seemed that of a fellow aristocrat. Robert Lee remained transfixed, though, lost in thought as more bedraggled troops walked past in the road's deepening quagmire.

Weak voices called out on both sides. "General, we with you." "So sorry, Mr. Lee – sorry." A crusty soldier with a head bandage and arm sling called out hoarsely, "You is so lyke my fa-der at home!" A private weakly saluted, "We'll see ya in Richmun', suuh."

As Colonel Fremantle rode up alongside Lee, the English attaché thought it might be an opportune time to present his case. "For your consideration, especially when you speak of strategic matters later with your staff, sir, know that in my role as an observer, I have the opportunity to give you a message recently arrived by courier.

"It is a spoken message for you from Lord Aplington acting for my own Queen Victoria. It is something about a League of some sort. My orders were to present this confidential message to you directly, sir. Not to your other officers nor to your Cincinnatus Society."

General Lee frowned at what he considered to be an imposition. "And what the hell is this supposed to mean? Say it straight, man!"

"My message from his honor, Lord Aplington, seems simple enough, although I do not know what it means. The message I am to convey is, "Ask General Robert Lee *'Is this the time for the Eagle to fly?'* He will understand."

Given his present feelings of loss coupled with his bone-numbing exhaustion, Lee's response was swift. He had little patience for this man's preening and shook his head vigorously, shouting into the rain, "This is not the time, Colonel. Our nation is rent in two. As you have seen, fathers and sons are fighting one another on either side, splitting their families and villages in two. Death and all manner of loss do not come easily for me. It seems we must either live without the sword or die by one. This sword is of our own making and does not concern Europe and any of their prying royal houses in the least!"

Fremantle brought his stallion around so that he faced General Lee directly before he asked, "What should I tell his Grace, Lord Aplington, then?"

"Make it simple, sir . . . Tell the lordship that my response is *'The eagle will not fly at this time.'*"

With a tight rein, Lee spurred Lucy on through the thick mud in the deepening gloom as lightning bolts sparked above the retreating Army of Northern Virginia like shellfire. "Come ahead, now, Colonel Fremantle, feel free to watch my deliberations with my general officers tonight at the tavern in Emmitsburg. I fear it is only Providence that can help our sorry state of affairs."

Marker on the Fairfield Road in Pennsylvania

The Confederate Army, the afternoon on July 4, 1863, began an orderly retreat by this road to the Potomac, which they crossed the night of July 13, after delay caused by high water.

Taneytown, Maryland
July 4, 1863

As was the case for the last two July 4th celebrations, the men knew that their dinner would again be for a small gathering rather than the festive event it had been in years past. The mood that day was sorrowful – the loss of so many longtime friends in the neighboring fields of Pennsylvania weighed heavily on everyone.

Late in the afternoon, after arriving by carriage during a drenching rainstorm, the elderly Alfred Adams made his way to the noisy backroom at the Taneytown Inn. The establishment was close to the Antrim Plantation, which had served as General George Meade's headquarters during the battle of Gettysburg. Adams greeted Major Harold Knox and several other Union Army members of the Society of the Cincinnati.

Thankfully for the weary officers, the three-day battle for the nearby town's railroad junction had ended late the previous afternoon. Word was rampant that 'the Rebs are fleeing the fight!' Assessing Confederate troop movements, the Union Intelligence Department had wired a self-congratulatory telegram earlier that morning of 'our great victory at Gettysburg junction' to General Grant's Army of the West in Vicksburg, Mississippi.

The officers and a few civilians at the Taneytown Inn dinner drank heavily of local ale that the innkeeper had himself commissioned from the personal stores of several Hanover neighbors. During the present ceasefire, the officers were able to fully relax for the first time in days and enjoy one another's company.

"What about Meade? Do you think he'll get right after Lee?" Professor Adams asked the others. The academician from Boston was well known to this cadre of Union officers. As a second generation descendant of John Adams, he had offered to host this hastily arranged version of their annual event. He knew that these direct descendants of officers who had served with Washington in the Revolutionary War had always enjoyed the tradition and camaraderie of the dinner, no matter what the circumstances.

"In my view, Professor Adams, I'm glad our new General is going to take several days off. My Michigan regiment is exhausted!"

"If he does," someone chortled, "they'll be sure to call him slow-poke Meade. Mind you, no disrespect, but . . ."

Several others sitting nearby laughed hoarsely. They had yet to see Meade really take charge and had heard rumors that he wasn't much of what was called a 'soldier's man.'

In addition to the members and a few guest-officers, Adams had invited an attaché from France, Major Andre Lemoix, who had been an observer of Colonel Chamberlain's unit during the fierce action on the Union's left flank.

While sipping on the sour ale, Lemoix unobtrusively came over to the dinner's host and said in a hushed manner, "Pardon me for interrupting, sir. I certainly thank you for inviting me tonight, but I must address a delicate subject with you sometime during the meal. Now is a good time . . . no?"

He didn't wait for a response. "Monsieur du Motier, I believe you know of him, is my employer in Aix and has given me a message for you. He was very specific that I say this to you en confiance, yes? It is for you alone. He quite firmly insisted that the message n'implique pas du tout, does not involve this Cincinnatus Society of yours at all."

Adams coughed nervously to collect his thoughts, then asked, "You have a message for me? Yes, you are correct, I do know the du Motier family quite well. It's been a while since . . . But what does he want?"

"I have no idea about its meaning, I only know the message. I am to give the Monsieur your reply." Major Lemoix glanced at the men seated on both sides before quietly saying, "His message is this. *'Is this the time for the Eagle to fly?'*"

Adams looked out the inn's windows and ran a hand through his thinning hair. Lightning periodically flashed as rain pelted against the thick lead-glass panes. He seemed to weigh his words before replying, "No – this is not the time, Major Lemoix. Simply tell Monsieur du Motier that and be sure to tell him that the others would agree."

Lemoix looked around. "These, these men in this room . . . they would agree with you?"

"Not these, sir, these are not the men. There are others."

After dinner plates were served, Major Knox pounded his tankard on the table and proposed a toast. "Men, here's to the Society of the Cincinnati, to our past and present warrior comrades! Men . . . here is to the Nation, to the Union, forever . . . and to our cause!"

As the men rose, a waitress came from the kitchen into the room, glanced at the diners and spoke words that rang out like the toll of a bell. "And drin' 'un dun to all da fallen lads, my sires . . . and to their fam's. Oh my — and for all the worl' ta' see — they jes' lyin' there. Hier's to der souls . . . bless 'em ev' one."

Vicksburg, Mississippi
July 4, 1863

Brigadier General Schuyler Hamilton and some fellow officers of General Ulysses Grant's Army of the West gathered in a canvas tent below the steep bluffs along the Mississippi. Hamilton had brought them together to informally celebrate their Society of the Cincinnati's annual dinner despite being camped near a contested battlefield. Since he was descended from two of the organization's original founders, the event had always meant a great deal. Both his grandfather on his father's side and his great- grandfather on his grandmother's side had served during the Revolutionary War.

Although Schuyler Hamilton was weakened from a year-long illness, his spirits were buoyed that night — the sixty-day siege of Vicksburg was over at last. One of the junior officers of General Sherman's Corps told the others how exciting it had been at headquarters that morning when they heard about Robert E. Lee's defeat at Gettysburg. Captain Frederick gushed, "The news arrived on the new fangled telegraph contraption. It had come all the way by wire, my fellows. Can you believe? It was like it had just happened . . . And what is more, it *did* happen this very morning!"

The other men sitting in the large field tent murmured as they poured themselves stiff portions of corn whiskey. "You shoulda seen both ol' man Grant and Sherman when they git the word. It turned 'm inta boys eatin' sugar!"

After more whiskey, the voices got louder.

"What a Fourth of July, eh friends?"

"Lots of rockets, flares! Bombs a'burstin in air!'"

"Drink hearty my frien's! Goooood relaxin' time tonight! Oh my, Betsy – weez comin' home sunh!'"

"With that feint against the cliffs and hilltop this morning, Gen'l Grant and my boys just pushed 'round the bluff from the south. Once we got up on the plain, we captured 'em all by comin' in from the rear. I'm 'mazed that dis in'ded so quick, 'specially after two monz of jes' sittin' here." The field officer's beard was soaked with his rye but he went on nonetheless. "An' to 'dink, some twenny tausand Johnny Rebs ar' now unda' our guard tonight. I hear tell!'"

Another inebriated Society member from the Indiana volunteers came to his side and added dumbly, "Ya wonder, sumtime'. After bein' Grant's hangman's noose 'round Johnny Reb's neck fir weeks, it jes' took news from Meade's boys up in Pennsy-vane-i-aye to get ol' Ulysses goin' and have us cinch his skiney 'lil rope tight."

Interrupting the celebration, Hamilton rose from his blanket roll and leaned against a center tent pole. "Men, fellow members of our Society, here's to good news at long last and hopefully more to follow!" He motioned for a Negro soldier to fill the officers' glasses again.

The others looked at Hamilton's paleness, startled that his health had declined so much since last year's dinner in Illinois.

Hamilton glanced to his side. "Colonel Fitzgerald, could you make a toast at this time. I understand that you are, after all, one of the descendants of Baron von Steuben's most trusted aides, William North. My father always told me that the Baron was reputedly the best toastmaster of all the Cincinnati."

The powder-stained artillery officer from Ohio's fifteenth volunteers leaned unsteadily against a tent pole and swung his mug in a semicircle. "Gentlemen, let us remember all the ones no longer here. Let's drink to America's patriots, past and present – to all the United States!"

September 1863

In late summer, Mr. Lawley, Colonel Fremantle, and Major Lemoix traveled together from Charleston, South Carolina and returned to Le Havre, France. The three Europeans carried the same message for both Lord Aplington of England and Monsieur du Motier of France. At a tavern on the dock, the three related that both General Robert Lee and Professor Alfred Adams had given the same reply: *'Now is not the time for the Eagle to fly.'*

25

Chateau de Rouen
Lausanne, Switzerland
August 1968

"That was a blister of a disturbance at your Democratic Convention in Chicago last week. It reminded me of those student riots last May in Paris. What was it all about, anyway?" An elegant gentleman airily posed the question in his high English accent as he sipped on a brandy.

One of the two Americans, Professor Lang Eccles, went to a picture window and replied, "As far as I'm concerned, Sir Edmund, it is yet one more example of the degenerating society that we have in America. First, we had three tragic assassinations – the Kennedys and Martin Luther King. Then our contentious Viet Nam War has created ongoing student protests, flag burnings and such. And now, all sorts of riots are happening in Los Angeles, Detroit and many other cities. The U.S. is spiraling out of control." The two European men could easily see that Eccles was quite exercised about the sorry state of affairs in his country.

The American paused and gestured out toward Lake Geneva. "In contrast, this place is almost unreal - so serenely peaceful and secure compared to the United States. It's rather other worldly isn't it?"

Eccles rolled his tongue by habit, trying to gauge Sir Farrington and Patrice du Motier's reactions. He and his friend, Robert Hamilton, had come to this chateau on behalf of a group of Americans. Several had recently voiced their gloom over the viability of the American republic. Eccles and Hamilton, the designated leaders of PATRI, had assured their fellow-members that they would address their concerns with two Europe League counterparts.

"Please, gentlemen, oh please." Sir Farrington snidely countered, "It takes more than an occasional news report or a newspaper article to disturb us."

"It is more, sir. We worry about this all the time on Wall Street. The markets haven't been doing well with the turmoil." Robert Hamilton was the diminutive CEO of the First National Bank. He added, "It has recently seemed that America's going to Hell in a hand basket."

"I believe," the English Lord wryly smiled, "that that's an expression borrowed from the French Revolution, though an 18th century historian expressed it differently when he observed that 'it was a *head* going to Hell in a hand basket.' "

"I partly empathize with your situation," Patrice du Motier said. "After all, we've also had our own problems, our difficulties. France got so close, so close." He affected a pinch of space between two fingers, and then added dismissively, "We all know that students turn crazy each spring. Cars and tires burning, so many hurt . . . yet it all went away on its own. The enfants returned to their mothers."

As he listened, Sir Edmund Farrington remained aloof. Since he was the thirteenth Lord Aplington, he sat in the British Privy Council and was a well-respected peer of the realm. He dared not show any emotion. "Come now," he said, "we have our own ups and downs in Northern Ireland, too, and don't think to characterize that as a problem . . . we simply call it a 'nasty disturbance.' "

Hamilton replied, "In America, gentlemen, our problems are much more multidimensional, more systemic than they are in Europe. It's not just the students at universities like Wisconsin and Columbia, but we also have all sorts of citizens, if you care to call them that, demanding a full ledger of rights, what they call 'entitlements.' "

"That doesn't sound any different than my fellow Frenchmen – but first we politely listen to their grievances and then merrily assure them that things will be different." Du Motier laughed sarcastically.

"You've got to understand, sir, Americans are much more assertive," Hamilton stressed. "Our parasites aren't just expecting some socialistic, goody-goody hand-out society – they are demanding it. Instead they should be made to realize that it's best for everyone in America to have market-driven, top-down capitalism. It works fine the way it is. After all, our laissez-faire system has always operated for everyone's benefit in the end."

Lord Aplington impatiently harrumphed, "Well, if that's still 'the way it is,' your America should recover on its own. It doesn't seem that the financial markets have collapsed too much, Mr. Hamilton, nor have ours over here. So, I really don't understand why you've come to meet with us here and now."

Langdon Eccles broke in. "You need to listen to me. Robert obviously hasn't made the point. Our American system actually *isn't* working as well as you imply."

"No, no, au contraire – I just heard Mr. Hamilton's words, too. As far as his Wall Street is concerned, your system usually runs as efficiently as a well-managed farm or orchard. Maybe all it needs right now is a little water, no?"

Eccles was clearly frustrated. "That may be from his perspective but borrowing on your metaphor further, I look at the quality of the fruit which that orchard is producing. The fruit has turned rotten, sir."

Claude, the chateau's butler came in and interrupted the discussion. "Sirs, Messieurs, dinner is served. Monsieur Rouen called. Unfortunately, he won't be able to join you but he does send ses amities, his regards."

He led them to an expansive dining room graced with a wide southern exposure. The tower of Chateau de Chillon could be seen in the distance to the east. Langdon Eccles remembered visiting the 12th century castle on a family vacation in the '50s and pointed it out to Hamilton. Warmed by his martini, he remarked offhandedly, "I can never forget that spot. What a place."

Lord Aplington suggested that they should settle themselves into the wide, wooden chairs around the table. "All this pleasant company has certainly stimulated me and my appetite." The robust Englishman suddenly seemed fraternal and advised, "Let's have our meal, gentlemen, lest I start to chew on the furniture."

After dinner the men walked out to the veranda to take their coffee. Terraced vineyards lined the slopes. Heat radiated off the deck's flagstones and served to temper the evening's cool breezes coming off the lake.

"While you two were in the loo," Lord Aplington admitted, "Patrice and I were discussing what the four of us were talking about before dinner."

Hamilton spoke for both Americans. "Without going into your private conversation, let me get right to the point if you don't mind. We have come to Switzerland with the understanding that you are the lead spokespersons of the Europe League. Our members have directed us to have you answer one question. Bottom-line, our PATRI needs to know this. Is now *'the time for the Eagle to fly?'*"

Patrice du Motier blew on his demitasse of espresso. He swallowed a sip before saying, "Sir Edmund and I can only convey your question. I presume it is more accurately your request, to the other Europe League members. Of course, there is no way the two of us can answer you tonight."

"Honestly, you can see that there may be barriers," Lord Aplington icily added. "What with the past French national crises, the cold war, Berlin Wall, our own present economic uncertainties, the sheer lack of European consensus about anything . . . I do not have the faintest idea how others on this side of the pond will feel about putting the steps in motion which might possibly activate the PACT agreement."

"Be sure to remind your members, whoever they might be," Eccles emphasized, "that the two of us understand that if your League affirmatively answers this call from America, it only is a first step. You would agree to meet us at the designated location." As he spoke, he pointed eastward towards the lights of Montreux.

"Yes," Patrice du Motier agreed. "The two of us are merely acting as message-bearers to our European members."

"Now, let me see if I have this straight . . . the four of us agree to see if the others agree or disagree." Sir Farrington chortled, nearly spilling his cup. "What a pig's mess!"

He leaned back and mopped his reddened brow. "More seriously, it strikes me that the only time that one of our two societies called for this sort of Swiss convocation was nearly a hundred years ago. At that time, as I recall, it was we Europeans who were asking for holding a conjoint meeting – and it was PATRI that turned our League's invitation down. Now it strikes me that the shoe's on the other foot, so to speak."

"I know what you're saying," Dr. Eccles agreed. "But that was then. This is now. In those days, it was during our Civil War and many of our PATRI members were in the South, in the Confederacy. Our members did not want any foreign interference of any sort. Now they might."

Robert Hamilton put his tea aside. "That's my feeling, too, Lang."

"And we," du Motier interrupted, "au contraire, I think you say 'on the other side of the coin,' we might not agree to your request that our own 'Eagle,' so to speak, should 'fly' – but we'll see soon enough."

The four turned to see Claude returning. "Anyone care for some cognac, some port?"

The guests of the chateau spent the remainder of the evening at ease, relaxing with each other as they talked about the ongoing Olympics in Mexico City.

The Frenchman took a grape and asked, "Tell me, I do not understand, what were those black hand salutes on the victory stand all about?"

"It was some power thing," Hamilton explained. "'Only a statement,' the sprinters said. I thought it was uncalled for, myself. They did win the medals but they didn't show great sportsmanship, I'd say."

"You are right on, old chap." Lord Aplington haughtily intoned. "It's style, gentlemen . . . style, form, and grace. That's what matters most. Whatever one's point, one's got to make his point most definitely with class."

He stopped and apologized. "Oh goodness gracious, there I go. It must be my royal blood talking again."

In early September 1968, a special delivery letter hand carried by courier arrived at the First National Bank of New York. It was addressed to Mr. Robert Hamilton and/or Professor Langdon Eccles. The message inside simply read,

No – this is not the time for the Eagle to fly.

Signed   *September 5, 1968*

    Sir Edmund Farrington, 13th Lord Aplington

Signed   *September 7, 1968*

    Monsieur Patrice du Motier

PART 2

The Eagle Flies

Gatsby believed in the green light, the orgiastic future that year by year recedes before us. It eluded us then, but that's no matter – tomorrow we will run faster, stretch out our arms farther . . .
So we beat on, boats against the current, born back ceaselessly into the past.

The Great Gatsby, 1925, F. Scott Fitzgerald

O beautiful for patriot dream
    That sees beyond the years
Thine alabaster cities gleam,
    Undimmed by human tears!
America! America! God shed his grace on thee
And crown thy good with brotherhood
    From sea to shining sea!

O Beautiful for Spacious Skies, 1893
Katharine Lee Bates

26

Washington, D.C.
July 2004

Admiral Thomas Winfield, III (Ret.) lowered the opaque window of the black limousine as his driver turned off at Observatory Circle in Northwest Washington and picked his way through concrete pylons before stopping at a heavy barricade. A Marine officer waved them through and saluted as their car drove onto the federal grounds. Well-manicured shrubs lined the curving drive leading up to the Vice President's mansion. Winfield mused that it looked like a veritable fortress. How could anyone living here imagine what was happening to the rest of our country?

Stopping at the front entrance, his driver opened the rear door, saying, "Good luck tonight, sir. I know that there's been a lot on your mind since your son got home, but still – ."

"I think I'll need it . . . and will happily take it, Ray. The luck, that is."

Winfield was the founder of Eurit Industries, a family-owned consortium of naval, aeronautical and defense communications headquartered in McLean County, Virginia. Much had changed in Admiral Winfield's life after his son, Captain David Winfield, had returned from a year's tour in Iraq.

David had been in the first wave of the invasion and had served in the Material Support, Liaison, and Logistical Headquarters for the IPC, the Iraq Provisional Council. Once home, Dave and his father had many discussions about his wartime experience. While explaining the reasons for resigning his commission in the Army Reserves, he revealed many disturbing realities he had observed firsthand in Iraq. These included problems of strategy, of mixed-messages for missions, of reconstruction efforts, and of the lack of adequate materiel. He added, "You can't believe it, Dad. Hired civilian contractors have better weapons than our soldiers."

On one occasion, David Winfield said, "It's a pisser, Dad. The most disturbing thing was the discrepancy between 2.3 billion dollars recorded being spent versus an actual expenditure of 800 million dollars. Can you imagine? A shortfall of one and a half billion dollars? And that was in only in Anbar."

After hearing his son's account, Admiral Winfield called the White House and told his long-time friend, President Anthony Drumin, of his concerns. Then, after his company auditors discovered many other instances of Iraqi-American corruption, he became even more agitated. Winfield was distraught that even his Eurit Industries might somehow have been complicit without knowing it. Provoked, he again phoned the West Wing's back line and suggested a frank meeting with the President. "How about dinner, Tony, this week. Your place or mine?"

The President hesitated. "I'm afraid neither, Tom. I'll be on a trip to Africa. It just came up. I need to join certain African leaders in Nigeria for some trade negotiations." There was another pause before Drumin observed, "But there's something in your voice – I hear ya, Tom. Maybe I can set up some sort of dinner over at Buchanan's place – whatever you guys talk about will be like I'm there . . . What do you say?"

Drumin reassured Winfield how much he always depended on Vice President Buchanan to take care of things. "I'm sure as two houns' lookin' up at a 'coon in a tree that you'll be able to figure things out with Dick, Tom."

Tom Winfield knew several attendees at a subsequently arranged dinner. Of course, there was Dick Buchanan, the host – a rancher from Nevada, the Secretary of Defense, Joseph Pierce, and then his old friend, General Lewis Medford, with whom he had served in Viet Nam. He admired Medford's deservedly bedecked dress uniform – Winfield knew that it took more than a flag in a lapel to make a true patriot.

The Vice President's Chief of Staff, Hubbard Petty, noticed that Admiral Winfield was sharing some thoughts with General Medford and slithering over to their side, he asked, "Gentlemen, what's up, eh?"

The two frowned at his intrusion. General Medford looked down and replied, "Nothing that you'd care to know about, Mr. Petty."

The short, baby-faced administrator caustically laughed. "You both understand, don't you, that everything around here goes through me?"

"Not quite, Hub." Buchanan saw that there was far too much bravado coming from his flippant aide. He knew that this sort of behavior would not be of any help in placating Winfield.

He came over and forcefully interjected, "Admiral, glad you could join us. My apologies – I don't believe you've personally met everyone here." Sipping on a vodka tonic, the red-faced Vice President draped an arm around Winfield and said to his aide, "Hub, I'll take over from here."

Buchanan caught everyone's attention and announced, "Let me welcome my special guest tonight, Admiral Thomas Winfield, a longtime supporter of the President and me. Most importantly, he is a true friend. Tom here has some pressing issues that he wanted to discuss with President Drumin. Since Tony is out of town, the President suggested that Admiral Winfield meet with us tonight instead."

Petty came back to their side and spoke like a well-oiled salesman. "What say if you let me personally take you around the room, Mr. – oh I'm sorry ... *Admiral* Winfield."

The aide first gestured to a stately Afro-American woman whom Winfield easily recognized. She had a welcoming professional manner. "Miss Crawford, please meet Admiral Winfield. Regina, as you know, has been a key player as the head of the National Security Council."

The NSC head warmly shook his hand. "President Drumin has told me so much about you, Admiral. He says you are from one of the most enduring families of Virginia."

"Well, almost . . ."

"The President says that the Winfields are nearly like the Randolphs and the Byrds in Virginia. Don't tell him, but I think he sometimes wishes his own family were as important. Well, you know, Presidents have this thing about their own legacy."

Winfield politely corrected her. "Like all of us, Ms. Crawford, I'm only one branch off my family tree, hardly a dynasty. Given our long history, though, I do appreciate your interest. Thank you."

Petty next summoned two men unfamiliar to Winfield. First, he introduced him to an Air Force officer, Major Ronald Greene from the National Security Agency. Winfield frowned, recalling rumors that the major was associated with a quasi-patriotic ultra-conservative association. As they shook hands, he couldn't help but cynically wonder whether Greene and others in these reactionary societies possessed a degree of covert influence in the federal government.

"Ron has been a godsend, Tom," Petty said. "With his background, he has scads of civilian contacts. He's the one that got AT&T and Google aboard for Dick's plan for the eavesdropping project. Greene merely called two of his relatives. Oh, by the way, you don't mind me calling you 'Tom' do you, Admiral?"

"Even if I did, it probably wouldn't matter."

Petty went on without skipping a beat. "Last but not least, we come to Paul Wolfe from the Wallis Institute. Paul, come over and meet Tom Winfield."

Petty stood like a boxing referee between two opponents eyeing each other before a match. "Vice President Buchanan thought that Paul, our resident think-tank guru, could answer any questions that you might have, Tom. On weaponry systems, rendition techniques, Mideast alliances and such . . . ."

When Winfield shook the scholar's unexpectedly hairy hand, he noticed a certain hardness – the technocrat's edgy nature was not far from the surface.

"Weren't you one of Tony's key players in the run up to Iraq, Mr. Wolfe?" he asked. Winfield noted a puzzled expression on the man's face. "Tell me, weren't you surprised there were no WMDs, weapons of mass destruction? With all that data – slam dunk, eh?"

"I think we were all blind-sided, Admiral . . . But no matter, Hussein had to go. Be that as it may, I'm sure Tony Drumin has already told you all about me."

As he stood listening, Winfield inwardly reflected that Wolfe and a few of the others present were the root cause of the mess that had consumed David and his fellow soldiers. The ex-admiral steeled himself. He knew that Wolfe and the others would soon be hearing him out.

A husky voice barked, "Dinner is served, sir." A white-jacketed Marine stood next to the doorway leading to the dining room.

Walking ahead of the guests, Petty motioned, "Admiral Winfield, you are the special guest tonight. You get to sit next to the Vice President. General Medford, I believe you and Colonel Greene are placed at the far end."

Midway through dinner, Buchanan leaned into the Admiral's shoulder and slurred, "Oh excuse me, Tom. Tell me . . . what have you been up to? And yes, how's your son David, Captain David? I hear he resigned. The war's too much for him, I understand."

Winfield jumped up, slamming his napkin on the table. "Dammit! I'm glad you finally asked, Mr. Vice President. It's about time you and the others here . . ."

Hub Petty glanced over and nearly choked on the vinegar dressing in his salad. The other dinner guests sat stupefied. When two Secret Service agents stepped forward, unsure how to react, Buchanan gruffly waved them off.

"It's about time you and the others here asked about Dave and all the other people fighting your war," Winfield barked. "I'll continue to call it that. 'Your War.' Ask about these men and women and their sacrifice, instead of painting rosy pictures! Instead it took a television show, Ted Koppel's *Nightline*, to honor the names of the fallen men and women. That idea certainly didn't come from the White House!"

"Oh, come now, Tom – you're starting to sound like one of them, not one of us."

Flustered, Winfield's face reddened as he looked about wide-eyed. Several friends tried to placate him.

"Not as bad . . ."

". . . And besides, we needed to . . ."

"Soon. Wait a bit – it's bound to get better!"

". . . You know, we have President Drumin's ear, and he agrees . . ."

Winfield paced the dining room like a caged tiger. "If you're afraid to hear what I have to say, you might want to leave this room right now!"

"But, Tom . . ."

"Save all this chatter, Mr. Vice President. Hear me out!" Winfield moved around until he stood behind General Medford. "After my son, Captain David Winfield, returned from Iraq he reviewed his tour with me. He told me of some, as he put it, 'heavy experiences.' Graft and foul play are rampant in that damned country. After he shared his disgust, I made myself a promise to make my own opinions known. Tonight is as good a time as any. The Iraq situation stinks!"

Dick Buchanan took off his glasses and quickly assessed the situation. He surmised that maybe it was best to let the old codger go on for a while. He could now understand why the President had him arrange a private dinner with Winfield instead of meeting at the White House. Drumin needed to distance himself from this, and besides, he needed Dick Buchanan to make sure it stayed that way.

Petty got up and moved next to Buchanan. The diminutive, rodent-faced sycophant was known for his aggressive tactics of deflecting any controversy affecting the Vice President. He leaned over and earnestly inquired, "What do you want me to do, sir?"

The Vice President stiffened. "Let it go, Hub."

Buchanan, originally from a small town north of Las Vegas, always valued having a trademark poker face, and was glad to employ it once again. "You've brought up serious charges, Tom. Let's see your cards, Admiral."

Winfield calmed himself down enough to address Buchanan's challenge. He went on detailing more of what his son had told him. Finally, he said, "David couldn't be sure whether the graft is of our doing or the Iraqis' – or both."

General Medford, trying to defuse the unpleasant confrontation, said, "As you know, Tom, we've seen this sort of thing in other conflicts and . . ."

Admiral Winfield cut him off. "But not to this extent, Lew. My company's auditors found that what is going on involves the most respected people and companies in America. I've told no one else of my investigations." He continued darkly. "Let me forewarn you. If any of you were found to be criminally involved, you would likely be impeached or court-martialed. The matter is quite simple for anyone to investigate. In fact, even though I am not a computer expert, I was able to trace some egregious examples of war profiteering merely tapping into my own P.C."

As Winfield spoke, Vice President Buchanan shifted uncomfortably in his chair, trying to judge some of the other guests' reactions.

Secretary of Defense Pierce had heard enough. "You're not suggesting?"

"I'm not suggesting anything, Mr. Secretary. I'm telling you. If a Congressional committee or an Inspector General subpoenaed me, I'd predict that my own Eurit firm's books would look pretty clean compared to other firms. Much of the reconstruction effort in Iraq is in the hands of noncompetitive fly-by-night bidders. You know, so-called friends, relatives, whatever . . . our own and the Iraqis' own."

Buchanan motioned Petty over and whispered, "Use the brown phone, Hub."

He then stood and said, "Folks, I suggest that we take a much-needed break before our dessert. Tom, I promise to pick up from here later. Hopefully, you do not feel that I am arbitrarily cutting you off."

Honoring the Vice President's request, the guests wandered off to the music room with iced teas or cordials. Everyone seemed relieved to be able to cool off after the table talk had turned so contentious. The director of the National Security Council offered to play a portion of a Bach concerto and soon she was graciously entertaining the others.

During her impromptu recital, a rusting Pontiac with a lone passenger drove into the nearby British embassy. A late model GMC Denali followed at a distance but drove speedily past the consular building as soon as the doors to the garage closed. In the subterranean space, the Pontiac's passenger was escorted onto an underground moving tram and transported beneath the Observatory Circle to the executive residence opposite.

Following the harpsichord performance in the front room, Hubbard Petty kneeled next to Admiral Winfield's chair. "There's a person who would like to meet with you in the library, Tom. I'll take you there. Vice President Buchanan will stay with the others, don't worry."

When the two men came to the residence's large library, Winfield had difficulty adjusting to the dim light. President Anthony Drumin stepped out of the shadows.

"Nice to see you, Tom."

"What? . . . Aren't you . . . ?"

"I know, I know . . . but the African trip was canceled at the last minute. The Secret Service said there might be a plot there, some coup or whatever. Who knows?"

Petty left the two men alone. Buchanan had told him during the meal that the President needed to work on Winfield by himself.

"Tony, I wish you had been here earlier. You could have heard some of my concerns. We've always been friends and I know you . . ."

"That's why I'm here now. What's all this about an investigation?"

Winfield understood as soon as he heard the President's question that the Vice President must have phoned Drumin earlier about his implied threats.

The President shook his head. "You know, friend, we just can't have any sort of oversight or what not. There's too much going on."

As President Drumin tried to explain his point of view, Winfield could not help feel sickened as he remembered what a long time family friend, Major Philip Lee Mason, had recently told him.

Winfield had been visiting Mason's nearby Maryland Army base, and as they ate lunch at the Officer's Club, the young career officer recounted that during a White House meeting, both President Drumin and Buchanan had browbeaten him. They were upset about recent testimony that Mason had given to a House Oversight Committee, testimony that put Drumin's administration in a bad light. He detailed for Winfield the conversation in the Oval Office. He had had to listen to these two rant and rave for more than an hour.

Mason told Thomas Winfield that he felt that his patriotism was being questioned. He had been ridiculed for his lack of loyalty to his Commander-in-Chief. He was reminded that the President demanded loyalty over everything else and was summarily warned, "Phil, you're just not a team player. You'll never be anything at all if this keeps up!"

Later that afternoon, the Admiral recalled that Major Mason had stretched his legs for relief, while he looked out over the vista westward towards Mount Vernon and his own residence of Woodlawn Mills, visible on the other shore.

"I can tell you this, Admiral," the major said frankly, "because we all respect you. I trust that you know I usually never talk about commanders like I am about to now, but it's a real disgrace when these two men think they're leaders and it's we who have to put up with their incompetence, even as they float around their palace. And that Defense Secretary Pierce, he's a piece of work, that's for sure! These close-minded guys always seem to know best. Isn't that the truth?"

Tom Winfield told his friend that maybe a columnist, the veteran columnist at the *Post*, John Madison, had put it right. A week earlier, the reporter had written a series entitled 'The Imperial Presidency' and in his concluding column described the total deference to Drumin's White House from both Congress and the Supreme Court.

"Yes, Admiral, I'd agree with that. Perhaps I shouldn't be saying this, but since our families have been close for years I'll say it anyway. These three guys don't have a shred of legitimacy regarding any other sort of dynasty, political or otherwise."

"Well then, do you know of one – I mean a legitimate one?"

Winfield was intrigued by Mason's answer. "Yes, but I can't tell you now, sir. It's not the right time."

Without a pause, Major Mason had gone right on to detail how the one-sided conversation at the White House had initially demoralized him. Yet afterwards, it had encouraged him to think about contacting others, like his friend Admiral Winfield, to restrain in as many ways as possible this kind of despotic presidency.

The following week quickly passed for Thomas Winfield. Now standing in the Vice President's library, the CEO of Eurit sensed that he, too, was the object of a similar belittling treatment. As he listened to Drumin alternately cajole, plead and praise him, he found it ironic that now it was his turn to be called 'mai frien' by Drumin. Winfield sadly thought that a true leader wouldn't speak like this, only a smooth-talking demagogue would. 'King' Huey Long, Senator Joseph McCarthy and Bull Connors came to mind.

Three days later, Admiral Thomas Winfield, III, suddenly collapsed while walking on a side path into his home of Woodlawn Mills. Although he was quite fit and presumed healthy, the tall executive had left work early that day complaining of vague stomach pains and nausea.

Evan Hamilton's secretary at The First Federal Bank in New York buzzed him on the intercom and said that a Major Philip Mason from Maryland was calling on line 97.

"Evan, bad news over there at Woodlawn Mills. Admiral Winfield suddenly died this afternoon."

Hamilton inhaled and pursed his lips trying to fathom the news. "How . . .? What happened?"

"We don't know yet. Frank is on site with the others. He'll sort it out with the paramedics and doctors."

"How's Mrs. Winfield . . .? How's their son, David?"

"I've jumped right on that. I've alerted the field teams to mobilize the protection-net for him and his family over in Georgetown. Admiral Winfield's other child, his daughter, and her family live in Connecticut. We're monitoring them, too."

"I suppose that we've always known that it could go down like this. Do you think the President and Vice President know anything about the Winfield legacy?"

"I doubt it, but they both knew that the Admiral suspected them of all sorts of shenanigans – influence peddling, kickbacks, outright power-grabbing. I suspect they were much more concerned about their own legacies."

Hamilton nodded and said into the phone, "I'll make arrangements to have my plane take a few of us down there. We'll be at your landing site about eight and can meet you over at Woodlawn Mills later tonight."

Shortly thereafter, three incendiary bombs were set off at the Eurit headquarters in McLean, Virginia. Independent FBI and NSC investigations determined that Admiral Winfield's office had been ransacked moments before the resulting conflagration. In addition to the extensive damage, there was no trace of his computers. A half-written note on executive stationary penned by Admiral Winfield had been found in the rubble by the NSC lead investigator and was addressed to President Anthony Drumin.

That evening, Vice President Buchanan and Hubbard Petty sat quietly in the Oval Office as Paul Wolfe read the note aloud. "I now can see through your threats to the country, to all of us . . ."

"I guess now he never will . . ." Dick Buchanan sat back in his plush chair and smirked at the others.

27

London

February 3, 2018 1200 GMT

One minute, commuters were walking towards Kings Cross Station – the next, scores lay dying on Euston Road.

Berlin

February 3, 2018 1300 CEST

"We have identified the hackers," the security chief of Pharmaseit announced. The multinational pharmaceutical firm had been the target of intellectual property theft amounting to more than five billion euros in the past year.

"Chinese again, I presume," Franz Koenig, the CEO, surmised.

"Not so – it is more interesting than that. They appear to be a group of loosely connected American scientists bent on destroying Swiss-German chemical firms. For the most part, they work at prestigious American universities."

"Which institutions, Rudolph?" the head of Pharmaseit's R&D asked.

"Good ones . . . Yale, Cal Tech. But it seems that they do their hacking from home computers. These folks seem motivated by professional jealousies and feel that their discoveries are being exploited. They regard us as opportunistic competitors who ruthlessly work outside FDA and U.S. patent constraints. The prime actors express an intense hatred toward all proprietary pharmaceutical firms, including our own."

Franz Koenig frowned and wondered, "I have friends who may be able to help – I will see. Eric Stahlen at the Reichstag is probably the best choice. His family is extremely well-connected throughout Europe."

"What do we do in the meantime, Herr Koenig?"

He gave a thin smile. "Give them false information. Change the formulae, the manufacturing processes, whatever. We have got to protect our interests."

Washington, D.C.
February 3, 2018 0800 EST

Janet Melone, the co-anchor of the morning show on ABN, the American Broadcasting Network, saw the blinking green light on the translucent prompter and said, "Good day. First with breaking news. We have just learned that there has been a terrorist bombing today in London. There are initial reports of multiple fatalities with many more injured. Thus far, the details are quite sketchy. A blackout has been put in place in the U.K. for reasons of security. We will . . . "

She stopped in mid-sentence and turned to some papers on her desk. "Since I have to wait on updates from London for the moment, let me take you to events in Chicago. Despite bitter cold, protesting municipal workers and opposition members of the Freedom Party are massing right now on Michigan Avenue. As you recall, government workers there have called for a general strike later this week. The Illinois National Guard has been brought out in force, some 2,000 strong. We now go to the scene with Mimi Sperling . . . Mimi?"

After getting an on-site report from the ABN reporter wedged amid the crowds, Janet Melone came back on camera. "Now I move to yet one more sad, sad story. Eleven people including five adults and six children were found murdered last night in their home in western Virginia. The adults were farmers thought to have recently emigrated from Cambodia. A message found at the scene suggests a possible hate crime."

A police spokeswoman behind a bank of microphones on a live video-feed issued a statement. "The note we discovered reads: *'People like these don't deserve America.'*"

On camera, Janet Melone's jaw stiffened exactly as a teleprompter directed her to do. She spoke and postured verbatim, "This is indeed a tragedy for all Americans . . . ('*pause/nod/stare at camera, frown*') . . . We will be right back."

When she returned on air, the anchor resumed her patented Barbie-doll look as if there was nothing going on outside her studio lights and said:

"News from here in Washington now. Senate minority leader Timothy Blackburn vowed yesterday that he and his fellow Democrats would block the Republican agenda at every opportunity during this Congressional election year. He promised to delay several key federal appointments as well as a number of proposed treaties." Melone shook her head, miming an off-camera aide's look of frustration, before sputtering, "Folks, it looks like we'll keep having more gridlock here in D.C."

Following some more updates from Capitol Hill, she shuffled a paper on her desk and motioned to a nearby monitor. "Let me now turn to Roz Joslyn, our Supreme Court analyst, concerning the fascinating case that the ACLU is arguing this week. As you remember, the litigants are raising the question of whether a fifteen-year-old boy should be entitled to any civil liberties that run against the wishes of his parents. The ACLU is challenging an Appeals Court ruling made in the parents' favor. Roz, this whole thing sounds like complete nonsense. Is it?"

"In a sense it is, Jan, and in a sense it's not." Roz Joslyn's analyses often sounded anything but analytical.

Melone had been forewarned that Ms. Joslyn's comments might be too opaque for her morning show's viewers. She was understandably relieved when a director off-camera circled his finger like a sweep-hand. She knew that she had to break in using her honey-is-best manner. "Thanks Roz – I'd have you hold it right there. Viewers may wish to follow you at ABNnews.com for more details. It's a busy news morning so we'll only take a short break."

After a self-promoting ABN advertisement that ballyhooed an upcoming music award program, Janet Melone resumed her coverage. "I'm starting to feel like Walter Winchell this morning – one thing after another. Initially, we had planned to give the latest from this morning's London bombing, but during the last break I was informed that there has been a hazardous material incident near the U.S. and French embassies in Athens. The embassies are located next to Greek government offices on the Vas Sofias. Let us join Allison Frank from ITN on location. Allison?"

"Thanks, Jan. What we now know is that three emergency responders have been killed by sniper fire. Thus far, more than twenty victims are being treated for what appears to be nerve poisoning. Federal police say it seems similar to the sarin attacks in Tokyo years ago. Somebody told me that after one of the snipers was captured, he yelled, 'This is an attack on all Western civilization . . . on the United States as well as Europe.' What I'm seeing here in the cradle of democracy is hard to believe, Jan. "

While she looked at the monitor screen, Melone had to compose herself before she said, "We'll try to sort out both of these stories throughout the day. I understand that Ian Fergusson is now on site in London. Go ahead, Ian. Anything new?"

"Janet, near as we can tell there are no leads yet, but Scotland Yard is saying . . . "

"Sorry, Ian. Can you hold it right there? Secretary of State Wilkerson and Secretary Dunn of the Homeland Security Department are about to give a press announcement. Let's go there live." Almost as an aside, Janet said, "For viewers at home, we will be canceling our usual morning programming, but stay right here with us on ABN . . ."

For the next ten minutes, the two cabinet members attempted to give an official response from the State Department auditorium. They commented that President Henson, who was en route to South Korea, was fully aware of the situation and would make a statement later. "In the meantime, our many allies have assured their support," Secretary Wilkerson said confidently.

"Which ones?" a foreign correspondent asked sarcastically from the front. The microphone at the lectern picked up bits of her harangue. "You have so many so-called friends in your club. Which allies are you talking about? Israel? Japan, China? Nigeria? Why should America need their support when the attacks are in my Athens? It is you who should be giving us support!"

The two cabinet members stood in silence, frozen by the foreign reporter's brazen outburst. Not knowing what to say, they had her escorted from the room.

Looking on her screen, Melone had never seen a member of the press act so outrageously. At first, she was at a loss for words, then weakly surmised, "The Greek reporter is obviously under a great deal of stress, and aren't we all."

Once the televised press conference ended, Melone placed a fresh piece of paper on her desk and looked directly at the camera. She did not need to glance at the note as she announced, "Word from Wall Street – the markets will be closed today."

She paused, then said, "Ian, now back to you there in London . . . "

Office Building of the *Washington Post*
Washington, D.C.

Given the day's events, the senior columnist of the *Washington Post* was more somber than usual as he sat at his computer and contemplated what to write in his weekly column. John Madison stared out his window at the Washington Monument as he pondered how much had gone over the dam that day. Was it only a temporary aberration or a portent of some new state of affairs? He realized much of this sort of thing had happened before – 9/11, hate crimes, random shootings like Columbine, the Lehman collapse, cyber attacks – and we were able to somehow move on. But now, there was instant messaging, Instagram, You-Tube/You Have It Going On all around the world 24/7. The chaotic news cycle never ended. Where was he to start? How was he to start?'

Over the next hour, Madison was barely able to collect his thoughts. Finally, he started to draft a column titled 'The End of Democracy?' The opening paragraphs read:

> Two hundred and thirty years ago, after bitter contention and debate, our founding fathers agreed on a social contract. They wrote a Constitution, which would be the basis of the United States of America, the world's largest democracy. Many of these patriots, my own family's James Madison among them, thought that this experiment might not last long – in fact, that it might not endure beyond their generation.
>
> When the first crises in the new Union occurred, some naysayers even suggested a return to a monarchy in order to preserve America. Yet the authors of our contract saw that they had framed ideas, which allowed our precious democracy to adapt to many unforeseen challenges that succeeding generations might themselves face. The Constitution was not written in stone – it could be amended.
>
> Once again, our democratic system seems under attack from within and without. To confront this challenge, we need to have

much stronger leadership than we have in our presently gridlocked government. The future of our Republic may be unclear to many, but it seems to me that the American people, armed with their democratic mandate, can rise to accomplish . . .

Madison stopped in his tracks. Accomplish? Accomplish what? Primo accompli; no, primo; no . . . Jumbled phrases from his high school Latin classes turned in his head as he silently bent over the keyboard. *Primus erat offici – the first duty of ancient Greek and Roman polity* . . .

He wondered, "But how do I say it? What do I say?"

Finally, he wrote in conclusion:

It seems to me that a firmer degree of order coupled with strong political leadership is urgently needed in America as a necessary first step. I say this reluctantly since this suggestion runs completely against the grain of my lifelong persuasion that has heretofore always favored liberty and freedom at any cost.

28

Paris

February 2018

"This is a lovely place, Francis, like many other old establishments in St. Germaine." Hugh Rochan, the CEO of Media Manor, was well-traveled, having residences in Dubai, England and Los Angeles. He enthused, "These bistros are so authentic one can smell it."

His companions for lunch were Francis du Motier and Sir Ronald Farrington. The three had come from an annual meeting of the Europe League in Geneva. Rochan was a direct descendant of Lord Fairfax, du Motier of the Marquis de Lafayette, and Farrington, the current head of the House of Aplington.

Du Motier gazed at the rain-slick cobblestone sidewalk and the green merchandise stalls lining the riverbank. The booths were partly boarded to protect the second-hand books and prints against the dank, windy conditions. After sipping his aperitif, he said, "We certainly had robust discussions last weekend in Geneva – more than usual for our League."

Sir Ronald agreed. "And none too soon, I might add. Americans really need to open their eyes and see what we see. I heard on my hotel room's tele' an hour ago that there were two more explosions this morning, adding to the growing litany of mayhem. The first occurred during commute hours on one of the ring roads of Moscow and the other on an elevated expressway south of Boston. One is left to wonder whether these presage a newly defined world order, or should I say 'a world disorder?' "

Rochan took a sip of his anise. "This is a terribly complex problem, much more than a case of isolated degeneration. All our societies have been affected. Didn't that terrorist weeks back yell something about the end of

Western civilization as we know it? With everything going down, I'm glad that our League decided to tender a call to meet conjointly with the American group, PATRI. At least we know who are its primary spokespersons."

M. du Motier added, "That's right, Hugh. My fellow keeper of the keys is Mr. Evan Hamilton, a banker in New York. And Lord Aplington, your mirror administrator over at PATRI is a Gladys Eccles, an educator in New England."

"I know Dr. Eccles's thirty-year-old daughter, Bridgette, an actress in San Francisco," Rochan mentioned. "I haven't met her mother but Bridgette is quite the looker. We've enjoyed some pleasant times together. Too bad I couldn't sign her up to work at Manor Media."

"Now men, back on subject," Lord Aplington said interrupting Rochan's whimsy. "Let me be sure. Remind me what such a meeting would accomplish. Why did we elect to propose it to the Americans now? I am always a bit reluctant to go into things half-cocked."

As the three men were served steaming hot soups, du Motier gave a measured response. "We certainly need to see how things sort out over the next several months, but . . . "

"But, but, but. No 'buts,' Francis," Rochan declared impatiently. "Lord Aplington, you remember that we all agreed that things are rapidly devolving in the United States, and by that measure, in the rest of the world. I hate to say it but as America goes, so goes Europe. Our Europe League and the PATRI must decide together whether to activate the PACT – the mutual assistance arrangement.

"As I said a week ago, it may be a stretch for these liberty-loving Americans to accept us promoting the idea of their country having a king. After all, we have no absolute monarchs ourselves in Europe at the present. But no matter, we have to convince PATRI to see that, at the least, Americans need a strong leader who operates outside the realm of politics."

"Oh yes, yes. They must understand that if it turns out that this so-called 'leader' happens to wear the title of 'king,' so be it. It is evident to me, Hugh," Lord Aplington went on, "that our own families have enjoyed more than a measure of unspoken influence over the years here on the Continent, with or without royal titles. So too, in America, there is PATRI – a cadre of influential families who have always led from the shadows."

Rochan leaned forward and surmised, "It will take time to organize a first get together with PATRI, months at the minimum. In the meantime, hopefully things won't get further out of hand, but no matter. We need to get cooking."

"'Cooking,' what do you mean?" Sir Ronald asked. "It is probably another of your idiotic idioms, Mr. Rochan. You news people are always, dare I say, cooking up new words. Now permit me to ask you both something. How do you propose we notify these PATRI leaders about our Europe League's request for a conjoint meeting?"

Francis du Motier nodded thoughtfully and stirred his lentil soup. "Firstly, we know that our invitation-message must be quite discrete. I don't guess how it will play out. For their part, it is possible that the Americans may not see the global situation as being so desperate as we do. In that case, they must be confident enough to refuse to meet with us. Remember, gentlemen, on two previous occasions, one or the other group has declined the other's request to meet as a whole."

"Bosh! Here the whole Western world is falling apart and in the meantime we're sitting still." Lord Aplington was livid. "I'm tempted to say that we should ram the proposal down PATRI's throat. The matter of using the PACT to activate the PLAN is not a free choice . . . It's not a choice at all!"

Ignoring Lord Aplington's outburst, Rochan tore off a big chunk of a sesame seed roll. "I know it's not polite to speak with food in my mouth, but . . ." He started to chew the bread nonetheless. "Let's ask Philippe Rouen to facilitate making our initial entreaties. During our retreat in Geneva, he was telling me about a new commercial property he has in Virginia."

"How might that be helpful?" Lord Aplington barely hid his disdain. Rochan had a well-earned reputation for having all sorts of freewheeling ideas.

"We could use it as a front. Communications to PATRI would appear to be coming from within America and not be traceable to any of us in Europe. We can test the concept by first employing it as a conduit for messages. If it proves secure, this channel might later be suitable for all sorts of purposes, like money laundering or moving other valuable assets, if it comes to that."

Something about what Rouen suggested prompted Lord Aplington to say, "Most importantly, I think we all agree that we do not want to broadcast our intentions. In order that our endeavor has any chance of success, it will require many well-conceived deceptions."

"If it's okay with you both, let me call Philippe now to bring him on-board," du Motier suggested, and stopped to dial Rouen's cell phone. "Philippe . . . Yes. Good. Permit me to ask you . . ." After speaking, du Motier first listened, then laughed. "How clever, you old rascal! No one would suspect. You're such a schemer." A moment later, he touched the phone's display and signed off, saying, "See you, Philippe. Thanks."

Sir Ronald wiped his mouth with a linen, "From the look on your face, Francis, I believe we'll be setting things in motion soon enough. Good for that."

"Philippe thinks your proposal, Hugh, is sparkling, just crazy enough to work. He agrees that his Twin Oaks Mall in Virginia is a secure place from which to do our tasks. I assure you, gentlemen, that as you fly back to your homes this evening, I will send a cryptic request to Mr. Hamilton in New York."

Rochan, finished with his first course, looked out at the Seine. Rain pelted off a quay on the other side of the walkway. "I trust that you and I, Sir Ronald, can get out from de Gaulle if the ceiling does not fall too much more."

"If the weather doesn't allow flights, Hugh, we can both stay over at Le Royal Monceau in the ambassador suites."

"You are quite generous, my Lord. Rank certainly does have its privileges."

29

Bowdoin College

Thursday February 27, 2018

Professor Gayle Eccles, the Dean of Faculty at Bowdoin, swiveled in a deep captain's chair behind her large desk. Portraits of John and John Quincy Adams, her distant relatives, hung on the blue wall opposite. "What were you saying, Evan?"

Evan Hamilton, the President of First Federal Bank of New York, repeated, "After I received a coded message two days ago, I made sure to check on the PATRI items stored in my family vault. They're all there. If you agree with me about the message, it looks like we may have an important decision to wrestle with."

"You said 'a message,' Evan?"

"Yes. From Francis du Motier in France."

Noticing the concern in Hamilton's face, Eccles whispered, "What were the words, the exact words, Evan? I hardly know what to ask."

"Well, the message was brought by courier from Paris and I had it then decrypted by my security team. It was what you might guess: *'The Eagle must fly.'* "

"How do you know that it's genuine?"

The fair-faced banker leaned forward and sorted through his case. "Here, these might help." He aligned several scraps of paper on the table.

"Come on. Get serious, Evan. These are receipts from a shopping center."

"At first, I couldn't figure it out . . . but then look closer. They're all from the Twin Oaks Mall, a shopping center located in Manassas, Virginia and were tucked in the envelope along with the message. It struck me as odd that these scraps were included, since this sealed packet came directly from Paris and not from Virginia."

Hamilton watched as she sifted through the sales slips. "And look, Gayle. They come from four different retail outfits at that shopping plaza. Then see this . . . All four stores happen to have the same business phone number 1-888-222-1797."

"It does seem peculiar, but then . . . so what?"

"I called General Philip Mason at Fort Marshall. Our compatriot told me that indeed this shopping center is located across the I-95 from Mount Vernon. It was built by a Swiss businessman, Philippe Rouen, and opened last fall."

"Let me see the receipts again, Evan." Dean Eccles scrutinized the slips before wondering, "And this phone number? Interesting, it must mean something, eh? See there, oh my – the date of the original PATRI meeting, February the 22nd, 1797."

"You asked earlier if I thought the message was real, that it was genuine."

"I don't see how du Motier's message and these slips are connected."

"Well, I did what you might not have done, Gayle. I called the 1-888-number."

"I suppose . . ."

"Frankly, I didn't know what to suppose. The number, it turned out, was – I know you're not going to believe this – an escort service. You can imagine the pitch. Massages for 'all tastes,' lap dances for 'special occasions,' and more so-called 'opportunities.' A husky-sounding woman advised, 'Hi, gentlemen, our special is good through March.' "

The dean raised her eyebrows and chuckled. "This M. du Motier appears to have you all figured out, my friend. He knows exactly what buttons to push."

"Seriously now, Gayle, here comes the interesting part. Out of the blue, this sultry voice continued. 'Our services include everything that international gentlemen would ever need. Tell the Boston Family to come to Mount Rose with all her friends. For directions, call General Information at the Twin Oaks Mall in Manassas."

"Are you trying to convince me that you heard all this and . . .?"

"Here you go, Professor, listen to a recording on my ancient dictaphone. I called back and made a tape so you wouldn't have to phone yourself and risk being overheard."

For the next few minutes, the two listened to a scratchy recording of the low-pitched provocateur moaning her invitations of delight. They were interrupted by a knock on her office door. Dean Eccles had Hamilton quickly put the recorder in his briefcase before calling out, "Come in, Mrs. Stuart, please do."

As she entered, Dr. Eccles's secretary apologized, "Excuse me a moment, Mr. Hamilton. I need to go over the dean's schedule and messages." Mrs. Stuart then poured them two cups of coffee and set out a tray of baked goods.

"Go ahead, Genevieve. I think I know about the two meetings this morning." Taking a bite of a biscuit, Dr. Eccles asked, "Are there any new matters to go over?"

Mrs. Stuart opened an appointment book to February 27th. A special delivery envelope was clipped onto the large calendar page. "There might be. This item came by overnight delivery and was waiting in the mail chute when I arrived. Very impressive this, Dr. Eccles." She handed the dean the thick envelope. "A red wax seal and all. Looks like it came from some sort of European university."

"Could be," Eccles agreed. "It appears to be postmarked somewhere in France. Their centuries-old universities still carry on with many traditions."

Hamilton remarked, "We certainly never get anything this fancy delivered to my Wall Street office. Who knows, Professor Eccles, the materials inside might even smell old and musty, like book stacks in a 14th century library."

On the pressed portion of the unbroken wax, Dr. Eccles discerned that there were two eagles – one perched on a crag above the other. Beneath was a Latin phrase *'Republica regni fit.'*

"That's strange," she remarked. *"'from a Republic comes a King.'* Probably bulk mail. This stuff comes in every day, Mr. Hamilton. But thank you nonetheless, Mrs. Stuart, for not already opening this one. We've all enjoyed the chance to see this fancy wax imprint. Still, my guess is that it's only another piece of whatnot aimed at us university types."

"On the other hand, maybe this one is legitimate. You might have been invited to visit the University of Paris by dear Professor Giroux." Mrs. Stuart coyly suggested.

"Could be, Genevieve, but I wonder. Mr. Hamilton is here and I don't want him delayed watching me read mail. Is there anything else?"

"Nothing this interesting, Mrs. Eccles. There are a few phone messages, but only one appears to need your reply this morning." She started towards the door. "Oh yes, don't forget, Dr. Eccles, that you're having lunch with President Widlow at the faculty club."

After Mrs. Stuart left, Dean Eccles picked up the packet and observed, "I admit, I agree with Genevieve that this looks intriguing. Do you want me to open the envelope while you're here, Evan?"

"Only if you think . . ."

"I honestly don't know what to think, but you must admit that it's probably more than coincidental that a descendant of Alexander Hamilton happens to be with a member of what the phone message called 'the Boston family' on the same day that this parcel arrives."

Her hands trembled as she broke the royal-purple wax seal. Evan exclaimed, "Amazing, Gayle. Now that I think about it, the Europe League's seal on the PACT copy kept in my bank depository looks quite similar, but I'm not sure it's the same."

"Let's see, Evan. " She opened the thick-bound wrapper as if she were an excited two-year-old manhandling a Christmas present. When she took out a formal-appearing invitation, her emotions sank like a stone in water. "Nuts, I was right. It is junk," she said. "Simply one more invitation to one more conference."

She flipped through the pages. "I had such high expectations after what you said earlier that 'the Eagle must fly' and 'tell them to come to Mount Rose.' "

"Sorry you are disappointed – you probably get these kinds of invites every day, Gayle." He leaned forward, "Still, let's see what the announcement actually says, even if it's only to satisfy our curiosities."

"Give me a moment, a moment." After skimming the pages, she said, "I've been invited to organize 'The First Congress of Nation Leaders,' yet I haven't heard of any of the European or Asian members on the steering committee. Evan, this is nothing."

"Come now, where's your detective gene? After all, those eagles on the seal certainly piqued my interest. Anything else?"

She read aloud the conference's tentative date, September 2018. It was to be held in a Swiss resort called 'Mont Épine,' Mountain of Thorns. Besides the glossy brochure, the envelope contained a handwritten note addressed to 'Professor Eckless.' The two read it together.

> *Alert all of your colleagues to this important date. The sponsor, The International Institute of Education, will provide transportation, registration fees, and hotel accommodations. We would very much appreciate, Dean Eckless, that you contact the following list of invited Americans . . ..*

Gayle Eccles and Evan Hamilton looked over the names. Unlike the listed foreigners, they easily recognized all the 'American Leader' invitees, and both suspected why this was the case. An accompanying photograph of the International Institute of Education had the new Twin Oaks Mall of Manassas looming in the background.

"Gayle, it's a stretch, but here's my hunch what these materials are all about. This brochure serves as a backup to echo the tape's recorded message. It's an old-fashioned CIA-redundancy technique. The use of two separate vehicles assures that a secret instruction will get successfully transmitted.

"The phone recording said that the 'Boston Family should come to Mount Rose with all her friends,' and now this brochure suggests that you, the senior member of your own Boston (Adams) family, are to organize a meeting in Switzerland bringing certain Americans, '*all your colleagues.*' The two messages sound pretty identical to me. Both communiqués are likely from the Europe League."

As she nodded in agreement, Hamilton added, "I think you have probably guessed from our many recent communications that given the worsening state of affairs in America and the rest of the world, I feel that our society should at least hear them out. We both know, in any case, that a full agreement with the League is necessary before any conjoint PLAN is initiated. What's more, these two messages seem to independently suggest if the 'Eagle' would fly, as we have always known, it would be to somewhere in Switzerland."

"It seems to me, Evan, that in order to somehow get PATRI somewhere, we'll need more specific directions. For instance, look again at this brochure. It's really strange . . . there's a conflict of terms. It says that this Congress of Leaders meeting is at the 'Mont Épine' resort, not the 'Mount Rose' mentioned in the phone message."

"And, Gayle, it also says Professor 'Eckless.' " Hamilton pointed to the misspelling. "Look again, Gayle. Mont Épine, the 'Mountain of Thorns,' is nearly synonymous with 'Mount Rose.' Both have prickly-sounding names. The Europe League is probably referring to the same location."

"I wonder, Evan. Given all this mysteriousness, what should be our first reaction to this apparent request from the Europe League?"

Hamilton deliberated for only an instant and held up the brochure. "I certainly wouldn't reject it out of hand. Since you are not only to be this conference's organizer but also already PATRI's, I'd suggest you give all the American Leaders on this list a heads-up call . . . Tell them that 'something will be coming down.' "

"That's going to take some time, but should I should tell these fellow PATRI members everything else when I make preliminary phone calls?"

"Not yet, Gayle. Don't tell them about the true purpose of your conference just yet. I need to fill in some more details before you do."

"Well, what are you going to be doing in the meantime?"

"It seems obvious to me that I should next fly to D.C. and wend my way to General Information at the Twin Oaks Mall. I'm sure that I'll get specific directions regarding the actual meeting-place when I am there."

"Evan, when you do, get back to me as soon as possible. It will take considerable time for me to arrange the logistics of this Swiss conference."

Hamilton put the brochure back down on her desk and reflected, "Once we know the setting, then you can openly invite these listed Americans as well as the prominent international leaders to 'The Congress of Nation Leaders.' A highly respected educator like you is perfectly positioned to promote this innovative conference. Put it together as you would normally do. It seems a wonderful cover for secretly getting the Europe League and us together. Only at the time of this invitation should you reveal the true purpose of your Congress to the members of PATRI. And demand that they keep that second part strictly to themselves."

Dean Eccles put her reading glasses down and laughed out loud. "Your conspiracy should be easy, Evan. After all, I'm now 'Professor E-c-k-l-e-s-s.'"

Later, as Evan Hamilton walked to his jet on the tarmac at the Brunswick airport, he phoned General Philip Mason in Maryland. "Phil – we're going to be on the move. When we do, be sure to keep an even closer eye on David Winfield and his family over at Woodlawn Mills."

30

Washington, D.C.
Wednesday March 5, 2018

Two middle-aged men sat in a corner of the Fox's Glen, a tavern on M Street along the Rock Creek Parkway, waiting for their friend, John Madison. They had enjoyed monthly get-togethers ever since their CIA assignments in Thailand.

Roger Divost was recalling the time he and Madison had last played a tennis match. "John whooped me badly last fall, bad knees and all. I even tried the old distraction trick by making sure that Georgi Breining was there decked out in all her glory. Even she couldn't get our bachelor buddy to take his eye off the ball."

"You've got to admire the way he's still able to chase down all sorts of stories despite his recent divorce," Ed Finch remarked. "No distractions there."

John Madison had recently been nominated for a Pulitzer Prize. He had written a series titled 'The Corruption of Power' that castigated several military-defense firms for their environmental contaminations. As a well-respected member of the Madison family of Virginia, he had long enjoyed privileged access around the District. He also posted a weekly blog and was spearheading new Internet applications for the *Washington Post*.

The tavern's door opened and a late afternoon chill swept into the room. Madison shook out his coat and rain hat before hanging them up. With a smile of relief, he crossed the crowded area to their table. "Thought I'd never make it, guys. It's bad all around the Beltway."

Finch slid over. "We left this spot open, John. It's closest to the fire."

The heat from the logs crackling in the hearth warmed Madison's pants and wet shoes. On nights like this, the friends relished the place's ambience. Besides the old wood-burning fireplace, original nineteenth-century daguerreotypes of Washington D.C. were mounted on the wood-stained side-panels.

"We've been talking about the government – what else?" Ed Finch confessed. "I was just saying that I heard a respected scientist testifying recently. I think she got right to the heart of the problem. She said that one consequence of America's representational government is that there is no guarantee that any ongoing NIH research will be funded regularly. Put in a nutshell, guys, every federal budget is ever changing with different policy wonks setting out to give their fluctuating approvals. How can any government-sponsored program possibly function if there is no consistency to planning? China, on the other hand, has a built-in advantage with their centralized one-party rule. When the Central Committee makes a policy, it's set in stone."

Madison thought it best to try and change the subject. He and Divost had often heard Ed Finch rant on and on like this.

"You guys might be interested in a series of investigative reports that I'm currently writing," Madison said. "It involves all sorts of shady dealings. Watch out, Roger, these players might try to use your lobbying firm's expertise and soon. And Ed, they could make contact with your own Naval Department. So here's the picture. When I was looking into a recent labor dispute, I found out that foreign interests were heavily investing in projects in Richmond, Manassas and Tyson's Crossing. Money laundering and influence peddling might be going on. You might already have read about the House of Rouen, a French firm, in my first report but Rouen's dealings are hard to prove. And there are likely others." Madison twirled the ice in his glass. "I even went so far as to go on assignment to Lyon and Geneva to get background information about this Rouen business, but came up empty, at least for now."

The tavern was suddenly flooded by strains of 'Hail to the Chief' playing from a television over the bar. The President of the United States could be seen walking arm in arm with a foreign dignitary down a red carpet in a gilded White House corridor. They strutted regally like preening cocks between two rows of formally attired Marines.

Divost hissed, "I swear . . . who does he think he is . . . the King?"

"Well, you know each time some foreign leader visits, they've come to expect it," Finch observed. "The problem now is that it's gotten to where our own President is expecting it too. When you come right down to it, I'm sure most Americans, whether they admit it or not, enjoy seeing all this pomp and ceremony too."

Divost leaned forward. "There's so much Madison Avenue and Hollywood in politics and news. It's never-ending theatre, John. How can you possibly compete?"

The short-statured newsman rubbed his hands. "Television news anymore needs a sexy presentation to get high ratings. Yes, Roger, the big networks are quite contriving. It's partly the competition, many people prefer blogs and the Internet, but there's a real risk with these formats. If news sources aren't cross-referenced, can a story be verified? Is it believable? Is it hearsay? Oh my, don't get me started."

With his drink in hand, Divost suggested, "Let's get to some real issues, guys. How about the latest breakdown with North Korea? My take is we've had too many different U.S. negotiators dealing with the same intransient North Korean representatives over the years. For instance, North Korea has had three dynastic chairmen in the past sixty years, while in the last twenty the United States has had five Secretaries of State and three Presidents. You wonder how much this degree of changing personnel jeopardizes long-term peace prospects in Asia. For my dollar, I bet it does."

Ed Finch agreed in principle. "Once again, too many cooks spoil the broth! My wife always says that civilization's downfall began when TV remotes were invented. Too many choices lead to too many changes. She's quick to remind me that I'm her one and only. 'Don't change the channel,' she says, 'stay tuned just where you are.'"

The two others laughed heartily. "Maybe that was the problem with my ex-wife," Madison said. "She always felt the need to change husbands whenever she wanted. Thank heavens she's got a new one now."

Now well lubricated, Divost's thoughts started to wander and he grumbled, "Things never get done in the bowels of Congress because every proposal is leaked before it can even break wind. I doubt the Founders could have written the Declaration or the Constitution if Sunday talk shows had existed back then. When our elected officials can't agree, what's the first thing they do? Make excuses, shift blame, form focus groups, call special elections, let everyone have his or her own say. It seems a case of the tail wagging the dog. Frankly, I don't see any kind of good leadership on the horizon."

When Divost mentioned the Founding Fathers, Finch couldn't help but recall a recent, unexpected phone call. Last weekend he had heard from Gayle Eccles for the first time in years. After listening to her abrupt message, he had been left to wonder whether their PATRI would at last be mobilized rather than simply continue to nest in the dreams of their forebears. He forced himself to snap back to the ongoing table talk in the tavern, realizing that he shouldn't appear to be distracted. As far as he knew, neither of his friends were fellow members of PATRI.

Madison laughed when Divost went on and mentioned 'headless voters.' "You're probably right, Roger. I recently read where more Americans can name the seven dwarfs than the last seven Presidents – or for that matter, any seven Presidents."

"Come on you two, get real," Finch chided. "From what I can see, I wonder if we'd be better off with a completely new system of government, make it less flexible. As I said earlier, I can't stand the way the country changes directions every few years, even every few months. There's no consistency whatsoever. Our slimy politicians change more than the weather in western Ireland. They always run around worryin' about their next election, and they'll certainly change their opinion if a moneybag or a new poll tells them to. It's like they're catching the wind like a bloomin' seagull."

"But remember when we were in Thailand, Ed, we saw what implanted political parties lead to," Madison countered. "Tortuous as it seems, our American democratic system protects against the kinds of abuses when callous leaders become too entrenched, because they usually turn into tyrants. When you balance it out, I always think that change 'by the people and for the people' has proven the test of time."

The heavy-set Finch realized he might be getting too exercised and stopped himself short, clapping Madison on the shoulder. "Oh, John, you always use big-sounding phrases. I was justa speakin' 'bout the weather, me lad."

After a waiter came by and took their dinner orders, Divost's face hardened as he described a recent mugging he had witnessed. "Many times, I wish we had vigilante justice," he snarled.

"Remember, Roger, vigilante justice is good only if you hold the long end of the rope. Effective as it might seem in movies, there are many innocent victims with that kind of justice. You don't want to make the victim a criminal and, by that, turn the criminal into a victim. True justice would then be on the *short* side of the rope."

"You're probably right John, but still . . . All these guys walking the street. They're taking our country over." Divost countered.

"A more effective approach, Roger, might be to do what they're doing all over Europe, have a lot more surveillance cameras. Somehow, we've got to find a way to have more civil order without sacrificing privacy, without losing personal liberties."

Finch leaned his beefy frame against the booth's bench. He couldn't side with either Madison or Divost, but he knew how he felt about the need for strict law enforcement. It was in his make-up. The ex-Marine glared as he declared, "Well I, for one, totally favor whatever policing methods are necessary. Obedience to the law comes first and foremost. You can't maintain any society without it. Whatever it takes – so be it."

"Chill out, you two," Divost slurred. "When you add everything up, all in all, things aren't too bad in the good ol' U.S. of A. Counting calories and having bottled water delivered to your table is pretty damned good."

Madison leaned forward. "No doubt, Roger, but many things could be better."

"You mean if Washington wins the Super Bowl or when lobster gets below $6 a pound?"

"Yes. Something like that. You could say something like that."

After their plates arrived, Divost and Finch focused on discussing the Capitals and the springtime chances for the Washington Nationals.

While they did, John Madison looked down at his iPhone. He had a follow-up conference call appointment scheduled for the next day. There was also a memorandum to return a call to a dean at Bowdoin College. While beginning to eat, Madison refreshed his memory concerning his conversation earlier that afternoon with Dean Eccles calling from Brunswick, Maine.

Professor Eccles had invited the *Post's* journalist to be part of a colloquium 'Journalism – Practices and Pitfalls,' that Bowdoin College was sponsoring in two weeks. She apologized for the late notice but explained that a distinguished participant had suddenly taken ill and she needed a replacement.

The dean mentioned that, in addition, she was inquiring about an exclusive hotel near Montreux, Switzerland that Madison had alluded to in a recent column. In that column, Madison provided an account of a certain Swiss Frenchman as background to a series of upcoming reports on the influences of foreign businesses in America. He had described the man, Philippe Rouen, as owner of a military consulting firm based in Alexandria who had also developed a massive shopping mall in Manassas, Virginia. The journalist allowed that thus far he had only scratched the surface.

Professor Eccles hoped that if Madison were able to come to Bowdoin for her colloquium, she could get additional insight into this particular Swiss hotel. She explained that she was asking about this resort since she thought it might be a wonderful setting for an academic conference that she was organizing for the fall.

Madison mentioned that he would get back to her as soon as possible about whether he could join her colloquium at Bowdoin. In any case, he said he would check his files on the hotel and, at least, describe it to her.

"It's great being with you guys – always is." Madison stopped eating and asked, "Do either of you know a Gayle Eccles? I googled her – not much there except her c.v. at Bowdoin College. Come to think of it, isn't that your family's school, Ed? What's also interesting is that it mentioned that she's a direct relative of John and John Quincy Adams."

Although Finch had known of John Madison's own prestigious American ancestry for years, he was quite sure that Madison had no idea of his own connection to Henry Knox, a famous general under George Washington and founding member of the Society of the Cincinnati. Finch almost choked on his food when he heard the name 'Eccles.' He couldn't imagine what these two, Eccles and Madison, were doing. Of more importance, had Eccles turned? And what about PATRI?

Finch thought it strange that he had also heard from Dean Gayle Eccles on a secure phone line days before. So this might be it, he remembered thinking at the time. Her phone conversation was short: "Be ready, Ed – for the Knox family, be ready for Montreux. I'll get back to you."

The line went dead.

The Navy Department civil administrator had assumed up until then that John Madison had nothing to do with his PATRI society, but now this? "Maybe I'm wrong," he thought. He paused to clear his throat with water before he finally answered, "I haven't met her, John, except for two or three occasions when she came down here to meet with alumni. From what I hear, she has been pretty effective since she became Dean of Faculty." Sweat formed on his brow as he stared across the table at Madison. "Why do you ask?"

Madison matter-of-factly replied, "Nothing important, Ed. She invited me to be a part of a colloquium on journalism at Bowdoin. Besides that, she wanted to get my input on a place that I wrote about located near Montreux, Switzerland, a rather quaint resort named Mont Épine. She said it would help with some sort of conference she was planning or some other such matter. I only thought you could give me some insight on her."

Later that night as she slept alone in her drafty house, a coastal Nor'easter blew hard against her windows. Gayle Eccles's bedside phone rang and she sleepily picked it up.

A muffled voice was barely audible. "Remember, Gayle. The pledge, Dr. Eccles."

31

Bowdoin College

Thursday March 27, 2018

The gray-haired dean escorted an expensively groomed middle-aged man from her Hawthorne-Longfellow office. "Oh, Evan, stop here a moment. I presume that this is Mr. John Madison." She guessed correctly. "I have been looking forward to meeting him, Evan. He's been so accommodating for the College."

Madison thought he recognized the man with her – Evan Hamilton, President of the First Federal Bank of New York. The journalist stood up in his Harris Tweed jacket and replied, "It is nice to meet you, Dr. Eccles."

She warmly asked, "Have you met Mr. Madison, Evan?"

Hamilton enthusiastically shook Madison's hand. "No, but it's nice to finally meet you in person. You look much younger than your byline photo. I hear through the rumor mill that you are a distant relative to THE Madison, James that is. Well then, it turns out that we all have something in common. I'm part of Alexander Hamilton's family tree and Dean Eccles here – she of the New England Adams clan. Given your own bloodlines, no wonder you have liberal inclinations, John."

Madison brightened and remarked, "Not necessarily so, Mr. Hamilton. I have to be somewhat objective in my line of work. But it figures for you both . . . banking, Wall Street, an American financial dynasty while with Dr. Eccles, she carries a legacy of academics, especially if Henry Adams is included."

Hamilton nodded. "I read your material religiously, Mr. Madison. I enjoy your liberal points of view – they balance my own strongly conservative outlook. I have to admit reading news rags has long been a part of my morning routine."

Professor Eccles broke in, "Evan, remember now, don't get sidetracked. You've got to get going. There's a lot for you to do. Besides, Mr. Madison and I need some time of our own to go over the journalism colloquium that he is chairing this weekend."

"Correct as always, Professor. I hope you both have a good day." On his way out, Hamilton gave a sweeping bow to her administrative assistant and remarked, "I appreciate your muffins as always, Mrs. Stuart. They make my visits so enjoyable."

Mrs. Stuart flushed, suspecting that the good-looking executive didn't limit his flirtations. "Mr. Hamilton, keep that up and you may find trouble on your hands."

"You've got that right, but getting out of trouble is what my family has always been known for." As Hamilton confidently strode through the door, the air literally seemed to be sucked out of the room.

For the next hour, Madison, an Adjunct Professor of Journalism at Georgetown University, and Dean Eccles discussed the tentative schedule for the colloquium that was to be held the next day.

When they completed their planning, Gayle gingerly brought up a new subject. "This is an aside, I realize, but do you recall that I asked you several weeks back about a certain place in Switzerland, near Lausanne? You had mentioned it in a column. I'm wondering, what kind of place it is?

"As I told you on the phone, Mr. Madison, I've been asked to organize the first meeting of an international university educators' group." Dean Eccles gave him the glossy announcement that she had kept in her desk, saying, "Tentatively, it is to be held at Mont Épine, the lodge above Lake Geneva that you wrote about."

Madison wistfully looked over the brochure and mused, "It is a beautiful setting – it really is."

"Since you have seen it, I hoped you'd be able to give me some insight into the place. I think there might be a small picture of it in the brochure, John, along with some other information. Take a look. See if it's the same place you wrote about."

Madison immediately recognized the exclusive Swiss lodge pictured on the registration page. As he spent time to scan the brochure, Professor Eccles had a brief interlude to recall the events that had occurred since Evan Hamilton's visit a month earlier.

She had made immediate contact with all the other members of PATRI, with an encrypted phone call, saying, "The time has come in order for the Eagle to fly to Montreux. More detailed instructions will follow. Be ready."

Meanwhile, Hamilton had been busy, too. After contacting a night supervisor at the Twin Oaks Mall, he had found out what were some of the Europe League's plans. During his nighttime visit to the shopping center, a rough-looking warehouseman advised him to bring "the necessary person" and "the defining materials" to the Mount of Rose, the Mountain of Thorns, east of Montreux, Switzerland. "It is an exclusive lodge – Mount Épine," he divulged.

The warehouseman gave him a further message from his employer: "We will be nearby waiting to meet you there in September when the moment is right for you and your group."

Soon thereafter, Dean Eccles had phoned each PATRI member for a second time on March 6th to give Hamilton's newly acquired information regarding the time and precise setting for their clandestine meeting. She revealed that it would happen during an international conference for educators to which all of PATRI would be conveniently invited.

When she called Ed Finch for the second time, however, he seemed highly agitated that a certain friend of his might have somehow discovered information about their clandestine society and its intents. As she talked with him about where the PATRI meeting would be held, the Department of Navy analyst had seemed extremely put off. She could tell that he was restraining himself when he angrily remarked, "Oh, yes Gayle. That suspicious friend that I just mentioned is one of my best friends, John Madison, the journalist for the *Post*. He let it slip out during a little get-together last night that you had called him yesterday to find out about Mont Épine, the same place in Montreux, too . . . What's that about, Gayle? Remember . . . the pledge!"

She had realized with a start that it had been he who had recently awakened her with a threatening, late night phone call. She responded curtly to his frosty accusation. "Why do you ask me, Ed? Don't you trust me with PATRI?"

She managed to remain calm and explained that since John Madison seemed to already be knowledgeable about Montreux, she felt it was necessary for her to come up with some reason to interrogate the newspaperman and find out for herself exactly what he did know. "Especially, Ed, in light of what Madison wrote in his article about foreign money interests with certain French connections and possible money laundering in Manassas and Richmond. Your buddy, John Madison, is already on to possible misdoings involving Rouen, with or without me. What do you say about all this, dear Ed? And how coincidental," she said, spitting her words, "the Twin Oaks Mall of Manassas – and Philippe Rouen owns it! It's the same place that Evan Hamilton had risked to go to meet the messenger.

"For the sake of all of us, trust me to take the next step. You see, Ed, I've got to find out what else Madison knows – about Rouen, the whole story. Whom does he suspect? The Europe League? PATRI? In order that we can go forward with our planned rendezvous in Montreux, I must check him out and, if necessary, lead him on a wild goose chase."

Gayle Eccles was finally able to reassure Finch. "I need to have a face-to-face visit with Mr. Madison, my dear Ed. As he told you, he's coming to Bowdoin soon and I'll have just such an opportunity. All of us should worry, myself included, that he could be a threat to PATRI."

Professor Eccles understood that her present interaction with the *Post's* journalist carried a certain danger. It reminded her of a saying ascribed to Sun Tzu, the military genius of ancient China: 'Keep your friends at a distance and hold your enemies up close.' Her purpose was simple. She had to know what he knew, up close and personal.

At last, Madison put the educator conference's brochure down. "If you expect to have a large attendance at your get-together in Montreux, the Le Montreux Palace could also accommodate such a meeting. But if your expected numbers are modest, from what I can see in this brochure Mont Épine would be ideal for this sort of thing."

"I doubt that there will be many people coming. It is the first year for this meeting," Dr. Eccles added, "but I do want to impress everyone with a memorable setting."

"There is one thing, though. I'm sure the room and facility costs are much more than you could possibly afford, especially with the Swiss exchange rate."

"That is something that we've been blessed with, support. An anonymous donor has already generously funded the Institute. He or she may actually be attending but we are not to know. I want to do what's best for the initial meeting."

"That sounds wonderful, Dr. Eccles. If this is to be a think-tank, a retreat-type of meeting, then you can be assured that you will not be bothered in any way there."

"Why is that, Mr. Madison? By the way, you can call me Gayle."

"They have so much apparent and not so apparent security on the grounds. The managers mentioned that if there is a so-called 'conférence secrète' held in Switzerland, it is usually held at Mont Épine, not in Davos or Geneva."

"I still don't fully understand why you were there?" The dean nervously held her tongue. She didn't want to seem prying, so added delicately, "You gave a wonderfully detailed and colorful description of the countryside and nearby castle."

"I was in Switzerland, as my first article suggested, to follow up on reports of certain irregularities in some construction projects and military contracts in and around Northern Virginia. Philippe Rouen's consortium is only one of many such foreign investors of interest. Since this Rouen lived near Geneva, I briefly visited his environs to try to get a fuller sense of the man.

"Unfortunately for me, it turned out that other than seeing the five-star resort and the historic Chateau de Chillon, there was little of importance to be gained for my story in either Lausanne or Montreux. If there is some sort of an illegal operation at Rouen's Twin Oaks Mall, it probably goes through Zurich or Madrid, far from his home in Lausanne."

The Bowdoin dean breathed an imperceptible sigh of relief. Thus far, it appeared that Mr. Madison was totally unaware of any connection between Philippe Rouen, the Europe League and their PATRI. Still, she felt the need to further reassure herself by knowing the extent of any other of Madison's ongoing investigations. She asked tentatively, "Correct me if I'm wrong, but I remember in your article you reported that there were many other hidden arrangements that involve European and Mideast banks. Is that right?"

"Yes, Dr. Eccles," Madison replied. As he spoke, she carefully studied his facial expressions. "I'm early into the investigation, but there are probably many other foreign groups that Rouen may be affiliated with that are also involved in this sort of stuff. I just don't know yet."

Eccles was taken aback and stared at her desktop. She sensed that although Madison seemed off their trail, she had to trust that Philippe Rouen hadn't gotten too careless. After a pause, she looked up, "And again Lausanne, Montreux?"

"They are indeed special places but nothing there of importance for me at the moment. Still, it was a wonderful assignment while it lasted. I think that the real story concerning this Rouen family enterprise is probably best discovered here in America. Sadly, I don't think there will be any reason for me to return to Switzerland anytime soon."

"You've been a big help, Mr. Madison. How can I find out anything else? About this place, that is." Her voice was measured. "I already tried to look this Mount Épine resort up on the Internet and came up with nothing. So you can see that your information this morning has been most helpful."

"I can't be sure but the lodge is likely far too exclusive to have a website. If you and your group do end up going there, however, I think everyone will really enjoy the place. Given the seclusion, I'm sure that you'll get a lot done."

With barely concealed relief, Gayle Eccles smiled graciously and said, "I am truly thankful for your information, Mr. Madison. It will be most helpful for the preliminary planning for my international conference. Speaking of getting things organized, let's see if Mrs. Stuart has settled any of your own arrangements here at Bowdoin."

32

Mount Vernon

March 2018

> The mission of the Mount Vernon Ladies' Association is to preserve, restore and manage the estate of George Washington to the highest standards and to educate visitors and people throughout the world about the life and legacies of George Washington, so that his example of character and leadership will continue to inform and inspire future generations.
>
> Mission Statement of the Mount Vernon Ladies' Association
> from the Official Mount Vernon Guidebook, 2001

Suzanne Winfield enjoyed days like this when she could stay closer to her home. Eight generations of her husband's Winfield family had lived on an adjoining estate, Woodlawn Mills, along the southwestern border of Mount Vernon. She had recently joined the Mount Vernon Ladies Association as a docent at the urging of her mother-in-law, Mrs. Nancy Winfield. That day she was on duty as a guide.

It was unusually warm for springtime and Suzanne sipped coffee on the portico while waiting for some other docents. The historic home of George Washington stood on a gentle rise. Rolling hills and vales fanned out in all directions like the spokes of a wheel. To the east, the house had an unobstructed view of the Potomac. The National Farmland stood out on the opposite shore.

"Suzanne, how are you doing young lady? It looks like you're lost in thoughts."

Startled, she squinted into the sun and saw Georgianne Breining and Betsy Wills coming around the bordering hedge. "Not really, Betsy. Since there's a lot happening at the University, I was thoroughly enjoying just sitting here."

"Ladies, please," Georgianne put in, "let's not waste the day flopping around here doing nothing. The traffic nearly spoiled it for me already."

"You're right, Georgi . . . guess it's time to get to our stations." Suzanne felt fortunate to have been assigned to her favorite guiding-location, the faux mahogany-grained Passage. It was the original part of the Mansion House occupied by George Washington's father and brother – Augustine and Lawrence.

"Where will you be this morning, Georgianne?"

"Up in Lafayette's room . . . or at least that's what I call it."

"How about you, Betsy?"

"Down in Washington's study near you, Suze'. I love that spot the best. I enjoy seeing the copies of the surveying maps and ledgers that are on display there."

Suzanne Winfield agreed, saying, "For me, the best item is Lawrence Washington's original deed to Mount Vernon hanging right over the writing desk."

Betsy seemed puzzled and asked, "I've never understood, though. The bottom edge appears rather torn. Do you happen to know why, Suzanne?"

"No, Betsy. I only know that that and the portrait of Lawrence Washington are the only permanent exhibits in the study." Whenever Suzanne saw the portrait of George Washington's brother Lawrence, she was amazed at how much he resembled her late father-in-law, Admiral Thomas Winfield. Each man had similar nasal and forehead features, the same patrician bearing. She had concluded long ago that with so many intermarriages between colonial Virginia families, it was likely that many genetic traits were shared through the years.

When she had mentioned this to Georgianne Breining, her garrulous friend facetiously rejoined, "That sort of gene pool sharing happens in many other places, too, honey. It's not limited to Virginia." The ex-Manhattan socialite related her own experiences with the close-knit villagers living near her family's summer home in the Adirondacks. "It's not much different in upstate New York than it is here, Suzanne. I've never heard that DNA is contagious, but it *could* be." Then she teasingly suggested, "Who knows really? You could possibly catch somebody's DNA just by swimming in a pool. That kind of stuff probably floats around like people do. Could be that's why folks at the Oakwood Country Club call each other 'cuz' or 'uncle.' Maybe, in fact, they are."

Suzanne moved into the main hallway. She noted the surveillance camera in a corner of the ceiling and was reassured that its green light was blinking. Mrs. King's fifth graders from Biglerville, Pennsylvania began to move into the hall. "Come in children. Thanks, Mrs. King. Please stand along the wall near the side door . . . Yes, that's right."

After the school children settled down, Suzanne explained that this particular spot gave a view into several roped-off rooms.

"Now squeeze around, see in there – this is the West Parlor. You've already been through the large formal dining room, the big green one. But this beautiful room in Prussian blue is where the family's day-to-day social life took place. See the furniture? They are the same that the Washingtons used in 1790."

"What are those things over the fireplace, there?" a boy asked.

"That is a painting of the farmlands around Mount Vernon about 1760. Above that is the coat-of-arms of the Washington family. General Washington added the motto – *Exitus Acta Probat* – under the shield. The Latin words mean 'The End Proves the Deed.' The coat-of-arms has been the Washington family symbol for centuries."

"What's that?" A curious girl gestured to a brazened hemi-octagonal glass display case mounted midway up the Passage's wall. It held what appeared to be an unusually large key. "That's a funny place for a key . . . Is it for the front door?"

"No, but that's a good question. Actually there's a story about it. This key was a gift sent from Marquis de Lafayette to the General and Mrs. Washington after he became our first President. This is one of several original black iron keys taken from the Bastille. The French Revolution began when the hated Bastille prison was captured. General Lafayette fought in that revolution, too.

"Lafayette and France had been important to the earlier success of our own Revolutionary War. This key was a symbol of the two men's friendship. He encouraged Washington to hang it in Mount Vernon – our first national home. Washington prominently displayed it here in the passageway, making it visible to all who entered his mansion. The General and Martha Washington treasured the gift since the young French aristocrat was like a son to them."

A Biglerville Elementary School parent added, "I believe that when Lafayette made a later visit to America years after General Washington died, he gave a different Bastille Key to Mr. Washington's Masonic Lodge up in Alexandria. The two men were both active Freemasons. That other key is still on display there."

"Yes, that's right. Now off to your next station."

Mrs. King saw that some of the children were getting restless near the sidewalls and looked at her watch. "Okay class, as Mrs. Winfield says, time to move on. Let's give her our thanks. Wasn't this great?"

The fifth graders beamed and applauded. "Yes thanks . . . That was really neat."

Suzanne backed against the curved banister and motioned for them to carefully ascend the stairs. "Follow along and be sure to see the room where Mrs. Washington did her sewing. Mrs. Breining will meet you at the top of the stairs."

Before leaving the Mansion House, Mrs. King's class passed through the first floor study. There, Mrs. Betsy Wills pointed out surveying equipment and an original framed document hanging above George Washington's desk:

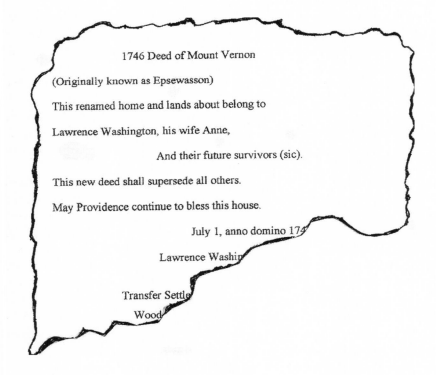

1746 Deed of Mount Vernon

(Originally known as Epsewasson)

This renamed home and lands about belong to

Lawrence Washington, his wife Anne,

And their future survivors (sic).

This new deed shall supersede all others.

May Providence continue to bless this house.

July 1, anno domino 174

Lawrence Washin

Transfer Settle
Wood

Woodlawn Mills, Virginia

After arriving back home at Woodlawn Mills, Suzanne Winfield lounged for a while with a steaming cup of tea and happily reminisced about bygone times.

During her first visit to Princeton years ago, she was glad for a chance to rest some before seeing her childhood sweetheart, David Winfield. A second-string halfback, David had invited her for Homecoming in 1999. The four-hour Amtrak train trip into the New Jersey countryside had allowed her to nap and get rejuvenated after freshman-year midterms at Georgetown.

Suzanne looked out on the path crossing the front lawn of the Ivy Club. In the distance, she recognized David shuffling through the fallen leaves. She ran off the porch and tightly embraced him.

"Hey there, good-looking. Welcome to the north woods. Sorry I'm late. The team dinner dragged on and on – many old-timers were fixed on the way it used to be. You know stuff like 'we played on both sides of the ball' and all that."

Suzanne tossed her head back and put a finger to his face. "Sssh, my friend. You're probably going to be like that when you're old and gray too."

Bemused, he shook his head knowing that she was likely right, "Let's not waste any more time. Let's go in. I want to show you the eating club." Once they squeezed into the club's library, he turned and asked, "First off, how's your Mom?"

Caught off guard, Suzanne felt overwhelmed by his show of concern and bit her lower lip. "She seems alright . . . for now, I guess. Oh Dave, it's been tough." Her eyes filled with tears. "Her oncologist says maybe another year."

Her mother, Sara Claridge, had been a striking raven-haired model from New York who had married an eccentric gentleman from Virginia's horse country. Her classic beauty had graced magazines and amazed her adopted Arlington society for years. Suzanne had often been told that she closely resembled her mother in her parents' wedding pictures. Now Sara was withering from terminal cancer. Suzanne inwardly winced at the thought that her mother would not be at her and David's marriage or at the birth of her first grandchild.

David coughed trying to dispel their moods before suggesting, "Come, let me show you something in here, Suze'." He took her hand and led her over to a book stack. "These are my father's gifts. Since Dad was class of '62, he gave these old editions and original manuscripts to Ivy."

"How about his other stuff?"

"Oh, the ones we discovered when we were rummaging around my home, the dusty letters written by Washington, Madison and Thomas Jefferson to the original Winfields? They're still at Woodlawn Mills. Dad tells me he's debating giving them to the National Archives."

"Dave dear, you do go way back." Suzanne Claridge pinched his flank. "You Winfields are amazing. No wonder we teased you and your sister at Episcopal School and called you our 'First Family.' I remember we used to say that next to the Lees and Washingtons come the Winfields."

The next night after the Yale game, they went to David's top-floor room. His roommate said that he'd give them an hour together. As they sat on his bed, Suzanne mentioned that a girlfriend had once told her that a drink or two took the edge off 'doing it.' Now that they found themselves closer to the actual IT, they nervously smiled at one another. Neither had thought to touch any alcohol.

Until that night, David had always been the forward one. And she had always kept him out in the cold. But that was then. "David," she said, "sometimes I wish we'd allow ourselves to . . . I know you always say we need to save ourselves for later, but I want you. So . . . yes."

"But . . . but, Suze'."

"We can stop anytime . . . oh Davey. I want to learn together . . . Make me your first – no one else." She leaned forward and took charge, touching him in new ways.

"But seriously now . . ." He took her face in his hands. His steady gaze asked whether her choice was the right one.

Suzanne softly pleaded for him to place his hand there, there, then everywhere on her sweater. "It's messed up already, don't worry . . . let me help you."

Sitting on his hard mattress, Suzanne kept her doe-like eyes focused on his face as she purposely pulled one, then her other arm out of the cashmere's sleeves. The sweater became jumbled around her shoulders like a yoke. After a moment, she huskily ordered, "You take the rest off, David . . . Yes, now . . . Do it for me."

His arms enfolded her and brought her closer, as if by doing so he could somehow mute her wish. As she came hard against him, Suzanne was sure that he could feel her body's heat through his shirt. Despite his arousal, he was almost afraid to see her unfolding nakedness. Closing his eyes, he awkwardly touched her bra. She backed away and whispered, "Be careful, David. It's my sister's favorite sweater."

"Well . . . let's see . . ." He tried unsuccessfully to lift the cashmere sweater over her head.

"It's caught!"

They stopped in their tracks.

"Nuts . . . I can't believe it! Stop there, Davey. Hold it a minute!"

"What?"

"Don't worry, I'm okay. It's not your fault."

"Well?" He put his palms out in surrender. "My hands are off, Suze'." He could think of nothing else to say.

The sweater remained bunched up over her eyes but Suzanne started to blindly sort out the problem. "Why did I wear jewelry? This is the pits!"

"What's that got to . . .?"

"It's caught . . . Lisa's sweater is tied up in my earring and necklace!"

"Suze', maybe this is telling us something."

They started to giggle about their predicament. "Is this hysterical or what?" she asked. "What a pain! Here I am, half-undressed with my love for the very first time, even getting myself all hot and bothered, and now . . . I'm freezing!"

"Here, let me help," David offered sheepishly.

"Oh no . . . no, no, no! Just sit there but don't look, my friend. I've got to do this carefully or Lisa will kill me!"

David looked on anyhow as she held the sweater over her forehead, tilted her head, and gently removed an earring and the necklace. Suzanne was grateful when she finally started to pull it over her hair and was even more thankful that her sister's cashmere sweater appeared undamaged.

"David, you once told me that you wanted to give me your frosh sweatshirt. Now seems as good a time as any."

A minute later, as she pulled his extra-large sweatshirt over her shoulders, Suzanne muttered, "I suppose we'll remember this for a long time."

Sitting there and collecting their wits, they were finally able to laugh at the situation. Suzanne summed it up saying that they'd probably long remember this as the "fumbled" start of many more Saturday nights together.

Here it was – nearly twenty years later and Suzanne Winfield woke with a start. Although dozing off for only a minute, she felt completely rested.

Then she heard in the background, "Mom! We're home!"

33

Woodlawn Mills, Virginia

July 2018

Mustard dribbled from his mouth as Bobby Winfield gagged on a half-eaten hot dog. His teen-age sister Caroline yelled, "Yuck! Why do you always take such big bites?" They and their brother Jeffrey were together with the family on a sultry Saturday afternoon.

Uncle Harrison Claridge came over to tease his niece. "Come now, Caroline, you're starting to sound like your mother. She used to boss me around, too." Having decided to have a barbecue for his wife's thirty-ninth birthday, David Winfield was delighted that his brother-in-law could attend. It turned out that Harrison was already coming down from Manhattan for a performance at the Lincoln Center.

Suzanne's sister, Lisa Sargent, was not there. She had recently remarried and was on an extended honeymoon in Europe. And David's sister, Marilyn Ashford, had a long-standing commitment to be with friends in Boothbay Harbor that weekend and was terribly disappointed that she wouldn't be able to attend the celebration at her childhood home.

David's mother Nancy sat at the poolside and took careful notice of her grandchildren. She picked up her digital camera and asked, "Harrison, might you please take a picture of us? First, let's wipe the mustard off your chin, Robert."

She clustered the children together and positioned them in a row. She made a habit of taking photos early at a party. "There, that should do," she determined after the pictures were taken. She wistfully thought that her dear Tom would have loved seeing the children growing up like this.

Standing off in the shade, Winfield felt relaxed for the first time in weeks. Managing his defense firm had become more grueling of late. He had recently lost several lucrative, longstanding contracts.

His brother-in-law's partner Randall came over and joined him. "Real nice place you have here, Dave. Harrison told me that it's been in your family a long time."

David smiled down at the unctuous New Yorker and replied, "More than two hundred years, Randall. It has passed from one Winfield to the other."

"Mount Vernon is right next door, isn't it?"

"Yes, in that direction." Winfield pointed to the east but thick foliage blocked the view. "You can see its cupola in winter when the trees are bare."

"Do you and your family have any connection? I mean with Mount Vernon?"

"No, not since some of the original Mount Vernon land was sold to an original Winfield. Or so the story goes."

"Do you have any special family traditions, secrets, you know, that kind of thing?" The diminutive actor's eyebrows lifted as he asked.

"Sorry to disappoint you, but I don't think so. We're sort of unusually usual." Winfield was not one to promote himself. "Let's see if we can get my mother anything."

"She's such a sweet lady, Dave, I really like her."

"My Dad would have agreed, Randall. He knew that Mom ruled the roost. The Winfield women have always been the jewels in our family crown."

As the two men approached Nancy Winfield, the grande dame looked off to the side and spotted her granddaughter trying her best to unobtrusively watch a muscular cook's helper flipping hamburgers on the grill. The Winfield matriarch smiled to herself and thought that it wouldn't be long before Caroline's generation would be taking over.

"Mom, let me get you something to eat. I'll fix you something and bring you a tray while you give Randall here a little history of Woodlawn. Any dressings?"

Several hours later, the backyard was silent except for the high-pitched cicadas in the bordering woods. David and Suzanne reclined in lounge chairs as barbecue smoke lingered like a guest overstaying his welcome. A near-empty bottle of Mumm's rested next to them.

Harrison and Randall had left earlier for the Lincoln Center. Nancy Winfield had had the estate's limousine take her and her grandchildren to an Amy Rush concert at The Barns at Wolftrap even though she had never heard of the singer.

Suzanne sleepily murmured, "It's only eight o'clock and they've all left us alone."

"Maybe that is their best birthday present to you."

"I doubt the kids would call it a 'present,' but I'm sure the adults see it that way."

'How so?"

She reached over and punched him playfully, "Oh come now, Davey dear, don't be thick. Your mother is a woman, too. She knows us."

"Why don't we simply lie right here and watch Maya and Greg clean up?"

"Come on now! It's my birthday – at least for the next few hours."

"And . . .?"

She gave him a cheeky look, "Mr. Winfield, sir, let's take a walk. I have a few more wishes to make. Maya, dear, we'll be back in a bit."

The housemaid yelled back, "Watch out, M'ss Winfield, not to get caught out there. The Weather Channel here is sayin' there's a line o' storm cells, mam, stretchin' from Winchester to Manassas. It looks like they comin', comin' our way."

"We shouldn't be that long, Maya."

The heat and humidity had been steadily building up through the day and perspiration soaked their clothes as they walked down a path to Dogue Creek.

"Darn, Suze', we can't stay here too long," Winfield fretted swiping fiercely at a swarm of mosquitoes.

"You're right – what a bummer. We should have brought our DEET."

He slapped again and suggested going back along the ridge path. "There's more of a breeze up there. That should keep the pesky critters away."

As they climbed the slope, the waning sun disappeared behind a bank of cumuli to the west. Low-pitched rumbles in the distance roiled the woodlands. Suzanne looked back at the creek and the hills of neighboring Fort Belvoir rising to the south.

"Maya's right. We should head back sooner rather than later," David said.

Suzanne squeezed his hand as the wind started to gust, blowing the poplar leaves in silvery rustles. "Oh love, let's be naughty . . . let's go hiding!" She stopped at the top of the ridge and turned him about. "There . . . " Pointing to their guesthouse a quarter mile removed from Woodlawn Mills's main house, she laughed and said, "That'll do!"

The storm hit with unexpected strength, blazing the sky with nonstop lightning, pelting the sills and balcony with sheets of rain and hail.

An hour passed – Suzanne couldn't believe it had only been one hour. Since the guesthouse was empty, David had suggested they leave the two sliding doors on the lee side of the balcony open. Despite that, he had had to keep getting in and out of bed on the windward side to open the dormers for air, or to close them whenever sheets of rain pitched through the louvers.

"Wouldn't you know, the darned windows," she giggled. "Down . . . then up . . . then down. That makes it tough when there's no air conditioning. Sort of like us at our age . . . first up . . . then down . . . then . . ."

The thunder faded into low-pitched rumbles rolling off to the east as the front moved off toward Maryland. Suzanne lay wide-eyed against David's moist chest and watched the dulled lightning popping within ill-defined clouds.

"I'm so glad we're here, love," she said, lightly kissing his body.

David passed his fingers over her sweat-drenched back and began to knead her. A random thought caused him to chuckle. "Suze', it's usually of our own making when we end up in a heat like this. But given these dog days of summer, we sure didn't need to add any extra combustion tonight."

"A funny thought, dearest Davey, but once again you were . . . you always are . . . so wonderful, wonderfully satisfying." Suzanne rolled onto her side and gazed at her husband's handsome profile.

Lightning continued to dance at the east-facing windows and bounce off the bedroom's two mirrors. David turned to face her and, as he did, placed a hand over her heart. "No honey, it's you. You're always there for me . . . for both of us when you let go."

She looked across her pillow and traced her forefinger down his nose. "Whenever you urge this sort of storm in me . . . oh my. Then this comes, like now – this sweet time, this incredible peace."

Turned slightly, Suzanne peered over and saw the cloud ridges on the far horizon. She could barely discern a light on the shore opposite, toward Fort Marshall – the Masons' home. Suzanne could hear that the dripping noises from the downspouts outside had slowed, and she contentedly placed her hand in his. "It's been great, but it's probably time to head back."

"Why don't we just call Maya and say we're stuck?"

"Why don't you, you lug?" Suzanne sat up on the bed and reached over to a nightstand to retrieve her apparel. As she put her earrings and necklace back on, she softly asked, "Davey, remember these? They're special . . . Remember Princeton?"

34

Wrangel, Alaska

August 2018

"What day is it?"

Maureen Nightbird-Reynolds squinted one eye open. It was early but the sun was already high at this northern latitude. Oilcloth drapes slapped against the window screens and hanging wind chimes tinkled outside in the morning breeze.

A deep voice moaned, "What day is it?" Michael, a longtime friend, blearily asked a second time as he rolled into the sunken V of her mattress.

Maureen pushed against his hairy chest. "I was wondering that myself, love. Let's see, you came down Friday and except for last night." She drifted her fingers lazily over his flank. "We've been here every hour since."

"So?" Michael was grinning. He always enjoyed her easygoing ways. "That must mean it's Sunday. My flight back to Prudhoe Bay isn't 'til three."

"Great," she said and deliberately moved her hand lower. "We can . . ."

"You're right, Mo', we can get some breakfast. It's my turn to . . ."

The marine biologist took a pillow and rubbed it in his face until he wrestled in self-defense. "You tease, mister. And if you tease, I will too!"

It would be another two hours before they seriously thought about breakfast.

"I'm going to take a bath, Mo'."

"Go ahead, Michael. Don't be self-conscious. You know that I love to look at you from all angles. Get on in there and I'll bring you coffee while you're soaking."

Shortly, Maureen heard him singing through the fraying plastic drapes that covered her tiny bathroom doorway. As she waited for the bacon to sizzle, the NOAA scientist signed onto her mailbox to check her weekend email. There it was – the promised follow-up message at long last. Maureen clicked onto 'Swiss Educational Conference' sent from *ecclesgbowsdean@ bowdoin.edu*. She hummed merrily to herself as she sat and read,

> *Itinerary – September 10, 2018 for:*
> *MN-Reynolds*　　　*Online Boarding Ticket #061742*
> 　　　*Anchorage – Seattle*　　　*Alaska Airlines*
> 　　　*Seattle – Chicago*　　　*American Airlines*
> 　　　*Chicago – Geneva*　　　*Swiss Airlines*

Maureen was a seventh generation direct descendant of Benjamin Franklin. As such, Gayle Eccles, the designated organizer of PATRI, had phoned her with two cryptic communications the previous March.

"Hey Mo'! Is the bacon burning?"

She jumped up and saw that smoke was drifting along her cardboard ceiling. "How perceptive, love. At least I'm not still smoking like I was a half hour ago."

As Maureen took the skillet off the burner, Michael walked in and pressed against her. Thankfully, she realized, he was turned away from her computer – she intended to keep him that way. "Do we really need food?" he whispered in her hair.

"Yes we do, friend – and you better do the eggs for me or I'll ruin them, too." She untangled herself from his grasp and faced him. "As far as I know, young man, cooks are dressed whenever they're working in the kitchen. Don't chase me around anymore – I'll look the other way." Maureen Reynolds gaily flipped him off. "So, Michael, your pants?"

As he pulled on his trousers, she deftly moved past him to shut down her computer, thinking to herself, "Michael must not know – know anything at all about my family."

Chicago, Illinois

August 2018

Karen Jay-York realized that she had forgotten to sign off after reading her emails. She went back to the den and saw her daughter Emily staring at the screen.

Itinerary – September 11, 2018
K York   Online Boarding Ticket #061861
Chicago – Geneva Swiss Airlines

And at the top of the message were the words:

Sent from: *ecclesgbowdeans@bowdoin.edu*
The subject line read: *Swiss Educational Conference*

"Mom.m.m.m! Are you're going away again?" the twelve-year-old whined.

"Just for a little while, sweetheart. Deidre will be here and can help you with your school assignments. There shouldn't be too many in September anyway."

The pre-teen, her mother and her mother's partner, Deidre Wolcott, had eased into a comfortable family-like arrangement at the York home along Lakeshore Drive.

Deidre, a twenty-six-year-old Jamaican native, worked as a postgraduate neuroscience fellow at the nearby University Hospital. For the past year, Emily had warmly accepted her new living situation, calling Deidre 'mother number two.'

"You ladies will get along fine, Emily." Karen York put her arm around her shoulder. "It is part of my job at the business school to attend these kinds of meetings."

"I can't stand you, Mom! Here you have Deidre, and I, I don't have anybody except Chloe. I hate you!" She was red-faced and still screaming as she stormed off.

"What's up with Emily?" Deidre came into the den. "You told me that you might have to go to a meeting next month. Is that what this is all about, Karen?"

"Afraid so, Deidre. She just can't understand why I must go anywhere at all. I suspect that it's only a phase."

The slight, cocoa-skinned lover soothingly stroked Karen York's neck. "The only thing I know is that I love our own little family right here. Don't worry, I'll take good care of Emily while you're gone, but both of us will miss you terribly."

As her tension began to ease, Karen half-turned. "Thanks, Deidre, I needed your touch," and then whispered with a sense of urgency, "I need you."

Newport Beach, California
August 2018

"Do I make you nervous? . . . I want you, Janet."

Hugh Rochan studied her reaction. A seemingly innocent smile curled suggestively as her eyes lifted. She was even more beautiful in person than he had imagined. Over the past month, he had studied many video clips of the young newswoman and concluded that it was her fresh looks that so enchanted him.

"A little, yes – nervous, that is . . ." Janet Melone had been flown to Los Angeles and now sat on his veranda overlooking the Pacific.

"I'm known as a man who gets what he wants," he boasted. "Tell me what you think about this, Newport Beach . . . about me?"

"Well, Mr. Rochan, I must say that I've never been propositioned like this before. Flying first class, a stay at a villa, being allowed to sleep in . . . Nice."

"And?" The sixty-four-year-old CEO of Manor Media waited.

"It's something I could get use to, being with you." She smiled and moistened her upper lip. "But seriously now, Mr. Rochan. I presume it is you that has something to offer . . . not me."

"Oh, Miss Melone, call me Hugh." He grinned broadly. "I didn't bring you all the way out here to seduce you . . . at least not in the usual fashion. But don't try me later. Despite my age, I'm a man after all."

The Washington-based newscaster couldn't begin to guess the real intentions of this surprisingly attractive billionaire, but she had heard rumors.

"What I have been so obliquely saying is this. My Manor Media needs you – and I think you need us."

"How so? I love being in Washington with ABN. I'm really quite happy with what I've got now – a fabulous job near my hometown."

"Let me tell you something. Washington is a peanut-size market, Jan. You probably aren't interested, but my family goes way back in the Washington area too, but they left years ago. I've always said if our family could have moved away, anyone can."

Melone could feel herself starting to feel more comfortable by the minute. The Englishman sounded warm and personal, not the least bit arrogant. As she picked at a blueberry muffin she asked, "When did they leave?"

"You've heard of the Fairfaxes?"

"The once-prominent Virginia family? Of course."

"That's my family – on my father's side. The Fairfaxes returned to England just before your Revolutionary War."

"Where do you call home now?"

"London – the Kensington District – then here, of course. And there are two others, one in Dubai and my family's estate in Kent, England."

"Do you have family, Mr. Rochan?"

"Yes, three children and two stepchildren, all around your age. Four work for me – I believe in nepotism. Then there are my two ex's and two sisters in the UK."

She noticed his deep blue eyes against the pale sky. "And?"

"Presently there is no lady in my life, not that I wouldn't want one. I think my life has probably moved on even though having family is very important to me."

"You're an interesting man, Mr. Rochan. I'd like to find out more about you." She leaned forward, making her breasts fall noticeably against her blouse.

Rochan took a bite of cantaloupe and politely attempted to avert his gaze. "Before I let you do that, Janet, let me cut to the chase. I've been viewing clips of your work at American Broadcasting. In a word, you're fabulous."

"It's nice to hear you're impressed. Thanks, Mr. Rochan – I mean Hugh." She sensed that her flushing might be evident.

Aware of the effect he was having, Rochan continued, "Yes, you've got it all. You're not only beautiful, but you convey sincerity. You are a person that people can trust . . . They want someone like you to look at, listen to, and most importantly, believe in."

"Are you saying that you've become a little obsessed with me?"

The British multimedia baron shook his head and laughed. "Oh no, no, no. If I wanted you for myself in a gilded cage, I wouldn't have been so roundabout. I'll say again what I said earlier, 'I want you.' I want you, Janet Melone, to be the anchor for my newly designed news program, the largest in the world."

For the next hour he outlined his dream of a new multimedia news venture that would revolutionize the industry. As the network's chief news anchor, he described, she would essentially be a 'news navigator,' but at this formulation, Janet Melone angrily interrupted. "Excuse me, Mr. Rochan, but I consider myself a journalist – not an actress."

"That is precisely what I want you to be, my Miss Melone. Your billing would be that of a first-rate newswoman, but your news show will employ a recently developed interactive image-menu. You will guide the viewers to see their options, what to look at and why. It is all in the public interest since it will give a larger number of story-choices." He smiled earnestly. "Your charming persona will capture viewers and thereby increase ratings and revenue streams for Manor Media."

"Sounds like I would be a hook. At least better that than a hooker."

"Listen, Jan – admit it. You are damned attractive. First and foremost, the viewing audience is primarily interested in looking at you, at honest believable you. They'll happily follow your advisements as you lead them through the news – that is, the news as my writers and I see it."

"When are you expecting an answer, Mr. Rochan?"

"Not right away. The program is still in the planning stages, but mercy me, I knew I'd forget something. Janet, the initial contract will pay five million a year which would double if the ratings do as well as I suspect they will."

She softly whistled. "Jimminy, can I at least give you a 'maybe' now?"

He smiled and said, "Of course," sensing that Janet Melone was almost his. Just then, his valet came in with a phone. "Sir, there's a call from your office in London."

"Thanks, Harold. Excuse me a minute, Janet."

Moving to the edge of the balcony, he barely made out his assistant Penelope's voice. "Mr. Rochan, a Monsieur Rouen called from Lausanne and left what he said was an urgent message. It was to remind you about the meeting in Montreux in September. He said that you should call him back within the hour."

Melone could overhear only his part of the conversation. "Thanks, Penny. I'm wrapping up here with Ms. Melone. Yes, the weather is fine, as always. I'll call him right back. My, you're working late, again."

When he hung up, Hugh Rochan walked over to Janet. "Sorry, Ms. Melone," he said curtly, "but some urgent business has come up and I need to make some calls. I think the two of us have made a reasonably good start this morning. Now, the ball's in your court. Once you get home, I hope that you will think things over and decide to join my new enterprise. Of course, feel free to call anytime with questions. Again, thanks for making time to come all the way out to California. I'll have one of my people get you back to LAX. "

Janet shook his hand warmly. "I deem it a pleasure that you even asked me to meet with you. You are obviously extremely persuasive, Mr. Rochan. I promise to give you a preliminary answer within the month."

As she turned and walked down a hallway to retrieve her luggage, she overheard him speaking into his phone, "Philippe? Hugh Rochan here. You wanted . . ."

35

Montreux, Switzerland

September 17, 2018

The delegates of the Congress of Nation Leaders had just finished a celebratory dinner in an imposing medieval castle, the Chateau de Chillon. Their sumptuous banquet had been held in a lavishly decorated Castellan dining hall featuring 15th century furniture. The castle, a picturesque historic site near Montreux, was located along the eastern shore of Lake Geneva.

Three floors below, the paraffin scent from a near-dozen lit candles filled a former dungeon. Thick, roughened stone walls trapped the hazy air under an arched ceiling, while the sound of waves hitting the rocky shoreline outside echoed through the prison's narrow apertures.

An imposing Frenchman stood before them, and his sharp voice resonated. "I am Francis du Motier, one of your hosts. I greet you. For the past half-year, I have been helping Dr. Eccles develop her conference here in Switzerland." He smiled knowingly and added, "Three of our members are delayed. I must wait a while longer before we begin our discussion."

Gayle Eccles realized that this might be it – finally the real meeting.

Her so-called educator's conference was being held at the Mont Épine resort, a short distance east of Montreux. Over the preceding two days of plenary sessions, the renowned invitees from around the world had met to discuss common problems and share different viewpoints.

Professor Eccles had scheduled free time that day in order for her guests to enjoy sightseeing and then a memorable concluding banquet. Although she was glad that the other seventy-odd invitees had deemed the convocation to be successful, she and Evan Hamilton could not help asking each other as the hours passed, "Where is the Europe League in all this? Where are they?"

That afternoon, during a paddle-wheel boat ride on the lake, Hamilton had whispered, "My guess, Gayle, is that it's not going to happen. Something must have come up. Most of us have to fly home late tomorrow."

The Europe League surprised them both when they finally surfaced. An hour before, as all the conference delegates were leaving the castle to board buses heading back to the Lodge, a man intercepted Ed Finch on the walk down the cobble-stoned drive and commanded, "Bring your people this way. Follow me."

Several resolute-looking servants came alongside and guided the American delegates down a wet uneven stairwell. Halfway down, Gayle Eccles whispered, "Evan, sneak past me. Take notice of each member as we go by to be sure they're all accounted for."

Flickering candles placed on several plank tables illuminated the dank dungeon. Shortly, a man and two women came through a side entrance leading from a wine cellar and joined the gathering. "Sorry to be a touch late, Monsieur du Motier. Elina's flight from Moscow was delayed." It was Hugh Rochan, the English mogul. He had driven with two fellow Europe League members, Catherine Bonard and Elina Pederson, from the Geneva airport.

M. du Motier coolly said, "Now let us begin . . . we have much to discuss. First, let me again say that I am Francis du Motier – a descendant of Gilbert du Motier – you know him better as the Marquis de Lafayette. As you might suspect, my other friends in this room belong to the Europe League. All of our members are here save one. Our Italian friend, Prince Bonapiento, unfortunately could not make it. The Prince is in New Zealand preparing for the America's Cup."

Gayle Eccles nodded and reflected aloud, "You can imagine, Francis, that Evan Hamilton and I have been wondering over the past few days whether you and your associates were even here – particularly after your previous messages."

"Yes, no doubt it was puzzling. I apologize for the delay here in Montreux, but you can understand that we had to be extremely cautious given the circumstance."

Hamilton officiously moved next to the Frenchman. "Mr. du Motier, we are missing two members ourselves. General Philip Mason needed to remain on a duty assignment and Gerald Schubert is too young to come. Dr. Eccles has volunteered to serve as their surrogate if any decisions become necessary."

An aristocratic Englishman rapped his knuckles on a table while clearing his throat with a bronchial cough. "Let me introduce myself – Sir Ronald Farrington, Lord Aplington. Pardon me, Francis, for so crudely interrupting. But Mrs. Eccles, is the *necessary person* that we asked you to bring, present in Montreux?"

"No," Hamilton forcefully replied. "Not at all, sir. At the moment, only two people are aware who this American is – and Dr. Eccles is not one of them." The others sat stock-still when he added, "He doesn't know it himself."

With a huff, Sir Ronald pressed the issue. "Why is he or she not here?"

"We thought it best to meet you first and agree with your plans before proceeding to address that particular request of yours," Hamilton explained. "We do not doubt your interest, sir, but Dr. Eccles and I didn't want to show you all of our cards at this initial meeting."

"Well, then, did you at least bring the *defining materials* that our message requested?" The English lord seemed quite put off.

"Hear, hear, Sir Ronald." The sculptress Catherine Bonard touched his forearm to settle him down. "They did bring themselves, after all."

"No, my dear. Sir Ronald is right. There are significant items that we asked for – is that not right, Mr. Hamilton?" Francis du Motier was clearly perturbed himself.

"I do have our original PATRI roster. Will that do? What else did you have in mind?"

"You know, sir, don't be coy," du Motier said as he counted on his fingers, "The several items stored in special places. If you did not bring them here, this is ridiculous. I totally understand Lord Aplington's frustration. This is very bad form. This stonewalling of yours makes for a terrible start."

Hamilton raised his hand in protest. "Wait, hold on a minute if you might. Let me suggest that we start from the top instead of immediately embroiling ourselves in such matters. After all, this is the first time there has ever been a full meeting between PATRI and your Europe League. Given that, may I suggest that before we do anything else, we should at least go around and introduce ourselves."

Hamilton turned to the side and took a yellowing parchment out of an attaché case he had brought in case the occasion presented itself. "This roster has been kept at my family's bank ever since it was first signed. It has been subsequently used to take a roll call whenever PATRI has a meeting."

Each person of PATRI announced his or her name and family connection to the members listed on the original roster of 1797. The Europeans then did the same with the 1795 Europe League Charter. When they were finishing announcing their names, Finch ratified that all PATRI members were present or accounted for. Hugh Rochan did the same for the Europe League.

Finally feeling more like himself, Francis du Motier thanked everyone for coming. "I apologize for the tone of some of my initial comments. We're all understandably tense. I imagine that I hardly need to give the motivation for calling this initial meeting with you, at this time and place. We, like you, are a diverse group, but we all share the similar wish to preserve our nations bordering the Atlantic."

As the attendees relaxed and began to settle down, they listened attentively to the Frenchman despite the chill of the dungeon.

"If any of you other Europe League members feel the need, please offer a correction to my words," du Motier deferentially suggested.

"Go on, Francis," Lord Aplington said in his clipped manner. "I, too, must apologize for my earlier behavior, but no, carry on. I thought you summarized our feelings very well at our League's meeting last February."

"Before you do, though Mr. du Motier, let me first say that some of us also talked quite a bit amongst ourselves these past months. For starters, we have met your request that *the Eagle must fly.* You can see we are here." Gayle Eccles glanced at all the Europeans and continued, "Now, it sounds like we will finally wrestle over the question of whether the *Eagle should land*, the penultimate decision. Let me thank you, ahead of time, for giving us the opportunity to meet and hear the basis for your League's thinking."

"Well then, I will try to state the views from our side of the Atlantic as succinctly as possible." du Motier asked the League member who owned the nearby Chateau de Rouen, "Philippe, do you mind first passing out the summaries of our discussions?"

As the men and women in the room looked over their material, du Motier began to explain the Europe League's reasons for wanting the PACT to go forward now, in 2018. "Of course, ladies and gentlemen, even though it is our League that thinks the action is necessary, both groups must see and agree that it is in America's best interest, as well."

Du Motier used a laser pointer as he directed their attention to an outline projected on a suspended white sheet. "There are many factors that affect present-day international alliances, especially our treasured NATO," he said, and advanced through the next frames. "The increasing military and economic strengths of China and India, as well as the ongoing terrorist activities in the Middle East, Africa, and parts of Central America, have adversely impacted our Atlantic community. Most importantly, though, we are concerned about the social and economic difficulties going on in your own America. These problems greatly affect us in Europe. "

The Frenchman went on and described in detail some of the most vexing examples. As he spoke, du Motier tried to gauge Hamilton and Eccles's reactions, and they appeared to be in agreement. "I have heard many times over the past year that, most of all, America needs a strong national leader. So I ask everyone tonight an easy question: Is that not so?"

Elina Pederson, a voluptuous ex-fashion model from St. Petersburg, affirmed him. "Da. We are connected at the hip to you Americans. If these problems were to overwhelm your America, they are sure to grow and threaten my homeland of Russia as well."

"Ja, Francis, Elina is right. I see it that way, too, maybe more so. Being a federal-conservative party member, I have long argued against the lure of being capricious – it is so easy to get hooked on taking the easy way out. Presently, America's policies are so, how do you say it, Mr. Hamilton – 'Willy-nilly?' " Eric Stahlen pursed his thick lips downward. "From Germany's perspective, many American political leaders only want happy solutions without having any real cost. They are like kids licking their candy while trying to steer little boats without rudders."

"We can talk on and on like this, but to summarize," du Motier intervened, "our Europe League's view is that our so-called 'Western Civilization' is increasingly at risk. Now, you must help decide whether instituting a radically new form of American federal government is the best option to combat the perils that threaten all of us. It should be obvious by now that we think so."

Francis du Motier turned the PowerPoint off, took a sip of wine and paced back and forth, and reiterated, "We feel that the United States needs a far steadier hand on what your famous American poet Whitman once called your 'ship of State.' "

"Mr. du Motier, please explain the implications of your Europe League's decision to my PATRI colleagues," Dean Eccles calmly requested. "I think that I for one know what you are driving at, but the others need to hear more."

"I'm not sure I want to know," Karen Jay-York muttered from the far end of the dungeon. "I was always afraid it might . . ."

Finch put a steadying hand on her shoulder and said, "Shssh, try to listen, Karen. It's our duty to listen –then decide." He thought it best to pour some more wine for them both.

"Dr. Eccles," du Motier said, pausing before cutting to the chase, "if you and your members unanimously agree, both organizations will somehow implement the Pan-Atlantic Community Treaty (the PACT) – dated January 1795."

Scattered murmurs and grumbling echoed in the cool dungeon. "What is this about? We haven't even talked amongst ourselves!" "Are they going to ask us to sign an agreement right away, tonight?" "Damn to Hell! We're all being bullied about – it's not even our own choice!"

Evan Hamilton addressed his fellow PATRI members. "I heard that last comment, Maureen. But no. In the end, it is our own decision whether or not to agree to go along with Monsieur du Motier and the Europe League."

"I feel we're being forced to agree with Mr. du Motier's suggestion," Nicholas Shippen opined, "but most of all, I'm distressed about his fuzzy-sounding thinking."

"No, Nick," Denise Donasti cautioned, "don't be so glum. I've always trusted that we of PATRI will make the right choice and do what's best for America."

"Remind me, Dr. Eccles." Princess Frederickson from Sweden had only vaguely heard about the PATRI overture in 1968, which her father and the other Europe League members had turned down. "If both groups do decide to take the first step together, what is that step? What does it involve?"

Dr. Eccles asked Hamilton for advice and he whispered in her ear, "For now, Gayle, only give generalizations about what would come next."

Gayle Eccles coughed nervously. "'A Note of Action' has been passed down through three American families – my own (the Adams) and the Lees and Hamiltons. This may help answer your question, Princess. Fortunately, my note is small. I brought it with me in case I had to justify my role in our discussions. Remember this was written in 1797, at a time when many of your royal forebears had absolute power."

She adjusted a nearby candle and read aloud from a silken scroll,

> "'In the future, when our PATRI, along with their allies from the Europe League, mutually agree that the PACT must be enacted, a legitimate leader will be enlisted to ascend to an American throne. A Second American Constitution to ratify this new government is hereby signed by all original PATRI patriots and is hermetically sealed in a Franklin-Glass. It should remain somewhere in the secure possession of the society's concierge until the due time.
>
> 'I charge the House of Adams to be the executor of PATRI – responsible with organizing meetings between PATRI and the Europe League."

The dungeon remained stark still. Gayle Eccles interrupted herself, quietly adding, "And having that first meeting is precisely what we're doing tonight. Going on . . .

> "'If and when PATRI and the Europe League agree to activate the PACT, the first step of the PLAN will be the confidential divulgence of a possible American King to the assembled members.

> Signed this day of our Lord, 27 February, 1797
> Geo Wash'"

"A king? This is bull," Maureen Nightbird-Reynolds blurted out. "There are no absolute monarchs in Europe anymore. What's the point to have one in the U.S.?"

Robert Laurens grumbled, "Besides, we can't decide a hare's ass if we don't know the name of this purported kingly candidate."

"I'm taking it with a bit of faith, too, Maureen and Bob," Dr. Eccles replied, "calm down. As Evan said earlier, even I don't have the faintest idea who this possible American king could be, but if and when we all agree on the need to enact the PACT, I guess I'll find out along with the rest of you. Isn't that so, Evan?"

Hamilton smiled thinly as he stood in the shadows and replied, "Indeed."

Gayle Eccles continued more deliberately, "I want to remind everyone that our American forefathers developed PATRI to work with certain European royal families in case – and only in case – the American experiment as a Republic failed. You should know, Monsieur du Motier, that ever since your call to me last March, Mr. Hamilton, General Mason, and I have debated for ourselves whether America has arrived at such a critical juncture. We finally have agreed with you that presently the U.S. has progressive signs of obvious decay. The three of us concluded that, at the least, PATRI should vote to embrace the PACT, and go on from there."

"What you are saying sounds crazy, even treasonous, Professor Eccles," Leone Gutierrez yelled. She hadn't understood much that evening, but she did know firsthand the evil things that happened with dictators in Central America. "This is not good, this – what I'm hearing. No, no, no. Not now – hopefully never!"

Other PATRI members clamored to be heard. Connie Marshall-Rubin turned away as if she was speaking to a stone wall, saying, "I usually go along with the crowd, but no, not this time. I've got to think this one over. It's pretty extreme."

"Things may be bad, Professor, but are they that bad?" Shippen asked sarcastically. "We usually weather-the-weather out in Kansas."

"Too many questions for me. I'm not sure what's going on. I feel like I'm being led by the nose." Finch was clearly having a hard time with all this. He angrily slammed his fist onto a nearby table for emphasis.

Hamilton held his hands out as if to restrain him. "Wait, wait – hold on a minute, Ed. Let me tell you and the others something important. Just a few minutes ago, I received a text from our fellow member, General Philip Mason, back in Maryland. It appears that armed insurrections have broken out this afternoon in several towns along both the Mexican and Canadian borders. Homegrown militias in three Western states have taken up arms against federal installations to further the causes of the Freedom Party. So far, they have only attacked several border patrol stations, but they are reportedly also moving into positions near a naval missile test site in Nevada. I believe you probably know the base, Ed.

"Beside that, Mason texted me in closing that despite this unrest, thankfully all is well thus far along the Potomac."

Hamilton sternly looked around, trying to see whether his words were sinking in. In addition to everything du Motier had talked about, now there was this.

Dr. Eccles decided it was not a good idea to call the question that night. It was too risky for her to try and have PATRI hurriedly decide whether to accept the Europe League's invitation for the '*Eagle to land.*' She and Hamilton could not count on the votes. She concluded saying, "Monsieur du Motier and Sir Ronald, it's obvious that PATRI cannot settle on this important issue tonight. Following our return to America, I will give you our society's decision within the month."

As the men and women started to leave the dungeon, Monsieur du Motier asked no one in particular, "Once again, if there is an American king, who is he?"

Evan Hamilton smiled enigmatically and replied, "As General Mason said, 'all is well on the Potomac.' Trust me, the end will certainly prove the deed."

Weeks later, an encrypted message arrived at the office of Lord Aplington in London and at the estate of Francis du Motier in Aix, France. It was short. *We have decided. The Eagle should land.*

36

Marshall Hall, Maryland

October 2018

"Who do you think *you are*?"

David Winfield was startled by the question.

"Sorry, Dave, I didn't mean to sound so condescending. What I meant to ask was, 'Do you know *who* you are?'"

Suzanne Winfield sat off to the side with the others as they sipped their after-dinner coffees. Her face glowed in the day's fading light and she lightly remarked, "I don't know how David would answer that, Mr. Hamilton, but I have a pretty good idea since I've known him the longest."

"Don't be so sure about that, Suzanne," Philip Mason responded and then smiled in her direction. "We've known him since he was born."

General Mason, a direct descendant of Colonel 'Lighthorse Harry' Lee and Lee's son, Robert E. Lee, had invited the Winfields to dine with him at Marshall Hall and meet a visitor from New York, Mr. Evan Hamilton. David and Suzanne relished coming over to the Mason home in Maryland since it sat directly across the Potomac from their own Woodlawn Mills residence. The General's colonial Maryland home, Marshall Hall, was listed in the National Historic Registry. Mason was the base commander of nearby Fort Marshall, an Army base located next to the Piscataway National Park. His sole duties were said to involve the Domestic Security Operational Force, DOSECOF, a military unit responsible for protecting the District of Columbia.

Evan Hamilton leaned forward and asked Mason, "Going back to what we were talking about in August, Phil, how are things around Washington these days?"

"It's been awfully iffy recently and with the upcoming midterm elections, we're not out of the woods. Dave and Suzanne would probably say the same thing."

"What happened? I only know what I read."

"I can only go into what's not classified. But let me put it this way, there's a lot more going on that's classified than isn't. Most times, it seems to me that America is going to Hell in a hand basket."

Hamilton thought it ironic that his own father had frequently used the same expression. He asked, "Anything new about the New World Patriots that I've read so much about?"

Philip Mason knew that he had to politely deflect Hamilton's query. He had years of experience feigning ignorance about one thing or another, it was part of his trade. 'Misremember' and 'I can't recall' were necessary parts of his professional lexicon. He had developed a well honed, natural-sounding Mason-speak. In fact, as the director of DOSECOF, he intimately knew of these 'Patriots.' He had had several of his elite Protection Force infiltrate the Richmond-based domestic terror group. They determined it to be an organization with roots in radical libertarian politics. Its objective was to destroy any vestige of American imperialism starting with the targeting of powerful Virginia families whom they labeled 'the silent American aristocracy.' In August, Mason had told Evan Hamilton that Woodlawn Mills and the Winfields must be protected at all costs, but had not specified the immediate threat. Because of his concern, General Mason had elected to remain behind when PATRI had met with the Europe League in Montreux in September.

"Frankly," Mason said, "I haven't heard much about them lately, but they're an example of the sort of thing that I see year after year around the District. Wacko groups like that are a dime a dozen."

While they sat comfortably in the living room, David Winfield hadn't been able to focus on their conversation, distracted by a nagging sensation that he hadn't grasped something Hamilton had said earlier. After hesitating, he interrupted, "Going back to what you asked me a while ago, Evan. Maybe I don't fully know who I am, but who does really? What were you implying?"

Hamilton got up from the sofa and moved to the large windowed doors leading to the back gardens. Looking into the setting sun, he pointed west to the two estates across the Potomac. Mount Vernon's red and white cupola blended into the autumn foliage, and beyond, Woodlawn Mills stood on a wooded knoll. "*There* is part of who you are," he said and turned back to David and Suzanne. "*You are a Washington.*"

Hamilton's words hung suspended like the chime of a faraway bell tower.

Philip Mason leaned over and touched Suzanne's shoulder, saying, "It must be quite a shock to hear this, Sue. I can't imagine what you're feeling."

"Uh . . . no." She sat stunned, frowning as she scanned her husband's face. "Dave, do you understand this? Any of this?"

He reached for her hand. "Suze', I'm as much in the dark as . . ."

Mason smiled like a Cheshire cat. "It appears that Mr. Hamilton and I have a lot of explaining to do, so . . ." As Hamilton moved back to his chair, General Mason asked, "How about turning on some lights, Evan?"

"Yes, and let's shed some light for the Winfields as well," Hamilton quipped.

Mason left to make a second pot of coffee, then laughed loudly from the kitchen, "Or would you folks prefer cognac or brandy instead?"

When he returned, General Mason and Evan Hamilton recounted how their own families had kept the Washington-Winfield legacy hidden. "It has been a near-sacred secret," they explained, "for your and your family's safety."

"Secret, why secret?" Winfield had asked.

Over the next hour, they told them about Lawrence Washington and the story of Lawrence's daughter Sarah. Then, they recounted the TIME at Belvoir, the other plots against the Washington-Fairfax family, and the subsequent history of the Winfields down through the years.

General Mason warned that additional dangers might be lurking in the Northern Neck. "Remember, Evan asked me earlier about a group called the New World Patriots? I had originally pleaded ignorance but," Mason confessed, "it appears that they've recently become allied with the Freedom Party. Believe me, they and other such threats have always been around."

Hamilton explained that because of these ongoing dangers, he and Philip Mason were the only ones to know the truth about David's historic bloodline. "We couldn't risk it to be otherwise," he said. "It's for your protection. And as of now, there are only the four of us who know, but for only a little longer. We have plans."

From that day on, Suzanne always remembered that Evan Hamilton had become strangely foreboding as he added, "You are a big part of that plan, Mr. Winfield." She realized that their lives would never be the same.

Hamilton continued, "There's so much more to tell you, but you'll get the idea soon enough. Our machinations will prove themselves in the end."

Suzanne thought to herself that 'machinations' was a rather harsh choice of words. Just then, an antique clock in the adjoining hall chimed the hour and she suddenly felt overwhelmed with exhaustion. The four of them had been talking for so long. "I'm sorry to say this, gentlemen, but I'm fading. Phil, is your offer to stay over still good?"

"Of course, Suzanne, take Becky's room. It's at the top of the stairs to your left. Evan is in the guest room in the back. I had Corcoran get some surgery scrubs and extra clothes at the PX today – hope they fit."

Yawning, she looked over her shoulder. "See you all in the morning. No more secrets, now. Dave, don't be too late."

After she left, General Mason poured glasses of Remy Martin and gave them to the others. "Here's to this evening – the end of the beginning and the beginning of the end." He looked intently at Winfield and added, "Dave, I'm sure all of this has been pretty intense for you."

"You've guessed right on that."

"I'm glad that you and Suzanne understand the critical nature of keeping all this confidential." Mason paced about the room before soberly adding, "Furthermore, I suspect that what we're about to tell you will again be more than you can imagine. Tonight, we are telling you, not asking you, to work with us and be America's leader. You and your family, David, have no other choice."

"Leader? How? You're not suggesting that I somehow get elected President. I'm not cut out to be a politician. It's not in my blood."

"Oh no, my friend, it may not take that particular avenue, but we'll have to see. How it will play out for America remains to be seen."

Over the next hour, as the other two men continued talking, David Winfield found it increasingly impossible to follow their conversation. Soon he faded as well.

Once upstairs, David Winfield carefully pulled the covers back so as not to disturb Suzanne. As the grandfather clock chimed twelve in the front hall, she sleepily turned on her pillow and reached for his hand. "Davey, I'm so tired I can't sleep."

"Shush, hon'. After tonight, there's so much . . ."

As he fell into the bedding, she rolled against his warmth and dreamily pressed against him. Her words were partially muffled by the thick quilt. "I always suspected there was more to you . . . more than just special. Love you."

David and Suzanne fell fast asleep.

37

Fort Marshall, Maryland

October 2018

"Take a look, Dave, do you know anyone on this list?"

Philip Mason turned a piece of paper around on his desk and pushed it over to his friend. The two were sitting together in the general's office overlooking Fort Marshall's parade ground.

Suzanne Winfield could not join them that morning; she had an important appointment at Georgetown University. One of her doctoral candidates was defending his dissertation to her colleagues in the Political Science Department.

"Well right off, I see your and Evan Hamilton's names." Winfield studied the sheet. "Let's see who else . . . There's General Greene from NSA – Eurit does a lot of work with him. Then Bob Laurens from Houston – we did some upgrades for him at the port refineries, a big deal on the Gulf. Give me a second . . . What's Ed Finch doing here? He's in the civil service, a squeaky-wheel kind of guy over at the Department of Navy, in material purchasing."

Winfield looked up and asked, "What's the point, Phil? I don't get it."

Mason smiled enigmatically and pulled a fraying parchment from a drawer. He pushed it across his desk right next to the other. "How about these?"

Winfield looked down at the barely legible signatures. "Give me a minute, I can't read it too well. Let's see: *'George Washington,' 'John Adams,' 'Alexander Hamilton,'* even *'Pierre L'Enfant.'* What is this all about?"

"And there's even my own ancestor," General Mason said proudly pointing to the signature of *'Henry Lee.'* "The names on this older-looking paper represent the real reason that I asked you and Suzanne to come today.

Sorry she couldn't make it, but I understand. I wanted to include Suzanne in our conversation today, but I expect you will tell her everything we discuss soon enough."

Adjusting his chair, Winfield noticed his friend's expression. He had never appeared so intense.

Philip Mason put the two lists aside and said, "Two weeks ago, I was charged by two organizations to make an overture to you, Dave. They delegated me this task since they knew we have been life-long friends."

Winfield turned his cell phone off so that he could give his uninterrupted attention. Mason sounded like he had a lot to say.

"The first step, Dave, was for Evan Hamilton and me to divulge your true lineage over the years, going back to Priscilla Winfield born as Sarah Washington, and hence to her father, Lawrence Washington. George Washington's oldest brother was the true scion of the House of Washington following the death of Augustine Washington, their father.

"Now to cut to the chase. I was asked by both of these groups to get you and Suzanne on board."

"On board? On board what?" Winfield asked. "And more importantly, why should we?"

"Before I start to answer your quite natural questions, give me a moment." General Mason leaned over and retrieving a folded document, unwrapped it, and spread it out on his desk. "I think these discussions may be more clear if you first see how my own Lee family fits in."

Winfield scanned the page.

A Note of Action

In the future, when our PATRI, along with their allies from the Europe League, mutually agree that the PACT must be enacted, a legitimate leader will be enlisted to ascend to an American throne. A Second American Constitution to ratify this new government is hereby signed by all original PATRI patriots and is hermetically sealed in a Franklin-Glass . . .

I also charge that only the Houses of Lee & Hamilton know the true identity of my rightful heir – Priscilla Winfield of Woodlawn Mills . . .

. . . the first step of the PLAN will be the confidential divulgence of a possible American king to the assembled members . . .

. . . Geo Wash'

Winfield was almost too stunned to blurt out, "A king?"

General Mason saw his friend's reaction and cut in, "No – no, don't jump the gun. Let's not start there, Dave. Go back to the beginning of this

Note of Action and we'll examine it line by line. Those two groups that have asked me to talk to you today are identified in the first line – PATRI and the Europe League."

"So?"

Over the next hour, Philip Mason explained the full details about each society – their origins, rationale and the original and current members. He said it had been essential for both groups to remain under the radar over the years As he expounded, Mason repeatedly pointed to the names on the two sheets of paper on his desk for emphasis.

"PATRI essentially represents a shadow government, Dave, for the purpose of preserving the original intents of America's Founding Fathers. It includes having this PACT of mutual assistance between our forebears and certain European royal families. The original PATRI society even went so far as to write what is mentioned here, 'A Second American Constitution.'"

Mason then further dissected his Lee family's Note of Action, going over it like an aggressive lawyer combing through a brief. He summarized, "My family's charge over the years has been to ensure the physical safety of the Winfields."

When he paused, Winfield broke in, "All this history notwithstanding, Phil, it still seems deeply convoluted. Why should I, no Suzanne and I, buy in?"

"Because you are the kind of patriots that each of these forefathers was. Remember that we told you that your distant relative, Priscilla Winfield's uncle, was George Washington – the original leader of PATRI. Since Washington had no issue of his own, you are already tied to us at the hip. But hang with me, Dave, there's another, more personal reason that I think should prompt you to join our cause."

"Give me a break, Phil. What's that?"

"I knew your Dad as a man who, like you, always fought for certain principles. Remember years back? He did what was absolutely right and look what happened to him. He died suddenly. So mysteriously? Unexplained? Hardly. My DOSECOF discovered it to be an assassination, though we couldn't put it down to a specific plot."

"Tell me the details. I trust you, Phil."

Mason shook his head sadly. "It's not worth it, Dave. Suffice it to say that things were done. The perpetrators have since been harshly dealt with, but recently we have identified all sorts of new threats to your family. For instance, those Eurit contracts you lost last spring, remember?"

"How could I forget, Phil – three of them worth three billion in all."

General Mason tapped on his desk with his pencil. "Since you guys are only one of thousands of firms involved with the Defense Department and the SEC, your own troubles can get lost in the woods. But Dave, we suspect that certain folks are specifically targeting you. One of your three losses involved hefty bribes from lobbyists and a hedge fund to two senators and three folks on the House Appropriations Committee. The other two apparently fell victim to several ill-construed rulings made by some shady federal judges. Once again, we've got some leads but it's hard to prove when the system is increasingly rigged against honest folks like you."

"After everything you've said, Phil, I still don't know. You can understand that Suze' and I were more than a little perplexed after the other night. I'd like to help you in any way I can, but we both have misgivings. Believe me, the two of us have not spoken about any of this to anyone – you and Hamilton made that demand quite clear."

"You say 'misgivings,' Dave. About everything we've told you?"

"I'll start with our number one concern, something you implied last weekend. Frankly, I'm not cut out for being the leader of your group, this 'PATRI.' It's not in my makeup."

Mason smiled knowingly at his friend. "Perhaps – but it's in your blood. It may end up with you becoming much more than just PATRI's leader."

Winfield hardly appeared to hear the general's words. "Look at it my way, Phil. You and Evan Hamilton didn't exactly say how I would fit into your plans. Before I'm committed, I need to know."

Mason stood and stretched. "I purposely kept your role ambiguous. Remember, last Sunday I said that 'it remains to be seen.' "

His childhood friend didn't appear any more open than he had been a few days earlier. Frustrated, Winfield asked, "Don't beat around, Phil. Give me a clue."

General Phillip Mason leaned back and said, "Since you asked, all right, I will."

"He said what? You gotta be kidding, Dave."

David Winfield met with his wife in her office on his way home after seeing Philip Mason at Fort Marshall. "I know – it makes absolutely no sense but this Note of Action that Phil showed me from George Washington was dated 1797 and addressed to his ancestor, Henry Lee. It seemed authentic enough."

"Was it verified, somehow?" Professor Suzanne Winfield had a well-earned reputation at Georgetown for analyzing source material.

"He made a phone call to Mr. Hamilton in New York City. Within minutes, a cyber secure PDF appeared on Phil's computer. Hamilton's family has long kept a note similar to Mason's except for one paragraph. And Suze', it was also signed by George Washington in 1797."

"So where's that leave us? I'm not at all sure, Davey. You tell me. Are you saying that these two guys want to go out and proclaim an American king? Good luck with that." Suzanne became frantic whenever she couldn't put her head around something. "Okay, I'll ask it again in plain English," she exclaimed. "Where the hell does that leave us?"

"Slow down, honey." He tried to calm her with a hug. "Lighten up."

That evening the two sat in their Woodlawn Mills' home library and while Maria took care of their children, privately discussed how their lives had turned so topsy-turvy. Philip Mason had also suggested that morning that David and Suzanne could at least take a certain baby step. "As long as the matter remains undiscovered, he said, it might answer a lot of our concerns."

"And what was that teeny step, love?"

"He seemed deferential for a general officer. He told me that he didn't feel comfortable in giving me orders, but he said that if we did what he asked, we would be doing, what he phrased 'a most necessary task.' "

"And what was that, dear friend?"

"Phil Mason only said, 'Somehow get me Washington's Bastille Key.' "

38

Mount Vernon

November 2018

Suzanne Winfield perched on a wide-based ladder and adjusted the mistletoe above the doorway. The Winfields and some friends had come to Mount Vernon in order to help the head curator Mary Roberts hang Christmas decorations. "Where did you put the wreaths and lights?" Suzanne asked after getting down and going into an adjoining room.

Mary Roberts remained kneeling as she unloaded two-dozen poinsettias. "Frank Yurkovitz told me there would be ten boxes for you folks outside on the back steps."

"Stay right here in the dining room, Mrs. Roberts. I'll find them. Please holler if you need help." Suzanne turned and directed her friends, "Georgi and Fred, how about working upstairs?"

As the two couples and curator placed assorted holiday decorations throughout the house, Frank Yurkovitz and his young assistant observed them via video from a control center at the Park's entrance. They could see David Winfield carrying garlands and red containers half-filled with floral clay from the porch.

"Suze', where do you want the planter containers?" he hollered.

"By the baseboards for now. We'll eventually place them along the stairwell."

Carrying a string of Christmas lights, he set up a tall ladder. "Hey, Suze'," he called out making sure that his voice would carry, "go tell Mrs. Roberts to call the control center. I need this monitor in the corner stopped for a few minutes so that I can hang some lights."

Suzanne returned shortly and announced, "Mrs. Roberts is about half-finished. In the meantime, she called the gatehouse. A Frank Yurkovitz is on duty and said that all you have to do is gently hold the camera to one side and touch a button on top – that will disengage the rotation. When you're done, he told me, you touch the same button and it will reset."

David smiled and waved up at the lens. "Even though I can't hear you, Frank, thanks. I didn't want the strings and wires to get caught."

The two guards in the control room saw his fingers moving in front of the recorder's lens, but once David brought the sweep to a stop, facing rightwards, they could only hear him working in the home's Passage.

"Suze', can you check on the Breinings upstairs now? I should be all right."

Fred Yurkovitz and his young assistant saw Suzanne appear on one of the monitors sweeping the upstairs' locations. Georgi Breining stretched and shook out her hair in one of the bedrooms. As she did, she moaned aloud and threw her shoulders back. Looking on wide-eyed, the elderly Yurkowitz wheezed, "She sure is a looker, Eddie."

"Which one, Mr. Yurkovitz?"

"Guess, Eddie. Goodness me, what a pair! . . . Uh, the ladies, I mean."

At that instant, the two watchmen heard Dave Winfield say, "Let me get the . . ." Suddenly a crashing noise was heard, and the guards nearly bolted from the control room. Winfield immediately called out, "Don't worry, that was my pliers, Mrs. Roberts! . . . it fell onto the floor. I'm all right."

When the corner monitor resumed its usual sweeping motion a minute later, Yurkovitz and Eddie were relieved to see that the Mansion's Passage appeared undisturbed except for the new lights hanging along the crown molding. They observed Winfield carefully going down the ladder. Once again, Yurkovitz stared lasciviously at Georgi Breining descending the spiral stairs along with Suzanne Winfield.

Shortly, Mary Roberts and David stood together outside on the portico rubbing pieces of green floral clay off their hands. "It looks splendid, Suzanne," Mary Roberts called back through the door. "This will make quite an impression this year."

Winfield put a closed plantar box aside and came next to Suzanne, whispering, "It's done, Suze' – it's done."

Outside in the guardhouse, Yurkovitz shifted uncomfortably and blurted, "I wonder, Eddie, if she knows that I saw near everything. Gosh darn, I wish I could have seen even more. That Georgi-woman is sure loaded!"

December 2018

David Winfield clumsily opened the Old Tomb's door with a duplicate of Washington's Bastille Key. "It works!" he exclaimed.

During his decorating of Mount Vernon's Passageway, he had removed the home's Bastille Key only for a minute, pressed both sides into malleable floral clay, and quickly cleaned the original key before returning it to its glass case on the wall. Then, he had secretly taken the clay imprint to a renowned lock and key company, J.R. Badertscher and Sons of Arlington, who had fashioned a copy.

David entered the narrow opening and adjusted his night scope eyewear. Inside, he whispered back, "It's here, Sam, on the lower ledge right where Evan Hamilton said it would be."

Earlier, Colonel Sam O'Donahue, a veteran member of the clandestine military unit DOSECOF, had stealthily led the two of them up from Dogue Creek. Although it was a foggy night, the colonel was glad he had packed some lightweight fog maker units to place in front of the Old Tomb's surveillance cameras.

O'Donahue and two of his crack commandos from the Fort Marshall barracks had been encamped at neighboring Woodlawn Mills for the past week. The visibility was less than ten feet when the four men took two kayaks from the Winfield estate's private launch site soon after nightfall. With their cloth-covered paddles, they silently navigated along Dogue Creek to the southernmost corner of Mount Vernon. Colonel O'Donahue and his men had often reconnoitered these waters and they well knew the vagaries of the Potomac's strong tidal currents.

The men heard sniffing, snorting sounds amidst fallen branches and crackling brush as their kayaks moved in the creek's shallows. Winfield understood that the three pairs of vicious watchdogs who prowled Mount Vernon had been surgically muted. This allowed the roving packs to sneak up soundlessly, and attack any unfortunate intruder.

"Closer, get closer," O'Donahue whispered, nearly upsetting his boat.

Winfield put his paddle aside and threw chunks of meat onto the shore. The dogs' scuffling noises in the undergrowth soon ceased. After beaching their crafts, Colonel O'Donahue was relieved to find the Dobermans and Rottweilers sleeping like babies. An expert at the National Poison Control Center had recommended a quick-acting chemical. Although the effects would be prompt, the specialist had warned that there might be problems with overdosing. O'Donahue's two sergeants had stayed back at the beachhead with injectable antidotes for the drugged sentry dogs.

Winfield awkwardly lifted a large box off the ledge, gave it to Colonel O'Donahue and hoarsely whispered, "Thank heavens it's not too heavy. Maybe twenty pounds or so. I'm amazed. It looks to be in surprisingly good condition."

O'Donahue scurried backwards like a lizard, his bent elbows and knees sliding on the thick moss as he cradled the box. He whispered in a ragged voice, "Let's quickly look around, Mr. Winfield. Anything else?"

"No, I see some old digging tools," Winfield said, "but nothing much else. Wait up, I'm coming out, but I need to be sure to lock the vault back up."

Once they were outside, Colonel O'Donahue urgently insisted, "We've got to be sure to take our fog makers with us, they could be traced. The surveillance camera lenses in this cold air will stay fogged up for a while and hide our retreat, but we need to be out'a here pronto. I'll take the box, you grab the canisters."

The two men gingerly edged backwards toward the creek bank. As they did, they covered their tracks using some fallen pine branches, and used a neutralizing chemical spray to erase their scents. Each was quietly satisfied after they made it down to the two sergeants tending the anesthetized watchdogs.

O'Donahue commanded, "Give the dogs the antidote, Ed — we've got to be off."

Woodlawn Mills

Colonel O'Donahue and David Winfield stared down at a twenty-four-inch-long box lying on a butcher-block table. A lone light bulb hanging in the well-stocked wine cellar harshly illuminated the locked container's side panels. On either side of the case, there were bronzed panels of ornate, Romanesque scenes.

The colonel rapped the sides and listened to its resonating tone. "I have never known ebony wood to sound like this. It's almost like it's reinforced somehow."

"Let's try to open it, Colonel, with the key that I had made. It already opened the door to the Vault back there. Interesting, though, that there are two large keyholes here, one in the middle and another on the right."

Winfield put his duplicated key into the right keyhole first. It engaged after several jiggles, but then it turned no more. The catch held fast.

"How about the middle one, Mr. Winfield?" O'Donahue suggested.

This time the key didn't even fit.

"Well, sir, it looks like no luck. Maybe this box of General Mason's needs a different key or maybe this is all a ruse."

"I certainly don't know," Winfield admitted. But standing in the harsh light, he already knew what Evan Hamilton had told him, "David, two Bastille Keys must be used simultaneously in order to open the Caesar Box."

Colonel O'Donahue impatiently looked at his watch. "Whatever – good luck. It's been a long night, Mr. Winfield, and my men need to get back to the base by sunrise."

"Thanks, Colonel. Thanks again for all your help." Winfield locked the wine cellar and walked Colonel O'Donahue and his men to an unmarked black sedan.

As they drove off, he yawned in bone-deep physical and emotional exhaustion, but as he made his way back inside his house, he felt heartened knowing that at least for the moment his task was done.

39

Washington, D.C.

January 2019

"Thanks for coming, Mr. Jefferson. As I told you, I'm writing an article about new faces in Congress. Lunch, of course, is on me." The *Washington Post* columnist warmly greeted the freshman Congressman. "When I heard the rumor, I couldn't believe the coincidence. After all, I'm a seventh-generation Madison. What about you?"

"Direct from Thomas Jefferson, eighth generation."

"Here we are, a Madison and a Jefferson back together in the nation's capital." John Madison laughed. "Yogi Berra certainly said it right, 'de ja vu all over again!' "

The youthful Representative smiled at the remark and said, "No matter our personal histories, it's a privilege to meet you, sir. I hope you get what you need today."

"First off, there's no right or wrong in this interview, Patrick or 'Pat' – can I call you that? I'm looking to do a series on the fresh perspectives that you and your fellow first-time legislators are bringing to the upcoming Congressional session."

The tall, auburn-haired Democratic Representative of the 12th District in Illinois had an appealing twinkle in his eyes as he said, "I'm afraid though, Mr. Madison, that many of my ideas may not seem particularly fresh."

The newsman had been looking forward to meeting the Illinois Congressman ever since Jefferson's stunning upset of an incumbent the previous November. He was currently on academic leave from Southern Illinois University where he was an Associate Professor in the College of Agricultural Sciences.

As the two were served generously layered sandwiches, Jefferson looked around and saw that many of the other patrons were in the midst of so-called 'power lunches.' He realized that he should have expected it. After all, he was in Washington now.

John Madison prefaced, "Hope you don't mind me taking notes during our lunch." Jefferson easily agreed and the columnist began, "First, give me a little background, Patrick, while we tackle these sandwiches."

"There's really not much to say," Jefferson mumbled as he chewed a potato chip. "Thirty-five, single, an academician . . ."

"Your family?"

"I grew up in Indiana. My Dad was the Dean of Engineering at . . ."

"Was?"

"He died two years ago in that accident near the Muncie regional airport."

"I think I remember. Yes, he and several other faculty from the University . . . it was national news. And the rest of your family?"

"My mother decided to move in with one of my three sisters. She thrives on being close to her grandchildren. Family's next to God for all of us Jeffersons."

"Where do they live?"

"We're scattered about. Wisconsin is home for Mom and my oldest sister. My two other sisters are in northern Ohio and me – Illinois." Jefferson stopped and took a bite of his tuna melt. "Wow, we don't have food this good in Carbondale."

During their lunch, Jefferson detailed how his upbringing, schooling and teaching vocation had played a large part in his recent election. "I've always been interested in politics, Mr. Madison. It's in my blood. But it's not politics as usual."

"How so, Mr. Jefferson? Can you elaborate on that?"

"Freedoms of all sort are pretty important to me. Look at Southern Illinois University or at any other university, for that matter. Academic freedoms are the keystone of any educational institution. This central credo has probably led me to have what some people call certain 'libertarian tendencies.' "

"I happen to agree with you, Mr. Jefferson, although there have been many times when I've seen the word 'freedom' used to justify near-anarchy."

"Whatever . . . but basically freedom is always worth it in the end."

"But taking that as a given, what are you most concerned about? What kind of government do you want?"

"I'll tell you what my family, friends, and most of the people in my part of Illinois are concerned about, Mr. Madison. Plain and simple – the size and power of the federal government that starts right here in Washington."

John Madison took a bite of his reuben and asked, "Could you expand on that?"

Jefferson paused. "There are all sorts of things attacking our basic freedoms. Internet censorship, NSA surveillance, and the unfair uses of eminent domain are only some examples. You know, you've seen them."

Madison wasn't too surprised that Jefferson sounded so intense. He had seen that kind of fire-in-the-belly before. "I don't want to question your credentials, Pat, but are you sure you're a Democrat? At times, it seems that your ideas sound more like the tenets of the Freedom Party but perhaps not as conservative."

Jefferson smiled and waved him off. "Remember though, Mr. Madison, even these Freedom Party folk occasionally have good ideas. Some people say that I'm such a 'red-state libertarian' in some of my views that I'm 'radical' in my thinking. That shows what labels mean – little, I'd suggest."

Jefferson wiped his mouth on a napkin before continuing, "I suppose that since I'm a college professor you probably expected me to be some sort of Democratic Party-firebrand espousing socialism. But no, wrong – I favor good old-fashioned, local-is-best traditional values. That's the way we are in the Midwest and that's who I am."

Madison nodded. "You should know that in many ways, I happen to agree with you, Pat."

Jefferson pushed his plate to the side as he added, "My point, Mr. Madison, is that I'm afraid America has gotten so diverse and unwieldy that the federal government feels compelled to do something for one group, while at that same time needs to placate another. I call it a 'we'll fix it for you' government. It is like a fussy farmer running after all his animals, going this way and that desperately trying to please them all, and in the end pleasing none.

"I believe you asked earlier, John, what kind of government I wanted? Certainly not anything like this. Why can't people be allowed to figure things out on their own? Most problems usually sort themselves out anyway."

Madison tried to more thoroughly understand Jefferson's thinking, "I take this to mean that most of all, you champion the rights of individuals and favor giving more powers to the individual states and local institutions rather than developing an even stronger federal government."

"Absolutely! We may sometimes get in trouble for espousing liberties, but in fact protests, even an occasionally violent one, are necessary for any sort of democracy to survive. Speaking out keeps us from falling into the hands of tyrants."

Jefferson hotly added, "When all's said and done, the folks that live around me in the Midwest don't want people living elsewhere telling them what to do. And that even goes for their neighbors!"

"What about your own Democratic Party's leadership? Aren't you afraid they'll force you to take positions you might not want to take?" Madison closely studied the young Congressman's reaction.

Jefferson smiled and matter-of-factly replied, "Mr. Madison, sir, if my party's caucus ever forced me to take a certain stand, any stand, I wouldn't do it. I don't like being told what to do even though the lobbyists certainly try. Does anyone?"

Sitting opposite, Madison scribbled: *PJ seems very pleasant, quite independent, sure of himself, he seems a kindred spirit echoing many of my own opinions, appears docile on the outside but tough and principled, needs to be watched . . . could certainly amount to something.*

Patrick Jefferson checked the time and said in apology, "Sorry, Mr. Madison, I nearly forgot. There's a group photograph for freshman Representatives in the rotunda at two."

"I understand, Pat. You've been a great interview. We've covered quite a bit. You go ahead, I'll handle the tab." As Jefferson eased out of the booth, Madison suggested, "We'll have to try to get together some other time. After all, we're sort of fraternal twins given our family connections."

"Right – I'd look forward to doing that," Jefferson replied as he stood to leave. "I'll email you soon but for now, I gotta be running. Again, thanks."

On his way to the subway, Patrick Jefferson texted Holly Rhyne: *R U OK 4 2NI?* He had first met Holly at a recent reception for new government employees. She had graduated from the University of Maryland two years ago and shared an apartment along the C&O canal with an airline attendant. With her bubbly personality, Holly, an intern for a prominent Senator from Kentucky, had taken the initiative and got him further settled. Her skill at social networking as well as her familiarity with the District helped her quickly locate a rental for Patrick only two blocks from her own.

As he reached the METRO platform, the vibrator on his iPhone hummed. He was buoyed by the message: *I M! C U @ KS @ 8.* KS, the Kapital Saloon, was their special watering hole on Wisconsin Avenue.

As he viewed her reply, Jefferson felt the gust of an oncoming train and made sure to step behind the yellow caution line. He laughed to himself, hoping that the silly grin on his face didn't break the photographer's camera later that afternoon.

40

Chateau de Rouen
Lausanne, Switzerland
February 22, 2019

"Does the key fit? . . . Yours, that is."

As Evan Hamilton and a second man kneeled together on a rug, David Winfield stood off in an adjoining room. A day earlier, he had given Hamilton a thick seven-inch key copy after he arrived from Washington with General Philip Mason.

Monsieur du Motier glanced over at Hamilton. They frowned in frustration as each attempted to use his separate Bastille Key on the box, which General Mason had brought to the meeting. Both men understood that the keys had to be simultaneously engaged in order to open the uniquely named Caesar Box.

"I'm sure these are the right instruments, but perhaps the catches are rusted."

Hamilton told the assembled persons that George Washington and Alexander Hamilton had placed certain items within this decorated container for safekeeping. Everyone else kept looking on, fascinated by the ornate carvings on the box's sides and lid. The two kneeling men continued without success to try to turn their keys.

The select men and women from the United States and Europe were gathered together once again on the shores of Lake Geneva, this time at the palatial Chateau de Rouen. The host was the scion of the House of Rouen and a direct descendant of M. Talleyrand, an important figure in both 18th century France and America. Although not of royal descent, for years his Rouen family had played a pivotal role in the financial institutions of Europe. That afternoon, the guests were gathered in the chateau's spacious and naturally lit Grand Room. Floor-to-ceiling windows looked out on snow-capped Alps glimmering against the late winter sky. In the foreground, terraced vineyards led precipitously down to the motorway and rail line running along the lake.

"What do you suppose is in this impressive box?" Denise Donasti asked Elina Romanov-Pederson who was standing next to her.

The Russian countess replied with an enigmatic smile, "The two of us perhaps could have a wagon load of ideas. Maybe there are bones in it, da?" Her attention was suddenly diverted by a late arrival and she welcomed Hugh Rochan warmly. "Oh Hugh, how are you, love? I missed you last night."

His corporate jet had been diverted on the way from California, making him the last Europe League member to arrive. Rochan greeted her with a kiss on both cheeks and exclaimed, "I am delighted to see you again, Elina. Your husband?"

"Not at all like you, my love, but then who could be?" She giggled while giving him a familiar embrace. "You're such a flirt."

The two men who had been struggling with the formidable locks finally gave up. Hamilton leaned back and asked, "Monsieur Rouen, could you see if one of your workers can get us what we call 'Liquid Wrench' or some other anti-rust solvent?"

"*Oui, mon ami,* certainly, yes." The slim, athletic-looking owner of the chateau left for a moment and quickly returned with a small tin container. He had General Mason tip the heavy container on its side so that he could liberally squirt the solvent into both keyholes.

"We certainly don't want to cut through it," the general remarked as he lifted the box onto a sturdy table. "We can't afford to damage any contents."

Hamilton and Francis du Motier reinserted their Bastille Keys. This time, there was an audibly synchronous 'click-click.' The four men exhaled in relief and du Motier exclaimed, "There, we've got it. The Caesar Box, open at last!"

All the others gathered around the immense oak table as General Mason propped the lid open. As he did, a musty odor escaped into the room.

Sir Ronald Farrington, the immaculately dressed Lord Aplington, stepped forward and along with Evan Hamilton, took immediate charge. He frowned as he handled the first of several enclosed objects. "One of these must surely be the PACT, our original agreement."

Farrington lifted out a semilucent, longitudinal glass tube closed at both ends. It was carefully cradled on a sling fashioned by two silk handkerchiefs resting between two tarnished brass cylinders. A hand-decorated porcelain urn was nestled against the near side of the wooden box.

"Let's see . . .we should probably start with this," Farrington said as he slowly turned the tube in his hands. He thought he could recognize a familiar design on a sealed parchment that was stored within the glass container.

"But how best to open it? . . . And should we?" du Motier asked.

"It looks like certain Franklin-designed storage tubes that I've seen at the Smithsonian," Katy Blitz, a respected curator at the National Gallery, commented.

"Mind if I take a look?" Dr. Maureen Nightbird-Reynolds came over and carefully held the cylinder. "Yes, it's similar to my own, an ingenious device that my distant relative Benjamin Franklin, and his grandson Frederick Reynolds, fashioned in order to keep important paper records from deteriorating. The technique cleverly utilized inert gases."

"I propose that we get on with it, *mes amis*," du Motier impatiently remarked. "It seems this box contains many other objects as well – so please go on."

"You make your point well, Francis." Hamilton took the glass cylinder from Dr. Nightbird-Reynolds and looked to the back of the room. "Monsieur Rouen, I hate to bother you, yet again, but it looks like we'll need some sort of scratch-file."

The Swiss chateau owner excused himself and soon returned carrying a pair of leather gloves, protective eyewear and a sharp file. "As you requested, Mr. Hamilton." He bowed in jest, adding, "Of course, let me know if you need anything else."

Hamilton dragged the file across one end of the tapered glass tube, and as he sharply snapped the end off, an odorless gas whooshed from the small aperture. Then, with the point of the file, he teased out a tightly wrapped piece of thick sheepskin.

"Let me take a look if you don't mind, Mr. Hamilton." Without waiting for a reply, Lord Aplington picked up the curled parchment and placed it next to the Caesar Box. Despite obvious aging and wear along its edges, the sheepskin had held up surprisingly well. He fingered the thick red wax seal and quickly confirmed his earlier suspicion. "Yes, just as I surmised . . . George the III's lion seal. My friends, this is authentic. I suspect that this first item from the box here may be our PACT."

"Come now, Ronald, why would . . .?"

"Even though it has been known by all of us to exist in some form, somewhere, our two societies have never known precisely where it was."

As Sir Ronald spoke, Hamilton and du Motier furtively glanced at one another. Both men knew that for more than two hundred years, the two PACT copies had been in the possession of their families, instead of being stored in this Caesar Box.

General Mason moved the ebony box to one side while leaving the sealed parchment package in front of Lord Aplington. "No wonder it's heavier than it appears, folks – look here," he said, pointing out the velvet-covered, thin steel-lattice grid tacked in place along the box's inner lid and walls.

Francis du Motier moved forward and remarked, "I have always been told that the most famous Marquis de Lafayette was a clever man. This box shows it to be true. After he received a note from George Washington requesting a particularly strong storage piece, Gilbert du Motier had expert craftsmen from Sorrento fabricate this very container.

"I understand that he ordered them to place an additional lock from a door of the Bastille, which he had stored at his farm, onto the right side of his storage trunk. The two locks each required a different key and George Washington already had the second key in his possession. Thereafter, the Marquis had his custom-made box shipped to Virginia – and this is what we have here." du Motier touched the purple velvet of the innermost lining and observed, "Obviously, this container was able to safely store certain objects for the purposes of his American friends."

As the Frenchman spoke, several guests moved forward and fingered the intricate outer carvings of the Caesar Box.

"Excuse me, but at this rate we could be here for another year or two," Ed Finch interrupted. "Let's back off and again give Mr. Farrington our undivided attention."

"Thank you, kind sir. Now, then . . . I recommend that we first ascertain the contents of this rolled up parchment piece – the one that I am holding."

"Why do this first, Lord Aplington?" Marquises de la Caves had just returned to the room and overheard his last comments.

"Looking closely, albeit perfunctorily, it is the only bit of all these items that I presume to recognize. The packet's wax seal has the distinctive emblem of the Hanover royal house. As I said earlier, this suggests to me that this may be the original PACT that we seek. It makes sense, at least to me, that this agreement has been sequestered in America for safekeeping to keep both parties satisfied. Do you have an opener, Monsieur Rouen?"

Gayle Eccles sensed that everyone was getting tense – they had come to a critical juncture. Once the seal was broken, it might be opening a Pandora's box.

When Sir Ronald got a letter opener, he deftly cut through the thick, lion-embossed red wax seal. "Oh, this is interesting," he observed. "Look at this – there is a smaller note held within another. What is this all about? I will read this additional letter after I first read what looks to be the important piece."

Lord Aplington put on his reading glasses. "Oh sorry, my friends. Although it is quite well preserved, this is not the PACT. Instead, it is titled

'The King's Promise.' It is dated 1787, shortly after the American Rebellion concluded. Since the seal of George the Third was intact, it seems to have never been previously read. Let me read it now,

"The King's Promise

'To: George Washington, Esq.

'Being that you are reading this, sir, I surmise that you recognize at this time that you need my assistance in restoring civility and order to my former colonies of America. Lord Fairfax of my Privy Council and his nephew, George William Fairfax recently of Virginia, assure me of your good nature and noble character. As with the Roman general, Cincinnatus, you can assuredly lead honorable men once again.

'On reading this, please allow that I intend not to be meddlesome but rather to be merely of service to you and your aims. Please communicate the manner of assistance that you might require directly to the Crown. All manner of support is at your disposal.

'His Highness, George III of England
Attested by Lord Fairfax   May 1787'"

Sir Ronald coughed, adding, "This does not seem to concern us today, but it is amazing to me that this was never opened by Washington in his lifetime, given that he had to deal with so much domestic turmoil in America's early years. This 'Promise' appears to have been written solely to Washington – and suggests a lingering sentiment on the part of King George for the welfare of his former colonies in America."

The Englishman took a drink of tonic and put the outer document aside. Then, he carefully unwrapped a delicate tie that bound the inner rice paper note. Farrington silently glanced over the letter and mused, "Interesting. How very strange."

Catherine Bonard had previously had experiences sorting through the voluminous letters of the French Court filled with her Bourbon family's intrigues. "Judging from where it lies tucked inside the larger parchment," she said, "King George and his Councilors would certainly have been aware of this particular note as well. They obviously must have allowed it to be included for some reason."

Sir Ronald Farrington raised his hand in order to be heard. "Allow me to review this small note as well, then." He read,

"'My dear Royal Highness, Your Excellency, King George

'You had raised several questions when last I saw you at Windsor. No doubt you were confused by my news and I trust by this explanation, it will be clearer to you.

'I have certain irrefutable knowledge that George Washington, Esquire, former General and the owner of Mount Vernon, Virginia, though childless himself, has a previously unknown direct descendent for his House of Washington. His niece, Sarah Washington, is the sole surviving daughter of his deceased brother, Lawrence. My dearly departed friend, Anne Fairfax Washington Lee, is her true birth mother.

'Because of important concerns for her personal safety, this Sarah Washington was raised under a pseudonym as Priscilla Farris-Fairfax. She is now known as Priscilla Winfield, the wife of Jonathan Winfield of the Northern Neck in Virginia.

'As you asked me recently, kind sir, this should serve to legitimize the person and her family line such that she or her heirs could rightfully serve as an American monarch for your plans.

'This is my response to your concerns about whether any such person exists . . . though my assurance is not, by itself, a necessary proof.

'Your most humble subject,
Sally Cary Fairfax

Attested by Lord Aplington; Sir Reginald Farrington
Somerset   May 1787'"

Sir Ronald Farrington took off his reading glasses and raised his bushy eyebrows, measuring the reactions of those seated nearby. "The letter seems to be properly witnessed and signed by a distant relative of mine . . . Yes, the Reginald Farrington referenced here was the sixth Lord Aplington, a member of the King's Privy Council."

Maureen Reynolds, an expert at deducing information, spoke out, "I'm not sure, but isn't the friend of Mr. Hamilton and General Mason that we all met earlier at breakfast a Winfield? Maybe I'm missing something, but still . . . "

Up to then, David Winfield had remained inconspicuous in a side reading room. He felt everyone's eyes fall upon him as he entered the chateau's Grand Room. "Yes, you're right. I am one of the same Winfields . . . of the Northern Neck of Virginia."

"That's why General Mason and I invited him here, Maureen," Hamilton said, pointing to the note of Sally Fairfax. "There will be much, much more that we'll discover in this box, I suspect."

Hamilton walked over to the new guest. "Let me point out that my friend, Mr. David Winfield, has not been previously known to be connected to our cause. Some of you – Bob, Ed, and General Greene – already know David from your earlier business connections, but most of you haven't heard of him at all. General Mason and I felt it best that during this second conjoint meeting between our societies, he should be here in person. In fact, were it not for his actions," he said, "this Caesar Box would not be here at all."

Leone Gutierrez raised a shrill objection. "Evan, if most of us have never met Mr. Winfield before, how can we be sure of his loyalty? After all, that's what we're about."

"Leone is right, Evan. Don't forget, he's not a member of PATRI like the rest of us." Karen York was perturbed about the evident loss of confidentiality. Each of their fifteen ancestors had taken an original binding pledge years before.

"Don't be so sure, Ms. York, not so. See here – " Hamilton retrieved the two- hundred-year-old roster of the original PATRI members at the 1797 meeting held at William Shippen's home. He had carried it from New York in his valet case and opened it on a corner table. "Look closely here to see who's missing. Which founding patriot of our society listed in our original roster dated February 22, 1797 has never been represented by a descendent over the years PATRI has met? That is . . . until now – *George Washington*!"

A collective gasp was heard in the high-ceilinged room.

General Mason stepped forward and added, "Now that the message is out, let me say that it has been my Lee-Mason family's singular duty over the years to guard the Winfields. It is a near-sacred task – protecting George Washington's bloodline."

"None of this makes sense to me at all." The statuesque Elina Romanov-Pederson threw up her hands. She spoke with a thick accent. "I need to know about the PACT that one of my ancestors supposedly signed, not some fancy nonsense like a personal promise from the King of England to General Washington."

Hamilton again unlocked his leather valet case and raised a hand to calm the fiery Russian. "Actually, Sir Ronald will not find the PACT in this Caesar Box. Acting as PATRI's concierge, its keeper-of-the-keys, I have brought the American copy of this treaty from my Hamilton family bank vault that has also stored PATRI's roster. Mr. du Motier assures me that the European copy remains hidden at his Aix estate for safekeeping. As of now, no one living, including Francis and myself, has read it."

Hamilton bent over and retrieved a bound document from a courier's folder within the case. He carried it over to Sir Ronald Farrington and said, "Now might be an appropriate time for all of us to see and hear the PACT."

"Before you do, Sir Ronald, does anyone besides me need a break?" Gayle Eccles spoke for the others. She had only known of the existence of the PACT through an oral narrative passed down by her Adams's family. She imagined that every person in the room would want to give his or her undivided attention once they started to hear Sir Farrington's reading of the actual document.

"Good idea, Gayle," Francis du Motier said. "Monsieur Rouen, could you point the way to the lavatory facilities for anyone that needs them?"

As many PATRI and League members took leave, the few remaining persons came over and met David Winfield during the break. Trays of croissants, fresh fruit and cheese as well as Perrier drinks were brought in from an adjoining pantry. In a reserved manner, several guests surrounded the imposing patrician of Virginia and asked about his background.

"When did you know?"

"Who told you?"

"What do you think about all this?"

Winfield bent forward and took a deep drink of sparkling water and politely answered each in turn. "I learned of this not more than three months ago from Mr. Hamilton and General Mason. I'm not sure what to think, but I am here to find out like the rest of you."

Philip Mason remained at his side ready to edit any unguarded responses.

"Yes, and . . ." Connie Marshall-Rubin, an attorney from Ohio, did not want this Mr. Winfield to duck her line of questioning.

"It was at General Mason's house. He had my wife and me over for dinner."

Marshall-Rubin remained skeptical. "So it's all hearsay. He told you what? That you have some sort of a Washington family connection? That's not definitive proof."

"On that you are right, but you can see that *they* were right about the key at Mount Vernon. General Mason and Mr. Hamilton certainly knew about that. Somehow, that should mean something."

Marshall-Rubin persisted. "Again, how do you personally sit with all this?"

Winfield understood her skepticism. "Truly, I'm accepting it on faith so far. I'm wondering as much as you and everyone else. What this all means, where it leads, Mrs., uh. ."

The civil service administrator, Ed Finch, saw Winfield's discomfort and came over to lighten the mood. "Dave, Ed Finch here. Haven't seen you in a while. Your company did a great job with the naval guidance system last year. But this George Washington connection of yours is something else. Let me say, it blows my mind."

"Good to see you again, Ed. You and your section at the Department have always been really committed to excellence – I like that. Phil Mason recently told me that you were in PATRI, too. That figures. I've always preferred warriors to worriers."

The raven-haired Spanish princess, Maria de la Caves, leaned forward and demurely asked, "How do you stay in such good shape?" She moistened her lower lip as she eyed the handsome American.

As Winfield smiled in response, Queen Frederickson sat nearby and was similarly taken by the imposing American. He reminded her of her late father.

Hamilton enjoyed seeing the impression that Winfield was having on the two European royals. He was glad others could easily recognize what General Phil Mason and he saw – an attractive, charismatic fellow, a natural leader. "But then," he thought, "that should be no surprise. It was in Winfield's genes."

Gayle Eccles clapped her hands and interrupted the women's musings. "Everyone, please, let's get back to the reception. We've got hours to go, I'm sure."

The dark, curly-haired Italian, Marcello Bonapiento, came up behind her and playfully tapped her waist. "You look so, so remarkable when you take charge, la incarico. I like women like that."

Dean Eccles pushed the playboy away and hissed under her breath, "Hush now, Marcello, I'm old enough to be your mother."

"I love all kinds of mothers, too," he whispered as he and the others settled back in their places around the Grand Room.

41

Chateau de Rouen

February 22, 2019

"For the sake of time and order," Dean Eccles encouraged, "we should get back to business." She was comfortable being PATRI's organizer, its moderator. "Sir Farrington, I believe you had the floor. Please resume and read the PACT that Mr. Hamilton gave you before the break. After all, it did originate with your forebears."

The English nobleman took his seat at the table. "Ladies and gentlemen, I too have only heard about this particular document and have never seen it. Like Dr. Eccles, I have a written Note of Action, as she calls it, stored in the Aplington vaults. My note is signed by King George III and tasks my family to be the Europe League's executor. It is in this role, that I now proceed.

"Before I read it, permit me to give a little background. During the break, I thought it would be wise to do so. Let me recall that The King's Promise, which I read earlier, was formulated right after the Revolutionary War in America. The Promise only involved England and America, and assured some sort of British assistance but only if requested by George Washington.

"In the years following, we all know that there was a great deal of diplomatic activity involving all the royal families of Europe, owing to the specter of civil collapse in France and elsewhere on the Continent. These royals feared that the French Revolution would spread to the rest of Europe and to the newly formed American Republic – with terrible consequences.

"George III and my own relative, the sixth Lord Aplington, secretly approached certain trusted representatives, first of Europe and then of America, to determine the possibility of formalizing a new relationship.

During their mission, the American envoys voiced their own similar concerns about the survival of their new Republic."

"Given this, what happened?" Nicholas Shippen asked. "How did this agreement, the treaty known as the PACT, come to exist?"

"Let me tell you what I understand. Firstly, as Dr. Eccles said, the PACT idea came from our side of the pond. Beside having mutual worries regarding America's political future, the European royal houses were interested at the same time in America's vast resources and its potential for lucrative trade."

He picked up the still-coiled document for emphasis. "The aim of George III and his royal allies was a proposal for peace, order and prosperity for the Atlantic countries, those that bordered on this promising ocean of commerce. This treaty was framed by the European royal houses, each of which much better understood the requirements of a durable government than did the founders of your fledgling American Republic."

When she heard his words, Denise Donasti whispered to Katy Blitz loud enough to be overheard, "Englishmen! They always think they have all the answers."

Lord Aplington ignored her sarcastic comment. "Evan Hamilton informed me that this American copy of the PACT was brought directly from the King James's Court by John Jay to President George Washington in 1795. During our break, Dr. Eccles told me that Washington was receptive to this rapprochement since he feared that his hopes for a civil American society would be dashed if a dangerously free-willed democracy were allowed to flourish. At the time, this seemed quite possible given that many of Thomas Jefferson's radical ideas were beginning to take hold. It is my understanding that George Washington knew that several Federalists in the state of New York had already floated the notion that a secret re-alliance with England might be useful to counter the incendiary ideas of their political opponents."

Gayle Eccles interrupted, "Let me add, though, that it was only after James Madison formally joined Jefferson and other political dissenters – persons termed 'republican-democratists' – that George Washington finally went ahead and selected a few of his like-minded supporters and formed PATRI. These patriots, our respective forefathers, were charged by President Washington to develop a shadow government that would guarantee the preservation of the United States."

"Excuse me, Lord Aplington, let me put in another word." Evan Hamilton stepped forward. "Washington had his former aide, Alexander Hamilton, store this private treaty in his New York City bank. It has been in my family's bank to this day."

"To offer further detail," Gayle Eccles added, "as PATRI's first order of business, President Washington was delighted to demonstrate this PACT document to the original members, which ensured support from European royals. I have it in our society's records that it has been read only once before to PATRI during the first meeting in 1797. And here it is, in front of us at last. Enough of this, we professors have a tendency to talk too much." She smiled apologetically.

"You're not the only one. I tend to go on myself," Farrington chortled. "No doubt, we are all curious about what it says. It should prove the basis of our subsequent actions. It looks to be a short read, so please hear me out."

Lord Aplington put on his reading glasses and read,

"PAN ATLANTIC COMMUNITY TREATY

'Wherein there is a natural and common bond of our peoples across the Atlantic waters and whereas there are clear and present internal dangers Roiling all of our Nations . . .
        '. . . we of the Europe League
pledge to fully assist in the formation of a new Government,
  a legitimate monarchy in America.
'This PACT will thereby ensure future order in America –
order that is so necessary for all of our civilized Nations.

       Europe League January 1795'"

Lord Aplington concluded by reading the names of six royal signatories. When he finished, he laid the PACT on the table, held its edges down with several books, and said, "Come forward, if you please. See for yourself."

Several persons moved around to have a closer look.

"I'm impressed," du Motier said. "This particular document is well preserved. On the other hand, my own copy stored at Aix is somewhat weathered after more than two hundred years."

Diane Fleming-James from Denver stood to be heard. "When we met in September, we all wondered about what the PACT would actually say. We supposed but now we know, oh my! . . . In the United States? I've thought about this ever since. Americans will never go for having a king."

"What's more, as I said when we first met last fall," Maureen Nightbird-Reynolds added, "since European countries don't have absolutely powerful monarchs anymore, why should we?"

"And beside, who would believe that the designated heir-apparent is one of the Winfields?" Karen Jay-York asked skeptically. "Just because Sally Fairfax's note to King George says so? That doesn't hold much water for me."

Someone in the rear of the room called out, "Remember, though, her letter implied that there might be some sort of 'necessary proof.'"

"The whole concept strikes me as being most unusual," Queen Frederickson of Sweden said with a frown. "If you actually do go ahead and enlist this so-called leader to be your president or king, or whomever, you should understand that monarchs arise only from known family lines, and from a family that is deeply respected over many many years. If there is such an inherited connection between the historic Mr. Washington and Mr. Winfield here, it is certainly going to take a foolproof demonstration of family bloodlines to convince anyone, including myself, that he is worthy to be the chosen one."

As she spoke, David Winfield could only wonder as well whether there was any definitive proof for what Evan Hamilton and Phil Mason had revealed to Suzanne and him at Marshall Hall in October.

Hamilton walked around the table and ran his hand along the decorated Caesar's case. "Certain members of my and Mr. du Motier's families have been told over the years that the proof of George Washington's lineage lay near at hand, at Mount Vernon itself. President Washington directed Alexander Hamilton to help him sequester items necessary to prove the direct connections between the Winfields and his elder brother, Lawrence Washington."

"But Evan, please . . . Sally Fairfax's personal letter suggesting a Washington connection to the Winfield lineage? You now say your family also knew about this lineage all along? The evidence has got to be far more than that. So far, like I said earlier, it's merely speculation." As a respected lawyer, Connie Marshall-Rubin's opinion was authoritative.

"Of course, so far you're right, Connie, but we can see that there are a few other pieces remaining within this box which may yet substantiate the Winfield legacy." Hamilton picked up the smaller of the two brass cylinders. "What about this, for example?"

He pointed out some scrawled writing on the side and read aloud, "*Exitus Acta Probat*. Ah yes, this is the Washington family motto."

He tried to unscrew the cap but it held fast. Green corrosion was tightly wrapped around the lid. "Sir Farrington, could you please pass me that can of solvent still sitting there . . .? It worked well on the locks."

"Let me help, Mr. Hamilton. Don't get your banker's hands all messed up." The burly Finch volunteered and put a newspaper on the table. He dripped some of the Liquid Wrench along the cap's edge and then with an audible grunt, wrenched open the metal tube.

"What is inside?"

"A small roll of cotton parchment, nothing else." Finch fingered it out of the crusted brass cylinder and gave the paper to Hamilton.

He observed, "This piece is much more frayed than the other documents that we've examined but I can still make out most of the writing."

"Vas' does it appear to be about, Mr. Hamilton?" Stahlen asked.

"Near as I can tell, it looks like a testament of some sort . . . and on the bottom is a barely discernible signature. It looks to be *Lawrence Washington – 1752.*"

"This seems like an Agatha Christie novel," Donasti remarked. "Now entering the plot comes a document written thirty some years *before* the Revolution."

Hamilton asked for attention as he took the parchment into the light of a nearby lamp. Late afternoon snow coming in from the west was beginning to fall outside on the terrace. The room had turned noticeably darker.

"What this note says, or at least what I think it says . . . Monsieur du Motier, could you please come here? See if we can read along together . . ."

The two men both had to squint to see the words as du Motier read aloud,

> "This is my last testament as dictated for my brother, George Was'."

After he read aloud various matters and assorted dispositions, Hamilton looked up as the Frenchman reached the end of the testament. "Lawrence Washington concludes,

> 'Finally, I direct my wife, Anne, her family and my brother, George, to be forever mindful of my only living child, my Sarah.
>
> 'I go, soon, to join the ages.
>
> 'When my time comes, Sarah's inheritance must be sure, nearby to our home of Mount Vernon.
>
> 'Most importantly, she will have my good name, a Washington, too.
>
> Lawrence Washington   May 1752.'"

After hearing the words, Shippen asked Hamilton, "I'm not sure how this testament of Lawrence Washington relates? Why did George Washington and Alexander Hamilton put this in the box in the first place?"

"I frankly don't know," Hamilton admitted. "I guess we'll have to hold off a minute, Nick. I am sure there's a reason. At the least, it might partly explain Sally Fairfax's note that was contained in the Franklin glass . . . That is, the message to King George III about Washington having a direct family descendent. His niece, as she wrote, was the sole survivor of his brother Lawrence." Hamilton paused to measure whether Shippen was following his train of thought. "Although George had two step-children, we know that he and Martha Washington had no issue of their own."

Dr. Eccles, with her extensive knowledge in American Studies, countered, "But, Evan, all four of Lawrence Washington's children died early on. This sounds like pure fiction."

"But as we all know, Professor, many things are not always as they seem. There may be a different truth, a different story." Hamilton stopped and stared out the window. He sensed that somewhere, there must be the necessary proof. Otherwise, why had Sally Fairfax written it?

"We can analyze this testament of Lawrence Washington until we're blue in the face," Diane Fleming-James said. "It is only a piece of a puzzle that may or may not go along with the other items in the box. It doesn't seem to make sense by itself, so let's see what else there is." The woman from Colorado was a Federal Reserve governor and enjoyed all sorts of analytical challenges. "I suspect that the full message held in this box, if there is one, will become clearer only after we get everything out at once. We need to put all the contents onto the table in some sort of chronological order."

"Brilliant, my dear Watson," Hugh Rochan said as he gave her a show of applause. It was evident to everyone that the media mogul was becoming increasingly impatient. "I, for one, hope that we can wrap all this up pretty soon. I have some conference calls to make to my office in Los Angeles and some people in New York before that."

Winfield was bemused observing everyone's waning energies. He imagined that they might soon be at a dead-end and have to finish for the day.

Instead, Lord Aplington brusquely pushed past Francis du Motier and impatiently said, "Not quite yet, Mr. Rochan. We should move on to the other metal cylinder. My hands are so very sensitive. Can you work on this one too? It's Mr. Finch, isn't it?"

Finch saw that thick built-up corrosion on this second tube might make for an even greater challenge. He dripped some solvent on the cap's juncture and with a firm grasp tried desperately to twist the base. "No luck, my friends. Is there anyone else that cares to try?"

The muscular Marcello Bonapiento attempted but winced in defeat. "Me neither, non la posso aprire. We will have to use a saw . . . the metal seems set."

Philippe Rouen called out, "Oh Henri, do we have a hacksaw in the tool shed?"

"We must, Monsieur," the vineyard foreman answered from the kitchen. "I will find it and be right back." In a matter of minutes, Henri returned. "I am very sorry, Monsieur Rouen. Jacques told me that he loaned out our hacksaw a week ago and . . ."

"Don't get it now. It's late, but we'll need it by tomorrow for this brass cylinder."

Henri came over to the table and also tried to loosen the lid. "Perhaps an acetylene torch that I have in the barn? That would cut through this metal."

"No – no, Henri," Philippe Rouen cautioned. "There are probably things inside that would get burnt."

"I see. Then, sir, tomorrow first thing, you will have your saw."

Lord Aplington put the unopened brass cylinder to one side and noted, "Now the last piece from our Caesar Box." He cradled a lead-glazed porcelain container.

"It is gorgeous," Catherine Bonard said, admiring the relief on the thickly glazed surfaces. "Just notice the exquisite detail of the figures on all four sides."

"Can you imagine what this container holds?" Robert Laurens asked, wondering whether the urn-like piece held someone's ashes. "It appears to be soundly locked with an unusual-looking octagonal keyhole."

"Might there be a key for it tucked in the case?" Gayle Eccles asked.

Lord Aplington ran his hand along and under the purple velvet lining, "None that I can determine, but . . . wait, no, maybe?" He held up a three-inch piece of steel fragment. "Pity, it looks like a broken-off bit of the reinforcing grid along the box's interior." The English lord was exasperated. "Once again, we're stymied. No doubt, we'll need a locksmith from the town to get this thing opened."

As everyone took pause, Philippe Rouen spoke out, "Pardon for my interruption, Lord Aplington. I think that we should call it a day. I sense that we have arrived at an impasse. Nothing further can be accomplished at the moment. You can now go and get any personal business done. Feel free to use the library. It is quiet there. I am sure that others have their own affairs to attend to as well."

Everyone stretched and as they started to get up, Rouen added, "I will have my man Henri bring a hacksaw tomorrow to open the remaining brass cylinder. At the same time, I have arranged for the locksmith of Lausanne to come up here. I am sure he would be familiar with such an eight-sided keyhole. We need to be very careful when we open this urn, as well – we don't want to damage its contents, either."

Sir Ronald Farrington nodded his own agreement. "In the meantime, do you have a secure storage location for all these materials, Philippe?"

"Yes – a fireproof vault in the wine cellar. They can be placed there. That should do."

David Winfield moved nearer to Evan Hamilton and whispered in his ear, "For some reason, that oriental piece there reminds me of a jewelry box that my mother gave to Suzanne years back."

"Why is that, David?"

"I don't really know." Winfield picked up the porcelain Chinese urn and fingered its keyhole, "It's really strange seeing this."

"Strange?"

"Suzanne's jewelry case is opened using a small, unusually-shaped octagonal key – just like the one that would have been needed to open this container."

As they walked out of the Grand Room, Hamilton turned and asked, "I was wondering, Dave, what do you suppose it would take to get that octagonal key of yours over here?"

"The one that I mentioned that opens my wife's heirloom jewelry case?"

"Yes. I know it's a hunch, but her key might also open the porcelain jar from the Caesar Box. Since that urn was stored in the Vault at Mount Vernon, it seems more than coincidental, don't you think?"

"Perhaps," Winfield said, "but I think there must be many other, similar colonial-era locks."

"I may be way off base, but still, could your wife bring the key and her jewelry box to Lausanne? I know it would be a hassle, but I think it could be important."

"Give me a moment, Evan. I'll call her now, it's one o'clock at Woodlawn Mills. I don't know what her plans are. She had mentioned midterms at Georgetown."

As Winfield dialed his wife on his cell phone, General Mason came around the corner. The Army Security chief had overheard the end of their conversation and volunteered, "If there is anything I or my staff can do for you, give me the word."

Hamilton held up his hand. "Stay here a minute, Phil, we'll let you know."

Later that night, Suzanne Winfield flew across the Atlantic in a mysteriously marked military jet that took off from an auxiliary runway at the Joint Force Andrews airbase. Her two hurriedly packed bags rested in an overhead compartment.

42

Chateau de Rouen

February 23, 2019

Early the next morning, members of PATRI and the Europe League watched a locksmith from Lausanne as he tried unsuccessfully to work the unusual octagonal keyhole's lock mechanism with a master-watering key. "It's a classic piece," he muttered, "something they knew about in the 18th century. I've only heard about locks like this. Each has a distinct lever mechanism so they can't be picked." He then suggested, "Let me call some friends in Italy where these sorts of devices were invented and ask if anything can be done short of breaking the urn."

Meanwhile, Henri had gone out on the porch with a borrowed hacksaw to work on the second brass cylinder. In a matter of minutes, he opened the tube and carried it back into the Grand Room.

After the foreman was excused, Lord Aplington pulled out several pieces of paper from the tube and set them out on the large table. The others gathered around as he looked over the contents. Sir Ronald exclaimed, "This one is some sort of business transaction. It is signed at the bottom, 'GWas'.' "

"Read it out loud, sir. Some of us can't see back here."

The British nobleman put on his reading glasses. "It looks to be some sort of property contract. There's an obvious tear at the top with an uneven edge. But, I'll read what is here on what appears to be the bottom of a larger document,

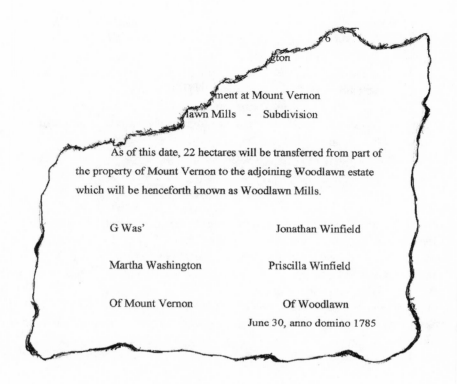

...ton ...6

...ment at Mount Vernon

...awn Mills - Subdivision

As of this date, 22 hectares will be transferred from part of the property of Mount Vernon to the adjoining Woodlawn estate which will be henceforth known as Woodlawn Mills.

G Was'   Jonathan Winfield

Martha Washington   Priscilla Winfield

Of Mount Vernon   Of Woodlawn

                                         June 30, anno domino 1785

Lord Aplington held up the torn parchment and asked, "What are we to believe about this? 22 hectares amounts to 2,200-some acres. That's a lot of land. Why did George Washington and Alexander Hamilton store this in the Caesar Box?"

Hamilton leaned over and scanned the parchment. "Seeing this, we could conclude that George Washington and his wife Martha had made rather comprehensive plans to generously support these early-day Winfields. By putting this deed in his Caesar Box, Washington demonstrated that he had fulfilled his older brother's dying wishes contained in Lawrence Washington's testament that we read yesterday. Given this and the other items on this table, it seems evident that Priscilla Winfield and her family remained extremely close to George Washington and were well-subsidized by him during his lifetime."

David Winfield came closer. He had not previously heard this part of his personal history. He had mistakenly believed that Woodlawn Mills was originally a piece of the extensive Fairfax holdings of Belvoir. The largest portion of his Woodlawn Mills estate was instead a generous gift of property transferred from Mount Vernon by George and Martha Washington.

He examined the deed for himself. "We have some original Winfield family correspondence in my home's library and several others that my father bequeathed to Princeton. From what I remember, these signatures appear to be in Jonathan and Priscilla Winfield's handwriting. My wife Suzanne would know, but she's not here."

Hamilton moved over and suggested, "Let me put this deed aside for a moment, Lord Aplington. There is another scroll from the same cylinder over there."

Farrington tried to read it but the script frustrated him. He gave it to Gayle Eccles. "Since you are a professor of the humanities, doctor, no doubt you have read many such materials. Can you help this old man out?"

"My pleasure, Sir Ronald. I do have plenty of practice reading all sorts of manuscripts – let me see." She proceeded to scan several pages of what George Washington had titled a 'Letter for the Ages.' "In this expansive letter," she said as she looked it over, "General Washington firstly notes that his legal will and testament had already been finalized, and that it is stored in the hands of his solicitor in Alexandria. He writes in the beginning, 'that this is a different sort of testament.' My first reaction as I look this over is that it shouldn't be too surprising, given Washington's surveyor's instincts, that he has left us a veritable roadmap.

"Let me try to read some of it.

> 'Besides this, my 'Letter for the Ages,' I have decided to include herein a copy of the Woodlawn transfer agreement to the Winfields in case there is future dispute of the lands of Mount Vernon.' "

Gayle Eccles pointed down at the table. "We have that deed sitting there."

She glanced over the other two pages and summarized the gist of the rest of the letter. "It appears that President Washington had a slew of ongoing concerns and misgivings. He states in his Letter that he wished to somehow document his inner thoughts so as to counteract any possible misunderstandings about his primary motivations, misunderstandings that might surface after his death.

"For instance, he writes here that in the years after he became President, he grew more aware of the 'larger requirement,' as he puts it, 'for a stronger national executive.' He expresses this rather vividly with several examples and then forcefully posits that his newly conceived organization of patriots is necessary for the good of the country because, as he writes, 'of the fractious winds of rebellion seen all around us. I am pleased,' he notes, 'that such a group (sic PATRI) is now in place.'

"Then, Washington goes on to say,

> 'Should there ever arise circumstances wherein PATRI and the Europe League agree together that the PACT and a transition to an American monarchy is required, Mr. Alexander Hamilton and I have left in the Caesar Box the necessary proof of Mrs. Priscilla Winfield's legitimacy . . .'

Gayle Eccles looked up and concluded, "' . . .for the royal house of Washington.

Signed GWas' April 1797.' "

David Winfield was stunned. These words of George Washington's 'Letter for the Ages' used the very same phrase that Sally Cary Fairfax had written, 'necessary proof.' He was left to wonder whether it might be sitting there in the unopened urn.

As Dr. Eccles put the note back down, General Mason came up behind Winfield and mentioned, "They landed at Geneva an hour ago and should be here shortly, Dave."

In a few minutes, the two friends slipped out to intercept Suzanne and were pleased to see two of Mason's DOSECOF escorting her up the terraced stone steps. Winfield gave his wife a warm kiss of greeting, took her carrying case, and suggested that she lie down in his guest room while his meeting continued.

Before going upstairs, Suzanne sleepily gave him a small silk purse, which held the octagonal key for her lacquered jewelry box from Woodlawn Mills.

"That's exactly the one that I asked about, love. Thanks." He kissed her again and asked, "And Caroline, Jeff, Bobby?"

"Fine. They love staying with Maria."

"Try to get some rest, you're probably exhausted. Mr. Rouen's people here can show you the way. You'll recognize my stuff. It's a lovely room."

"They are the same. Both locks work with Suzanne's key!" Winfield exclaimed a short time later. He and Mason breathed a sigh of relief. The Chinese porcelain urn from the Caesar Box now lay open on the large oak table.

Hamilton and the others eagerly crowded forward. "That was a splendid hunch on your part, Dave," he marveled. "Good thing you like gadgets so much."

"Perhaps, but ever since I was a little boy, I have been fascinated with the unusual shape of the keyhole of my mother's jewelry box. And then yesterday, there it was again, when I saw this Chinese piece with a similar keyhole."

Gayle Eccles and Francis du Motier listened to Winfield's remarks with interest. She concluded aloud that it was now obvious, at least to her, that the histories of Woodlawn Mills and Mount Vernon were inextricably linked.

"How do you mean, Dr. Eccles?" Robert Laurens asked. He couldn't follow how she had jumped to this conclusion.

"Well, Bob, think about it. An unusual key brought from the present day Winfield estate of Woodlawn Mills opens a stored Chinese urn, which has laid hidden on the neighboring Washington estate of Mount Vernon since the eighteenth century." She held her hand up. "Everyone, please be patient. You can huddle about but no touching. If you don't mind, Lord Aplington, I'll do all the handling of this fragile piece."

"Please do, Professor Eccles," Sir Ronald agreed. "Your dainty touch is sorely needed."

Gayle Eccles lifted a strange assortment of objects from the glazed china container and carefully spread them about the table. There was a four-inch garland-circle comprised of human hair of two distinct hues – auburn hair was woven together with strands of deep brunette. An infant's skullcap lay in the middle of the wreath and held fine, wispy clippings of blonde baby hair. Inside the cap was a slip of paper with the scripted words: 'Always a Washington.'

"What do you suppose this is all about?" Maureen Nightbird-Reynolds asked.

"It used to be a common practice here in Europe, my dear," Catherine Bonard explained. "This is what is known as a memory box. A young mother would be given one of these special containers at the birth of her first child. It was traditionally used to hold mementos of her children, usually lockets, caps, baby hair, those sorts of things."

"And here, yes," Eccles said carefully fingering the garland of hair, "here are three lockets lying about." She lifted them out of the memory box, placed them on the table, and proceeded to read the etched engravings on each locket aloud:

"LW & AW
JW 1744
    LW & AW
    FW 1747
LW & AW
MW 1748"

Dean Eccles delicately sprung the catch of each exquisite locket. She observed to the others that all three contained small locks of fine baby hair.

"As Madame Bonard said, this is what was customarily done, my friends," Queen Frederickson confirmed. "In those days, a woman's memory box was like the scrapbooks of today, used to store a mother's treasured family history. This was particularly popular during this time period when there was a very high childhood mortality."

"So these lockets?" Katy Blitz asked. With her interest in all sorts of art, she was spurred to edge forward. After she scrutinized one of the silver pieces, she said, "These probably once belonged to Lawrence Washington's wife, Anne. Each of the three has different initials and dates along with the same initials of the parents: *LW & AW.* "

"Gayle? I believe you told us yesterday that they had four children? Why are there only three?" Maria de la Caves of the Europe League had been intrigued by the Bowdoin College professor's earlier thumbnail sketch of the Washington family history.

Suddenly Winfield exclaimed, "My God. Hold on a second. I've seen a similar locket, but it's not here. I think it is in my wife's jewelry box that I had her bring from Woodlawn Mills. I'll go upstairs and look for it."

He roused Suzanne and asked her to come down to the chateau's Grand Room for a moment. As she combed her hair and freshened up, Winfield asked her to do him a favor and bring her lacquered jewelry case down from their guest room.

Once they came downstairs together, Winfield enthusiastically introduced her. "I would like you all to meet my wife, Suzanne. I called her last evening and she has flown all the way here to bring a family heirloom from Woodlawn Mills on quite short notice. She's understandably a bit weary."

Winfield reached over and picked up the small octagonal-headed key. He turned to Suzanne and said, "Sorry, love, that I had to wake you up so soon, but the other ladies present would agree that a man should never open his wife's jewelry box. But trust me, there is a purpose, perhaps only satisfying a curiosity on my part. Suzanne, take this. It should fit – after all, it's yours."

Winfield gave her back her personal key, the same one that had just opened Anne Fairfax Washington's 17th century Chinese porcelain keepsake. The piece remained ajar on the table. Suzanne put her lacquered jewelry box down next to it, inserted the double flute key and easily opened her treasured family keepsake.

"Do you mind, dear, seeing if that necklace piece is still in your jewelry box, the one my mother often showed me when I was a boy?" He looked warmly at the others in the room and added, "My mother always told my sister and me how special the piece was when we were growing up."

"This one, David?"

"Yes, that old silver locket is the one I remember. Can you show it to the others?"

"May I?" Gayle Eccles stepped forward and delicately took the fragile-looking, thin silver piece from Suzanne. She opened a tiny catch on its side and observed, "This one has a small sample of hair, as well, but the engraving is a bit different." She moved it into better lighting.

"What are the letters?" Lord Aplington asked.

The professor squinted as she closely examined the locket. "Let me read them,

> "*AF*   on the top of the front and then . . .
> *1750 - PFF - 1752*   on the bottom
>   . . . and barely seen on the back is this:
> *lw & aw*
> *sw 1750*

"The letters on the back are hidden in an etching of bowers and are easy to miss. The engravings are quite worn down."

"It stretches my imagination," Sir Ronald Farrington harrumphed, "but one wonders. The Washingtons . . . the Winfields. And the initials *PFF*? Who do they stand for? They don't seem to have anything to do with anyone."

"Quiet down, Sir Ronald," Eccles ordered. "What about the Sally Cary Fairfax letter to King George III lying there right in front of you? You read it to us yesterday. It was stored, wrapped inside the King's Promise."

She continued, "Remember, Sir Ronald, Sally Fairfax wrote in her letter that Lawrence Washington's daughter Sarah had to be renamed Priscilla Farris-Fairfax for her own safety. So now look, look closer. The initials of both of the girl's names are etched on this silver locket, *PFF* on the front and *sw* on the back."

Gayle Eccles staggered backwards and held Suzanne's locket aloft. "Oh my! This might be the 'necessary proof.' "

March 2019

When the twenty-some assorted persons in the new alliance returned to their homes on both sides of the Atlantic, each understood that for the PLAN to be successful, the legitimacy of David Winfield must be certain. They agreed that only a Washington could possibly be such an American king.

When they had adjourned, Lord Aplington reminded them what was still lacking – the foolproof evidence that Sally Fairfax had mentioned in her letter to King George, the 'necessary proof.' It would take much more than supposition and circumstantial evidence to establish David Winfield's true bloodlines, to prove beyond any doubt the connections that made him George Washington's heir.

Two weeks later, General Philip Mason made an encrypted conference call on a secure phone line to Evan Hamilton in New York, Gayle Eccles at Bowdoin, and David Winfield at his office in McLean, Virginia.

The general could barely control his voice. "The genetic reports just came in on the forensic analyses. The tests were blinded and run independently in Zurich, at the Institute of Pasteur, and at CellGen here in Maryland. Along with the six samples of hair from the Caesar Box, Dave, I included your and Mrs. Winfield's samples that we obtained in Lausanne."

"And . . .?" Hamilton's throat went dry.

"They are the same."

"The same person? How can that be?"

"No, no my friends, the same *family*. All six of the samples and those of David and Suzanne prove with a 99.999% certainty that David Winfield descended directly from Lawrence Washington."

PART 3

The Ascension

"The ex-King said, "Yon star's indifference
Fills me with fear I'll be left to my fate:
I needn't think I have escaped my duty,
For hard it is to keep from being King
When it's in you and in the situation.
Witness how hard it was for Julius Caesar.
He couldn't keep himself from being King.
He had to be stopped by the sword of Brutus.
Only less hard was it for Washington.
My crown shall overtake me, you will see;
It will come rolling after us like a hoop."

Excerpted from: *HOW HARD IT IS TO KEEP FROM BEING KING*
WHEN IT'S IN YOU AND IN THE SITUATION

The Poetry of Robert Frost,
Edward Connery Lathem (ed.), Holt, Rinehart and Winston,
New York (1975), pp 453-462

". . . Prudence, indeed, will dictate that Governments long established
should not be changed for light and transient causes . . ."

The Declaration of Independence, 1776

43

East Hampton, Long Island

July 2019

'Is the System Broken?' Suzanne Winfield reflected on how appropriate the title had been for a think tank conference that she had just hosted at the Seacrest Hotel in the Hamptons. Over the previous two days, some thirty legislators, governors and news commentators had privately met to discuss a variety of national and foreign affairs. Without their knowledge, the attendees were in fact being used as a mini-focus group for PATRI's purposes. During the confab, they had also been given the task of mulling over plausible rationales for having a third political party in the United States.

*   *   *

"What were some of your participants' main points?" Evan Hamilton was settled into his favorite, all-weather summer sofa. The morning sea breeze promised a temperate summer day along the shore outside his summer home. "And beyond that, what was the thinking about a third party, Suzanne?"

Suzanne glanced around the outside deck. Members of the newly named exploratory committee of the American Federalist Party sat with their coffees and teas. "I've summarized them as bullet-points here. Concern over government shutdowns and the lack of civility topped the list." She passed a printed sheet out to the others. "It's pretty much what I would have suspected. They didn't seem to feel a third political party was necessarily the answer, but then again, that opinion was sort of expected."

"Sorry, but before we get too deep into our discussion," Hamilton said, "I should introduce some folks around the room. You've probably heard of these three people that I asked to join us, but just in case . . ." He gestured in turn to Roland Peters, an aide to several Republican administrations and a respected, conservative political analyst; to Sheila Linden, a well-known polling expert and past member of the Democratic National Committee; and finally to Sidney Rosenthal. "You may not know Sid Rosenthal, here. He was an instrumental player in the last New York City mayoral race nearly won by his Independent Party candidate."

Each of the three guests nodded. Hamilton had already given them a generous retainer fee and, accordingly, they were all delighted to be there.

Sheila Linden spoke out first. "The three of us already understand from both Evan and Gayle Eccles that today's get-together is mainly to have exploratory discussions about the feasibility of an American presidential campaign by a newly formed third party. It's been tried before, but it's never succeeded. Strom Thurmond, Ross Perot, and Ralph Nader are three recent examples. It will be very long odds to get the prize."

"But for starters," Roland Peters said indifferently, "I guess you want to hear our gut reactions to the points made at Professor Winfield's weekend conference."

"Yes, Sid, you've got that right," Hamilton said, taking charge again. "We want to see if there are enough reasons to develop a third national political party. First, though, we need your professional opinion in this regard."

Rosenthal wiggled in his chair. The others had heard rumors that this aptly named 'mayor of the Bronx' always preferred to cut to the chase. "Oh bosh – reasons, reasons! At the end of the day, you never tell a voter the *reasons* they should support you – you figure it out beforehand but then go ahead and tell them whatever you think they want to hear. Let's get down to brass tacks. It's not what you call 'reasons' at all, Mr. Hamilton, that makes for a successful election. It's this – Who's your candidate?"

"Sid, hold on – hear him out," Linden chided. "I have always felt that a political party, especially a new one, must first have a solid lattice of worthwhile ideas before it can possibly seek any sort of popular support. Selecting a prospective candidate comes later, in my book."

"Hogwash, Sheila," Rosenthal flashed back, "it's the candidate that always matters, never the issues . . . Ya gotta sell me on the person, not their ideas, to get my vote. Bottom-line, it amounts to Mr. Voter saying 'I like that guy' or 'I could enjoy a beer with him.' "

Evan Hamilton enjoyed hearing this boilerplate, political-insider repartee. He was excited that Gayle Eccles had tapped into a lodestone of invaluable pragmatism. "Please, please, I agree with you both. We need both approaches. As you know, national voter registrations show there are 20-25% Republicans, 25-30% Democrats and 40-50% Independents. And yet, these many Independents do not have any sort of a national party they can identify with. Now we can use this to our advantage and give them one."

"Please don't get too sidetracked," Peters advised. "We are only here until noon. Mrs. Winfield, could you describe the main points on the sheet that I'm reading which illustrate America's so-called 'broken system,' especially the ones that your attendees agreed upon?"

During a lull following Suzanne Winfield's hour-long presentation, Hamilton raised a question to the three politicos. "What do you think are the most vital ingredients of a successful campaign organization?"

"Money and media, with a capital M!'

Hamilton laughed out loud when he heard the unanimous answer. "At least you three old sages finally agree on something."

"Of course we do," Peters remarked. "It is the most important ingredient, Evan. National election campaigns are hugely expensive. Even with Super-PACs, it's still a pain to raise all that dough. It takes up nearly 70% of our time."

Rosenthal agreed. "At the end of the day, it's the money that gets the prize."

"Let me assure you that the resources will be there," Hamilton said as he thought about the vast financial network that Philippe Rouen had already developed.

A voice interrupted, "Excuse me, Mr. Hamilton, you have a call in the kitchen."

Evan excused himself and went to a sunny nook. "Hello . . . oh, Francis." Francis du Motier was calling from his village near Aix, "How is it going, Evan? Monsieur Rouen and Sir Farrington have been with me this weekend. The three of us have been talking extensively about your idea of entering the U.S. presidential election."

"Hopefully, the election of Winfield will succeed without first having to resort to the military fallback-contingency that I mentioned months ago. For now, our PLAN seems to be progressing, Francis. Three political consultants are here today. Do you and your fellow Europeans have any recommendations at the moment?"

"Only one – keep us out of it until the PLAN is completed," du Motier warned.

"But Francis, I told them that there are plenty of resources. Are you backing out?" Hamilton's hands tightened on the phone.

"Not at all, Evan. But none of our support can be discovered. We Europeans must not be seen as foreign intruders in your PATRI group's election campaign."

Hamilton stared out the kitchen window onto a view of the open Atlantic and said, "Yes, you're certainly correct about that . . . Any other matters?"

"No, mon ami, but of course give my salutations to Mr. and Mrs. Winfield."

"I will, Francis. General Mason's men are keeping a close eye on them here. Good day, my friend." He looked outside at four bland-looking houseguests sunning themselves on randomly scattered lawn chairs. He was relieved to see the DOSECOF detail. The Winfields were well protected.

Evan Hamilton returned to the porch. "Sorry, the phone call was from some friends out of the area," he said to no one in particular. "Now where were we?"

"Mrs. Winfield's list of the issues seems rather generic, Mr. Hamilton," Roland Peters said. "Assuming money is not a pressing problem, the first order of business would be to find out what this party is to be called and then, second, to ask again if you already have someone in mind as your candidate."

Gayle Eccles crossed her arms. "I'll speak to that, Evan. Some of us came up with the name 'American Federalist Party' since our primary aim will be to espouse a new brand of federalism. It would offer a fresh way of governing our country, more centralized and accountable."

The outspoken Republican consultant objected. "Many folk would say the federal government is too big already. Pay close attention to the libertarian demands of Freedom Party members, Dr. Eccles. They'll surely try to dismantle anything like this."

"We're not saying that big government is bad, per se, Rollie. What we're saying is that the problem is inefficiency. We believe that the federal plan which we propose will make government in the United States much more effective."

David Winfield described what he thought characterized success in business, and then added, "A President should do it the same way – listen to others, yet forcefully manage from the top down."

"That's it in a nutshell," Hamilton said. "Currently, we're faced with having too many checks and balances. They strangle any federal administration. I believe Dave says it right. If a U.S. President needs to bypass our inefficient Congress to get things done, so be it. At the end of the day, for our national government to be effective we need more, not less centralization. Hence the name, Rollie, the 'American Federalist Party.'"

Sheila Linden frowned. "It won't work – government's not a business. I promise I won't take any of what you say out of this room, but your ideas, Mr. Hamilton, sound unAmerican. You remember what's the danger of extreme federalism? It's tyranny."

Hamilton rejoined bitterly, "Ah yes, Ms. Linden, but unfettered liberties lead to widespread anarchy. Which is worse?"

Before she could answer, Suzanne Winfield took a step forward and waved her copy of the discussion points from the 'Is the System Broken?' conference. "Allow me to interrupt. I really must summarize for you the consensus of the invitees. You've heard it said, 'if it ain't broke don't fix it,' but given the weight of the evidence, the conference attendees decided otherwise – that our American system *is* broken and needs fixing. This list," she gestured, "in front of you is a litany of the very problems they felt should be addressed and remedied by a more efficient federalist system."

The Democratic activist rebutted her strenuously. "Well and good, Mrs. Winfield, but these people were a captive audience. I still have reservations."

"Sheila, calm yourself, be polite," Rosenthal interrupted, "especially since the three of us are being paid to be just a sounding board for our hosts. We're not being asked to comment today on policy making, at least not yet." He lightly tapped his arthritic fingers together, contemplating the future. "You've only given us one name, that of your prospective party, Mrs. Eccles. What about the other name? That's the most important piece of your construct."

"I suppose you mean the name of our proposed candidate?" Hamilton asked. "Ah yes, I agree, that's certainly the important piece. It's to be Mr. David Winfield here, sitting right next to you, Roland. Admittedly, most people do not know him, but he has the right stuff evidenced by his renowned leadership in the business community. Gayle and I did a thorough background check. Trust me when I say his lineage is noteworthy. Professor Eccles, his wife Suzanne and I have been ghostwriting David's autobiography in which we detail his guiding beliefs. It will serve to introduce him to the public arena."

Linden had only heard of David Winfield as being the chairman of Eurit Industries. "Remind me, I'm not sure. Aren't you the late Admiral Winfield's son?"

"Yes. He was a great father . . . a really humble man."

"That he was," Peters agreed, "A wonderful man, a solid patriot."

Gayle Eccles spoke further, "When we were trying to decide whether we were going to mount this effort, Sheila, we decided that we needed a candidate who seemed to come from out of the Beltway but at the same time within it. Dave fills that bill nicely."

"How far along are you guys with all of this?" Rosenthal broke in, pushing the conversation along like an alpha dog.

"Well, having you three here today is a big step," Hamilton responded. "We wanted to pick your brains, use your expertise, to see if we're missing anything at the start. We've got only fifteen months before the general election to pull this off."

Peters spoke out. "With time a bit short, as long as money is no problem your first priority is getting on each state's ballot and . . ."

"That's certain," Sheila Linden agreed. She could tell that she was beginning to get enthused in spite of herself and blurted, "It's very, very important to know what's going to be our, I mean 'your' strategy. Remember, it's still an Electoral College system. Some states are worth much more than others, so get on their ballots first. You can throw popular votes out the window. Initially, you need to go after the states where you have the best chance, to keep either of the other two parties from getting a majority of the Electoral College votes."

"Thanks for the civic lesson, Sheila." Rosenthal feigned a yawn. "I'm sure Mr. Hamilton and the others of his new party have already given thought . . ."

"Oh no, quite the contrary," Hamilton replied. "That's why you're here. Speaking for Gayle and me, we'd be happy to offer each of you a key position with our campaign to get things rolling. I'll need you to get back to me on the offer, but let me know soon. The clock's already running."

"To help us make up our minds, or at least my own, Evan, who is already on this American Federalist Party's staff? I assume that you are the Winfield campaign's chief-of-staff, the way you've been talking."

"Fortunate that you ask, Mr. Peters." He knew that the Republican was well known for his shrewd managerial style. "So far, we have a small but loyal group, but none with the decades of political experience that you three have."

"Let's start with who you've got as your nuts 'n' bolts guys. That's my favorite group of campaign workers ever since I was known as a young boy-wonder in the Bronx." Sidney Rosenthal was widely considered the guru of precinct politics.

"We've been fortunate to sign on a really first-rate husband/wife team as our day-to-day campaign managers, Victor Marino and Hildy Baker. They already brought over twenty of their consulting group in Washington to join the staff."

"I know them, Evan. Good choice."

"The financial part will be run by Karen York of Chicago. We're delighted that she's in the fold. Oh, Dave and Suzanne," he said parenthetically, "did you know that one of Ms. York's forefathers was John Jay, one of the original cabinet members?"

Suzanne Winfield smiled sweetly as if hearing this for the first time. "Evan," she said with an unaffected Southern accent, "I wasn't aware of the connection, but I'm sure that many of us may be related to other important persons, too."

Rollie Peters rubbed his chin and said, "Not me, I'm afraid. But all in all, it seems like you're well past an exploratory phase for this Federalist Party of yours."

"We certainly hope so. I'll go on now and give you a few of the other key players." Hamilton gestured toward Gayle Eccles and said, "Dean Eccles is in charge of personnel and resource allocations. She has plenty of experience in this regard."

Dr. Eccles added with a trace of sarcasm, "Yes, and my first assignment was to get you three consultants all here today. You are such busy people!"

Hamilton named several others that would be involved. "There is Ed Finch, our national security advisor, but since he is in the civil service, his son Patrick nominally will fill this position. With Ed's years of homeland security and military experience, his input will be vital."

Peters spoke out, "Finch, yes, a good man. My wife and I are friends of Ed and his wife Sandy at the Oakwood Hills Club."

"Then moving on, Nicholas Shippen. Roland, I think you know him too, right? Yes, Kansas City. He will be our Domestic Affairs campaign manager. His agribusiness already utilizes an immense tracking system. Using this as a template, we hope to design a similar network to guide our decision-making during the campaign."

"This Mr. Winfield seems a well enough chap," the crusty Rosenthal said as he looked skeptically in David's direction. "But honestly, he's a big unknown. You're really going to need to go full court with public relations . . . and make him a celebrity."

Gayle Eccles had anticipated that this might come up. "Well, there is Denise Donasti, Mr. Rosenthal. Evan, remember that I told you last week that she was a 'maybe?' She texted me this morning. It's now a 'yes.' "

Hamilton grinned with sudden relief. "What Gayle just said is big . . . really big. I think you said earlier, Mr. Rosenthal, that 'money and the media,' are the keys to any election. Well, we've now got Mrs. Media, herself."

"Who?" Rosenthal asked blankly.

"You may remember that in years past, Mrs. Donasti went by her maiden name, Schuyler, when she modeled and appeared on Broadway. She's now settled on her family's estate near Albany, but she's still as outgoing as ever."

Hamilton always had a special fondness for Denise. They shared a common heritage going back to General Philip Schuyler of George Washington's Continental Army.

"I can easily place the name along with her face, Evan," Peters said. "We tried to have her do some public relations work for a New York gubernatorial race but she turned us down. Ever since she retired from the theatre, she has been a bit reclusive. Anyone running for higher office in New York or anywhere on the East Coast would covet having a Donasti-Schulyer connection."

"She is quite private, but by chance we discovered what might persuade her to help us. You're right, Rollie, she has all sorts of connections."

As he spoke, Hamilton couldn't help but think about Hugh Rochan and his London-based Media Manor enterprise. He was sure that Denise and Hugh would work well together. Rochan would provide the coverage while she would script and rehearse David Winfield's campaign speeches and interviews from her actor's studio in Poughkeepsie.

"You've made quite an impressive start, Mr. Hamilton," Roland Peters said. "Are the two major parties aware of your intentions?"

"Not yet. As you know, both seem quite consumed by the run-ups to their own campaigns. One party can't make up its mind whether President Henson should run for reelection. He seems to have more than a few enemies and, besides, there are some recent rumors about his health. At the same time, the Democrats are enjoying their usual bickering. They already have six presumed candidates attacking one another like horses pulling at their bits.

"The simple answer to your question, Mr. Peters, is 'no.' We're under their radars. Even if the Republicans and Democrats were aware of our existence, they'd consider us small fish. Nonetheless, we feel that now is the time for us to start getting organized. Our small team is highly motivated. We'll do whatever it takes."

Realizing that his time was running short owing to other commitments, Hamilton hurriedly closed the meeting. "I appreciate having you three here today. Speaking for me, it has been very helpful."

He stood up and concluded more officiously, "After you get back home, feel free to get back to me if, or when, anything else crosses your mind. If you do decide that you want to sign on with our new Federalist Party, we would certainly pay you handsomely to make that happen. Remember, we're doing this for America. None of this is for ourselves alone."

In a while, Hamilton watched the last cars drive through the expensively manicured hedges of his estate. "How do you think it went, Gayle?"

"Interesting, a very interesting morning. For all their years of working within a two-party political system, something tells me that these folks might be excited about the prospect of trying to succeed with a third."

Hamilton picked up one of Suzanne Winfield's summary sheets. "'Is the System Broken?,'" he read half-aloud. "We know the answer to that, Gayle, don't we? And we're the ones to fix it."

44

Washington, D.C.

Sunday AM, November 2019

Hugh Rochan had been able to arrange an interview for David Winfield on the prestigious Sunday talk show of a rival network. The nationally known talk show moderator had arrived with minutes to spare.

The newswoman came over and shook her guest's hand saying, "Thank you so much for coming, Mr. Winfield. We haven't had a first-time interviewee for months, so this should be interesting for both of us." She often relied on gut instincts and sensed that, given his formal bearing, he would be a most appealing guest.

"Just so you and I are paddling in the same waters, so to speak, my producer said the main subject is about a new book you've written. Is that right, Mr. Winfield?"

"That and . . ."

"We only have a few minutes before we're on – my studio assistants gave me some talking points to ask you. Let me check my notes."

As she did, a loud voice boomed through the studio, "Ready on the set!"

An overweight man wearing a thin headset off camera watched a digital countdown and then pointed at the show's moderator. "Good morning to all of you and thanks for joining us on the Sunday Report. I am Judy McIntyre. Welcome. I am fortunate to have Mr. David Winfield with me today. His recent book titled *In This We Believe*, subtitled *One Man's View of America* has been very well received. I thought his book would make a good jumping off point going into Election 2020."

She turned slightly in her chair, "Welcome, Mr. Winfield. First, let me ask about your background for our viewers. Tell us a little about yourself."

Winfield folded his hands and calmly acknowledged her question. He remembered some of the pointers that he had practiced with Denise Donasti. "How you look and act on TV," she had advised, "will be much more important than what you say. People vote for the messenger, not the message. Simple Speak . . . make whatever you say clear, concise, and short. And whatever else, be sure to look presidential at all times."

Winfield made eye contact with the show's moderator. "Thank you for having me, Ms. McIntyre." He engaged her as if only the two of them were on the set. "To answer your question, I should start by saying that my family goes back here in Virginia for more than two hundred years . . ." He briefly described his position at Eurit Industries, reviewed his and his family's longstanding involvements in philanthropic and cultural activities in the District, and alluded to a growing personal interest in politics.

"I want to focus on your book this morning. You titled it *In This We Believe – One Man's View of America*. How did you come up with the title?"

"Actually, it was my wife Suzanne's idea. It is a play-on-words from the famous Edward R. Murrow radio show, *This I Believe*, which was popular in the '50s, but I trust that the views of America which I hold dear are held by the vast majority of Americans."

"Your book could be very appropriate heading into another election cycle, Mr. Winfield." McIntyre hesitated before asking, "Being as you are not a politician, why did you write on this particular subject now?"

"First and foremost, I felt it was a story that needed to be told. As background, over the past few years I've become steadily more frustrated with our government. I felt the need to spell out some of my dissatisfaction . . . to state what works and what doesn't. I sense that an increasing lack of civil discourse has become the behavior of the day. In the book, I underscore our country's core beliefs in the hope that they will inspire other Americans to demand a more proper governance."

"How did a busy business executive like your find the time to . . . ."

"To answer that, I need to recognize three superb collaborators – my wife, Suzanne, who is an associate professor of government studies here at Georgetown, Professor Gayle Eccles, a dean and political science professor at Bowdoin, and finally Mr. Evan Hamilton, an esteemed bank CEO from New York."

"Your book sounds rather erudite, more like a textbook for a university, Mr. Winfield. How do you expect to appeal to a wide readership?" She tilted the book so that a nearby camera could zoom in on its glossy front cover.

David Winfield smiled. "I use a technique called 'Simple Speak,' Ms. McIntyre, which allowed my ideas to be more clearly worded and hopefully, be better understood by the general public. The book is surely not an action-novel, but I think that some of it should pique the interest of many Americans."

"Can you give an example?"

"I have a chapter, for instance, on the blatant inaction regarding infrastructure – the lack of highway repairs, maintenance of water and sewer pipelines, and such. If simple repairs can't be addressed, what can be? I describe several instances of public works calamities. For instance, twenty per cent of Boston's drinking water leaks out of outdated pipes and is wasted. Many such examples are caused not only by the inaction of state and local officials, but also by the ineffectiveness of national leaders." Winfield somehow began to feel strangely energized.

McIntyre easily recognized his building passion and remarked, "This morning, you seem like a man on a mission, Mr. Winfield. Even though many might call you 'elite,' you convey the commonsense values that should be so important for us all. In a word, what motivates you to carry this torch?"

"I'm primarily motivated by what I trust should motivate us all – to help ensure that we leave an America that is worthwhile for future generations. Right at the moment, I'm concerned our system is broken, that America is in danger of being thrown off . . ."

McIntyre interrupted him. "I'm not sure where you are going with this, and I'm not sure we have the time. So let me ask my question another way. What are those certain 'core beliefs' that you mentioned earlier, that people should expect their elected officials will foster and protect?"

"I brought some notes so that I wouldn't overlook anything. Do you mind?"

"Not at all. Our regular viewers know that I use Teleprompters. Go right ahead, Mr. Winfield."

"Let me see, the beliefs that Americans should task their leaders to uphold are those mentioned by the Constitution. Such as a belief in the establishment of justice, a belief that a common welfare will be provided for all of our citizens, a belief that there be a common defense. I cite five or six other such examples."

As the interview proceeded, Winfield forgot all about Denise Donasti's advice and started to speak more expansively. "For instance, Ms. McIntyre, if we believe that justice is good, and I think most of us would agree that justice is a cornerstone of America, then we should have leaders that provide it just as the founders did. We once created a national system to perform this judicial function, but . . ."

McIntyre raised her eyebrows, trying to follow his train of thought. "'But' is probably the most important word in the English language, Mr. Winfield, and the most overused word here in Washington."

"I was simply trying to say that too many functions of government, local and national, have been privatized or neglected over the past fifty years. In fact, many of these projects are funded by no-bid contracts, sweetheart deals shepherded by lobbyists. It seems the federal government, in particular, has sloughed off many of its responsibilities in favor of outsourcing to the so-called 'free marketplace.' "

"And?"

"Things that we deeply believe in and cherish aren't being addressed effectively here in Washington by either party, the Republicans or the Democrats."

"The Beltway and District are good for some things, Mr. Winfield. After all, we both live here so I suppose it's good in that sense." She half-laughed. "But seriously, for a non-politician you obviously have a natural calling for civics. I like that. Let me get to a rumor that has been circulated here in Washington. Is there any truth that you might consider running as a third party candidate for President?"

Winfield kept a poker face and opened his hands, palms out. "I haven't heard about that idea, so I guess it's just a rumor."

McIntyre was known to press after her guests' half-answers. "Whether you've heard about the rumors is not the question, Mr. Winfield. Do you suppose there is any chance for a third national party next year, and more importantly will you be leading it?"

He grinned enigmatically. "What I think at the moment is, I don't know."

"Any plans in the next several months?"

"Just personal stuff like getting this book out. And then, of course, work and family matters, Thanksgiving and such, the usual."

McIntyre looked up at the camera. "We need to take a short break for our sponsors and when we return, Josh Jones will summarize the overnight news. I'd like to thank Mr. David Winfield for his comments about his recently published book, *In This We Believe — .* "

The green light over the camera lens turned red as the segment ended and the program's familiar theme song aired. As the Winfields left the set, Judy McIntyre waved, "Thanks so much, Mr. Winfield, good luck with the book. Hope to see you again."

Suzanne affectionately hugged him and whispered as they walked away, "She's right, she'll probably see us again, Davey . . . I think you did great!"

As the two left the television program's sound stage, they could hear Josh Jones's voice broadcasting overhead through the ready rooms and hallways: "It's been another eventful night. First, three terrorists were caught in Washington state shortly after crossing the Canadian border. At this time, it is not clear whether they are being interrogated in Seattle or have been taken elsewhere.

"Yesterday at a conference in Shanghai, it was announced that the economic contractions in China would continue but at a faster pace. Labor unrest and civil demonstrations are escalating in the western provinces, threatening the extraction of rare earth metals there. This will certainly have a far-reaching, global effect.

"Here in the United States, Governor Gardner of North Carolina has called out the National Guard in anticipation of a probable statewide wildcat strike by health workers on Monday.

"The White House announced that it plans to hold a conference next week, sponsored by the business advocacy group FreeWill, active in all Republican-controlled legislatures throughout America. Many states want to enact further stringent anti-union measures and some governors have proposed consolidating their efforts.

"President Foster Henson will be traveling to Minnesota's Mayo Clinic early next week for a thorough health evaluation. You may recall that several months ago he had some temporary weakness, but testing at the Bethesda Naval Hospital was unremarkable.

"Finally, the Senate minority leader, Democrat Harvey Jones of Nevada, spoke earlier today on the Manor Media network. Here's what he had to say."

> As a video clip was shown, the Senator said, 'I am astonished that the President and his Republican Party plan to halt all federal investigations of financial institutions. This goes beyond the pale. It appears that the Grand Old Party is once again in the pockets of the banks and their so-called Freedom Party Caucus. In addition, I understand that President Henson plans to eliminate the Environmental Protection Agency beginning in 2020, stating that the EPA infringes on legitimate mining rights currently under control by the States. Accordingly, in order to combat this reckless disregard for our federal government, I have informed our caucus that we will block any such dismantling legislation until after next year's elections.'

"It sure seems there's always more than enough gridlock, doesn't it?" Josh Jones commented. "If you want more information, please go to our website, *SUNDAYAM@Washnews.com*. Now, back to Judy."

"Thank you Josh. The 21st century continues to confound all of us."

Judy McIntyre looked at her notes. "Since there are already so many announced presidential candidates, this morning we have asked four panelists to give their views for the coming year. They include Roland Peters, the well-known strategist who has been involved with the past three Republican administrations, Sheila Linden, a former member of the Democratic National Committee and currently a lobbyist for the District of Columbia, John Madison, the respected columnist and Associate Editor for the *Washington Post*, and finally, to give a viewpoint from outside the Beltway, the highly regarded freshman Congressman from Illinois, Patrick Jefferson. He has first-hand experience regarding our current political situation. First, Congressman Jefferson, tell us . . ."

The Winfields walked together out the heavy, automated doors to the parking lot. Suzanne took his hand and in her customary teasing fashion pouted, "Sadly, I'm afraid that from now on, we'll have to watch out for ourselves in public."

"Well then, Suze', how about going on home and getting private, instead?"

45

Woodlawn Mills

November 2019

"Overall, I think you did pretty well, Dave. There were times, though . . ."

The committee of the American Federalist Party was gathered a week after David Winfield's appearance on the McIntyre – Sunday Report. Karen York and Nicholas Shippen had flown in that afternoon, while Denise Donasti, Gayle Eccles, and Evan Hamilton had come down from Westchester, New York. Four others had driven to the estate from their homes in the greater Washington area. A tape of Winfield's interview with Judy McIntyre played repeatedly on a nearby flat screen.

Roland Peters leaned forward and remarked, "David, you've got to be precise and much less wordy for anyone to possibly become interested in your message."

Donasti had stressed this same point over and over. "Mr. Peters is absolutely right. Don't let your audience get lost in your words. Remember, David, we've all told you. It's how you look . . . not what you say."

Hamilton, Finch, Eccles and Victor Marino sat in a semicircle in the library while the others voiced their opinions. Hamilton was delighted that he was able to convince Peters and Sheila Linden to come to this recap session. The New Yorker enjoyed hearing the fresh opinions and perspectives of these two strategists, especially now that they were members of his team.

Sitting with them, he thought back to what Sheila Linden had said recently when she went with him and his wife, Francesca, to the Lincoln Center. "Mr. Winfield is someone I could believe in – a campaign with him would be fun. If I decide to come aboard, don't tell anyone, at least not yet."

Hamilton had also visited Ed Finch in D.C. The two played golf as a threesome with Roland Peters, a longtime member of the Oakwood Hills Country Club. Somewhere on the back nine, Peters paused before addressing his ball and addressed his companions instead. "I've been thinking ever since that get-together you had at your Hampton place in July, Evan. Your idea of a third political party may not be so far-fetched . . . sounds very interesting." The elderly politico hitched his pants and stared far down the fairway, mumbling, "Nice and straight, keep it in the center . . . right down the middle."

As the three golfers walked off the tee, the veteran Republican operative had said, "I'm almost tempted to join up with you guys just to give this old man one last thrill, but if I do, don't tell anyone."

Hamilton was gratified that these vital recruitments had been accomplished in the space of that one midautumn week. He had lined up two of America's most esteemed political operatives, and what was equally important, from both the Democratic and Republican parties as well.

"Now there was the matter of convincing Mr. Sidney Rosenthal," Hamilton ruminated, "the only one with experience at managing a third party campaign." He knew that some people thought Rosenthal was a loose cannon, so he was not surprised that Sidney hadn't yet decided to join their enterprise.

Hamilton surveyed the others in the room and confidently announced, "I'm glad to see most of our key players today, except for Hildy Baker and I hope to get Sidney Rosenthal's commitment tomorrow." Other than this last nagging question, the New York banker felt satisfied thus far with the progress of their efforts.

Just as everyone was comfortably settled, Suzanne Winfield came into the room and loudly announced, "I don't think I can go through with all this."

While the television droned in the background, her words fell like a bombshell. David didn't fathom her outburst and could only ask, "Suze'?"

"It's too much for me to handle." Her face flushed as she wailed, "The children, our privacy, everything . . . oh."

Winfield got up from the sofa, hugged her and quietly led her into the adjoining kitchen. He searched her face when they were alone, trying to understand. "Suzanne, all sorts of other folks have traded in their private lives when they felt a call to public service. And they did it understanding that there were risks."

"I know, I know," she sniffled, "but it's different when you're married to that person. My first and only duty, Dave, is to you and our children, not to some nebulous cause. I really don't know. I guess I'm selfish – but part of me is afraid."

"Honey, I understand where you're coming from, but why now? You seemed to have been on board with all this before. You know I would never do anything without you agreeing to do it with me."

Suzanne sobbed into his shoulder. "Forgive me, Dave, for not telling you sooner. I didn't want to bother, but Lisa called this morning and said she has a serious health issue. Given our mother's cancer history, Lisa said she needs more tests, but she's scared. I can't get her off my mind, and she's my best friend. It's gotten to me."

"It should, sweet one. No wonder. I'm stunned to hear about Lisa. What do you suggest I do? Call things off?" He pointed at the doorway. "Though frankly, I don't think we should bag this one meeting. Right now we don't know for sure what's going on with Lisa. Until now, you've been as committed as I was, Suze'."

In several minutes, Suzanne finally controlled her sobbing and gathered herself together. Using a dishtowel to freshen up, she reminded him that, whatever else, first and foremost she had his back. "When we go in, Dave, let's be honest with everyone. I'm sure they'll see that I had more pressing issues on my mind. I'll call Lisa later tonight – and go and visit her tomorrow."

Suzanne followed him back into the living room, and once there gave a silent smile of resolve to the others. Winfield explained her outburst and said that he had promised to support her in any way possible, even if it meant postponing the campaign. For now, he said, they both wanted the afternoon meeting to continue.

After hearing his comments, Gayle Eccles came over and gave Suzanne a hug. "It's quite understandable, you're human. Thanks for being so real with all of us. And you, David, I love a man who understands priorities. Speaking for all of us, we wish you both well with this difficult situation. We'll work it out together."

Somehow, the gathering was able to eventually settle back to the business at hand. After another hour dissecting Dave Winfield's talk show appearance, the group agreed that there was little reason to postpone the formation of the American Federalist Party and Winfield's candidacy – provided he and Suzanne gave the go-ahead.

"After what you shared earlier, Suzanne, how does this really sit with you?" Karen York was by her side.

"You know what? Dave and I have been talking about this nonstop for months. Before I went off earlier, we were of the same mind. Deep down, I think we still are." She looked over at David to reassure herself before saying, "In fact, I know that my sister Lisa would also be in favor of me going ahead . . . if she knew. Please understand, though, that my attention may not be too focused for the next several months."

Overhearing her, David squeezed her hand. "Of course, I'll give you whatever space you need, Suze'. I suppose we always have the option of withdrawing, if our family circumstances don't allow us to continue." He then asked, "What, then, would be the next step, Evan, now that Suzanne and I have given our okay?"

Hamilton leaned forward and suggested, "Vic here should speak first."

"Concerning practical matters, we do have a little time to gear up," Victor Marino, the campaign's co-chairperson said, "but given the reality that David is a virtual unknown, the sooner we announce the better. He's like a thoroughbred who up until now has been in a stable eating oats. He needs to get out on the track."

"I agree," Roland Peters responded. "The first order of business, it seems to me, is to start getting recognition of both the Federalist Party and Mr. Winfield. Timing is everything."

"And when do you two experts suggest?"

Peters answered, "I'd even recommend this week if the Winfields are feeling up to it. You can feed off this McIntyre talk show, arrange book signings, and get him all sorts of radio interviews. Make sure as many people as possible are introduced to your 'great American.' Sorry for my usual hyperbole, but you've got to get out and tell his story, and tell it soon."

When she heard this, Sheila Linden recounted that on the other hand, she had had a few unfortunate experiences with candidates who announced too early. "At the end of the day, there is no sure thing, but I think we can make a great case, with all the political feuding going on these days, for announcing David's candidacy whenever we choose. I think many Americans are ready for his message."

"What would the steps be after that?" someone asked.

"We would then rapidly coordinate the campaign state-by-state," Peters, the veteran Republican strategist, answered. "That's why Evan and I were hoping that Sidney will join our efforts soon. With the vast networking that Sheila and I have developed over the years, if we get Sid's tactical expertise, we would have a sound start. The reality, though, is that a national effort like this will need a whole host of paid staff and volunteers."

Sheila Linden interjected, "The two major parties are already out beating the bushes heading into their primaries starting in January. That's another big reason it might pay to announce our campaign as soon as possible. Head 'em off at the pass."

As he listened, Hamilton was pleased that Sheila had used the words 'our campaign.' The phrase seemed to affirm her ownership.

On the couch, Winfield reached out and held Suzanne's hand again. "Ready honey?" he asked softly.

"Sorry that I blew up earlier, love. Thanks for being so understanding. Yes, I believe so, but I'm still worried that Lisa will be alright."

Two weeks after Thanksgiving at an arranged press conference in the Grand Ballroom of the Washington-Sheraton hotel, Dean Eccles announced the formation of the American Federalist Party, the AFP, and introduced David Winfield as the new party's candidate for President. His attractive wife stood attentively at his side and prior to making brief remarks, he introduced her and their three children.

When he was done, Gayle Eccles resumed her comments at the microphone. "David Winfield's recent book, *In This We Believe*, is an inspiring introduction into the character of this man. Over the coming months, you will soon get to know all about him." The irony of her expression 'all about him' did not escape the notice of Hamilton and Winfield.

Meanwhile, Sheila Linden and Roland Peters looked at the Federalists' televised news conference along with Sidney Rosenthal. Their longtime rival had finally thought the better of Hamilton's stubborn invitation to work for the new American Federalist Party. Rosenthal had sent him an email saying that he "loved a battle," and with that, had elected to join the AFP as well. The three watched as Gayle Eccles made her announcement.

"Well folks, the cat's out of the bag. Now we can begin," concluded the grizzled veteran from the Bronx.

"The end's a long way away, for sure, but this will be a lot of fun working with you guys for a change." Linden laughed as she and the other two toasted their jury-rigged collaboration with plastic cups filled with tap water.

The next morning, John Madison's syndicated column in the *Washington Post* was titled:

Mr. David Winfield – Do You Know Who You Are? (Do We?)

The column concluded,

It is far too early in this process to fully analyze any candidate let alone a virtual unknown. But Mr. Winfield, I sense, somehow carries an out-of-date aura of well-intentioned elitism and old-fashioned patriarchy. If you say or even if you don't say who you are, Mr. Winfield, we will find out soon enough.

One evening early in 2020, President Foster Henson made an unexpected televised announcement from the Oval Office. "My fellow Americans, over the past four months, I have been experiencing certain neurological and muscular symptoms. After many tests, experts at our finest institutions have consulted with one another and reviewed their findings with Mrs. Henson and me. I must tell you tonight that I am in the early stages of amyotrophic lateral sclerosis, otherwise known as 'Lou Gehrig's Disease.' My neurologists predict that my condition will progress slowly over the next two years and then much more noticeably for my remaining lifetime. In the immediate future, I will be mentally fit – and able to perform the duties of the Presidency.

"For any information about this condition, I invite you to check any number of websites on the Internet.

"I have informed the leaders of the Congress and the justices of the Supreme Court of my physical condition. Vice President Snyder will continue to perform his present duties but he has no plans to seek higher office.

"Therefore, my fellow Americans, I feel that it is incumbent for me to announce tonight that I will not be seeking re-election next November.

"Thank you. God bless America and good night."

President Henson looked steadily at the camera as the picture dimmed.

46

Atlantic City
May 2020

Janet Melone had barely finished her lead-in from a broadcast booth high above the crowds. The Rochan network's news anchor gazed over her shoulder at the auditorium and commented, "Quite a sight. It's incredible that this has all come out of nowhere. You were just saying, John," she said as she turned to John Madison, her network's expert commentator, "that you think this American Federalist Party may be the most legitimate third party America has ever had. Why do you feel that way?"

The *Washington Post* columnist smiled like a Cheshire cat and pointed at two persons sitting in an adjacent booth. "You have it right over there, Janet. Roland Peters and Sidney Rosenthal, plus other folks they know. They wouldn't have joined any kind of third party if they thought it was pointless."

"More on this later, John. Now back to the podium. This David Winfield phenomenon is truly amazing." As the cheering mounted, Melone looked on and while trying to remain detached, found herself inwardly admiring Winfield.

"Remember, we have to be objective in what we say, Janet," Madison reminded her off mike after he saw a telltale flush on the newswoman's neck. "Being elected President takes more than good looks or at least it should. It's more important to hear what he has to say over the next half year."

Down on the podium, Evan Hamilton quieted the conventioneers and spoke: "Since many people don't know our motivations and purposes, I am pleased to explain what the American Federalist Party stands for. It stands for honoring certain patriotic principles that were held dear by the original

American founders. Our new party was formed not only to honor, but also to preserve these precious national values.

"Many of these tenets have been increasingly threatened by the idle talk of libertarians along with so-called 'nullifiers.' These men and women often wrap themselves in the flag of patriotism, justifying their extreme viewpoints by using a catch-all credo: 'Nobody is going to tell *me* what to do.'" Hamilton's voice became pitched as he added stridently, "It's as if they think there are *no* limits, my friends, to anything. No room for community at all. Their incessant demands run counter to the very compromises and agreements made by our founding fathers."

He paused to let his words sink in and then resumed. "We count it fortunate to call ourselves 'the new federalists.' It is our goal to constitute a stronger government. This new emphasis will enable those of us in 21st century America to better preserve our country. To do that, it is imperative that we first elect a true leader."

Standing off stage, Suzanne held tightly to David's hand.

"This evening, we have nominated such a leader, such a patriot, for steering us through these unsettling times. It is my honor to present . . . the American Federalist Party candidate for President . . . the next President of the United States . . . David T. Winfield of Virginia!"

Grinning broadly, Winfield strode forward and shook his friend's hand. He and Suzanne then warmly waved to the wild cheers of more than three hundred delegates in the Atlantic City auditorium.

Looking on, Janet Melone mentioned on air, "This should be exciting, John. It looks like Winfield is ready to speak. Again, we're coming live from the American Federalist Party's first convention, and here is their nominee, Mr. David Winfield."

Once the noise started to subside, Winfield gestured to Gayle Eccles sitting in the front row. "Talk about a patriot, there's your Vice Presidential nominee, a renowned teacher, mother and friend. Now for a little known fact. Besides being our Vice Presidential nominee, Dr. Eccles is a direct descendant of our country's first Vice President, John Adams. That seems to be a very auspicious sign. Let's keep it in the family, yes?"

The delegates stood to cheer again, while Eccles smiled demurely and waved from her seat. She did not want to steal any attention from David Winfield's moment.

"We know that professors often have quiet demeanors," a relaxed Winfield began, "but I assure you that we will hear plenty from Dr. Eccles this fall." Knowing laughter greeted his comment.

Winfield paused to gather his thoughts. He was employing his well-rehearsed facial expression to command attention. During his training sessions at Denise Donasti's Actors' Workshop, she had also advised that with iPads, cell phones and other such devices, he had to watch out for being recorded even if he thought he was out of earshot or off a mike. If he wasn't careful, he would be bound to hear himself on a replay within minutes.

Continuing on, Winfield kept the conventioneers spellbound as he described contemporary America. "The central question I believe is this. Do we make ourselves worthy of the sacrifices of past patriots whom Mr. Hamilton has mentioned? Is each of us able to claim to be a contributing citizen as much as he or she could be, a worthy part of the whole? Friends, I fear not. But we can be."

He pointed to the boldly lettered phrase on the banner hanging from the rafters. "My fellow Americans, read those words *'E pluribus Unum'* – 'from many one.' As we strive for *'certain inalienable rights,'* we must remember that these 'rights' apply to our whole citizenry, not only to a selected few. "

The delegates looked up at him with near reverence.

"Every four years," Winfield continued, "we select a person to be our President. That person takes an oath before assuming this awesome position. And what exactly does that oath say? My friends, the person taking this oath of office pledges to uphold and defend the Constitution of the United States. The larger issue for all of us, it seems to me, is to explore what it is that we're asking that person to uphold? Should it end with them simply mouthing the phrases found on the documents stored in our National Archives?

"It's not so simple. The President and our elected senators and congressmen and women who take this oath are charged with performing certain duties. If our elected officials neglect these constitutionally derived functions, it stands to reason that the Constitution is not being upheld. Even worse, it is being defiled and abandoned!

"What are the several functions of government that our elected representatives are required to do for us that are spelled out in this precious document? Do you know some? They are clearly written down. Here are but a few, codified by James Madison and his compatriots.

"'The Government of the United States is hereby created in order to form a more perfect union.' It's obvious that we're not at the end of that road. Our elected officials are charged to form and reform and then, reform again and again whenever the occasion demands." Winfield was clearly exercised and added loudly, "My fellow citizens, our government should constantly be in the business of pursuing a more perfect union in each passing generation. Sadly, many times our elected representatives have failed to even try.

"Moving on, we are obligated to 'establish justice.' . . . Then, there's the need to 'ensure domestic tranquility' and 'promote the general welfare.' And let's not forget, to 'provide for the common defense.'

"So you can see, my friends, these are some of the guiding principles for our treasured Republic. Our leaders must honor them. Our elected leaders do, after all, at least *say* the words promising to 'uphold the Constitution.' But it is too often evident that there is rampant failure on their part to actually *do* what our Constitution demands."

David Winfield stood still. "In closing, I'd like to share a few lines from a poem by Robert Frost. *'Two roads diverged in a wood, and I – I took the one less traveled by, and that has made all the difference.'* Friends, my fellow Americans, that road now awaits us. Good night and God bless."

"That's all?" Janet Melone wondered aloud. As her network cameras panned the podium, she said, "I'm puzzled, John. It was awfully short. At times, it sounded like the kind of banal speech that we've grown used to hearing every four years, but I'm not sure. He seemed to have both a lot to say and yet left a lot unsaid at the same time. What was your take?"

Madison adjusted his loosened tie, knowing they both would soon be back on camera. "I thought his speech was provocative in a way, Janet, but the proof of the pudding for Mr. Winfield will not be our reactions tonight but what happens next."

"How do you mean?" Janet Melone realized that even if she were pushed, she would be able to quote only snippets of what Winfield had said. She had been much more impressed by his mannerisms. He had great presence – of that she was sure.

Madison lightly commented, "There'll be plenty of time to assess him during the campaign, but despite a certain skepticism on my part, I agree with your gut reaction, Janet. On first sight, this guy seems impressive. We'll just have to see."

An hour later, the nighttime conventioneers had gathered at the Freeport Hotel in the Livingston Ballroom for a large reception, and in the Empire Room for a final press conference.

In the ballroom, the expensively dressed Westchester socialite, Francesca Hamilton, interrupted Suzanne Winfield who was speaking with Denise Donasti. The two women were standing alongside Katy Blitz, the associate curator of the National Gallery of Art who had arranged the Federalist Party's social events. As Francesca gave Suzanne her customary cheek kiss, she said, "You look darling, dear. Quite some speech your David gave. By the way, how's your sister?"

"Thanks for asking, Francesca. Lisa was really fortunate to have caught it early. She's done quite well on low-dose chemo ever since her surgery. Her doctors say she should have more than a 95% chance of a complete cure."

"I'm so glad to hear that, what a relief for you. How are the kids?"

"Don't ask. One fifteen-year-old daughter is more than enough for me. The boys are a piece of cake compared to Caroline."

Denise Donasti took a sip of her Chablis and agreed. "When our daughter finally had children of her own, she and I became the best of friends, Suzanne, so don't give up. Before I forget, your decorations and setups are lovely, Katy."

Suddenly they were interrupted by a loud voice yelling from an adjacent doorway, "Is there a doctor or nurse here? We need help! Now!"

David Winfield was wrapping up his first press conference in the Empire Room when another shout rang out. "Quick! Someone call 911!"

Other loud voices called out from the back of the room. Ensconced behind a bank of microphones and television cameras, Winfield could not see what the commotion was all about.

"Get back . . . stand back!"

"I'll grab him here," a husky bystander said. "Somebody help me try to hold him up."

From where John Madison stood, he could see the frightened cyanotic face of a struggling Evan Hamilton. The man had a desperate look as he speechlessly clutched at his windpipe and contorted like a Raggedy Ann doll in the stranger's grasp.

The people in the Empire Room fell eerily quiet. No one could believe what was happening. Hamilton's eyes rolled back as he lost consciousness. Madison automatically moved over to the stricken man and spoke to the other responder, "Here, let me get next to you. I'll try to keep his arms up."

"He was just standing here and started to choke . . . Let's go!"

Kneeling behind the collapsed man, the muscular stranger wrapped his long arms around Hamilton's midsection, joined his hands against the front of his abdomen, and abruptly jerked his fists upward. Nothing happened and he shook his head. "Keep holding him up." The first responder kept his forearms snuggly in place. "Let me swing my hands down a bit under his ribs. There! Here we go!"

Following a second forceful thrust into Hamilton's belly, a piece of chicken meat flew out of his gaping mouth. The burly young man and John Madison eased his body to the floor. After a low-pitched gurgle emanated from Hamilton's throat, an explosion of vomitus ran over his face.

"Stand back . . . he's barely breathing . . . *he needs air*!"

Nicholas Shippen, who had been standing at one end of the raised platform, came over and informed David Winfield what a Secret Service agent had just told him. "It's Evan – he's choking."

"Oh God, no," Winfield reacted. "Let me see him . . . Will he be alright?" The tall Federalist Party nominee jumped off the mini-stage and made his way through the crowd with the help of two plainclothesmen.

Hamilton remained sprawled on the floor. Someone loosened his necktie and his color soon started to return. Madison and the now identified *Philadelphia Inquirer* reporter continued to kneel by his side. A white-shirted man hunched over them and said, "I'm a doctor. He's got a pulse. Keep his face turned to the side a bit and pull his jaw forward, like this. We have to be sure he doesn't obstruct his airway."

By the time Winfield reached the circle gathered around his stricken friend, three uniformed paramedics wearing Atlantic County Fire and Rescue badges had barged into the room. They parted the crowd as they wheeled in an emergency stretcher. One attendant carried a large, advanced life-support package. They cut off Hamilton's suit, shirt and tie in seconds.

The rescue workers settled into a well-practiced rhythmic routine.

"Keep his airway intact."

"No obstruction right now."

"I hear breath sounds bilaterally."

One paramedic started an i.v. while another used a noisy suctioning device to clear Hamilton's throat. Although he had initially been unresponsive, he now coughed vigorously whenever the suction catheter was used.

"Coming around, that's good. We need an alert patient," the female emergency responder murmured. "So far, guys, he hasn't bought himself a tube."

Hamilton strained as he flailed about on the carpet and twisted his head to the side with a grunt. Again, fetid stomach contents erupted, soiling his face and the paramedic's vinyl gloves. As they started to clean him up, Hamilton had a grand mal seizure, soiled his pants, and once again lost consciousness.

An hour later, Francesca sat surrounded by nearly a dozen friends and strangers in the Critical Care waiting room of the Atlantic County Hospital. Her husband was now intubated and sedated. He had just been wheeled downstairs for an emergency CAT scan of the head.

"It's routine just to be sure nothing is going on," a nurse explained.

"What do you mean, nothing is going on," Francesca cried out. "That's my husband and plenty is going on!"

Nearby, David Winfield and Gayle Eccles talked together in the corridor. The smell of hospital disinfectant filled the air. "The doctors aren't sure, Dave. They think he might end up with some degree of brain damage."

"Have they told his wife about their concern?"

"Not yet as far as I know. When I talked to them they said there was no reason to. At best, they told me that it'd take at least a week of serial observation and testing. The doctors didn't want to alarm her – it's early."

"Suzanne and I are going to help Francesca contact some of her friends. She's obviously shaken."

Gayle Eccles touched his elbow. "Get me his son Everett's number, will you? I've known the young Hamilton for several years. Especially at this late hour, I need to be the one to give him the news about his dad."

Later, while Winfield started to phone some of the contacts that Francesca had provided, Eccles went outside and contacted the groggy-sounding twenty-six-year-old Everett Hamilton in Manhattan. "It's one in the morning, Everett. I'm sorry to call you in the middle of the night, but your father is very, very ill . . . Less than an hour ago. Yes, he's all right for now but he choked and had some sort of seizure . . . He's in the Atlantic County Hospital here in Atlantic City. I'd come down as soon as you can. He is being kept sedated . . ."

"And mother?" He seemed in shock.

"She's being given some tranquilizers. Your sister is here and using her cell phone right now, so you'll have to call her later."

"Thanks for letting me know, tell them you reached me. I'll be out of here as fast as I can but I'll need to borrow a friend's car. It may take a couple of hours driving down the Garden State."

"One other thing, Everett. There are certain materials held there at your family's Federal Bank." Gayle Eccles was nervous. "Do you know anything about this?"

"Yes . . ." There was a distinct hesitancy in the young Hamilton's voice.

"Everett, can you hear me? Do you know about these items?"

"Yes, I know. Dad showed me our family's 'Note of Action' some years ago."

47

Cape May, New Jersey
May 2020

As the couple lay beneath a comforter on a creaky four-poster bed, their faces began to dim in the day's waning light. Despite the chill of the room, the covering warmly wrapped them together as if they were tucked in a cocoon.

"The best . . . that was the best. I've never . . . " he murmured, kissing her hair.

"Somehow, I think you've said that before," she giggled.

He squeezed her fingers lightly before turning away. "I'll be back in a minute, Maureen. I've got to use the bathroom."

"You can bring another condom if you want," she suggested. "There are two or three more in my overnight case."

The mattress lurched like a rocking boat as he slid out of the bed. "'Want' is one thing, 'able' is another, Maureen. Let's just talk for a while when I get back."

"That's fine with me," she agreed. "I haven't snuggled with anyone for a long time, I'd enjoy that. Do your duty, mister, but then hurry yourself back to the scene of the crime."

When he left, Maureen Nightbird-Reynolds turned to lie fully on her back. She could hear the high-pitched bleating of seagulls through the half-closed windows as they floated on the evening breezes. The marine biologist from Alaska inhaled the familiar salt air and listened to the rhythmic thunder of the rolling Atlantic surf. She loved that the waves broke a lot closer to the shore in New Jersey than they did on the Pacific coast. The sounds reminded her of summers at her grandparents' cottage on Cape Cod.

She could not help but think how the weekend seemed like a fairy tale. She had been introduced to John Madison at one of the Federalist Party's hospitality suites. In only a few hours, the handsome divorcee had persuaded her to unwind with him for a few days in Cape May. He had described a delightful-sounding B&B, the Congress Inn, in the Victorian-styled town and supposed that since it was off-season, they could easily get an accommodation.

Maureen lay still in the dark room, exquisitely relaxed in her recovery. The scent of his cologne surrounded her as she dreamily concluded that he reminded her of no other man she had been with in her life.

During the two-hour motor trip to this quaint Oceanside village, the investigative journalist had, by habit, employed his interrogative skills. While he drove, he asked question after question. Since she was a delegate, why had she joined this new political party? What did she see it accomplishing? Who was this Winfield anyway? Was she related to him somehow?

Maureen was amused by his many queries as they passed through the sandy terrain of southern New Jersey. She told him that she joined this third political party because Dr. Eccles had personally asked for her support. "She knew that I was a favorite graduate student of her late husband," she mentioned. "Dr. Eccles told me that I would be the first representative from Alaska."

"I'm not exactly sure, though," he wondered, "what your American Federalist Party hopes to accomplish."

Nightbird-Reynolds mentioned some of the changes that many people at the convention had been talking about. She told Madison that because there were so many good people already in this party, a New Day might be coming. "Just like my mother's favorite song from her '70s hippy days says, John, 'Everybody's talking 'bout a new day in the morning, new day in the morning comin' o −o −o − on.' " Maureen had leaned back in her car seat like a teenager and brightly sung the rest of the lyrics to him.

While cruising down the Garden State Parkway, Madison admitted that so far, he only superficially knew David Winfield. She was startled when he asked point-blank, "Do you want me to tell you what else I've found out about your Mr. Winfield?"

Maureen had swallowed hard when she heard his question. Her mouth suddenly felt as if it were full of cotton and resin. She was afraid to have Madison go on and tell her what she suspected he might say. The twenty-something NOAA biologist suspected for a moment that this crafty columnist knew it all − knew of PATRI and its shadow government. She worried that he had been able to sort all this out given his own wide connections. If he had, it would take only a stroke of his pen to destroy PATRI's well-planned patriots' dream.

Madison said that he hadn't been able to trace the Winfields prior to the 1770's. He found that the pre-revolutionary records maintained at the DAR's Constitution Hall were sketchy. The original Winfield, he discovered, had immigrated to America about that time and this man, Jonathan Winfield, worked on the Fairfax estate of Belvoir. "The succeeding Winfield generations have resided to this day on a large Virginia estate nearby, called Woodlawn Mills. You probably know this already, Maureen."

By the time they got closer to Exit 1, Maureen was finally able to breathe a little easier. She realized that Madison had told her all that he knew. His background research did not appear to even scratch the surface of what there was to know about David Winfield, and thankfully nothing at all about PATRI. She leaned over and affectionately touched his forearm, saying, "You're good, aren't you?"

"At what I do, I suppose so. But we always do a lot of background checking, Mo'. That's the way it is in journalism." Madison added, "Everyone has a story, Maureen, but Winfield's particular tale is starting to get quite interesting."

As she continued to wait for him to return to their bed, Maureen revisited the other events of that day in her mind's eye. There was the motor trip down the Garden State Parkway, the half-eaten Italian dinner, their first embrace, and finally, the amazing lifting feeling of his touch. It had seemed like the moment of release riding on a roller coaster.

The bathroom door swung open and glaring light flooded her face. Maureen blinked her eyes and moaned, "Turn that off, love. With all those watts, how do you expect me to be able to see you in a romantic light?"

Clicking off the wall switch, Madison groped his way back to the elevated bed and snuck back beneath the heavy quilt cover like a letter into an envelope. "You're still? . . . You're so . . . " He stroked the warm moisture on her thigh and smelled her musky fragrance. The forty-six-year-old groaned in mock frustration about his present impasse.

"Relax, John. Remember what you told me a minute ago. We're going to lay around for a while and hold onto each other until you get resuscitated."

"You might be able to help me do that, Mo'."

"No thanks, not right now," she said as she lackadaisically fingered his soft penis. "I might as well use the facilities, myself. I've got time."

Once she rejoined him under the quilt, she positioned herself against his side and traced swirling patterns on his chest. Madison tenderly kissed her nose and conceded, "I think you're right, Maureen. While we are waiting for my revival, we can enjoy talking about whatever."

"Why not, John? Better to talk about 'whatever' than old boyfriends and such."

"Well, if you'd rather, I could tell you about all sorts of ladies that I have known . . . That could be a turn-on."

"Forget it, buster. Just promise you'll let me check on your condition every now and then." Maureen gave his stomach a playful pinch and giggled, "I love that saying, 'When you were good, you were really, really good – and when you were bad, you were better!' It certainly fits you, young fella."

"You're really quite the lover yourself, lady." Madison laughed and moved over to kiss her deeply. As he pulled away, he asked almost as an afterthought, "Off the subject a bit, but did I already mention that I have a son? Peter is graduating next month at U.VA. You'd like him – he's more your age."

"That's nice but I already like his father." She caressed the stubble on his chin and continued, "Now speaking of family, I heard a rumor at the convention. I didn't know you were a member of THE Madison family. Is that true?"

"As long as you don't hold it for or against me, Mo', but yes, it's true. Not directly, though. I'm related through one of his nephews." Madison faced Maureen but in the near-darkness could not see her expression. "It's never struck me as being particularly advantageous. I've tried not to make much about it. You know, we newspaper types have to appear to be unbiased."

"Well, since that's the case, what do you think about our Professor Eccles being introduced in Atlantic City as a direct relative of John and John Quincy Adams?"

"I already knew. Why do you ask?"

"I was just wondering what one relative of an American founding father thought about another."

"I suppose it shows that family and their connections can go a long way."

Maureen bit her tongue. She recognized the danger in continuing on with this kind of pillow talk. She was relieved, but only for a moment, when Madison propped himself on his elbow and slid his hand beneath her billowing hair on the pillow.

"Mo', enough about me . . . tell me about yourself. Anybody as interesting as you in your family?"

No other first-time lover had ever confronted her so directly. The marine biologist had always kept her own lineage secret from a partner – she might seem too threatening. Her father had always advised that she hold her Franklin-family history to herself. He said she was safer that way. Maureen valued this habit of hers, particularly so that evening. Although

John Madison had also descended from a founding father, she knew that he was not a fellow member of PATRI, for reasons she did not understand.

Maureen tilted her head and replied, "Only my mother's father was important, John. He was a tribal leader of the Yakahima nation in the state of Washington. Grandfather Nightbird was well-respected for his leadership in settling many issues that affected the Puget Sound."

"I guess that accounts for your interest in marine sciences, not to mention your high spirits and feistiness, Mo'."

"Well," she corrected him, "that last part comes from my father's side of the family. They had all sorts of interesting characters."

He turned to closely face her. "And you're the latest and greatest in these long lines. I'm glad we're together, Mo'."

They warmly kissed and soon she felt him again start to stir against her. "Me too, John and . . . would you like to know me even better?" Maureen reached beneath the down covering and was glad to feel his arousal once again. Her thumb and forefinger touched his shaft, making an encircling ring. His breath quickened, then caught and held as she purposefully grasped his hardening tumescence. As she did, she found herself becoming aroused as well, especially when she felt his involuntary straining and heard his deep moans. As she often felt with a fresh lover, it was as if she were exploring some new tropical shore.

In the midst of their building foreplay, Maureen realized that it was best to voice a word of caution. "One thing, John. You already found out an hour ago that I'm one of those screamer-types. You know, like a babbling brook when you are . . . there with . . . then in me." She had to catch her breath as his fingers rhythmically covered her moisture.

"That's okay as long as the neighbors don't mind."

"Oh, shush up, puppy." Maureen stroked him even more forcefully, prolonging his pleasure. She marveled at the results of her handiwork and, while keeping precious hold, opened a packet with her left hand using her teeth to grip the foil-cover. "This one is ribbed. Can you believe it's called a 'Rib I'?" She nearly inhaled her laugh. "I love what it does for me." She backed away and put a dollop of lotion on her hand before deftly unrolling the prophylactic onto his fullness.

"I'm glad you're here with me, Mo'. You're amazing!" Madison thrust his hips upwards to help her set the sheath firmly. "Let's be at it," he laughed lustily, pushing them on their sides in a tight embrace.

"Remember, guy — if I accidentally say or do anything you don't understand, don't try to understand. It's just part of who I am." She touched his lips to make him promise. "Kiss me deeply. That always brings me on."

48

Georgetown
May 2020

"Pat, what do think about this American Federalist Party?" Holly Rhyne asked as she sat in a booth at the Kapital Saloon with Patrick Jefferson and her friend Cary. She had not seen him for weeks since she started taking a night course in political science at George Washington University.

"Overall, I'm not sure what to think, Holly," Jefferson said. "At first glance, David Winfield seems impressive enough but honestly I don't know. On the other hand, some of his chief supporters like Evan Hamilton and a few others sound strange, even a little frightening. I can't buy their conviction that America needs an even stronger government here in Washington. I understand, though, that Hamilton is still critically ill, so I doubt he'll be a factor during the election."

Holly took a sip of tonic. "But still, Pat, I have enjoyed hearing some of Winfield's comments. He sounds almost as idealistic as you, friend."

"Saying something and doing something are two entirely different matters. In John Madison's recent columns, he also appears to be questioning what Winfield and his movement is all about. For now, I'll try to keep an open mind."

"There you go, my stubborn friend. At least you could give him credit for highlighting the Constitution in his acceptance speech."

"And why would he not?" Jefferson asked. "It's a frequently used tactic of politicians. Most times it's simply coating-the-cake, so to speak."

"Are you guys debating again?" Cary McAllister quipped as she sipped her Chablis. "What is this all about? You both are always over my head." Cary was a longtime flight attendant for Virgin Flight. She and Holly shared a condominium down the street off Wisconsin Avenue. Although Cary could hold her own on a wide range of subjects, her attention usually started at 10,000 feet and climbing.

"We're not debating, we're talking about David Winfield and his chances. By the way, what do you think, Cary?" Jefferson had a reputation for being a good listener.

Cary took a gulp of her wine. "Not my type. He's too good to be real. I deal with men like him all the time. They *say* the nicest things and then *do* another."

"But he and his wife are reported to be a sweet couple," Holly said.

Jefferson played with his mug of beer before adding, "I'd agree that physical appearances are certainly in his favor but that's only skin-deep. We don't know everything. I've got to admit, though, that in contrast to some of his own Federalist Party, he makes a good sales pitch to moderate voters when he stresses the dual need for protecting individual rights and promoting the common welfare. Given the current state of affairs, that's a good middle-of-the-road strategy for any political campaign.

"In rural Illinois, for instance, we put a premium on having all sorts of freedoms, yet enjoying neighborliness at the same time. People around Carbondale like it that way."

Holly Rhyne sighed. Whenever she heard about Patrick's home in Illinois, it sounded idyllic. Even though she worked for a conservative Republican from Kentucky, she shared little of the Senator's close-minded, self-serving morality. "Why can't the rest of us be more like you are in Carbondale? Seems like we have a lot to learn from you folks. If we can't imitate that, then can we at least get a more workable and friendly political system around here?"

Jet-lagged, Cary listlessly echoed. "Yes, Mr. Congressman, can we?"

Jefferson grinned. "I'm not wise enough to know or I would have proposed it by now to my Congressional leadership. My concern, frankly, is that Congress has been squabbling over the same problems, the same landscape for years. It's become as badly entrenched as the senseless torn-up battlefields of World War One."

He paused before reflecting, "America was built on compromise and reconciliation, so we ought to focus on having justice, mercy, humility, the Golden Rule and such. For instance, if I respect your rights and freedoms, Holly, I will help society as a whole because it becomes more civil and peaceful. And if I take care of your need, I help society too because it becomes more humane and healthy as a result. It should not only be about *me*, Holly – it should also be about *you* and *us* and so on."

"Hurrah for Pat," Cary slurred loudly. "You've got my vote for President!"

"I wouldn't dare to suggest that, Cary. Having principles is one thing, putting them into action is another. At heart, I am the sort of professor who is content with teaching and research, with mentoring. I am certainly not an administrator-type like Dean Gayle Eccles. Look at her, a candidate for Vice President."

"With Gayle Eccles on board, it appears that the Federalists have a good team," Holly opined. "What about your Democratic Party, Pat?"

"We are in a quandary, too many candidates. I suspect Governor Martinez from California has the inside track but we'll see in August."

Cary McAllister yawned. "Sorry, buddies, but it's well past midnight London time. I'll leave the light on, Holly."

"Wait up, I'll go with you, young lady." Holly leaned forward and lightly kissed Jefferson. "I've got some reading for my poly sci class, Pat. I have finals in a week."

Patrick Jefferson picked up the tab and called out as the two women were leaving, "I'll check in with you sometime next month, Holly. Starting in a week, I'll be busy fulltime with Committee work. We're dealing with Republican proposals for severe cutbacks looming for NOAA and the NIH. I swear I never see what these guys are all about – money, jobs, money, always the same. Nonetheless, it's been great seeing you both even for a little while. Take care."

49

New York City

Fall 2020

It was the sort of crystal clear day that hinted frost would soon be on the pumpkin. As she walked on 5th Avenue to the studio, Janet Melone thought that New York City always seemed at its best on crisp autumn days. The Manor Media network's national news anchor was looking forward to meeting her two chief investigative reporters that morning, Fred Rodgers and Bryan Schupak. They had hinted over the past month that powerful foreign interests might be involved in influencing the upcoming national election.

"The best example we've found so far is a certain French-Swiss family, the Rouens, who have set up a business, no it's probably a front, with Robert Laurens and his sons in Houston. You know Laurens. He doesn't run for elections, Janet, he runs them."

"Although some of the European funds can be traced, Jan, we suspect that those on the public record are only a small fraction of the total transfers."

Melone leaned forward. "I thought Philippe Rouen invested in shopping centers here in the U.S. Now he's into oil? That's all Laurens does. It doesn't add up."

Rodgers, her respected business investigator, replied, "I agree, Jan. From what I've seen, there's little evidence that Rouen is into oil deals with Laurens."

"Rouen told us on a conference call that it was merely startup capital for a friend. Strictly business, he stated," Schupak said. "But there's 500 million dollars in Houston that is unaccounted for. That's quite a friend!"

"It's hard to get answers from this guy, Janet. Since Energy Resources capitalization totals roughly ninety billion, Rouen's additions amount to less than one percent, a small piece of the pie. It makes it nearly impossible to audit."

The news anchor was puzzled. "So how does this relate to the elections? From what you've told me, we can't feature a story like this. It's rumor at best. We've had foreign investors in the U.S. for years. Foreign money is hardly on most people's radars."

"On the face of it, you're right, but . . ."

By instinct, Melone convinced herself to listen further. She knew that these two reporters were good, at least their salaries were.

"Bryan found out some interesting information last week from a Veronica C," Rodgers continued.

"Who's Veronica C?"

Schupak had recently been honored for his exposé of widespread hacking in the entertainment industry, an exclusive story that had required him to hack the hackers. "She is a friendly retainer of mine," he answered, "who happened to have had what I would call a more than casual liaison last weekend in Cleveland with Ms. Karen York, one of the Federalist Party big-wigs."

"And?" Melone put the lead of her pencil on the tip of her tongue, a habit of hers whenever she became intrigued during a business conversation.

Rodgers emphasized, "To remind you Jan, Karen York is one of their key operatives. She's the financial director of the AFP."

Schupak went on, "It was fortunate for our investigation that Ms. York has a taste for female companionship. Victoria C told us that one evening she and Ms. York had consumed a fair share of wine. As the two women lay in their hotel room, Karen York loosely related, among other things, that 'oodles of cash' were always available for the American Federalist Party through discrete bank transfers from Texas or the Caymans. She went on and on, mindlessly blabbering that the Winfield campaign never had to worry about campaign finances. Our gal Victoria continued to draw her out and after York's defenses fell, she blurted that the Internet was a great way to cover their tracks. 'According to the Election Commission,' she said, 'we have nearly two million donors through our website. Who's to guess we really have only one donor, instead.' "

"We're still working on the story, Jan," Rogers added. "Somehow, the connections so far lead to Energy Resources in Houston . . . and we suspect that the Swiss-Frenchman, Philippe Rouen, is the key player involved in all this."

"Think about the impact," Schupak said. "It would be a bombshell to report that our American presidency is being put up for sale to a bunch of Europeans."

"You're right, Bryan," Janet Melone conceded. "It'd be quite a story. But we've got to do better than to depend on the words of some besotted person."

"This is precisely why we called for this meeting today, Janet. If you think the piece has merits, we need to go over our next steps. Maybe get York's phone tapped."

"No, no. Mr. Rochan would never go for that. You could always start with the Election Commission. After all, they're charged with auditing campaign financing."

"We've done that — it's mud," Schupak replied. "Winfield has two million donors on file, like Karen York told Victoria C, but who is going to take the time to trace them?"

The newswoman put her pencil down. "It's obvious to me that one of you guys has to interview a sober Ms. Karen York. I'll put a call in to Hugh Rochan. With his connections, the boss might be able to help. He'll know what to do. Besides, he's always keen to break any kind of racy story."

"That'd be great if you would, Jan. Not a word to anyone else, though — especially if our hunch turns out to be a dead-ender. If it's bogus and we go right ahead and broadcast the story, there'd be more than mud on our faces."

Bryan Schupak cautioned, "For now, no one should know but us . . . and this Victoria C, whoever she is."

An hour later, Janet Melone got Hugh Rochan on the phone in Dubai and asked whether he could suggest anyone who might know about a link between Philippe Rouen and Energy Resources in Texas, and their possible connection with the Federalist Party. "I've tried reaching John Madison over at the *Post*. One of my staff remembered that he had written about Rouen's multinational firm in the past, but unfortunately Madison can't be reached, Hugh. He's out on holiday seeing a friend in Alaska."

There was a discernible pause before Rochan dryly asked, "Why are you interested, Janet?"

"A hunch, just a guess, Hugh."

"Give me some time to think about it," he said with a certain hesitancy. "I forgot to ask, Jan. How's your newscast shaping up for tonight?" He sounded to her strangely impatient, his voice distant, as if he wanted to change the subject.

"To put you at ease, tonight's program is full of pretty standard material."

As she described her main stories over the phone, Rochan tapped his fingers silently, marking time. He finally cut in, "My advice, Jan love, is to stay with the basics. Don't go on any witch-hunts. Most people prefer soft news. Stay with what you're good at doing. Your viewers are probably tired of all this boring political news anyway. Instead, be sure to give 'em plenty of touchy-feely stories to hold their attention. We need the ratings, Jan. You need the ratings."

"Thanks for the advice," she said, "but still, if you do come up with any ideas let me know. By the way, when are you coming to the city, Hugh? My mother is here for three weeks. She thinks you're wonderful, but then most women do."

Rochan had not planned on making any trips to New York, but on the spur of the moment he said, "Strange that you ask. I'm coming over this Thursday, Jan. I'll drop by to see you on Friday. Perhaps your mother could join us for a late dinner."

"Hugh, it's funny. Just now, it sounded like you suddenly came up with a bright idea. You're so sharp. It's amazing the way your creative ideas pop up. What's the deal?"

"What you just said, Jan, caused me to wonder. Why not have taped studio interviews with each of the three Presidential candidates separately?"

"Do we have time to schedule this? Election Day is only four weeks off."

"We can talk about it in detail on Friday." Rochan's mind was wrestling with myriad thoughts. "I was going to visit my old friend, Evan Hamilton, anyway. He is still recuperating at his family home there in Pelham. I've been told that he's been left with only a little residual weakness from his stroke."

"I can still picture seeing him choking at that news conference in Atlantic City. It was surreal. Lucky that John Madison and the other guy knew what to do."

"Yes, yes, very fortunate, indeed. Now getting back to my idea, Janet, have your scheduling folks call and see if each Presidential candidate will tape an hour session with you. We'll run a program of all three the following week."

"And why would they agree — especially on such short notice?"

"Because I'm me and I'm persuasive, that's why. Get this, Jan. While we've been talking, I even thought of a new format. It's sort of sexy, but I'll need to detail it to you in person. For now, get your producers to tell the three campaigns that each man would be asked the same questions."

Hugh Rochan felt certain that Janet Melone had forgotten the original purpose of her call. Certain, that is, until she concluded, "Still — try to think about any possible ties of this Swiss-French family to Laurens's business, Hugh. Rodgers and Schupak singled out a Ms. Karen York as their original source. Remember, our two guys are topflight reporters. They wouldn't run off half-cocked."

Rochan somehow managed to keep his voice steady so as not to raise any concern. He couldn't appear to be obstructing her inquiry in the least. "You know, Jan, your interests are always at the top of my own. But again my simple advice is to stay with programming that got you to the top in the first place."

"I'll see you on Friday morning, Hugh. Around eleven. I've got to go over my news-story board by two, though, so I'm afraid no lunch."

"We'll see you then, Jan. Tell your guys Rodgers and Schupak that I'll do my best. I'll let you know if I come up with anything."

Right after they had hung up, Hugh Rochan got on a conference call with Francis du Motier, Sir Ronald Farrington and Philippe Rouen at various locations throughout Europe, and reviewed this new dilemma with them. If their financing of the American Federalist Party were discovered, he tersely noted, PATRI's PLAN would be ruined.

Ronald Farrington heard the news from his country estate in England. "Obviously, I am glad we found this out now, Hugh. Rather a close call, I would offer."

"Rather 'round about, in the least," agreed Francis du Motier. "Has this Ms. Karen York always been such a loose cannon?"

"I am not sure," Philippe Rouen said, "but I think that no one except the four of us should know about her unintended but decidedly unfortunate leak. We've got to stem it right now. No matter what, nothing can happen to this York woman. That would really sound alarms for these two journalists of yours, Hugh."

"What do you suggest, Philippe? They're hot on your trail at the moment."

"Since I am the one who is being followed, I am delighted that these two reporters do not in the least suspect that we know about them. Goodness, let me have fun. I'll simply give them a different trail, a detour we call it, to follow instead!"

"How might you imagine doing this?"

Rouen thought out loud. "Hugh, first tell Ms. Melone something like this – You contacted me to give an interview with her Bryan Schupak. It can take place at the offices of my shopping center in Manassas, Virginia, the Twin Oaks Mall. On that day, I will arrange that by coincidence Bob Laurens will be there, up from Houston. After I introduce him to this Schupak, I will get Robert into some off-handed discussions, stoking an interest in diversifying, perhaps investing in some of my retail businesses. For good measure, I will bring along Francis. He can add to the mix and assure Laurens how nicely he has done by adding Rouen malls to his other holdings in France.

"To ice the apparent deal, I will invite Ms. York as my paid acquisition expert and also Connie Marshall-Rubin as my corporate lawyer in the U.S. When we meet, I will explain to the reporter that the two women are helping with initial discussions with the Houston oilman. Laurens and these ladies will prove convincing, especially if we keep them in the dark concerning our little charade. Robert Laurens will be seen as a prospective shadow partner. Of course, I will emphasize that these preliminary negotiations must be treated as confidential, as mandated by the SEC. That should satisfy Schupak's investigative appetite for a story and allay his suspicions as to the connection between Lauren's Energy Resources and my House of Rouen. I bet it will throw him completely off track, my friends. Business is business, after all."

Philippe laughed out loud over his clever ruse. "Hugh, trust me. M. du Motier and I will lead your Mr. Bryan Schupak on a wild goose chase. You and Sir Ronald can be sure of that. The two of us Frenchmen are such wily fellows!"

"I am going to New York this week. Anyone want a ride?"

"Are you going to see Evan Hamilton, Hugh?" du Motier asked.

"Among other obligations. He is supposed to be making a good recovery."

Rouen spoke from his chateau in Lausanne. "I will be going to Washington tonight, sooner I think is better. I will be tied up in Richmond and Virginia, so be sure to give Mr. Hamilton my regards. I am sure he will understand my priorities."

"And you, Sir Ronald? You have been uncharacteristically quiet, I might say."

"Would it be too much of a bother to pick me up in Paris, Hugh? I can meet you and Francis there. I really want to catch up with the Federalist Party strategists and ask these consultants how the Winfield campaign is going."

"Of course, Sir Ronald — just don't give them any of our secrets." Rochan added, "Remember, good as they are, none of those three, highly compensated political consultants have a clue about us and PATRI, so . . ."

"I know, I know," the English Lord assured him. "But we certainly need their expertise for the success of Mr. Winfield's election to the American Presidency."

"Enough then— we're set. My personal Airbus A320 will pick you two up at Orly early afternoon this Wednesday for the flight over."

"Sorry you are not able to join us, Philippe."

"Moi aussi, mes amis, but think of me heading to Dulles on Swiss Air instead. I have my business to attend to in Virginia. See you there, Francis. Au revoir."

50

New York City

Fall 2020

Later that week, Lord Aplington went to meet with the three American Federalist political consultants in Evan Hamilton's thirty-fifth-floor office in lower Manhattan. The meeting was billed as an information-only session. Gayle Eccles had assured him that the three advisors had no knowledge about either PATRI or his Europe League. As Roland Peters and Sheila Linden entered the bank's conference room, Sidney Rosenthal and Sir Ronald were already there while a worker set up a-v equipment.

"Many more Europeans than usual are keenly interested in your presidential elections this year – particularly your brand-new Federalist Party. When I get back, I want to give some of my friends a general overview of how your and the other two parties' campaigns are going. I hope you don't feel this is too intrusive. I've cleared my visit with Dr. Eccles." Sir Farrington then matter-of-factly asked, "We heard about some novel campaign strategy for your AFP, Mr. Rosenthal. Are you staying with it?"

"We certainly are, Sir Ronald. Most days, we feel like David facing off against Goliath, but in fact there are two Goliaths. We had to develop a wedge strategy for our third party. We're still using it."

"'Wedge?' Between what and what?"

"We want our Federalist Party to somehow fit between the Republicans and Democrats. Let them duke it out, and in the meantime, we take the middle ground."

"None of us, Lord Aplington, provide the message," Roland Peters said. "That's up to Mr. Winfield and his campaign directors – Evan Hamilton and Denise Donasti. Hildy Baker and Victor Marino remain in charge of day-to-day operations."

Sheila Linden dimmed the overhead lights and turned on the projector:

General Introduction

1. *The American Federalist Party – formed in 2019*
2. ......

"Get on, Sheila. None of us need this," Sid Rosenthal interrupted.

Ignoring him, she continued, "First, the favorite Joseph Martinez, the Democratic governor of California, is running very strongly with his liberal base. As always, Wall Street and the religious right favor the Republican, Senator Doren Winchester. He has the solid support of the South and Midwest. And then . . . there is our David Winfield."

"And what about Mr. Winfield?" Farrington asked with barely concealed interest.

"Winfield is the wedge," Linden replied, switching to the next frame. "A third party has never won an American presidential election." She highlighted the details of previous third party campaigns.

"Early on Sir Ronald, Hildy Baker and Mr. Marino saw that we couldn't succeed with a fifty-state strategy. We did not have the time or volunteers to organize committees and produce a competitive campaign in many states for Winfield."

"So . . ." She switched to another screen:

How to Elect a Third Party Candidate

1. *Make message unique and simple – tell a story*
2. *Get name recognition – mass media*
3. *Get independent financing – the big M – don't make deals*
4. .....

As she talked, Rosenthal looked over at the Englishman's half-closed eyes. "Rubbish, Sheila," he fretted. "Lord Aplington didn't come all the way to hear something he could have dreamed up. He probably wants to understand the nuts 'n' bolts of how we're planning to pull this whole thing off. Right, sir?"

With a start, their English visitor grinned sheepishly and said, "Right you are, Mr. Rosenthal, I – I suppose so. Yes, Ms. Linden, what have you and your Federalist organization been doing these past months to elect your man Winfield? It seems to me that the odds are pretty high against him. Ladbroke's isn't even covering it."

"Sir, you anticipated my last two frames." She pointed her laser to a projection of a map of the United States, "As you know, Sir Ronald, our presidential voting system is a bit complicated. In contrast to your Parliament, our Congress does not select our President. We choose electors in each state, none of whom holds an elected office. They are the ones who officially elect the President. The winning candidate must get an absolute majority of the total national electoral vote.

"Given this, here is the strategy that we came up with." Sheila Linden modified the projected map with a colored overlay. "The graphics will show quite well the daily progress of the campaign. As a baseline, the states are either blue (for the Democrats) or red (for the Republicans) based on the 2016 results by each party."

The actual 2016 electoral counts were depicted on the screen by white numerals in each of the colored red or blue states on the graphics. "We decided to focus only on certain states in order to have the best chance of picking up electoral votes. Since there are a total of 538 electors, if we can *prevent* either of the two major party candidates from getting the absolute majority number of 270 votes in the Electoral College, we will have taken the first step to getting our man Winfield elected."

"Then? What's the second step?" Lord Aplington was struggling to follow along.

"You'll see. The fun really starts when the deadlocked election is sent from the Electoral College to the House of Representatives. This next step is outlined in the U.S. Constitution. If we can get to that point, a few constitutional experts have told me that Mr. Winfield could actually win it there."

"Show Sir Ronald which states we're after, Sheila," the pragmatic Rosenthal suggested. "But sir, a reminder. Dr. Eccles told us that you have agreed to keep all this confidential. You should share only the generalities of our discussions with your friends back in Europe, not the specifics."

Sheila Linden pushed a control and a colored overlay fell on eighteen of the fifty states and shaded them purple instead of their former blue or red tones. "These are the ones that we are after. We can tie up the Electoral College with victories in only a few."

Roland Peters nodded and added, "We only have to get a certain number of these purple states in order to successfully wedge Winfield between Martinez and Winchester. Hence, sir, the name 'Wedge Strategy' that Sheila used earlier. "

Sir Farrington adjusted his bifocals and surveyed the projected map.

Linden remained standing, pointing to a few purple states. "Now in 2020, we estimate that we will need a hundred or so electors in order to keep either Mr. Martinez or Winchester from winning the election outright." Numbers within each state flashed on the screen. "The overlaid white numerals, Lord Aplington, are each state's allocated number of electors. There is one elector appointed for every Senator and Representative in a given state, plus three electors appointed for the District of Columbia."

"It changes every ten years," Peters added, "depending on a state's population determined by a census count. That explains why what we call the Sunbelt states have had large increases in electors over . . . "

Sidney Rosenthal impatiently interrupted once again. "Come on now, Roland, our distinguished visitor doesn't have time for a detailed American history lesson."

"If you don't mind, Ms. Linden, please carry on," Sir Ronald said, "but try to make it simple. The screen is starting to look like a schoolboy's geography lesson."

"In almost all the states, it's a winner-take-all. The candidate with a plurality in any given state wins all that state's electoral votes. I know it sounds confusing, but try to stay with me . . ." Linden was reacting to Lord Aplington's puzzled expression.

"I'll do my best, Miss Linden. It's important for me to understand enough to give my peers an assessment of your Mr. Winfield's real chances."

"Right now, going back to what I said, we're concentrating on these eighteen states – the important ones for our candidate. Although relatively few in number, they actually make up about sixty per cent of the total national population."

"And if you win them all, you win, right?"

"No chance of that, Sir Ronald." Peters shook his head. "As you will see on the next map, many states are already colored blue or red. These are likely not going to be competitive in the general election. For instance, take red-Texas – that's Republican, or say blue-California – we give that state to their governor, a Latino Democrat, Joseph Martinez. That's ninety-some electors gone already."

"We're being realistic with what's going on," Rosenthal added. "As of now, we'd be happy to get enough of a total number of electors to tie things up."

"Presently, what are your estimated counts? I believe that you mentioned to me on the phone that the Shippen firm in Kansas City was outstanding at polling and trend analysis." Lord Aplington leaned back in his chair and drummed his thumbs together.

Sheila Linden pushed the hand-held control again. Yellow-tinged numerals appeared in some of the purple states. "These are Nick Shippen's current projections. In a three-way race, we feel we can win the plurality vote in these eight states. For instance, New York here and Mr. Winfield's own home state of Virginia. If we total up the states with yellow lettering, Sir Ronald, we have about a hundred electors for Winfield. If that holds up, there's a chance that neither Gutierrez or Winchester will win the Electoral College, and the Wedge will have worked."

Sheila Linden turned off the PowerPoint and raised the room's power-blinds. The morning light flooded the room and caused them to blink and shield their eyes.

"Thanks for all your time. Trust me – I will not mention the specifics to anyone." The English nobleman got up to excuse himself, mentioning that he had a meeting shortly at the United Nations with the U.K. delegation. "This is fascinating. It's vaguely reminiscent of the blind Cyclops' tale in the *Iliad*. This 'Wedge Strategy' of yours is brilliant. No matter how you call it, I wish you the best. 'Cyclops' – whatever." Farrington smiled as he left, thinking that with luck, the PLAN might succeed after all.

Meanwhile, some of the leading members of the American Federalist Party gathered in Westchester County at the elegant home of Evan Hamilton.

"It's wonderful to see you looking so well, Evan," Francis du Motier said in greeting. "Do you feel as good as you look?

"Sometimes yes, sometimes no, Francis," Hamilton lisped. "My rehab' therapist says that I should be well recovered in another two months."

An unfamiliar man was introduced as 'Bill Finch' to the European visitors. They were told that he had taken the year off from his computer engineering graduate studies at MIT and used his expertise to design the AFP campaign's software.

Karen York remained semi-reclined on a wicker-backed sofa and looked over her shoulder. "Tell everyone what other help you've been, Bill. No, you're so shy. I'll tell them."

As she spoke, du Motier and Hugh Rochan warily eyed each other. They already knew that the others in the room were PATRI members, but they were not sure if Finch's son knew anything at all about the secret organization. Finally in an aside, du Motier mentioned, "It seems obvious to me, Hugh, that his young Finch fellow must know about PATRI, what with his important contributions to the Winfield campaign."

"It's so neat – how he did it and so very helpful," Karen York enthused. "The monies from Switzerland, from Philippe Rouen, are not residing in Houston. You only think so. Actually, the transmissions are stored in a cloud somewhere between Texas and the Caymans. Once the transfer monies are finally on the Islands, Bill Finch's system takes over."

"How does it do that, Ms. York?" Francis du Motier was fascinated.

"I still don't completely understand it myself," Hamilton interrupted with a laugh. "Thanks for asking, Francis. It sounds so simple and yet I've already heard it five or six times and can't explain it."

Karen York continued, "For years, the two major political parties have used 'bundling' to increase contributions. In the tawdry world of campaign financing, it previously was the way to go. Lately, we've also had super-PAC's thanks to our U.S. Supreme Court, which are clandestinely funded by so-called nonprofit corporations and anonymous billionaires. It's now near impossible for the Election Commission to monitor the 'fat cats,' much less any other contributor. "

"We have the same expression in France, the 'grans chats,' du Motier laughed.

The financial director brightened. "We gave the problem to Bill Finch this past June, and lo and behold, he designed his special software in two weeks. He fashioned a system wherein there appears to be a massive community of contributors, but instead they are virtual donors. All of these fictitious names are assigned as being one of hundreds of 'Winfield Patriots.' The monies from these pseudo-donors are delivered to the Caymans, then are periodically withdrawn and placed into American Federalist Party accounts on the U.S. mainland. Names and identifying demographics of actual people were randomly pulled in order to serve as a credible back-up should there be any investigations by voting monitors. There are so many of these so-called 'donors' giving such small amounts that the federal Election Commission would not be able to trace them even if it wanted to. There's probably no time before the election anyway."

Philippe Rouen had called in earlier from Virginia on a secure phone line and was patched into a speakerphone in the meeting room. He sounded irritated. Before Karen York could complete her explanation, he delivered biting comments. "I am sorry to interrupt but let me understand one thing, Mrs. York. My account in Switzerland has already transferred in excess of two billion Swiss francs, some one and a half billion Euros."

Francis du Motier felt his palms moisten. The Europe League completely relied on Rouen's financial judgments. After a long pause, Rouen asked, "And?"

"Not to worry, my dear Philippe," Karen York replied. "Bill Finch and I have already cleared ninety percent of it into various AFP accounts here in America. Most of it has already been put to use. Another $300 million U.S. is currently still in the Caymans. The monies are being used solely for David Winfield's campaign that I can assure. I can also assure you and your compatriots that they cannot be traced."

"Thanks very much for that, it's a relief to hear this directly. Before I sign off, Mrs. York, let me have a word with you about a completely unrelated matter. Are you able to help me out tomorrow morning with some business that just came up? You know my address here in Manassas. It involves a private business deal that I can't go into right now. I really would love your expertise, Mrs. York. I'll pay a good fee since this is such short notice."

As the semi-seduction continued, du Motier and Rochan sat back and marveled at their wily friend's warm and insistent appeals.

"Well, I think that's possible, yes Philippe," Karen York responded. "I have an appointment in Reston late afternoon, so morning would work. I'll be at the Airport Sheraton in Crystal City later this afternoon. I'll come down tomorrow, about nine."

When Philippe Rouen finally hung up, Hugh Rochan asked Hamilton if they might take a break so that he and M. du Motier could make some private phone calls of their own, perhaps from a den or bedroom.

"Certainly, down the hall several rooms on the right – use one of the open phone-lines. While Hugh and Francis are doing their business, anyone want a beverage? How about you, Denise? Nicholas?"

In the den, Hugh Rochan called his Manor Media New York office, "Jan, I think you will like this. I have arranged an interview tomorrow for your reporter Bryan Schupak with Philippe Rouen. He will be at his office in Manassas, Virginia. You said Schupak had leads about something. See if he wants to follow up on this, will you?"

Janet Melone was grateful – the Boss could certainly get things done. "That's great, Hugh. I'll get in touch with Bryan. I'm sure he'll be interested."

"Tell him that I don't think it's much." The media mogul looked at the room's ceiling as he carefully measured his words. "Probably business stuff."

"Thanks so much, Hugh, but Bryan does seem to have a pretty intriguing lead, boss. You've always told me a great story could make . . ."

"Right – and a bad one could break . . ."

"Remember, you also always tell me there's no harm in trying."

As he completed his call to Melone, Rochan thought that Rouen's little subterfuge should work out well. Philippe and Francis would be able to get this frisky reporter off their back by feeding him a good line. This Schupak fellow will see it as just another private business matter, Rouen imagined, as one of many such deals between American and foreigners.

In the meantime, Francis du Motier contacted Robert Laurens by phone and patched him through to Philippe Rouen in Richmond.

"Ro'bert? Philippe here. I am so glad that Francis was able to reach you. He's still on the line."

"It must be important, my friends. You know that I love my Thursdays."

"Pardon, mon ami, I want to discuss some business. No, not that matter . . . it's a proposal for an acquisition you might be interested in."

"Why don't we do it tomorrow, friend? Phone me after ten my time."

The conversation went silent before the Swiss-Frenchman insisted, "It needs to be in my Manassas, Virginia offices. I am afraid that the proposal cannot be done over the phone, Robert. I'll have Karen York and Connie Marshall-Rubin there as well. They have worked with me in the past and I need their expertise. You know them, of course."

Francis du Motier interrupted from Westchester, "Robert, are you still there? Right now, I'm in New York on a business trip. I'll be meeting with the four of you in Virginia too. I've often dealt with my friend in acquiring retail property in Nice. He's good . . . try to hear him out."

The oilman grumbled but deep down he knew that he was always interested in making any kind of a deal, anytime, anywhere. Finally, he conceded, "For you, Philippe, only for you. I'll make it."

As Laurens, du Motier and he finished their conference call, Rouen sat in an office building next to his Twin Oaks Mall. The Swiss-Frenchman of Lausanne smiled to himself. He reckoned that by this time tomorrow he would scramble the trail so much that this pesky Mr. Schupak would surely lose his way.

51

New York

Late October 2020

The three presidential candidates had agreed to come to Manor Media's midtown Manhattan studio for interviews with Janet Melone. A final televised program that included all three interviews would be aired as "Conversations with the Candidates."

The ground rules stated that Ms. Melone would separately interview each man for an hour. None of their un-edited comments would be shared with the two other presidential candidates. Employing this device, the news anchor hoped that her viewers would get a more valid comparison between the three candidates.

Hugh Rochan had detailed his nascent idea to Janet Melone on a recent trip to New York. He wished to preclude the possibility of the men making the usual formulaic evasions. Melone suggested that the taped comments on any given subject should be aired one at a time.

In addition, the sequence of the responses to the questions would be randomly changed throughout the final three-hour televised program. Clinical psychologists had cautioned Melone's executive producer that if each man's comments remained in the same sequence, the viewer might be subconsciously affected. The consultants mentioned that randomization would counter what they termed a first, or conversely a last 'answer-effect.'

The psychologists argued that some viewers normally fatigue over time. He or she might tire of listening by the time of the third candidate's answer. If so, that viewer would favor the initial respondent. Conversely, another person might give more credence to the candidate who had the final response. In that case, the viewer would consider that candidate's statement more favorably, since it was the 'last word.' The psychology experts emphasized that shifting the order of the three men's taped answers throughout the final televised program would be the only way to ensure a 'level-playing field.'

Doren Winchester and David Winfield looked up as Joseph Martinez, the Governor of California, came out of the recording studio. A twenty-something production assistant followed him into the Green Room.

"Good to see you both." Martinez flashed his well-traveled photogenic smile. "I'm sure you'll both love the experience," he quipped.

"I guess both of us won't be leaving town 'til noon," Winfield smiled. "Mr. Winchester and I are giving you a head start, Joe, so you owe us one."

"One what, Dave?" Joseph Martinez asked.

"We'll figure that out by November," the Republican, Doren Winchester said. He stood and expansively suggested in his distinctive West Texas accent, "As a favor, how 'bout considerin' givin' me your Califor-nyah votes, Joe?"

"Out of my control, gentlemen."

"At least O-hi-er's? . . ."

"You've drawn next Mr. Winfield." A fresh-faced assistant stood there with her clipboard. "Please follow me."

The Democrat Martinez turned as he was leaving. "Have fun, Mr. Winfield, these are your kind of questions. All fluff . . . hardly any substance."

Soon after his taping session with Janet Melone, David Winfield joined his wife and Sidney Rosenthal at Herman's Chophouse on West 52nd Street.

"How did it go, honey?" Suzanne looked stylish in a Calvin Klein business suit that would be considered conservatively attractive in any part of America.

"Pretty well, Suze'. It went just like you predicted, Sidney."

The wizened strategist took a sip of his lime and tonic. "Let me guess – she asked about your approaches to the economy, foreign policy, and . . ."

David raised his hand. "Not so fast, it wasn't anywhere near that specific. The way it started, it seemed that I was merely being asked to paint a picture of what a Winfield administration would look like."

"It would look great," Suzanne predicted.

As Sidney Rosenthal continued to watch Dave Winfield's facial expressions, he jumped into a rapid-fire interrogation. "Give us an idea of what really happened, not this cock-a-maney stuff about 'painting,' David. Miss Melone won't mind since we're in your confidence. What's more, you know that her boyfriend Hugh Rochan would have our heads if it got out."

"Obviously," Winfield answered. "All in all, the questions themselves were a bit unexpected, yet interesting at the same time, even though Joe Martinez had called them 'all fluff.' Let me try to remember a few, Sidney."

"What did she ask that took a whole hour?" Suzanne teased. "I'm curious. That good-looking lady didn't get your phone number, did she?"

"No, no. Basically the whole thing was taped as if it was a private conversation between Janet Melone and me, not at all like a debating format. Her first question was about management skills: 'How would you run your Cabinet meetings?' "

Winfield continued telling them how he had performed. "I would create temporary mini-cabinets or assign action-subcommittees. This sort of delegation would permit those cabinet members whose authority overlaps on a given issue to have collective responsibilities in coming up with recommendations. I called it an 'open-wall approach' between the various Departments and their agencies."

As they sat at their table, he said that he mentioned that Ronald Reagan had successfully used a similar governance style during his administration in the '80s. Winfield said that he told Janet Melone that he had no problem crediting the Reagan model. He surmised that he might have scored some points from both Republican and Independent viewers. Sidney Rosenthal had to agree.

After they ordered lunch, he reviewed Ms. Melone's next questions:

"'Who is your favorite President – and why?' I said George Washington, and then detailed my reasons. 'Who is your favorite member of a recent administration – and why?' I suggested that a recent Secretary of Defense was the kind of person that I would covet for a Winfield cabinet member. 'Who is your favorite member of Congress?' and then, 'Who is an outstanding jurist – and why?' "

Winfield added, "These questions led her to ask me what kind of qualities would I look for in my cabinet and judicial appointments. Janet Melone wasn't asking for any specific names but she focused mainly on the personal attributes that I most admire. It wasn't your usual political question, Sidney, but I was delighted that she asked anyway."

"Sounds like Ms. Melone was testing whether you could think on your feet, David," Rosenthal surmised. "Did she ever get you to detail some of the ideas that we've talked about? I thought they were rather fresh and appealing."

"Yes, Sidney. I was able to sneak one of them in when she asked how I could possibly get through Congressional deadlock, especially since I was a third party nominee. I expressed Gayle Eccles's idea about inviting different Senators and Representatives of both political parties to the White House weekly on a rotational basis. I mentioned that it would help if Congress members of different persuasions enjoyed more friendly interchanges. I stressed that civility would be given a very high priority in a Winfield administration.

"In addition, I brought up the notion of the federal government encouraging more regional cooperative efforts. I cited the effectiveness of the TVA as a good example of how a regional program had succeeded in the past, reminding her that in the '30s more than one state was affected by the Southern flood plains. It required a solution that was more extensive than any one state could do on its own. To give a current example, I pointed out the desperate water shortage impacting the Western states. I argued that, like the situation that caused the creation of the TVA, one or two Western states couldn't handle this present problem alone. Any decisions affecting the Colorado River, for instance, impact the whole region and its seven states."

"Did she seem to see your point?"

"I think so, Sidney, if her facial expressions were any clue. But I might have confused her a bit when I went on and tried to explain my initiative for encouraging more democratic rules for Congressional committees. I said that if it were up to me, minority party members should be allowed to set some of the Congressional agenda."

"You said it was unstructured – you weren't kidding, Dave." Rosenthal had never heard of anything like it. "What else did Miss Melone ask?"

"She asked about my views for education reform and then a few other topics before we talked about foreign affairs. I mentioned that in this day and age I favored having closer ties with Europeans than with any others in the international community. I reminded her that, by and large they have been America's closest allies over the years – in fact, since our nation began."

Winfield smiled thinking back on his remark. He took a drink of his iced tea and then continued, "Near the end of the session, she asked if I had what she termed 'outside-of-the-box' thoughts on any other issue. Ms. Melone seemed amused when I off-handedly mentioned that my wife might be able to answer that question better than I could."

Suzanne laughed and agreed. "Probably so, David, what with some twenty years of marriage. But let's hold on a second, our food is here." A waitress served their three pastrami-on-rye sandwiches.

"Wait 'til you try these kosher dills – they make any day in New York City special," Rosenthal declared. "But seriously, David, getting back to what you were saying, how did you answer that thinking outside-the-box question?"

After swallowing his first bite, Winfield was able to mumble, "That's better. Now as to what I suggested. First, election campaigns should be much shorter, like they are in Europe. Ms. Melone seemed outwardly skeptical that this could be accomplished in the U.S. and so she went on and asked me, 'Any other bright ideas, Mr. Winfield?'

"I couldn't tell if she was being sarcastic or what, so I just moved on to the idea of reestablishing earmarks in the Congress. I tried to summarize the main points, telling her that a Federal Earmark Fund would finance these projects. I explained that this would be a new type of earmark. All elected Senators and Representatives would be encouraged to competitively submit proposals to a review board. Ms. Melone understood the idea better when I compared it to the way research grant applications to the National Institute of Health are handled. Each Congressperson's proposal would receive an unbiased scoring graded by merit. Thereafter, the monies from the Earmark Fund would be allocated on the basis of this grading system, up to but not exceeding the total available dollars for that budget year."

Winfield took another swallow of his cold drink before saying, "She followed up by saying something like 'interesting, interesting – those are interesting thoughts.' While still on camera, she admitted that she had, indeed, asked me to think 'outside-the-box' and then off camera, confessed to me how impressed she was by my novel ideas.

"I thought this part of the interview went reasonably well, even though she seemed puzzled at times. I doubt that either Martinez or Winchester came up with any ideas that were as off-the-wall as mine." David laughed.

Sidney Rosenthal wiped his mouth. "We'll just have to wait and see if this weird program format of Hugh Rochan's did you any good, David. Come now, be honest. It sounds like you are feeling fairly positive about the experience."

Winfield took another bite of his sandwich and motioned thumbs up. Rosenthal gave his own opinion. "I agree. It sounds like you had a fascinating morning."

David swallowed his mouthful and took a deep drink before responding, "It was. I think we should do fine – all of us."

Denver

The following Sunday evening, David, Suzanne and several of the senior Federalist campaign staff were wrapping up a get-together in a large suite at a Denver hotel. The people had gathered to watch the Janet Melone special entitled "Road to the White House – Conversations with the Candidates."

"You did really well, Dave. You held your own with both of those guys."

"I liked your answer about President Washington being your favorite President," Diane Fleming-James, the Denver native, said coyly. "If people only knew."

He frowned and squeezed her hand. "Enough of that, Diane, we're in a crowd." Winfield pointed at the young aides milling around the room.

The Federal Reserve governor of Denver had drunk her share of wine and was starting to feel it. "Shssh – shssh," she said, placing her index finger clumsily over her lips. "Well, all right then, Mr. Winfield." She pouted like the original Marilyn.

Her husband, a handsome Afro-American plastic surgeon, came over and put his arm around her. "We should be going soon, Di'. I've got an early case tomorrow."

"Just a second, Dr. James," Winfield said, "You don't want to miss the show's last question. I hope I get the last word."

Soon it was evident that was to be the case. First Martinez's and then Senator Winchester's taped concluding remarks were aired on the screen. Suzanne looked nervously at her watch. "Only five minutes left in the program, Dave. What happens? Do you remember?"

"I think so, but . . ."

After a brief public announcement by the League of Women Voters, a relaxed David Winfield appeared on screen as he set himself for Janet Melone's last question.

"Now for my final question, Mr. Winfield. First, let me say it has been an honor to be with you and the others today. So in conclusion, tell us what will you be thinking, if you do win the election, as you take the oath of office next January?"

Winfield carefully measured his response. "My thoughts, Ms. Melone, would focus on the words of the oath itself – the need to preserve, protect and defend the Constitution of our United States. This precious document is much more than words cast in stone. After all, it was written by our Founding Fathers so that each future generation could discover its full meaning for themselves."

The American Federalist Party's campaign staff in the Denver hotel suite was on edge, checking each other's reactions as they watched their man Winfield. They knew this was a special moment for the campaign.

"I always tell my children, Janet, that change is often good. Yet, as you and I know, change for the sake of change can be overrated and on occasion dangerous. The Constitution has given us the ability to legislate changes whenever our people feel they are necessary – in the form of Amendments to the Constitution itself." He cleared his throat. "This so-called living document has ensured that all generations have been able to honor the Founding Fathers' deepest intents.

"Getting directly to your question, Ms. Melone, if the people do decide for me to take the precious oath to uphold this Constitution as their President, I imagine that when I stand there, I would reflect on those patriots that started our nation in the first place . . . And to the many subsequent patriots that kept our Union intact over all the years."

David Winfield spoke directly to the camera in a firm yet humble voice. "Finally, I suppose that as I gazed out from the Capitol steps next January, if the opportunity falls to me and my family, I would be mindful that there are many, many patriots still in our midst.

"Our wonderfully diverse country must and will go on with all of us bound together, 'E pluribus Unum.' With that, I would be honored to raise my hand and pledge my oath."

52

Woodlawn Mills, Virginia
November 3, 2020 6PM EST

An imposing entourage of Secret Service vans escorted the Winfield family in their estate car through the gates of their Fairfax County home. David and Suzanne had gone with their immediate family to a special election-eve vesper service at Christ Church of Alexandria. The service had been private, limited to church members only. Winfield glanced in the rearview mirror. "Thanks, Mom, for suggesting we go tonight."

Nancy Winfield softly replied, "Your father would have loved being with us, especially this evening." She turned and reminded her grandchildren, "Christ Church is where your parents as well as your grandfather and I were married."

"Is it true, grandma, that George Washington went to our church?" Nine-year-old Bobby Winfield loved to hear about all sorts of local history.

"I do not personally recall, young Mr. Winfield, he was before my time," his grandmother said with a chuckle, "but most people think that he did. Maybe you and I can look through the church registry someday and see for a fact."

"Hey, look!" Jeffrey Winfield exclaimed pointing at a mass of television trucks that had pulled up on the front lawn. "When did they come?"

"Duhhh . . . while we were at vespers," Caroline said, poking his shoulder.

"Kids . . . manners, please. Your father hasn't stopped the car." Suzanne then added, "Jeffrey, we expected them to show up by now. These trucks and vans will be here all night with reporters while we're inside watching the voting returns."

David Winfield pulled up before their four-car garage. He got out and resolutely walked toward the reporters, while the others entered their home by the back door. The network broadcasters were in the process of interviewing Evan Hamilton in the glare of elevated halogen lights. A production assistant hired by Denise Donasti came up to David and hurriedly applied facial makeup as he stood off camera.

"Thanks, Polly, I know I probably needed that, but . . . ouch."

"You look well enough to me, Mr. Winfield, but you know our Denise." She wiped the excess cream from his temples. "I do like your new hairstyle, Mr. Winfield. 'Presidential' is what I'd call it."

"We'll see tonight if enough voters think it's presidential," he laughed.

Hamilton glanced over and saw that Winfield was ready. "Here's the guy you really want to talk to," he said, gesturing in David's direction with his good arm.

Winfield smiled as he stepped forward into the lights and recognized several of the reporters by name. Four Secret Service personnel stood in customary postures nearby, and a separate cluster of eight Spartan-looking men and women took up positions of their own. The Department of Homeland Security knew the Winfields had employed a private security contractor for years, and after thoroughly vetting the firm, had given them clearance to remain on site. But they were replaced that day by an unmarked DOSECOF unit remaining in the shadows on orders from Fort Marshall.

In addition, General Philip Mason had received confidential information from two operatives who had infiltrated a cell of the Virginia-based New World's Patriots. They reported that the anarchist group had discussed a plot to injure certain candidates on Election Day. Despite hearing that this attack had probably been aborted, Mason wanted to be sure that David Winfield and his family remained safe. Accordingly, he had boosted Woodlawn Mill's security. Another twenty DOSECOF elite warriors were hidden, guarding the access roads to the estate.

Winfield adjusted himself on a temporary dais, before saying, "Thanks for being here tonight." He looked directly at the cameras. "Let me first say that this is where it starts for everyone of us – home. We just got back from church and my wife and family had to go inside for dinner. Perhaps they'll be out later. Certainly, Mr. Hamilton and I both intend to meet with you periodically throughout the evening."

After this short greeting, Evan Hamilton came forward and announced, "Now let me brief you all on the logistics. My wife Francesca and Mrs. Winfield have organized things for you. First, you'll be happy to know that the garage is warmed by space heaters. You enter by the side door and you'll find pots of chili, breads, fruits and liquid refreshments, and of course plenty of coffee. Maria here at Woodlawn Mills is a great cook. She has arranged several card tables with chairs for you. Hold on, I nearly forgot – the lavatory." He paused and asked, "Are we still off camera? Good. It's inside on the way to the kitchen. Any questions?"

"Mr. Winfield mentioned giving periodic statements. Can you expand on that?"

Hamilton pulled his cuff back and looked at his watch. "It's now near seven o'clock, Eastern Standard time. The polls in the East will be closing soon. Let's say I'll be out here every hour on the hour to give you a brief statement. Mr. Winfield, though, probably won't be with you again until near eleven. We need to wait for the results from the western states before he can possibly comment."

"Whenever you come out, can you at least give us some forewarning?" a Washington-based reporter asked. "I may be in the middle of a bowl of Maria's chili."

"Sure can, Alistair. If there are no other questions, that's it for now. Remember to use the side door of the garage over there. Well, as they say, 'Let the show begin.' "

Winfield and Hamilton turned and walked through the home's stately white front door. Halloween pumpkins and cornstalk decorations still stood on either side of the warmly lit doorway.

The news teams were impressed by the stately appearance of the bricked Georgian estate, a colonial home dating back to the late eighteenth century. Suzanne had placed an electric candle in each of the windows as a remembrance of the spirits of the many persons that had lived thereabouts, a custom she had admired in the homes of their former neighborhood in Georgetown.

Inside, Bobby Winfield greeted the two men as they entered the large family room. The hewn uncovered beams running throughout the ceiling made it seem like an early American inn. "It looks so exciting out there," the boy said, pressing his nose to a windowpane. "I wish Mom had let me have my friends over tonight."

Caroline poked him. "It's a school night, little boy. You're lucky to even be allowed to stay up past nine. Bobby, you think you've got it bad? I bet that Jeffrey and I are going to be bored out of our minds."

Her youngest brother looked around as if in agreement. The group of adults really did appear stuffy. Bobby quietly made up his mind to eat quickly and then escape to play video games upstairs.

While they waited for dinner, Hamilton went over, rubbed his wife Francesca's neck, and announced, "This is quite a night, friends – all these years later."

"What do you mean 'all these years,' Evan? The Federalist Party has only been around for a year," Sheila Linden corrected.

Hamilton swallowed hard – he feared that he had spoken too freely. Only four people in the family room, other than himself, were aware of PATRI – his son Everett, Phil Mason and David and Suzanne Winfield. Since his stroke, Hamilton knew he often had a hard time holding his thoughts, especially if he became stressed.

Winfield put his hand out. "Evan, you probably meant 'months,' although I agree, at times that this campaign of ours has seemed like years." He chuckled and, as he did, asked his son Jeffrey to come over and help his grandmother. Both Philip Mason and Everett Hamilton had to inwardly laugh at Winfield's deft deflection.

"Sure can, Dad. Can I get you a tray for your chili, Mom-Mom? It's really good." It was evident that the thirteen-year-old had inherited his mother's manners.

"That would be lovely, young man. I'm glad I'm sitting here next to the fireplace – my favorite spot." Nancy Winfield, the matriarch of Woodland Hills, arranged a comforter on her lap and pleasantly smiled at the others. She could see that the three Hamiltons had gone to serve themselves in the dining room. General Mason and his wife Betsy sat on a sofa next to her.

An outgoing woman was sitting nearby in a wing-backed chair. 'Mom-Mom' Winfield fretted. She had been introduced that afternoon to this woman and a second political consultant. Nancy Winfield thought that she was Miss Sheila Lent, or was it 'Linton,' something like that, and the other, a Mr. Peterson, or was it was 'Peters?' She realized that she would have to try her best to remember their names that evening.

Maria and Jeffrey brought in two tray tables, followed by two bowls of chili, salad and fresh baked bread, and placed them in front of the two women. "I don't ever eat this well at my home in St. Petersburg, Jeffrey," she told her grandson. "Maybe I will decide not to go to Florida this year."

"Like heck, Mom-Mom, you can't stay here. We want to spend our school winter holiday there with you."

"Miss Linden. That's it – Sheila, I think – I'm always amazed how much energy these children have. Just like their father had at their age."

As she politely listened to her, Linden looked across the room. The men were gesticulating loudly and for a moment she wondered whether some unexpected early election results had come in. She discovered, however, that the men were instead discussing Monday night football's game-of-the-week.

8PM

Suzanne Winfield had had workmen place three flat screen televisions about the room with a smaller one in the kitchen. That evening, four different broadcasters competed noisily with one another and their squawking carried throughout the room:

> "And the polls just closed at . . ."
> ". . . a projection from Rhode Island . . ."
> "Alice Reems will be reporting from the Joseph Martinez headquarters in Los Angeles later . . ."

"How are we to decide what to listen to? I can't hear any one of them clearly," Nancy Winfield spoke out. "There's too much chatter."

"That's easy to remedy, Mrs. Winfield, I am having problems, too." Sheila Linden stood and clicked the mutes of all the remotes. "There, how is that?"

The room turned silent and the others immediately asked, "Hey, what's going on? What happened?"

"The noise was bothering the two of us. Either we lower all the sets' volumes or we choose a primary broadcast at any one time. I favor going this route. We can always switch the sound to another channel if that one looks more interesting."

"I vote for the Melone coverage on Manor," someone shouted from the kitchen.

"Count me in for the Public News, the PNN coverage," Betsy Mason countered while she sipped her wine. "They've got the best analysis here in D.C."

"We'll still be able to see all the other sets at the same time but if anyone absolutely must, they can go to our bedroom," Suzanne suggested.

"You guys are so old fashioned," Caroline Winfield quipped as she carried her dinner bowl in and sat near her grandmother. "I checked out Electionnight.com on Dad's computer upstairs. Whoops, sorry Dad. I forgot to ask."

"Thanks for telling us, young lady, even if you're more than testing your limits." Suzanne frowned. "But since you're always online with your friends, I'll give you a break, but only tonight. In the meantime, I guess we should ask if you learned anything."

Caroline felt relief that her mother had given her a reprieve. "Well, . . . they have a map of the U.S. and you can get real-time results from any state by just clicking on that state. Dad, you were close in Connecticut but Mr.

Martinez won there by 5%. They commented that the only good news for the Winfield campaign there was that you came in second and not third."

As Caroline began to eat her steaming chili, Judy McIntyre's familiar voice carried over from a set. "One of the things we're watching with interest is how much of a vote Winfield's Federalist Party will ultimately get. Look at this," she said, pointing to a large U.S. map. "Rhode Island, we project as blue – for Joseph Martinez and the Democrats."

Another person came on camera. "That was expected, Judy, but not by such a close margin. Frankly, the surprise I'm seeing is this. David Winfield, an unknown only a year ago, got nearly 36% of the vote in the Ocean State and the American Federalists only campaigned there for the last two months."

McIntyre listened as her studio guest analyst, a columnist from the *Boston Globe*, went on. "Look at some of the other early returns from the East. This could be an interesting night, perhaps even historic. As we all know, Judy, the winner of any given state needs only a plurality of the popular vote to take all of that state's electoral votes. What is fascinating so far is the early strength of Winfield in Massachusetts. No doubt, having Gayle Eccles from New England on the ticket has been helpful."

"How does the rest of the East look at this point?"

"Well, we've projected six races to this point. Connecticut, Maryland and Rhode Island – they're all blue. West Virginia and Delaware are red – Winchester was favored there. And only Maine is green. For the viewers, that's the color we'll be using tonight for the new Federalist Party – green. Incidentally, Judy, if Maine continues to hold for Winfield, that would be the first victory of any state by a third party since Strom Thurmond's Dixiecrats won several Southern states in the campaign of '48."

The Public News Network anchor continued her line of questioning. "Remind me, how many states did the States Rights Party end up winning in '48?"

"Four all told. Thurmond got 39 electoral votes out of these states. He and Ross Perot, who received close to 19% of the popular vote in 1992, must have served as some sort of an inspiration to this year's Federalist campaign. Both of the previous campaigns showed that a strong third party presidential candidate was a real possibility."

"I, for one, have been impressed by this Mr. David Winfield," Judy McIntyre said, before she heard her producer off-camera warning her to stay objective, on target. Dropping her line of thinking, she abruptly nodded at her studio analyst. "I agree with you, Frank. It is shaping up to be quite a night for all three candidates."

Roland Peters flashed an 'OK sign' as they watched the election results in the family room, remarking, "We finally have their interest now, eh Sheila?"

"You bet, my friend." Then she saw out of the corner of her eye that one of the other screens was tuned to the main Manor Media channel. "Let me switch to Hugh Rochan's network for a little while. Does anyone mind?"

An unfamiliar voice announced, "So far this evening, we've had some results settled, but remember, it's early, only eight East Coast time. In the large middle-Atlantic states, we can't call any candidate a winner yet. That goes for Pennsylvania, New York, North Carolina and Virginia. I must admit, though, it's a surprise to see the American Federalist Party doing so well their first time out of the chute."

The camera flashed to the news anchor, Janet Melone, who asked in her well-worn, innocent-sounding voice, "What do you think this means, Chase? Maybe it's not too surprising. After all, Winfield seems to have a lot of connections . . ."

"If he gets enough actual votes to matter, especially if he captures one of these large states, it will be obvious that he and his party will be a force for the new administration to contend with, whether it be Democratic or Republican."

"I will say," Melone remarked with barely disguised admiration, "that no matter what, these new brand Federalists are already a force. It looks like they're putting the two-party system on notice tonight."

Suddenly there was a scream from the top of the stairs. Caroline, who had returned to her father's office, bounded back down the steps two at a time. "Hey, you all. Electionnight's website just said that Dad is going to win Virginia!"

"It's not on here, yet. Wait, let's go back to PNN."

On one of the room's television screens, they watched Judy McIntyre scan some newly arrived script on her desk before she finally looked up and announced, "There we have it. Using our polling numbers from a variety of bell-weather precincts, we are able to predict that David Winfield will win his home state of Virginia." The Dominion State flashed green on the large map behind her. There were now two green-colored states— the home states of the Federalist Party's candidates.

McIntyre went on, "What will be important now is how the New York and Pennsylvania votes play out. We've never had to run projections when there are three candidates running so closely. I doubt that we'll get any sort of resolution for hours."

"That's not what Gayle just said," Peters interrupted, coming in from the back hall. "I talked to her at her Boston hotel minutes ago. Dr. Eccles said that Sidney Rosenthal has special tracking software of his own, and he also called some of his precinct lieutenants this afternoon. He had assured her that it was 'in the bag,' saying that 'my boyze and gals are comin' through jes' like I promised.' " Peters said that Gayle Eccles admitted that she wasn't quite sure how Rosenthal had done it, but if what he called 'his folks comin' through' got the New York vote, then somehow his street-smarts had worked after all.

No sooner had he relayed the information, one of the muted television screens pictured a flashing outline of New York State. "Sheila, turn the sound onto that channel quick! Evan Hamilton exclaimed. "That might be it."

As the announcer spoke, the image of New York flashed green behind him. "We have good evidence, since more than 60% of the votes in the Empire State have been counted, that the Winfield-Eccles ticket, coming in with 36% of the tabulated vote thus far, will narrowly defeat Martinez here in New York. We know it's early, but we'll make the call."

There was a loud cheer in the room. "That's a big help, Davey. Part of our strategy seems to be working out."

"29 electoral votes in one bunch! We're up to 46 total already, and eleven more if we take Massachusetts."

Peters let out a whoop and celebrated out loud, "Our wedge, the Wedge, we gotta keep it going – the Wedge!"

Caroline Winfield came running down the stairs once again, "What was all the shouting about? I just saw on the Internet that some polling places in New York City are being placed under lock 'n' key by election officials."

Even as she spoke, the color of New York State on the television screen in front of them suddenly faded. A pale-hatched graphic, representing that it was 'undecided,' replaced the green tint. The third television network's commentator furtively stole a glance at his monitor before saying, "Sorry, ladies and gentlemen, we spoke too soon. A recount has been ordered in three of New York City's boroughs. We understand it is something to do with issues involving electronic ballots. Thankfully, there's a paper ballot backup system in place, so the officials should be able to sort this out within the next day or two. This will keep us from naming the winner in New York until we have the actual voting numbers."

Roland Peters thought to himself, "Tracking methods, my gosh. I hope Sid knows what's up and doesn't get caught with his pants down over his tracking methods."

53

Woodlawn Mills, Virginia
November 3, 2020 9PM EST

Additional returns from around the country indicated that Doren Winchester's strong conservative base was starting to come through for the Republican ticket. In the meantime, Massachusetts barely decided in Winfield's favor and was now labeled green on the map. The people sitting together in the Woodlawn Mills family room glumly took notice that New York remained back in the undecided column.

Evan Hamilton suggested that as Winfield's chief-of-staff, he should go out and give a brief comment to the gathered reporters. Suzanne Winfield got up and walked with Evan and Evan's son along the hallway towards the garage, and then stepped outside into the subfreezing night air. The reporters had set up their recording cameras so that the estate would be framed in the background.

Inside the home, the others suddenly saw on the TV screens the three standing outside in the glare of floodlights. Dave Winfield thought he could even hear Hamilton's comments coming directly through the front window as the Public News Network broadcast began with a voice-over. ". . . Live from candidate David Winfield's home of Woodlawn Mills." He sat down next to his mother as everyone eagerly watched Hamilton's first live press update.

"What did Evan say he'd talk about, Dave?" Philip Mason asked nervously.

"Just some generalities. Quiet now, let's see how he comes across."

Everyone in the family room listened intently to what was transpiring outside the home.

"I am Evan Hamilton, Mr. Winfield's staff manager. This is my son, Everett, and of course, most of you know Mr. Winfield's wife, Suzanne. Thank you all for being here on this frosty night. First, I want to give a short statement from the campaign and then I'll entertain a few questions.

"In our view, the early results appear to be promising. We're getting a moderate amount of votes. David Winfield's message has obviously been heard. As has already been noted, this is the first time in over seventy years that a third party has won any electoral votes. We have three states, so far, and both New York and Pennsylvania are very close. There's a chance to pick up electors in these key races, too.

"We're encouraged by the diversity of groups supporting Mr. Winfield. In many parts of the country, voters in traditionally red and blue states are voting for him. We suspect that there are a lot of independent-minded people seeking a voice. It appears that David Winfield has touched a responsive chord all across America."

Hamilton smiled thinly and then said, "Mr. Winfield will speak to you in another several hours. Ladies and gentlemen, the night is young. And now, Mrs. Winfield wants to give a personal greeting."

Suzanne stepped forward and with her honeyed accent offered a few well-mannered pleasantries, saying, "My family and I sincerely welcome you and the many viewers to our home. Besides your presence, one other thing unusual tonight is that our three children didn't do their standard dose of homework." She smiled warmly. "You can understand that they are more than a bit excited. They are keeping their fingers crossed along with the rest of us. Thank you very much for your fine journalistic efforts. We're glad you are here tonight."

Hamilton stepped back to the microphones. "Thanks, Suzanne. Are there any questions for me?"

An aggressive-sounding newsman on the frost-covered lawn called out, "Mr. Hamilton, it has appeared for many months, as it does tonight, that David Winfield will not be elected. What does he hope to accomplish, to become a modern day Don Quixote?"

"I think that he, and we, expect him to be the next President. Why else would he have run?"

Judy McIntyre back at her studio was listening to the live feed. She directed a question into her PNN reporter's earpiece. "Ask him, Jake, to whom Winfield and his neo-Federalists would throw their support if there is an electoral stalemate?" When Hamilton got around to recognizing him, the young on-site reporter asked Judy McIntyre's question aloud.

Hamilton looked squarely into the cameras. "We're not ready to talk deals with anyone, Jake. We American Federalists are not out to be kingmakers." He clenched his teeth and went on. "I'll say it again. We're about electing a President tonight and not a backroom politician. It's awfully early for any speculation. Let's see how things play out. We'll be back later tonight. I'll let you know."

When he concluded, the networks resumed their studio coverage. As Hamilton moved off the platform, a Latino correspondent yelled out, "While we've been standing here, I just heard that our experts have called New Jersey for Martinez and the Democrats. Any comment?"

Everett Hamilton brusquely stepped forward and answered off-air for his father. "This was expected," he dryly noted. "The mid-Atlantic has been Democratic for years. Let's leave it at what my father said. We need to see how things work out."

Evan Hamilton's breath clouded in the chilly air as he added, "I understand Maria set out more hot spiced cider with the coffee and doughnuts. Help yourselves." He stepped back and gingerly went back inside through the stately, holiday-decorated front door, flanked by his son and Suzanne Winfield.

As the three entered the family room, they saw a commentator reporting from a balcony of a hotel ballroom. In the background, people were moving about like ants on the crowded dance floor.

"We're at the Hotel Bel Air in Bel Air, California – the Democratic national headquarters here in Joseph Martinez's home state," a reporter said, holding her microphone close to her face. "You may have heard a big shout behind me when they announced that Martinez took Rhode Island and, just now, the state of New Jersey. Within the last hour, Republican Senator Winchester fell short to David Winfield in nearby Delaware after having an early lead. Joseph Martinez's margins of victory elsewhere in the East are in the six to ten percent range, which certainly suggests to the crowd below me that this may be his night. It is only early evening out here in Los Angeles. Governor Martinez and his wife are expected to make an appearance later . . ."

"Alice," Judy McIntyre cut in, "let me show an update of our national map." The screen flashed onto the fifty states. Three more in the Northeast region turned blue. "So far, it looks like the Democrat Martinez will probably be elected, but we must recognize that this is his party's prime territory. At this hour, Republican Senator Doren Winchester has only two red states in the East, but we all know that the Republican strength is in the South and Middle America. His campaign managers expect him to make a comeback there."

The senior anchor commented from her Crystal City studio, "What frankly surprises me so far, though, is how many votes the third party candidate, Mr. Winfield, has received. He's gotten nearly 27% of the national total – that's more than Ross Perot's percentages in '92. I believe Perot ended up with no more than 20% in that election."

The veteran analyst, Frank Jessup, cut in. "Yes, Judy, what you say is true but Mr. Winfield has to carve out a bunch of electoral victories in key states – that's what matters." Jessup was the elder statesman of American political commentary and a regular on her show.

Judy McIntyre nodded in agreement, pointing to New York and Pennsylvania. Both still had hatch-marks and no color tints. Their outcomes were still in limbo. She gestured at both and asked, "Like these important ones in the East, Frank?"

"That's what counts, yes. We have not only these two states but also most of the other large states to hear from. It's obvious to me there's a real horse race going on tonight, Judy. Only an hour ago, New York was projected to be going American Federalist and now we know that there is a recount going on in some of New York City's boroughs. I think anything can happen. I've never seen it quite like this."

Winfield moved so that he and Hamilton could see the television from the same side of the kitchen table. Sheila Linden and Roland Peters joined them. Winfield eyed both strategists as they drank mugs of steaming coffee. "Are there any unexpected results, so far? How does it look?"

"We're doing better in Pennsylvania than I thought we would, Dave," Peters replied. "I suppose it was your trip last weekend to Bethlehem and Pittsburgh. That little jaunt brought in a few blue-collar votes that we hadn't counted on . . ."

"I'd say New York is a bit unexpected, too," Linden said. "I didn't think we'd be this close. But when Sid and his folks are on their game, just like Frank Jessup said, anything can happen."

She left the men in order to answer her mobile phone. In a moment, she was back and flashed a 'V' for victory. "That was none other than Sidney himself. He succinctly told me not to worry. Turns out that it was Martinez's operatives that called for the recount. They had counted on getting more of New York City's votes and they were getting desperate. The long and short is that David was already trailing in the three boroughs that are being recounted. Sid said that the recount shouldn't cut too much into David's lead in the rest of the state."

Hamilton spun a cup of tea in his hands saying, "We still can't depend on it."

"In this game, Evan, you can't count on anything. But Sid knows what he's doing, 'dooein' as he puts it, so you're in good hands."

Suddenly they heard excited shouts coming from the other room. Suzanne, Betsy Mason and Francesca Hamilton were high-fiving and gleefully dancing in a circle.

"Wow, he did it! Davey, come in here quick!"

As the kitchen klatch came back into the family room, they stared wide-eyed at the screen. Pennsylvania was now green. An unidentified reporter intoned, "We at ABN have been able to confirm our analyses and, yes, we can now give Pennsylvania with its 20 electoral votes along with Vermont to the American Federalists."

Roland Peters cautioned from the back of the room, "Whoa, hold on folks. We have to worry about the rest of America. Their votes haven't even been counted. I, of all people, should know that ever since the '80s, the Republican Party has enjoyed a rock- solid base in the South and Midwest. In fact, a group of stalwart conservatives and I were the architects of that 'Red State' strategy. "

"Nevertheless, Roland, it's still heartening to see those green colors up there." Sheila Linden had predicted Winfield's wins in Maine, Virginia and Massachusetts, but this? First Delaware had slipped in and now the Keystone State and Vermont.

10 PM EST

Over the next hour, later results served to dampen their initial enthusiasm. After Winfield's earlier victories in six states, the other state colors on the national map steadily turned blue in the East and red in the South. Then, states in the Central and Mountain Time zones began to report. In short order, red color tinted the national map solidly from Georgia to Utah. Roland Peters was right. Senator Doren Winchester's strength was taking hold.

New York still remained hatched – colorless on the electoral map. "It's still too close to call in the Empire State," Judy McIntyre, Janet Melone and other network anchors continued to announce as the night wore on.

11PM EST

All three Winfield children were dressed in their pajamas and had sorted themselves onto a number of cushions on the floor. Maria spread Afghans over them. Suzanne came over and told them, "The election race probably won't be settled until late tomorrow morning, so you shouldn't stay up."

Bobby and his teen-aged brother took the hint and fumbled their way upstairs. However, Caroline decided to stay curled up on the rug next to the sofa. Over the next half-hour, the drowsy teenager watched television and listened in a fugue-like state to Joseph Martinez speaking from the hotel in Los Angeles. During his televised celebration, Caroline thought she could see a group of Hollywood celebrities standing in the background as he predicted, "It looks good, my friends. Our Democratic Party of Jefferson and Jackson is headed for victory. We won't know for sure until tomorrow but we should be all right."

"Just like Mom said," Caroline thought, "it's probably going to go on and on and on. And they didn't even show Tom Ellervie, my favorite from America's New Talent." She crawled even deeper under her blanket.

After an advertisement, the flat screen showed a far different celebration coming from a formal ballroom. The network had seamlessly moved to a boisterous group of Republicans congregating at the Renaissance Hotel in Dallas. Red, white and blue streamers floated down on a cluster of well-heeled people wildly cheering from a raised platform.

Once again, Caroline tried to keep her eyes open. She was not aware of much else besides echoing in the background as her eyelids fluttered. She thought she could recognize Senator Winchester's drawl but it sounded as if he were in a tunnel. "It looks good, ya all. Our Republican Party is headin' righ' now to victory, my frien's. We won' know 'til tomorrow. I think we'll be all right, ya hear?"

"I swear I heard all that before," she thought as she tried to stay awake. "Mom's right. Both of these guys had just now said the same thing, 'we won't know until tomorrow.' "

Her mother's voice startled her. "Caroline, honey, you might want to stay up a bit longer. Your father and I are going to go outside and meet with the press in a little while."

When she heard this, Caroline managed to rouse herself and slip onto the thick sofa next to her dozing grandmother. She looked around and could see that, except for Mom-Mom, the other adults seemed overly caffeinated. General Mason and his wife sat on the couch while Everett Hamilton and his mother sprawled on two easy chairs. Everyone was looking intently, as her father appeared on the television screens. She couldn't keep from glancing at the inside panels of their large front door. "On the other side stood the press," she thought, "the public eye." She had the distinct feeling that their home would never be the same.

An off-camera commentator hissed in excitement, "Here is Mr. David Winfield, the surprisingly competitive third-party candidate for President. His campaign staff told us that he'd make some comments. And now, Mr. Winfield . . ."

David squarely faced the reassembled group of news reporters. "Thank you all for coming tonight and staying with it," he began. "My comments will be brief and then I will answer some of your questions."

As they looked on the monitors in each of their two separate television studios, Judy McIntyre and Janet Melone unknowingly were struck by the same impressions.

McIntyre: *He really does look presidential.*

Melone: *It's a shame that he won't win.*

McIntyre: *He has such leadership qualities!*

Melone: *He and Mrs. Winfield certainly look like a first family.*

David Winfield began speaking. Suzanne and Evan Hamilton were barely visible behind his tall shoulders. "I think that we've done credibly well for a Party that came into existence only six months ago. With the results thus far, I sense that our candidacy and the Party's positions must have struck a chord. Despite being on the ballot in only forty states, the American Federalist Party has won six of these, and at the moment we are leading in four others in the West. In addition, two populous states are still being closely contested, New York and, surprisingly, Texas.

"Let me be sure to congratulate both Joe Martinez and Doren Winchester on their fine campaigns. I also want to sincerely thank the volunteers, supporters and my own staff for their help in this campaign. And of course, my wife – you Suzanne are the source of so much strength."

As Winfield drew Suzanne close, Evan Hamilton stepped to his side and asked the bank of reporters, "Now, are there any questions? Yes, you there in the front."

"Since you are obviously not going to win, what have you accomplished, Mr. Winfield?" The reporter had asked the same prickly-sounding question earlier to Hamilton.

Winfield smiled and humbly shook his head. "Allen, I think you and I know that Evan has already answered this. You see, we're not sure that we have lost. After all, we've won a platform, a stand from which to speak for many Americans who are sick and tired of two-party politics, of gridlocked government-as-usual."

Another reporter called out from the back, "Supposing you do lose, though, do you plan to join the newly elected administration in some capacity?"

"I doubt it," Winfield said. "You can imagine that any CEO has a hard time not being in charge. When we are not the bosses, it's very difficult for us not to rule a roost. You folks should know that I've always preferred to be the maker, the shaker . . ."

Sensing Winfield's built-up petulance, Hamilton tapped him on his sweater. His comments had turned gratuitous, and risked sounding arrogant. This whole episode was rapidly turning into a lose-lose situation.

Feeling Hamilton's cautionary touch, David pulled a U-turn. "Actually, what I mean is, I'll probably just resume my position at our family company here in Alexandria." His tone softened as he backed off and explained that he had already reconciled himself to the possibility that his run for elected office was nearly over. "It's evident," he conceded, "that if Joseph Martinez picks up either New York or Texas later tonight or tomorrow, he will have enough electoral votes to win outright. In that case, I'll support him like all Americans."

While viewing David's press interview in the toasty family room, Nancy Winfield, Caroline and the other guests stared wide-eyed as a message scrolled on the TV screen: 'Alert . . . Two analysts have now projected that both Texas and New York remain too close to call.'

Outside, David continued his comments. ". . . Yes, I'm realistic enough to understand that our American Federalist Party may indeed be a one-campaign happening, so to speak. It's my hope, though, that should we not succeed this time, as the song said years ago, *'There'll be one child left to carry on.'* Our basic message will eventually lead to much-needed changes in America."

"Mr. Winfield . . .?"

"Please everyone. Let me interrupt if I might." Evan Hamilton abruptly pushed to Winfield's side. Listening to David's words, he was increasingly concerned by what his friend might say next. Hamilton leaned in front of the microphones to speak. He feared Winfield might blurt out an apparently meaningless remark, a statement that could turn on them and unwittingly disclose PATRI and its present PLAN.

"We've all had a long night. With these and a few other states still up in the air, I'd suggest having a midday news conference with you all tomorrow." Hamilton looked down at his watch and said perfunctorily, "Oh, it's already Wednesday. Later today, then . . . Thanks for coming. Good night."

When the three came back into the home, that despite the late hour, they saw that an amazingly fresh and energized Judy McIntyre was still at her anchor desk on Public News. She gestured toward the studio's three-colored map of the United States.

"To summarize again where we all find ourselves. At this juncture, as expected, Joseph Martinez still leads the popular and electoral counts by a wide margin. Let's show you the numbers."

A graphic flashed onto a large screen behind her:

National Vote	% of Total	Electoral Votes (270 needed to win)	
46,400,200	40%	Democrat (Martinez)	243
38,650,000	32%	Republican (Winchester)	149
31,325,000	26%	American Federalist (Winfield)	54

"These are the totals so far. Although he's quite close, Mr. Martinez is not yet assured of a victory in the Electoral College." With a desk control, she pointed to the next graphic summary:

Outstanding Electoral Votes as of Midnight EST

Texas	38
New York	29
(4) Others	25

ORE -7   OKLA -7
NEV-6   NEW MEX- 5
Total Left Outstanding = 92

"It's interesting that the leader, Mr. Martinez, must win *either* Texas or New York in order to carry the general election outright. He can't do it by winning all of the remaining four smaller states alone. If he doesn't win either of these two large states, we can see that, at best, the Democrats would come out two electors short! So here we are again, another horse race. But instead, this year it is not Florida or Ohio. It is Texas and New York who will determine the outcome."

> The executive Power shall be vested in a President of the United States of America . . . elected as follows.
>
> Each State shall appoint, in such Manner as the Legislature thereof may direct, a Number of Electors, equal to the whole Number of Senators and Representatives to which the State may be entitled in the Congress; but no Senator or Representative, or

Person holding an Office of Trust or Profit under the United States, shall be appointed an Elector.

Article. II. Constitution of the United States of America

November 4, 2020 1 AM EST

Nancy Winfield had gone to bed hours before. David and Suzanne sat quietly with the others in the family room. Everyone felt thoroughly spent from the past twenty hours, much less the past six months.

Evan Hamilton got up and stretched his right arm by pulling on his weak left elbow. "I suppose Francesca and I should obey my doctor and turn in. He told us that aspirin, exercise and plenty of rest are all I need, so I think we'll go horizontal 'til morning."

"Evan, aren't you going to stay up and see if Joe Martinez wins?"

"Heavens no, unless he performs a miracle and overcomes Winchester's three-point lead in Texas in the next ten minutes. We probably won't know New York's results until 9 or 10 this morning at the earliest. David, do you have a way over to the guest house for us?"

"Yes, there's a golf cart. I'll get Jesus, Maria's husband, to drive you over."

In a short while, the others also found their way to their assigned sleeping quarters. Suzanne had decided on the bedding arrangement. The two politicos would join the Hamiltons in the guesthouse, while Philip and Betsy Mason would be in the guest bedroom in the main house.

The estate's large main dwelling became still as everyone warily went his or her separate ways. Sheila Linden stifled a yawn, "It's only one o'clock? This the first time I remember going to bed before an election is decided. I can't believe that we're all turning in already, but here I am starting to nod off like the rest of you. I still feel as if I should try to see this through."

"Don't worry," Roland Peters cracked, "your age is merely catching up with you, Sheila, as it is for the rest of us." They put on their coats waiting for Jesus to return with the cart. "Trust me, like you said, nothing's going to happen overnight, so we might as well sleep through 'nothing.'"

"My room over there has a small TV, so at least I can stay up alone even if it is only more of the same. I admit I'm bushed . . . but still, I'm curious, my friend."

After the golf cart came back and took her and Peters to the guesthouse, Sheila Linden turned on her bedroom's small flat screen TV. The long-time

Democratic strategist lay back exhausted on the fluffy bedspreads. She had lowered the set's volume by remote so as not to disturb the Hamiltons sleeping upstairs above her. Minutes later, while she stared at the television screen, a news bulletin scrolled along the bottom. 'Public News Network now calls Texas narrowly for Winchester over Martinez.' A second message followed. 'Upset – Winfield takes Nevada and New Mexico.' Soon thereafter, a new message moved across the screen. 'Doren Winchester claims Oklahoma. Martinez captures Oregon.'

Sheila jumped out of bed, crept down the hallway and softly tapped on Roland Peters' door. "Roland, are you still presentable? Come quickly."

The Republican operative hurriedly put on a guest bathrobe and slippers before he snuck into her neighboring bedroom to see whatever it was that was going on.

"We were right with the 'Wedge,' my Mr. Peters," she gloated and without a thought, gave him a hug and kiss on his cheek, nearly toppling them onto her bed. "It's now one-to-go for us, Rollie. New York, that's the one."

"Remember, Sheila, since we're being professionally affectionate at the moment, it's not that Winfield *wins* the election with *one more* state. It's that Mr. Martinez does *not* win with *one less!*"

54

Harrisburg, Pennsylvania
December 8, 2020

> The Electors shall meet in their respective states,
> and vote by ballot for President and Vice President . . .
>
> Amendment XII (1804)
> The Constitution of the United States

The President Pro Tem of the Pennsylvania Electoral College, the retired Judge Richard Wier, pounded his gavel and brought the assembled American Federalist Electors to order. "Do you understand the question before you, Electors of the Commonwealth of Pennsylvania?"

Hearing nothing, the retired State Supreme Court judge squinted over his reading glasses at the quarter-filled desks and whispered to the recording secretary, "That's good, Helen. This year proves no exception. Less work for lawyers, once again."

The judge looked down at the small gathering. "You will be individually casting a vote on behalf of your fellow citizens. I will now hear a motion to proceed."

Murmurs of "so-moved" and "I second it" echoed off the walls of the near-empty chamber of the State Senate.

"After you hear your name, please come to the front desk and sign the written ballot with our secretary, Miss Radnor. When you sign the document, it will ratify your vote for the American Federalist, Mr. David Winfield, the winner of the 2020 presidential election in Pennsylvania. We have a notary sitting next to Miss Radnor who will certify each of your signatures. I hope each of you remembered that you must present a photo ID this morning. After we finish that, we will repeat the same procedure in order to attest the ballot for Dr. Gayle Eccles as Vice President. I trust this is understood."

A wide-girthed, uniformed sergeant-at-arms jabbed his mace onto the floor and bellowed, "The clerk will call each person's name. When you hear your name, please call out your vote as 'aye' and come directly to the front of the hall."

Helen Radnor adjusted her glasses and read out, "Ms. Abbott, Carol Abbott . . ."

Over the next hour, in the same manner, twenty votes of the assembled American Federalist Party members were cast for President and Vice President of the United States.

"Miss Radnor," the President Pro Tem formally directed, "you and I must sign and certify each ballot using the Pennsylvania state seal. Before so doing, could you read the total tallies that will be sent to Washington?"

With assistance, she stood and read: "As according to our Pennsylvania election rules, the vote of December 8, 2020 is unanimous for the office of President. Twenty votes are for Mr. David Winfield, none for Mr. Joseph Martinez, none for Mr. Doren Winchester. The following Electors cast and signed their vote for Mr. David Winfield: Carol Abbott, Doris Adams . . . and finally, Allen Weslowski."

She then proceeded to do the same with a separate ballot for Vice President Gayle Eccles, who had received all twenty Pennsylvania electoral votes.

After the two presiding officials and notary public signed the bottoms of the two documents, Helen Radnor pressed the state seal onto their signatures and placed each electoral ballot into two special envelopes.

Judge Wier climbed back up onto the podium and said in his most official manner, "Thank you all for coming. I know that it is a busy time of year. Your work for your candidates, party, and the Commonwealth of Pennsylvania is deeply appreciated by both your fellow citizens and myself. The Electoral Ballots that you have just signed will be directed forthwith to the seat of national government at the Capitol. Thank you again. This concludes our business, ladies and gentlemen."

... they shall make distinct lists of all persons voted for as President

... which lists they shall sign and certify and transmit sealed to the seat of government of the United States, directed to the President of the Senate . .

Amendment XII (1804)
The Constitution of the United States

Pennsylvania, Highway U.S. 15

Holly Rhyne and Cary McAllister had left Georgetown earlier that day to drive to a baby shower in Hershey. The first-time mother-to-be was a close college friend who now worked at the Penn State Medical School.

"Let me catch you up on some goings-on, Cary," Holly said as she sipped from a coffee cup. "When you were gone last week, they had another garbage slowdown so watch it with our trash. Something about not having enough money in the D.C. budget for the rest of the year. The fire department is next."

"Sounds like same old same old, Holly," Cary sighed. "So much for having public workers, but I can't blame them. They're getting the shaft. Hey, have they found out anything about those two suspected arsons in Alexandria last week?"

"Nothing for sure but the two homes were owned by Pakistani and Kenyan families. Investigators suspect the work of some anti-immigrant terrorist organization."

"Give me a break," Cary groaned. "These kinds of weirdos always brag about having freedoms – as long as it's them and nobody else exercising their freedoms. Frankly, they ought to be put away somewhere."

"You know, I agree with you, but since there are no definite links, there's nothing anyone can do about these guys." Holly took a sip of her coffee as she drove and suggested, "Let's change the subject, it's too depressing. Thankfully, there's more to life.

"I'm really excited that Patrick is doing so well. Although he easily got reelected, he doesn't have a clue as to how the presidential election will turn out. Right now, he's betting it will be Joe Martinez."

"Politics, schmalitics," Cary groaned. "That's all you guys ever talk about."

"Sometimes it's more than that," Holly laughed. "We're not all talk, trust me. Pat will be visiting his family in Wisconsin until Christmas, but I've already asked him to have dinner with my parents and me after he gets back. They've been interested in meeting him."

"Now that's more like what I call 'news,' " Cary said knowingly. The long-time flight attendant was skilled about matters of the heart. Her job depended in part on it.

Holly kept her eyes fixed on the highway and matter-of-factly said, "Well, a lot of other people are interested in him too, besides my folks. He got almost 65% of his Congressional District's vote. Patrick told me that he hopes to have the opportunity to meet Mom and Dad, but he's not sure when. He said he'd be really tied up when the new Congress is seated in January. Senator Hunt told me the same thing. He said that the presidential selection process next month looks pretty formidable."

"But still, you've got to be careful what you wish for, young lady. If Mr. Jefferson gets too busy or too popular, you'll never see him."

"That's a chance, but still . . ."

"But enough, my turn to change the subject. Holly, you ought to hear about my latest escapade. I was lucky to get back at all last night."

"You did look awfully tired this morning. I was almost afraid to ask. What happened?"

"You may not know it, but Heathrow was shut down again Friday, this time right after my crew had boarded. We first had to sit there for hours and then . . ."

After she had told her drawn-out tale, Cary sank exhausted into her seat and exclaimed, "God, Holly, it was one thing after another. I should have studied chaos theory when I was younger. Maybe I would have been able to understand how things like this happen."

"Sounds like another day at the farm to me, Cary. At least you made it home." She laughed. "By the way, talk about chaotic, do you know the latest about Alice Krensky? She and Frank are having problems again. She'll be at the shower. I thought I should let you know. This time, to make matters worse, Frank got laid off a week ago."

"These deals are always tough, Holly, no matter how you cut it. But with their kids and all, Alice and Frank don't need him losing his job too. Go ahead, sketch out the plot but spare me the details. I'm starting to fade."

After trying to listen to a few fragments of the Krensky saga, Cary reclined and nodded off. Holly decided to put on a soothing tape as she drove them into Pennsylvania on US 15.

55

Capitol Building, Washington, D.C.
Tuesday, January 5, 2021

> ... The President of the Senate shall, in the presence of the Senate and House of Representatives, open all the certificates and the votes shall be counted; – The person having the greatest number of votes for President, shall be the President, if such number be a majority of the whole number of Electors appointed ...

Amendment XII (1804)
The Constitution of the United States

The outgoing Vice President William Snyder, acting as the President of the Senate, brought the Joint Session of Congress to order. The legislators knew that they were making history. There was a buzz emanating from the floor as the freshly sworn-in members of the 117th Congress wended their way to their seats. The horseshoe-shaped Gallery above them was filled to capacity.

Snyder's voice called out, "The Congress is now in session. As the first order of business, we will review the vote of the Electoral College. The sealed ballots from each of the fifty states are in the metal boxes on the sergeant-of-arm's table here in front." He cleared his throat. "The clerk will open each ballot and as she does will announce that state's official tally. An appointed member from each of the three political parties will monitor these counts from the front table. Will these individuals please come forward now?"

After the three appointed Representatives came forward, everyone, including the few newly elected Federalists, sat forward in their seats in the vaulted chamber of the U.S. House of Representatives. The sergeant-at-arms gave the first sealed certificate to the clerk. With more than four decades of legislative service, Mrs. Walters thought she had seen it all . . . until now.

"Let's see," she began. "Alabama is entitled to nine votes. It casts nine votes for Mr. Winchester." She went on, "Alaska is entitled to three votes . . ."

Evan Hamilton thought to himself as he sat in the Gallery that thankfully there were no surprises – yet. Still, he worried that an Elector might cast a 'renegade' vote. He felt his throat catch when she paused, and then announced, "New York casts 29 votes for Mr. Winfield."

After several more minutes, the clerk loudly concluded, "Wyoming is entitled to three votes. It casts three for Mr. Winchester."

Hamilton sighed, "It's done, almost according to Hoyle."

Vice President Snyder intoned, "The state certificates are now all in; the Electoral College is complete. Will the clerk please read the total votes of each candidate for the office of President of the United States."

The tension in the chamber was palpable. Everyone strained to hear her words.

"Yes, Mr. President." Mrs. Walters nervously adjusted her glasses and moved closer to her microphone. She spoke clearly:

"American Federalist Party, Mr. Winfield	–	94 votes
"Republican Party, Mr. Winchester	–	194 votes
"Democratic Party, Mr. Martinez	–	250
"Needed to win	–	270 votes."

"Mrs. Walters, thank you. These tallies are now in the record. Could you and the three monitors with you please sign and certify these Electoral College results."

A large commotion ensued as the members in the Joint Session faced the new reality. There was, indeed, no winner in the Electoral College.

"We must next proceed to the process of counting each state's vote for the office of Vice President. Mrs. Walters, please keep the designated monitors near at hand."

In the balloting for Vice President, the votes were the same as they were in the Presidential balloting. There was no winner in this election as well.

Despite his vigorous calls for order, it was minutes before Vice President Snyder could quiet the second uproar. C-Span caught his perturbed expression as he opened a leather-bound copy of the congressional rules. For weeks, everyone had known that it would come down to this – now it was a reality.

"My colleagues, hear me out. Our forefathers had the wisdom to fashion what must be our next steps. We have a unique problem today, but we do not, let me repeat, do not have any sort of a constitutional crisis. I know that many of you lawyer-types have already thought ahead about this possibility, and have sent petitions to the Supreme Court. But no, that is not the way at all."

"Martinez should be the winner!" voices called out. "He had the most votes . . . Where do we go from here?" Others shouted, "We Republicans should stand up and be counted!"

After the President Pro Tem brought the legislators back to order, he said firmly, "Ladies and gentlemen, take your seats. Let me read to you the salient passage from the U.S. Constitution applicable to our present situation.

> ". . . if no person have such majority (sic of Electors), then from the persons having the highest numbers not exceeding three on the list of those voted for as President,
> . . . the House of Representatives shall choose immediately, by ballot, the President. But in choosing the President, the votes shall be taken by states, the representation from each state having one vote . . . and a majority of all the states shall be necessary to a choice.

"This, friends, comes from the 12th Amendment to the Constitution. My history-minded friends tell me it was necessary following the Jefferson-Aaron Burr Electoral deadlock in the 1800 presidential election. All three of the current candidates have received some Electoral votes for President and are thus eligible to be selected by the current House of Representatives. Is there a motion to that effect?"

A Republican Representative from New York, a constitutional law expert, was recognized. "Mr. President, I am sorry to be sticky, but the Constitution is quite explicit on this matter. No further motion is necessary in order to have this special election. You've already just read aloud the roadmap. What I do move, however, is that the rules of the House governing this election be modified to allow for caucuses and free interchanges between the elected Representatives of all the states."

"Thank you, Mr. Aiello. Is there a second to this procedural motion? Remember that only the Representatives of the 117th Congress can vote on this motion, not the Senators."

Over the next two hours, an intense debate about the Aiello motion ensued. Many Democrats, whose party had regained a large majority in the

House, argued to call for a rapid vote. A speedy call-of-the-question might improve Joseph Martinez's chances in this direct House election. If there were to be any sort of caucus, however, the Democrats argued that it be of the traditional, party-based kind.

The Republicans, on the other hand, saw an opening to select Doren Winchester if they could unite and employ their 'Heartland strategy.' Although many of these so-called 'Red States' had small numbers of Representatives, each state, regardless of its population, was to be allowed one full vote in this special House election. The Republicans calculated that these sparsely populated states would wield a disproportionately large influence – and thus swing the House vote to their candidate, Doren Winchester.

A voice vote of the House members about the Aiello motion allowing states to have their own caucuses finally was taken. Remarkably, the outnumbered Republicans, aided by many independent-minded Southern Democrats, won the vote.

"The ayes have it," Vice President Snyder announced loudly as he looked for objections. "Although your votes will be made on a state-by-state basis, intra- and interstate caucuses will be allowed before the actual fifty state-votes are received. Every caucus can make up its own rules. Remember, these caucuses are not to be based on party or special interests. Are there any other questions? We will meet again tomorrow to see if we have cloture. Is there a motion to adjourn?"

During the rest of the day and evening, there were nonstop meetings throughout the Cannon and Rayburn office buildings. Most of the state caucuses left themselves open to any Representatives from neighboring states that wished to attend. One such Representative, a Democrat from Delaware, was her state's lone Representative. She chose to sit in on the Pennsylvania meeting. As a first-time Congresswoman, she enjoyed listening to some of their arguments. She was heartened when she heard someone in the caucus say, "We eighteen Representatives should not cast our votes as Democrats or Republicans – but as Pennsylvanians." Even though David Winfield had won the state's twenty electoral votes since he had won the popular count, the Delaware legislator knew that there were no newly elected Federalist Party Representatives from Pennsylvania in the new 117th Congress, and besides, only a few in the whole House of Representatives who would vote for him. She could see that without having many Federalist Party supporters, Winfield had a distinct disadvantage in this sort of House election.

In an unexpected, but what she thought honorable move, the Pennsylvanians reached an accord. They unanimously decided to respect their citizens' popular vote, and accordingly decided to cast their one Pennsylvania state-vote for David Winfield.

"That seemed reasonable," the Democratic Representative thought to herself as she walked back to her apartment. Her fellow Delawareans had made a similar decision for her, David Winfield had handily won Delaware's popular vote. As she walked along, she decided that despite being a Democrat, she would cast her and thus Delaware's one state-vote for him and his American Federalist Party.

Meanwhile, the Virginia caucus was turning raucous. Virginia had long been a battleground state and the usual enmity once again surfaced as claims and counterclaims of voter fraud and misuse of campaign funds roiled the room.

"There's no way our one state-vote goes Republican, even if you outnumber us seven to four," a heavyset Afro-American Congresswoman from Newport News shouted.

A Democratic Representative from Richmond angrily agreed. "Forget Winchester! For the moment, if it makes you any happier, you can also forget about my man, Martinez. It was David Winfield who was Virginians' first choice, not your Republican carpetbagger from Texas. He ran third."

"There may be another way," the senior-ranking Republican reasoned. "I heard that some Representatives in the other state caucuses are independently voting their hearts and minds instead of toeing their party's line."

"Well whatever, Paul. I'm not voting for a Democrat."

"Nor am I voting Republican!" another shot back.

"How about Federalist?" the Republican Representative asked rhetorically. "David Winfield has some things going for him. I rate him a 'good conservative,' not like some of the ultra hotheads in my own party. As Mr. Hill pointed out, he did win the Virginia popular vote for President. He is a native son and a neighbor of mine here in Fairfax County. He's a good man – I like him."

"But there are no elected American Federalist Party Representatives from Virginia to vote for him in our caucus here, at least by a standard count."

"That's what I'm trying to imply. For the good of our dear state going forward, all of us can compromise and vote for Winfield regardless of our party affiliation. Let's agree that we can be American Federalists for a day. I doubt Mr. Winfield will win anyway, but meanwhile we can be loyal Virginians and support our own native son. It's in our better nature."

Never ones to rush to judgment, the Virginia Representatives decided to continue their deliberations over a working dinner. Boxes of half-eaten pizza and empty sodas soon lay scattered around the tabletop along a back ledge.

At eight o'clock, the eleven members of the Virginia contingent finally reached agreement. They were persuaded to cast their one state-vote for David Winfield.

Someone concluded, "This means, folks, that our fellow citizens have the last word instead of the self-interest of us Democrats and Republicans."

"This may be only for the first ballot, friends," a senior legislator reflected. "For all I know, we may be casting the only state-vote for Mr. Winfield in the whole damned Congress and what we've decided to do is only theater."

The two Representatives from Maine had their own mini-caucus at the nearby Dug-Inn restaurant. A crusty, twenty-term Representative from Augusta said that he didn't much care for Doren Winchester and 'his brand of Republicanism' anyway. He grew flustered as he explained, "Those rigid, know-nothing conservatives have been taking over my Grand Old Party for years . . . Now they've completely lost the way."

The other, a newly elected Federalist, excused himself to go to the rest room. While in the hall, he called his former professor from Bowdoin. "I've got his vote, Dr. Eccles. Maine will be for Winfield. You were right."

"That's great," she exclaimed. "From what Evan Hamilton just told me, the word's starting to get around that there might be eight or more states out there that could break for David. Each one is one vote! I'll be sure to let you know, Andy".

"I'm sorry, Dean Eccles, that you're not in the running for the Vice Presidency," he said. "It's too bad that the rules only allow the Senate to choose between the top two vote getters. You're obviously the best . . ."

Gayle Eccles's voice crackled in his ear, "Thanks, Andy. Next time . . . maybe."

The seven Colorado Representatives met for most of the afternoon on the third floor of the Cannon Building. They continued to have deep-seated disagreements – not only about this election but also about many other issues. One was a Democrat representing Denver, two were Republicans, and two were Independents. For the first time there were two others, a pair of recently elected legislators who were members of the American Federalist Party. After much discussion, the seven decided to take a straw vote. Unexpectedly, David Winfield came up barely short with three votes while Martinez had one and Doren Winchester, two. One of the Representatives was undecided.

Shortly after this first vote was tallied, the undecided Congressman blurted out, "Whatever. I know that I could never vote for Martinez or Winchester." The pony-tailed legislator from Durango went on, "Those two don't see things my way. Never have, never will."

"Vote with us, then Mike. If we deadlock, Colorado will have no leverage. Besides, you once told me you liked Winfield. How about it?"

Brooding, Mike Grayson twisted the cup in front of him, "Okay, you've got it. Count me in for Winfield and your Federalists . . . at least on the first ballot."

The next morning, back in the House of Representatives, Mrs. Walters rose and with a clear voice announced, "This is the result of the first House of Representative ballot for the President of the United States held on January 6, 2021:

"Mr. Martinez – Democrat – 21 states
"Mr. Winchester – Republican – 15 states
"Mr. Winfield – American Federalist Party – 10 states
"Undecided or Deadlocked – 4 states

"Mr. President." The clerk looked up at the rostrum. With his jowls, Vice President Snyder looked like an English bulldog sitting behind her. "More than 26 state-votes in the Congress are needed to select the next President. By that mandate, no candidate has received the majority in order to be certified as the next President."

A loud sigh, more like a groan, could be heard in the hallways outside the chamber. For the past month, Patrick Jefferson and his fellow House Democrats had calculated that since their party had the largest number of Representatives, Joseph Martinez would easily be able to win the House's special election. It was apparent that he had not . . . yet.

William Snyder gaveled everyone to attention and said, "Ladies and gentlemen, curb your reaction, if you please." He looked out at the members of Congress. "I, for one, appreciate everyone's work over the past two days. It falls to all of us to carry on with our Constitutional duty. I admonish you to return to your deliberations. All other Congressional business is suspended for the moment. When you are ready to cast your second ballot, your leaders will notify me to schedule another session of the House of Representatives in this chamber."

The acting President of the Senate looked in several directions and semi-snarled, "Do I hear a motion to adjourn?"

"So moved . . . . aye . . . aye."

His gavel sounded like a gunshot as the morning session ended.

56

Washington, D.C.
January 12, 2021

It was bitterly cold outside the restaurant on M Street. Evan Hamilton and his son Everett quietly talked at a secluded table with the jut-jawed House minority leader, Republican Thomas (Buckeye) Moore from Ohio. "I'm hoping to cut the cake with you, Tom, but it's got to be only between the three of us." Over the years, Moore was used to such confidences, and was widely known as a consummate wheeler-dealer.

The younger Hamilton watched the two older men. It was as if they were engaged in a chess match. His father leaned forward and asked in a conspiratorial tone, "Your chances of electing either a Republican President or Vice President are nearly zero with or without us, Tom. Don't you agree?"

Moore smiled inwardly, knowing that Hamilton was right. He appreciated that the man sitting opposite was shrewdly showing his cards one by one. A veteran of countless campaigns, the Republican was still smarting from the results of the general election. "If only President Henson hadn't cozied up to that damned Freedom Party," he thought to himself. "All he did was rile up the Democrats. We lost the House and even Winchester hadn't won the presidency like he was supposed to."

Moore nodded wordlessly and Hamilton went on, "In the Senate vote for Vice President, there are only two candidates – your chances are better there. In that chamber, each Senator's vote matters, Tom. Presently, you have forty-seven Republican senators to count on. If we give you four more votes, two Independents and the two newly elected Federalists, your man would be able to squeak in and get the Vice Presidency."

Hamilton took a small spoonful of his steaming chowder and stopped to see if his description of the situation had sunk in.

"What happens if we agree? I suppose there's something in it for both of us."

"That there is, my fine fellow. Like I said, we give you four votes in the Senate selection – and a Republican is the Vice President. On the other hand, we need some of your Republican members to give their state-votes for our own man, Winfield, in the House presidential election."

Red-faced, Tom Moore tried to slowly but surely chew his forkful of chicken salad, yet nearly swallowed it whole. "We can't do that, Mr. Hamilton," he sputtered. "In the first ballot in the House just completed, we had fifteen votes and still do as of now. You only have ten. We should be asking you for *your* state-votes, not the other way around."

"There are a lot of things we can do with those ten votes. We don't want to give them to Martinez unless we have to." Hamilton was used to striking hard bargains as well.

The Republican minority leader nearly choked on his rutabaga, and after drinking some water, replied, "You seem pretty sure of yourself, Mr. Hamilton. You're not even one of us." He saw how the man had developed his well-earned reputation as a Wall Street dealmaker. "What's the catch?" he asked.

"The way the Senate votes are lining up, that Democrat lady Rosenfeld will probably beat your man, Richard Thompson, for the Vice Presidency if we don't pitch in with those four votes. And with the House vote for the President in stalemate, anything could happen there. At the end of the day, I think you'd prefer David Winfield to any Democrat, especially Joe Martinez. Am I right? Finally, Tom, there's the matter with a Miss Gina Pinelli – do you remember her?"

"Not really, no . . . Should I?" Moore looked uneasy. He thought it strange that Hamilton would mention this particular K-Street lobbyist.

The banker pulled out his iPad. "Seems she's living somewhere in McLean. Let's see. 2860 Willow Drive, phone 703-476-1131. You two go back a way. Is she a business partner? I hired a private investigator a while ago. I didn't want to bother your missus . . . not yet. And we have these." Hamilton pulled out several glossy photographs and fanned them out on the table like playing cards.

Moore frowned as he eyed the pictures. "You do know how to negotiate, Mr. Hamilton. Your reputation is well deserved." With a tight grimace, he folded his arms and leaned back from the table.

A short while later, Tom Moore strolled into the large Greenwood caucus room with his Republican Party whip. He had called for a meeting of Gulf State Representatives the previous day after the lunch with the Hamiltons.

Soon thereafter, he had received a phone call from Bob Laurens in Houston. During the conversation, the oil executive strongly encouraged the Ohio politician to "do what's best, Tom." He had said, "I heard from Helen Foster of Louisiana that she and other Republicans are pleased to be meeting with you at a so-called Gulf Coast caucus tomorrow." There was a pause. "I guess Evan Hamilton told you what to do." Hearing the Houstonian's deep-throated sarcasm, Moore was afraid that his longtime supporter also knew about his private life within the Beltway. Before he could reply, Laurens had concluded, "Maybe you and your wife Dotty can fix to come to our place on Padre Island one of these days. My Mary always likes to see you two."

Minority Leader Moore was encouraged as he glanced around the room. The people there were so much like his people of Ohio, what he called 'the good folks.' The brunch included the Republican Representatives from Texas along with those from Louisiana, Mississippi, Alabama and Florida – a total of over fifty in all. At Moore's suggestion, stretching the adopted House rules, the few Democratic legislators of the region had been left off the invitation list. The gathered Representatives had many shared interests: oil leasing rights, shipping in the Gulf, Southeast Conference football, and a deep distrust of East Coast cities with 'those damned liberal Democrats up there.' Every state in the Gulf state caucus enjoyed a large Republican majority, and accordingly, Doren Winchester had easily won each of their five state-votes on the first House of Representative's ballot.

The House minority leader was glad that the food caterer had already come and gone. "Please, be sure the doors are closed over there," he commanded.

"As many of you guessed," Moore began, "we are here to fashion a compromise, my friends. We could first try to get the support of the American Federalists for our man Doren Winchester, which is something that I'd prefer to do, but that raises all kinds of problems which I'll tell ya' all about in a minute.

"On the other hand, we could flip it around and instead give Winfield and the Federalists our own support in the House election. Winfield's chief-of-staff, Evan Hamilton, has offered us the following. They'll give our Vice President candidate, Rich Thompson of North Carolina, the necessary four Senatorial votes that would ensure his election in the Senate. For that, we would give the Federalists the state-votes of your five Gulf States and hopefully block the election of Martinez."

"Aren't you selling our man Doren down the river, Tom?" a longtime member from Mississippi asked "Can't he still win? I'm afraid I don't understand the numbers."

"Good point, Ross. Let me make it clearer." Moore pulled over a writing tablet perched on an easel. "Can you all see?" He circled some figures. "Right now, Joe Martinez has twenty-one solid state-votes. We have to be *very* careful to keep Martinez from getting more – he's almost there.

"Here's the deal. If the Democrats see us Republicans trying to take the votes of the Federalist-voting states, they would pull their people in faster than Pro Bass boys pull in hooked bass. Those states might have initially voted for Winfield on the first ballot, but my hunch is they'd never end up supporting our man Doren instead. The Democrats would get the five state-votes that they need lickety split by having these Representatives switch their state-vote from Winfield to Martinez." Tom Moore circled the number '21' on the sheet, crossed it out, and wrote a '26.' "And . . . Joseph Martinez would have twenty-six state-votes and become the next President of the United States."

At that instant, Tom Moore's cell phone went off. "Excuse me," he said to the others. It was Nicholas Shippen's familiar voice from Kansas City.

"I was in D.C. last night, Tom. Had dinner with my Kansas Representatives and the four of them agreed with me to solve their deadlock. Evan Hamilton was right – it took convincing but the two Republicans and two Democrats compromised. They'll be giving the Kansas vote to Winfield. All four thought it'd be best to at least be counted on the next ballot."

Moore snapped his cell phone cover shut, fuming as he put it back on his belt. He wasn't pleased about Winchester's situation but knew that he had to make the best of it. He felt comforted only by the fact that he was starting to build roadblocks against Joe Martinez. "Get anybody elected but that tooty Democrat," he thought. Moore turned his attention back to the caucus's brunch and asked, "Well now, do ya' all see where I'm heading with this?"

"What do we get out of a Winfield administration, Tom?" somebody shouted. "So we get a Vice President . . . what else?"

Moore had one of his lieutenants check to be sure that none of the Democrats from the Gulf States had entered on the sly. Then, he continued, "I've heard from the top that there'll be several high-ranking Cabinet posts. Defense, Treasury to start with. Our two parties coming together will initiate a new form of government for America. Better to be part of that, I figure, than to give the whole damn election to the Democrats and come away with nothing. We gotta do it, that's all there is to it."

"But this sounds like you are giving up on us and proposing joining a coalition. The notion sounds pretty poorly conceived." The long-time Representative, Thomas Eustis Pettigrew Wilson of Louisiana, was widely known as an independent skeptic. He had no problem confronting the Republican minority leader from Ohio or anyone else. In fact, many other times he had doubts about Tom Moore's true intentions, and even more, about his honesty.

"Call it what you will, Eustis. In the end, both political parties will get different spheres of power. Remember, it's the Democrats who are our primary opponent. As I see it, this is the only way we can keep them out of the White House. So . . . are you in?"

Moore silently stared his fellow Republicans down. One, then several hands went up. Then, a highly respected Representative from Mississippi stood, demonstratively put his hand on the conference table, and announced, "All in, Mr. Moore. You have our agreement. Count 'em for the American Federalist Party."

Moore breathed an audible sigh of relief. He would remember to call his wife Dotty later in Columbus when he knew she'd be home from work. A vacation to Padre Island with the Laurens, he thought, might do them both a world of good.

January 15, 2021

Three days later, William Snyder again stood augustly before the House of Representatives and faced the congregated legislators. "We must carry on with the people's business. I understand that the Senate next door is taking their vote today for the office of Vice President while we are meeting.

"Before we receive the results of your second ballot, though, let me remind you that the terms of President Henson and me expire at noon next Wednesday, January 20th. This end date for the terms of our offices is clearly specified in the Constitution. However, the start date for the newly selected executives is not cut in stone, so to speak."

Patrick Jefferson stood and signaled from his bench in the left corner. Over the past week, he had been increasingly upset by the whole scenario and was starting to have second thoughts about his own decisions. Being an avowed centrist, he was getting increasingly frustrated by the ongoing partisan debates. Jefferson sensed that most other Americans probably felt the same way. They likely wanted a speedy resolution as well.

"At this time, the chair recognizes the Democratic Representative from Illinois, Mr. Jefferson."

"A question, sir. Since no one has faced these present circumstances before, could you direct the clerk to read the passage in the Constitution concerning the transfer of executive authority?"

Someone sitting next to him laughed, "You gotta be a veteran around here, Patrick, to know rules of that kind. You're hardly old enough to vote."

Vice President Snyder leaned over and asked Mrs. Walters. On cue, she opened the large leather-bound binder on her desk. "This comes from Amendment XX of the Constitution passed in 1933.

> "The terms of the President and Vice President
> . . . shall end at noon on the 20th day of January . . . .
> . . . If, at the time fixed . . . a President shall not have been chosen,
> the Vice President elect shall act as President until a
> President shall have qualified; and the Congress may by
> law provide for the case wherein neither . . .

"And now, going back to Amendment XII:

> "And if the House of Representatives doesn't settle by March
> 4th . . ."

William Snyder could tell that many of the members of Congress were perplexed after they had heard Mrs. Walters's words. "I'll try to restate what she read in plain English," he intoned. "I spoke to the Attorney General last month in case this situation arose. I took some notes so first give me a moment."

Snyder looked down at his papers and said, "The Constitution gives quite explicit directions on your vote from hereon. But since your decision appears to be progressing rather slowly, let me say that there is a timeline that you need to know about. Both of the current executive offices are transferred as of this Friday, but the federal government will not be left in a vacuum. If both a new President and Vice President are not selected by the 20th, Congress will need to name a temporary President. You are aware that the rules of succession have always named the Speaker of the House if neither executive position is filled. If the Vice President is selected, but not the President . . ."

As his deep soporific voice went on and on, the President Pro Tem of the Senate became frustrated and abruptly cut himself short. "Read it yourselves or get a lawyer! Oh that's right," he chuckled, "I forgot. Most everybody here *is* a lawyer."

Snyder gestured as he continued, "Mrs. Walters has in her possession all of the sealed votes that each state's Representatives delivered to her office last night." After the three appointed monitors came forward, the Pro Tem calmly advised, "Go ahead, Mrs. Walters. You and the sergeant-at-arms have the floor."

The roll call lasted less than half an hour before she summarized:

"The Second House of Representative Ballot results for the President of the United States on January 15, 2021:

"Mr. Joseph Martinez – Democrat	21 states
"Mr. Doren Winchester – Republican	10 states "

A collective gasp roiled the chamber as Mrs. Walters concluded,

"Mr. David Winfield – American Federalist	16 states
"Undecided	3 states."

"Mr. President," she said, turning to William Snyder seated on his throne-like chair above her, "the Second Ballot results indicate that no person has reached the necessary majority of state-votes to be certified as the next President of the United States."

Snyder spoke loudly against the subsequent uproar, "Is there a motion . . .?"

January 25, 2021 10AM EST

Twenty-eight Representatives from ten small states gathered in the Mix Caucus room. The vast majority of these twenty-eight were Republican, and on the first two ballots most had dutifully made sure that their state-votes went to their party's candidate, Doren Winchester. Three states, however, were still registered as being undecided.

"Thank heavens for the Constitution, ladies and fellow gentlemen," a legislator from South Carolina cried out. "It always gives us a gosh darn chance to go up against the big boys. People livin' up North and out there in California just don't see things the way we do. How could they? We're the real Americans."

The House minority leader and the Republican whip from Utah stood behind their respected colleague from the Palmetto State and nodded in perfunctory agreement.

"It's got to get done," Tom Moore thought to himself. "What had Evan Hamilton said? 'Use your small state strategy, Tom. You Republicans have used it many times before.'"

'Big' Jim McClellan from Charleston went on, "All of us in this room have always counted ourselves fortunate, but perhaps never so much as we should feel now. There are only twenty-eight Representatives from the ten small states in this room, and we make up only 5% of the whole House membership, but looky here. We control ten state-votes in this historic presidential election, a full 20% of the whole. Think of that for a second. That's what I call leverage! It's a blank check, friends. It's been handed down to us for years to use any time we see fit."

"Jim, you're right," one Kentucky delegate said. "It's literally in our hands, the people in this room, to crown the next President of the United States. We are — we still are — the kingmakers."

"As long as it's not Martinez," a Republican Representative from North Dakota hissed. "He's a skunk."

"They all smell like one, Frank. Your guy Winchester is not much better," the lone, nominal Democrat from Idaho retorted. The man from Boise had been reelected with the crucial backing of the libertarian Freedom Party.

"When you think about it, Andy," a long time Representative from South Dakota pointed out, "all you Democrats living in small states haven't gotten much from your own Party over the last eight years. As somebody just said, your Party mainly worries about big stinking cities and ends up giving away all sorts of foolish hand-outs."

"And then, they go ahead and give our taxes away like there's no end in sight!"

"Seriously folks, let's think about what we're doing. I would prefer to believe that America and Americans come first — not either party." Jeb McClellan of Sioux City spoke with authority. "I was speaking to some colleagues from Pennsylvania and Delaware at lunch today. They're planning to vote for Winfield again. The folks in their two states voted last November for a person not a party, they explained. They'll still honor that."

After listening from the back of the room, Tom Moore interrupted. "Let me say a few things if I may to your Small State caucus. Please understand, I've been working some things out for all of us," he winked. "My staff has crunched the numbers on the probable state-votes going forward."

One of his aides carried an easel to the front of the caucus room and adjusted its legs. "My colleagues, as I've already said, given the current stalemate there's no way short of a miracle that Doren Winchester can come out a winner and beat Joe Martinez. This is true especially if all the states that are now committed to the Federalist Winfield release their support." He pointed to a graph resting on the easel with the results of the second Congressional ballot for President on a state-by-state basis.

The Ohio Congressman held onto the easel for effect and emphatically waved his Sharpie pen. "Thankfully, for those of us in this room, Joe Martinez is stuck for the moment. Six of the sixteen states that are now currently committing to Winfield are located in the Northeast and Mid-Atlantic, but their continuing Federalist loyalty is 'iffy' to say the least. As I mentioned to another group a week ago, when push comes to shove, those crucial six Eastern states will switch to Martinez if Mr. Winfield drops out or if this voting keeps going on. In this latter situation, the Representatives from those six states will succumb to what I call 'legislative battle fatigue.' We all know Americans are not known for patience, so I want to break the logjam before that happens and strike while the iron is hot."

Moore took a swallow of his bottled water before adding, "Don't be too partisan, friends. You know that we can't count on any of these states to ever support our candidate, Doren Winchester. If what I'm saying comes to pass, Martinez will soon get the 26 state-votes necessary to win the whole friggin' thing. So the compromise I'm proposing needs serious and speedy consideration. The future of our Republic is in your hands."

Moore wet his lips and glanced around the room like a wide-eyed predator. It was essential that they understand his personal, not political recommendation. "If you small-state Republicans and red-dog Democrats can get together and give Winfield your state-votes, you'll be able to get the win not only for the Federalists, but more importantly, for what I call your precious 'Heartland of America' interests as well."

A bent-over veteran Congressman hoarsely observed, "Your reasoning sounds like that ol' song, Tom. 'Know when to hold 'em, know when to fold 'em.' "

As he took another drink of water, Moore caught himself thinking about a recent phone call from Evan Hamilton. The New Yorker had said that he hoped to fly down for the next ballot and added darkly, "Tom, talk up Dave Winfield at your meeting Monday." Moore knew that he had done just that.

One of the freshmen Representatives asked from the back of the room, "So you're saying, Mr. Moore, that as of now our choice is between this third party Winfield guy and Joe Martinez? According to you, Doren Winchester is pretty much out of it."

The question snapped Moore out of his reverie and he replied, "That's exactly what I'm saying to you and the others, young lady. Winchester's chances are dropping like a stone 'n water. I tell ya', time's runnin' out. If you want to have an impact and get somethin' outta' this, I'd suggest makin' do and givin' your state-votes for Mr. Winfield."

"What I'm hearing you say, Tom, is that we've been backed into a corner," a Representative from Wyoming growled. "But see here, now. We're not going to be kicked around. First and foremost, most everyone here enjoys having his or her freedoms. I'm frankly not sure what David Winfield even believes in."

Following up, Jim McClellan asked skeptically, "Bottom-line, Tom, we may have missed what you said earlier, so let me ask. What do we get for our votes?"

"We're already getting something, Jim," Moore answered. "The Federalist Party essentially got our Dick Thompson selected as the Vice President over in the Senate this past week. So they made good on one of their promises so far, right? It's a matter of tit for tat. Giving us choice cabinet appointments would be next."

A sharp-speaking woman stood up. "I still can't agree with your deal, Mr. Moore. It goes against the grain of the Utah residents who voted for me."

Tom Moore held his arms out as if he was trying to stem a tide. "But if we don't come through with our side of the deal, Ms., Mrs. Johnson, we'll wind up getting absolutely nothing except an impotent Republican as Vice President and a Democrat, Joseph Martinez, as President. Do you want that?"

As Moore's rhetorical question hung in the air, a junior legislator from South Carolina leaned over and whispered to a colleague from South Dakota, "I suppose if push comes to shove, we could go through with his suggestion. After all, our man Thompson is now only a heartbeat from being President.

"Correct me but didn't Winfield's father, the Admiral, die young?"

"Yeah," the South Carolinian winked. "I was told it was unfortunate . . . if you know what I mean. Who knows? Whatever. It may run in the family."

A member of the Arkansas delegation loudly offered his own verdict. "If it's not going to be Doren, then never, no way, can it be Martinez. As for Winfield, well I don't really know but I suppose I could get used to him. Seems like a regular guy . . . somebody I could have a beer with."

An impeccably dressed Congresswoman stood and said she felt compelled to make her own observation. "Much as I hate to admit it, he does look a lot more presidential than either of the two other men." Although the lone Congresswoman from Alaska was a longtime Democrat, she had been increasingly impressed every time she had seen David Winfield and Gayle Eccles during the recent campaign.

The previous night, she had heard from a constituent, Dr. Maureen Nightbird-Reynolds, who had detailed exactly what a Winfield presidency could do for Alaska. She also mentioned that the Representative was on Winfield's short list to head the Department of Interior. "Besides that, he is as good as he seems to be, Sarah. In fact . . . maybe better."

Congresswoman James looked at the others in the room and announced, "I think that now is a good time for all of us to give Mr. Winfield serious consideration."

"Why don't you all take a straw vote, folks," Moore suggested after a long pause. "I've got to meet with the Senate leadership at eleven, and I wanted to give them your sense. Any changed votes?"

"Hey now, Tom. Hold on. No, no," Jim McClellan protested with a stop sign gesture. "We don't want no outside pressure 'cludin' you, pardon me. Why not leave your notes and numbers up there on the board 'n we'll go right ahead 'n have ourselves a free 'n open discussion while you're at that other meeting."

Tom Moore realized that he shouldn't appear to be too pushy. The legislators from these small states had to believe it was their decision. He couldn't force any votes on this crowd even if he wanted to – many had lingering ties to the Freedom Party.

"That's fine, ya' all. Do what ya' gotta do. Like I said, I have to be going. I'll have one of my aides stay. She can call me directly if you have any questions."

An hour later during his meeting with the Senate leadership, Congressman Moore's cell phone rang. He was sure his aide was reporting in from the Mix Caucus Room. On his caller ID screen, though, he saw an unfamiliar number (212) . _ . _ . _ – New York.

He barely made out the words, "Tom . . . is this Thomas Moore?"

The Ohioan was perspiring even though the office windows overlooking the Mall were frosty. "Evan Hamilton, here, Tom. I just arrived at Reagan with my son, Everett. We are taking Miss Pinelli out for lunch. Care to join us?"

Moore remained speechless.

The voice on the phone remained intimidating. ". . . I thought so, but nevertheless, Everett and I will be in the chamber tomorrow to see the House vote. We have reserved seats in the central balcony. Look for us then, Mr. Moore."

Congressman Moore's phone went dead.

57

Capitol Building, Washington, D.C.
Tuesday, January 26, 2021 10AM EST

Mrs. Walters read the South Dakota ballot: "The South Dakota Representative, Mr. Bornmeister, gives his vote, his state's vote, to David Winfield and the American Federalist Party." A silent wave of shock registered throughout the hall following the House clerk's announcement of this, yet another, unexpected state's vote.

Representative Patrick Jefferson nervously looked around. He had borrowed a *Washington Post* and was starting to read that morning's column by his friend John Madsion entitled 'Where Now America?' He could not see across the wide chamber. Many of the other Representatives stood milling about their desks in disbelief as the clerk continued to read the voting results from the dais.

The Minority Leader Tom Moore sensed that, if he was lucky, the end might be near. He turned and gazed up at the Gallery. There they were, Evan and Everett Hamilton seated next to Gayle Eccles, and he recognized that they were becoming increasingly animated. Every minute or two, Eccles, the defeated Federalist Party Vice Presidential candidate, would wave down to various Representatives from New England.

A low-pitched murmur crested on the House floor with the announcement: "Utah votes . . ."

"Let's see what else is going on." Everett scrolled through the news on his iPad, whispering to his father, "The Market's down 150 . . . What's this? Hey Dad, there's a terrorist alert. Where? Let's see . . . right here along the Potomac. A cruiser and three destroyers were brought up from Portsmouth last night."

Everett put on a small earpiece and listened intently to a more complete radio-fed narrative: "General Philip Mason, commander of the District defense forces, the DOSECOF, is taking this step as a precaution. The terrorist group has not been identified but some indications are that it may be a new offshoot of the New World Patriots, the domestic fringe organization. General Mason asks for any information and reminds everyone to stay on alert. Currently, the code for the Capital is High Alert but may be raised to Imminent later today."

When the young Hamilton told the other two about the bulletin, they nodded as if they already knew. Gayle Eccles said, "That happened four years ago, too, Everett. Every time there's an inauguration, nut cases make all sorts of threats."

Everett rubbed his hands and said bitterly, "We ought to just put them away, threat or no threat."

"At least, we can trust that Phil Mason and his troops will do the right thing," she reassured him.

"Even better, when David Winfield finally becomes President, we won't have to put up with any of this."

Evan Hamilton agreed with his son. "About time somebody took care of these measly characters."

From below, Mrs. Walters called out: "Representative McMillen casts his one vote, and thus the Vermont state-vote, for Mr. Winfield."

Tom Moore nervously shuffled some papers on his desk as he stood with one hand tucked in his pocket. He kept his head down so that no one would notice him biting his lower lip. The Democratic Speaker of the House and his party's Whip stood across the aisle from him. The three men had each been ticking off the state-votes one-by-one as each result was called out. The two Democrats kept looking over at their Republican rival with furrowed brows and puzzled expressions. One after another, his small so-called 'Red States' were surprisingly voting Federalist. They wordlessly mouthed, "Tom, what's going on?"

Finally the vote of the lone Wyoming legislator, a Red Dog Democrat, was to be announced. His state-vote had been listed as 'undecided' on the first two ballots. His colleagues in the House tensely awaited the decision of this maverick Representative from another sparsely populated Western state. Before he heard it, Moore was sure what that vote would be. Even though he couldn't count on votes all the time, he sure knew what made people tick.

"Wyoming casts its state's vote," Mrs. Walters announced nervously, adjusting her glasses, ". . . for Mr. David Winfield of the Federalist Party." She could not have been more shocked than if she had announced that Winfield had won an Oscar.

"Would you and the three monitors bring all the ballots to my desk, please?" the newly sworn-in Vice President Republican Richard Thompson of North Carolina asked.

With the Senators in attendance as guests in the House Chamber, the whole Congress remained hushed as the five officials passed the fifty ballots between themselves. Minority Leader Moore along with the others surmised that Winfield was close if not there. The tension in the vast room was as electric as the charged air before a thunderstorm in the hills of western Ohio.

Affirming nods among the people clustered at the rostrum seemed to signify that some decision had been reached. Vice President Thompson looked straight ahead and sternly gaveled the stunned House of Representatives to attention. The resonating wood-knock was hardly needed. The House Chamber was eerily quiet.

Finally, the Vice President's voiced boomed. "I now request that Mrs. Walters, clerk of the House, present the results of this morning's vote."

The gray-haired clerk coughed dryly and nervously adjusted her microphone.

"This is the result of the third House of Representative ballot for the President of the United States held on January 26, 2021:

"Mr. Martinez – Democrat – 21 states
"Mr. Winchester – Republican – 3 states"

A buzz filled the room liked a stirred-up hornet's nest. The Vice President had to pound his gavel repeatedly before order was resumed. Finally he turned and directed the clerk, "Go on, please, Mrs. Walters."

"And . . . Mr. David Thomas Winfield – 26 states
"Undecided – no states. "

She looked up and continued,

"According to the rules of the House of Representatives and according to the individual state-votes taken today, it is certified, Mr. Vice President, that on the third ballot of the special presidential election by the United States House of Representatives, Mr. David Thomas Winfield has the required absolute majority and thus is elected as the next President of the United States."

Members of the House and Senate, along with the visitors in the Gallery, responded with a kaleidoscopic range of emotions. Exuberant shouts were coupled with silent puzzlement. Resounding cheers were mixed with expressions of disgust. Animated shoulder thumps ran alongside frozen bewilderment.

It was evident to the observers in the Gallery that many Representatives from both sides of the aisle were now reaching out to join the few Winfield supporters scattered throughout the chamber. Surrounded by surging colleagues, Representative Tom Moore looked up but could not identify any guests in the Gallery. When he finally did spot Gayle Eccles celebrating with the Hamiltons, he felt a vibration from his iPhone. Buck' Moore bent over to read a text message: 'CU@3-RPLACE-GINA.'

Evan Hamilton turned in the front row and gave Gayle Eccles a warm hug. "We're going to have a wonderful time at David's coronation, Gayle. America is finally going to get what it has always wished for!"

58

Capitol Building Washington, D.C.
January 26, 2021 8PM EST

The recently inaugurated Vice President, Richard Thompson, called out loudly to the Joint Session: "Will the Sergeant at Arms and the appointed members of Congress please escort the President-elect into the chamber."

As if on cue, the Representatives and Senators of the recently seated 117th Congress of the United States rose to their feet and looked back in anticipation. The traditionally subdued robed members of the Supreme Court and the stolid chiefs of the various military services also stood expectantly in the front row.

Given a perceived vacuum in American leadership, events in the United States and the rest of the world were turning ugly. Military units had already begun to enter and surround the District of Columbia to contain a confirmed threat from a homegrown militia. Because of this emergency, the Congress had speedily agreed that Presidential power needed to be transferred to David Winfield on this very day of his election. Pomp and circumstance would have to wait. All of America and the world were focused on this spellbinding inauguration of the first third-party President of the United States. Despite the uncertainties of the past month, the American Presidential succession was finally about to take place.

The three Winfield children were seated in the middle of the crowded upper Gallery. Bobby and Jeffrey gawked at the spectacle below and leaned far over the rail to see if their parents had already arrived. David Winfield's sister, Marilyn Ashford, sat next to her seventy-eight-year-old mother, Mrs. Nancy Winfield, who had flown up from her winter home in St. Petersburg the previous day.

Several members of PATRI were able to get VIP tickets and stood in the row just behind them. They included Robert Laurens and his wife up from Houston, ten-year-old Gerald Schubert and his mother from New York, and Ed Finch from the nearby Naval Department. Katy Blitz had just left a fund-raiser at the Phillips Collection and was the last to arrive. She joined Karen York and the others in the balcony. Everyone remarked upon the unusual degree of security that night throughout the District.

Four foreign observers stood behind them – Francis du Motier, Sir Ronald Farrington-the Lord Aplington, Philippe Rouen, and Hugh Rochan. They had flown in that afternoon on the spur of the moment after having been invited to the proceedings by Gayle Eccles and Evan Hamilton. In spite of jet lag, the Europeans were heartened to notice the cordial reception being accorded to the Winfields.

Those PATRI members who were absent from the inaugural proceedings tuned in from separate locations throughout America. Each suspected what this ceremony would really be all about. Diane Fleming, who had a compulsory Western Federal Reserve Board meeting, watched from her hotel room in Aurora, Colorado. Nicholas Shippen sat with his wife in their large Mission Hills residence in Kansas City. An unexpected ice storm that morning had resulted in the closure of MCI. Denise Donasti was at one of her daughters' homes in Albany, helping to take care of an autistic grandchild recovering from a cold. One member of PATRI, however, was unable to view the ceremony in Washington. In the late afternoon of the Pacific Northwest, Dr. Maureen Nightbird-Reynolds worked aboard a NOAA research vessel, the Oscar Dyson, taking samples of the threatened Tanner crab in the cold depths of Glacier Bay.

A grizzle-haired, uniformed veteran of these Joint Sessions opened the pair of large padded doors up the left aisle, then turned and brusquely pounded his mace onto the floor's carpet. A foot-long bronze eagle holding several wheat shocks in its curved beak topped the ceremonial mace. The hollow thump-thump made by the Sergeant at Arms resonated off the walls of the chamber.

"Mr. Vice President, members and guests," he bellowed. "Please welcome the President-elect of the United States, Mr. David Winfield and Mrs. Winfield."

The swirling legislators pressed forward and soon engulfed David and Suzanne. From above, Katy Blitz observed how regal they appeared despite the stark illumination of hand-held strobe lights. She thought that Suzanne looked absolutely stunning in a conservatively cut, red-and-white Versace outfit. The senior Senators and Representatives of the honor cortege placed themselves in a wedge-like formation to escort the couple down the packed aisle.

Given his height, David Winfield could see over most of the assembly and nodded greetings to several legislators that he recognized. But Suzanne felt hemmed in, and grew uncomfortable with the sweaty glad-handing, the vacuous faces surrounding them. Walking with David behind the Congressional phalanx, she suddenly felt faint as hands stretched out to touch her. Reaching into her suit pocket, she drew out a capsule of smelling salts. She often had to do this during the recent campaigning when David had pressed into enthusiastic crowds. Surreptitiously breaking it, she inhaled the biting ammonia powder. One sniff jolted her into alertness.

The Sergeant at Arms continued to lead the procession by fits and starts down the sloping aisle. With a long and practiced flourish, he held his mace high so that everyone in the chamber could measure the cortege's deliberate progress.

Another fifteen minutes passed before David and Suzanne finally ascended the podium. From there, they waved at their family and friends in the visitor's section. David thumped his chest with his fist before stretching it out in a thumbs-up fashion. During the campaign, he had used this gesture many times as a sign of esteem and respect. Tonight, he was especially mindful to recognize the few newly elected Representatives and the two Senators from his own Federalist Party.

He bowed deeply to acknowledge the black-robed Supreme Court jurists impassively standing off to his right. The somber jurists appeared to be paying little attention. To them, the proceedings were strictly theatre.

In contrast, on the left he saw his friends Generals Ronald Putney Greene and Philip Lee Mason, officiously applauding along with the Chairman of the Joint Chiefs of Staff and the four Service Chiefs. Next to them in the front row were the first named members of Winfield's executive staff – Evan Hamilton, chief of the White House staff, and Gayle Eccles, transition coordinator. Because of his progressive neuromuscular weakness, former President Henson and his wife elected to remain seated off to the side.

After the gathering settled itself, the Sergeant at Arms once again pounded the staff of his eagle-topped mace onto the podium's floor, and then ceremoniously moved to the Speaker's right, placing the staff into its marble pedestal. As he did, he announced in a bellowing voice, "Mr. Vice President, Madame Speaker, Chief Justice Brewer. I present to you, Mr. David Winfield of the Commonwealth of Virginia for the purpose of taking the oath of office of President of the United States."

The Speaker of the House, Democratic Representative Julia Minor, rose along with everyone else and led a final round of thunderous applause from her position high above the Winfields. Suzanne smiled with a special radiance from the rostrum as she held a worn bible in one hand and her husband's hand tightly with the other.

Nancy Winfield, looking on from the balcony, squeezed her daughter's hand and tearfully observed, "Your father would have been very happy, so proud tonight, Marilyn, to see David and Suzanne looking so well. You three are in the prime of your lives. It's wonderful to see you all flourishing."

Shortly, the Chief Justice took the Speaker's nod as his cue and came forward and stood with the Winfields. The Speaker of the House pounded her gavel and brought the crowded assembly to order. "You may be seated. Please sit down. As we all know, we are having this special and historic inauguration this evening due to the extraordinarily tight security measures that have been imposed around our Capitol. I have been informed that America may now be facing a Condition Imminent. It did not seem wise to any of your Congressional leadership to delay the oath of office and the transfer of Presidential power until a more customary ceremony could take place outdoors on the Capitol steps. Thus, we meet tonight.

"Justice Brewer, you may now proceed with the oath of the office of President."

The Chief Justice of the Supreme Court stepped closer and instructed in a soft tone, "Mrs. Winfield, you may stand here to the side and hold your family bible." Then he turned to face the newly elected President. In an official-sounding voice, he continued. "Sir, I now ask that you place your left hand on the bible and raise your right hand. Each President of the United States has taken the oath that you are about to take. Think hard, sir, about these words. They come to you from the ages – the same words that are written in the nation's original Constitution.

"Please repeat after me:

> *'I do solemnly swear . . .' "*
> "I do solemnly swear . . ."
> *" 'That I will faithfully execute the office . . .' "*

After completing his oath, David leaned over and warmly kissed his wife. The Speaker of the House and Vice President Richard Thompson came down and, along with Chief Justice Brewer, heartily congratulated David and Suzanne Winfield.

Everyone in the hall felt profound relief that the American system of government had once again managed to work. Somehow the Congress had been able to compromise and avoid a Constitutional crisis. They had avoided a deadlock in the selection of the President, a stalemate that they could ill afford in these perilous times. Given the growing threat of domestic and international terrorist attacks, they and most Americans felt that the selection of a President, even if it was a third party President, had been accomplished just in time.

During a subsequent ovation, the Speaker of the House came forward and put her hand on Winfield's shoulder. "And now, sir, please address us all – those in the chamber and your fellow citizens watching around the country."

Once again, thunderous applause broke out as nearly everyone voiced their support for their new President. After a due interval, David Winfield held both arms up with outstretched hands and encouraged everyone to be seated. He took a sip of water, squared his shoulders and prepared to speak. It was evident that he would be speaking extemporaneously. He retrieved no scripts from his coat pocket and surprisingly used no Teleprompters.

Watching from the Washington studios of Media Manor television, Jan Melone had been giving an explanatory voiceover to her television audience to fill time before his speech. She had commented to viewers how absolutely stunning the first family looked, almost like an American monarchy. Her producer, Hugh Rochan, had called to check in earlier in the day. It was only after she started to speak on the air that she thought it strange that he had suggested, nearly verbatim, so many of her introductory comments.

During this down time before Winfield's address, the news anchor was taken aback. Hugh Rochan could be seen on camera sitting directly behind the Winfield family in the balcony. Seeing the Englishman, Janet Melone could only wonder as she said, "This election is important worldwide this year, especially in Europe. We know that all peoples bordering the Atlantic have so many things in common, and . . ." She interrupted herself. "Here now," she whispered, "is the President of the United States."

Winfield paused on the dais. He had learned from Denise Donasti's tutorial sessions to be sure to take proper time before speaking. After squaring himself behind the lectern, he smiled broadly and began.

"My friends and fellow countrymen and women, President and Mrs. Henson. I am humbled to stand here as your 46th President of the United States. I pledge to be a leader, your leader, of what I call a New Society for all Americans – a society that will be more efficient and better equipped to deal with the tumult and confusion of our times.

"The original framers of our republican experiment in government wrote our Constitution during their own tumultuous era. Many of these men meeting in Philadelphia during that unbearably hot summer of 1787 said that it was far harder to make a nation than it had been to declare their independence in that same city in 1776. By their work and words, though, they envisioned that future reform and revisions would always be needed in order to continue pursing their goal. Each future generation, they stated, will need to take its own measures in making a 'more perfect Union.'

"Here we are, fellow citizens, more than two hundred years later. It is now our time in our nation's history. The mantle of leadership has fallen on our shoulders. We must all still look to perfect our Union by choosing to be a part of this remarkable nation.

"But, and I would emphasize the word 'but,' we are presently far from the perfect Union that these original American patriots wrote about. Indeed, recall that Washington, Adams, Madison, Hamilton and many of the other founding fathers during those early years had serious doubts about the prospects for a long-term successful national government. Where do we stand now, my friends?"

As David Winfield spoke to the gathering, he was keenly aware that millions were watching him on live TV and Internet feeds. He continued, "Have we established justice? . . . I mean *real* justice? Have we provided for domestic tranquility, for *all* of our citizens? Have we understood, really understood, the blessings of liberty to ourselves and for others? Have we made adequate provisions for the general welfare of our many states and regions? Have we taken care to provide for the common defence? Have we allied ourselves properly throughout the world?

"On all these issues, I suggest not."

President David Winfield paused for several moments as he fingered the lectern, letting his questions linger in the air.

Sitting at his customary place near the backbenches, Democratic Representative Patrick Jefferson of Illinois frowned, wondering where this first American Federalist President was going with his comments. Even more puzzling, he thought, was the lack of uplifting phrases that everyone always expected to hear at moments like this. Instead it seemed that Winfield's speech was a downer of sorts, but Jefferson couldn't precisely pinpoint why he was feeling that way. He decided there was nothing he could do about it, in any case, and so continued to try and follow along.

At the same time, elsewhere in the District, John Madison was watching Winfield's speech as he composed an analysis of the inauguration in real time onto his *Washington Post* blog. He looked up quizzically when the television monitor abruptly went silent. "That seems strange," he thought. "Only the audio portion is shut off, whereas the picture is still on air."

"Where is Winfield going with all this?" the *Post* journalist wondered aloud in the pressroom after the sound cut out. "Damn! I need to hear his words!" What made it more frustrating was that Madison could not recall a single time in the past year when David Winfield had looked so wooden, almost as if he were a puppet. The journalist was annoyed that he could only analyze the newly inaugurated President's body language rather than hear what he was saying. Madison was puzzled to see on the muted screen that his features had become dark and sphinx-like.

Staring at President Winfield on the monitor, Madison recalled that he had heard from an agitated Hugh Rochan that morning calling from London. Rochan was inquiring about Madison's morning column entitled 'Where Now America?' that had been mounted on the *Post's* website the day before the final House vote was taken. The column had been about the direction that Madison feared Winfield might take the country if he was somehow elected President. At the end of his call, Rochan had parenthetically asked in a near-threatening tone, "Where are you going with this, Madison? Just stay on the facts, John, on the facts."

Within minutes, as suddenly as it had switched off, the television's audio was fully restored. Without giving it much thought, Madison and the others in the *Post's* copy room continued their tasks as they again listened to Winfield. Everyone suspected there was going to be plenty to write about that night and knew they needed to stay on the story.

President Winfield's speech once more was fully carried on the television. ". . . and that should be our goal."

"I apologize for sounding so serious in this my initial speech as President, but we find ourselves in difficult, no, in perilous times, ladies and gentlemen. We did not find these times – they found us.

"Let me pause at this juncture, though, and take pleasure in reintroducing you to Dean Gayle Eccles, my colleague and friend."

Winfield smiled and made a sweeping gesture in her direction. Gayle Eccles stood up in the front and waved to the gathering.

"We all know you lost the Vice Presidency by not qualifying for the Senate election proceedings, Gayle. But I promise to do something about that after you complete your work with my transition team."

He motioned again to the front row on his left. "And let me reintroduce Mr. Evan Hamilton, my campaign director, who is, as of this moment, my new White House chief-of-staff. It should be reassuring to America, as it is to me, that both of these present-day patriots are direct descendants of two of the most important of our original Founding Fathers, John Adams and Alexander Hamilton."

Winfield encouraged them both to come up to his side on the elevated rostrum. As they did, the Representatives and Senators stood and loudly applauded. Thomas Moore of Ohio energetically led his fellow Representatives in response, pounding on the shoulders of nearby colleagues.

There was a palpable sense of relief throughout the whole Joint Session of Congress. The collegiality that most of the lawmakers were feeling was probably owing to the sense that they had been instrumental in preserving the United States. A more cynical observer might have proposed that what they felt was not collegiality at all, but rather a dumbed-down state of euphoria brought on by shared exhaustion.

While members of Congress were engrossed in self-congratulatory rumblings, a military aide discretely came over to inform Generals Greene and Mason that the temporary audio NSA-jam to the networks had worked. The junior officer quietly mentioned, "Give us the go ahead anytime, sir . . . We'll be ready when you are."

59

January 26, 2021 9PM EST

As people milled about on the House floor, Evan Hamilton came up briskly and authoritatively stood before the Joint Session. It was just a matter of time before some of the members of Congress recognized his presence on the dais. They were left to wonder what he was doing there so soon after David Winfield had taken his oath of office. An awkward silence spread through the chamber like a virus.

Winfield moved back to stand next to Suzanne. They appeared to be unsurprised that Hamilton had joined them. His newly appointed chief-of-staff looked foreboding as he began. "I am told that the audio for the television broadcast has now been fixed. It is good to know that everyone at home will again be able to hear what we have to say."

Hamilton leaned forward, grasping the lectern. "Thank you President Winfield for your kind words. On the occasion of your inauguration, I am honored to tell America even more about you."

Hamilton turned and looked back at President Winfield who had remained standing with Suzanne at the side. "Let me start by saying that even though there are many other patriots in our midst, none has greater legitimacy than our new President. But allow me to point out two other such American heroes. Please stand if you will. General Ronald Putney Greene is a seventh generation Greene, descended from a hero of the Revolutionary War, General Nathaniel Greene. He and his family have a long history of dedicated military service. This currently involves his leadership of the NSA at Fort Meade, the National Security Agency. Next to him is General Philip Mason, one of the Lees of Virginia, a legendary American family that also dates back to the Revolutionary period. Presently, General Mason directs the security forces protecting Washington, D.C. from his headquarters at

Fort Marshall along the eastern Potomac. Gentlemen, we owe you and your families a great debt of gratitude. Thank you both.

"At this time, I have asked General Mason to bring certain items to the podium regarding President Winfield's family which I will detail later."

Phillip Mason walked to a side door. When it opened, a field grade officer proceeded to lead two platoons of soldiers past him into the Joint Session. Winfield thought that he recognized the officer as Colonel O'Donahue, but from where he was standing, he couldn't be sure. As the detail crisply took its place, it suddenly dawned on people that the customary Capitol security personnel were nowhere in sight.

Two of the soldiers carried a two-foot-long, ornate box and a third carried what appeared to be a worn leather valet case. The three brought the items up the steep carpeted stairs onto the House podium and put the box and valet case on a side table. Following this, the three soldiers sharply turned about and rejoined their platoon, still stiffly standing at parade rest along the chamber's wood-paneled walls.

General Mason returned to his seat. Except for General Greene, none of the other seated officers recognized the strange markings on the troopers' uniforms. A patch on the upper sleeve contained the acronym 'DOSECOF,' Mason's clandestine Domestic Security Operational Force.

Hamilton continued speaking. "What I have to tell you about David Winfield is a long and convoluted story, my friends. Some will say it sounds like fiction. It might make for a good book someday, but it is much too long to repeat in its entirety tonight."

He turned to David and Suzanne Winfield and said, "I think that now would be a good time to sit back while I recite some of your narrative, David." Hamilton gave them two glasses of water and the couple returned to their chairs at the rear of the rostrum.

When they were comfortably seated, Hamilton again turned to the audience. "Ladies and gentlemen of Congress, in order for each of you to better follow my discourse, Dr. Gayle Eccles and I have made an information binder for each of you. I have instructed the Congressional pages to hand them out at an appropriate time. First, though, please let me make some initial comments."

Hamilton smiled thinly and gestured to the table next to him. "Suffice it to say that there are several objects in this container, which is known as the 'Caesar Box,' which will substantiate Mr. Winfield's legitimacy to be our President."

Hamilton peered over the crowded hall to be sure he had commanded everyone's attention. As he again pointed to the large box, the television camera zoomed in to capture its ornate decorations. "This ebony case," he explained, "was tightly locked from 1797 until very recently. It was stored for more than two hundred years at Mount Vernon in the family Tomb, the Washingtons' original Burial Vault.

"Ladies and gentlemen, George Washington and Alexander Hamilton used this Caesar Box for the purpose of securing certain vital documents. By doing this, Washington's seminal ideas and deepest wishes have been preserved through the years. Washington and Hamilton cached them in this clever container with the belief that they might some day prove critical to the survival of America."

Irregular murmurs resonated through the room like the rush of a river heading downstream. What the legislators were now hearing from Hamilton seemed ludicrous and nonsensical. Many wondered aloud, "What is he talking about? What does this have to do with President Winfield?" Still others simply concluded that the man had lost it.

"Some of you appear confused and are probably asking yourselves, 'Where is he going with all this?' My reason for telling David Winfield's story hinges on the fact that for much of America's history, the presidency and the power behind it have rested in the hands of a few selected families – not only the Adamses, Roosevelts, and others, but certain family-owned dynasties in the private sector as well.

"It has seemed that at times Americans have wished for a larger-than-life, might I even suggest 'regal' figure as their President. Well, friends, we have one now in David Winfield and his New Government."

People throughout the chamber erupted loudly with questions. "What is Hamilton driving at? Is this a New Government or a New Order?" "Aren't we the duly elected officials of the government? Evan Hamilton is only an appointee – he's a scoundrel to be speaking so presumptively." "What the hell are these 'vital documents' that Hamilton talks about?"

Hamilton looked back at President Winfield for reassurance and, after getting a dull-witted nod, turned to the front and glared as if he were a matador. Incandescent with self-righteousness, he raised his arms in a Nixonesque manner and shouted, "Hear me out, friends! What I will tell you next is critical."

He knew there were many more details regarding the Washington-Winfield connection that he had to explain, before he could possibly divulge the real reason why David's legitimacy was important. "First, let me draw your attention to this leather valet case on the table. I brought this item of interest from the cellar vaults of my own First Federal Bank of New York."

Hamilton pulled a billfold out of the leather valet bag and demonstrated it with a flourish. After withdrawing a parchment-piece, he announced, "This the attendance roll of the original members of an organization known as PATRI, dated February 22, 1797. This was a secret American group of federalists who were gathered by George Washington in response to a direct correspondence he had received from certain Europeans. The original PATRI members met only once, and were selected for the express purpose of ensuring the perpetuation of dearly-held patriotic beliefs."

The chamber became deadly quiet. No one could guess what he might say next, since to many Hamilton seemed increasingly outlandish. Those in the half-domed room clearly saw that David and Suzanne Winfield, in contrast to nearly everyone else, appeared surprisingly unsurprised as they sat passively in their chairs.

Nancy Winfield leaned over in the Gallery and whispered to her daughter, "Marilyn, do you think David and Suzanne are all right? It's almost like they've been drugged or something."

"I know, Mom. I was thinking the same thing, but it's been awfully stressful lately for both of them. Suzanne told me they've been up since four this morning." Marilyn smiled and tapped her mother's shoulder, silently motioning at her nephews sitting next to them. Both boys seemed to be nodding off as well.

Up on the dais, Evan Hamilton could tell that he had everyone else's rapt attention. His revelation about the existence of PATRI was completely unexpected. "It is important to distinguish this group from another organization also formed soon after the Revolution, the Society of the Cincinnati. This latter society continues to be an open, well-respected organization, comprised of the descendants of Washington's Revolutionary War officers. I suspect that many of you are currently members. But let me be perfectly clear. The aims of the Society are quite different from those of PATRI.

"As well, membership in PATRI has been secretly passed down only to certain descendants of sixteen original patriots who were convened, as I've said, at President Washington's urgings. I am one of them. My direct ancestor, Alexander Hamilton, was one of the lead members.

"Let me give you an idea of some of the other original PATRI signatories – John Adams, John Marshall, George Washington, and another dozen well-known patriots. President Washington was the only original member who had no known direct descendants. PATRI has no other purpose other than the preservation of America as Washington himself would have wanted."

Hamilton sipped some bottled water as he gazed about the expansive room. "As I mentioned, Dr. Eccles and I will shortly distribute an informational booklet. It is a guide that will document what I say later to make it easier for you to digest the facts."

As he glibly continued to speak, many Senators or Representatives didn't think he was worth listening to. They needed his so-called 'booklet' for reference. Many of them stopped trying to even understand his near-ramblings, and so instead sat checking their text-messages.

Suzanne and David fought to stay focused, vainly trying to stifle their yawns. David could not understand why they were feeling so groggy, but figured both of them had heard all of this before anyway.

Up in the Gallery, Sir Ronald Farrington - the Lord Aplington, took his own liberty to send a text message to fellow Europe League members: *'So far, so good, friends. EH will soon present the crux of the matter.'*

Patrick Jefferson shifted uneasily in his seat on the House floor. Nature with a capital 'N' was calling. He regretted having some extra espresso at dinner. As Hamilton continued to talk on and on, the Congressman from Illinois became even more uncomfortable. He hastily put down his *St. Louis Post-Dispatch* and excused himself as he slid by two of his colleagues.

"Take good notes," he whispered. "I've gotta go to the restroom."

As he passed through the leather rear doors, he met two pages and asked one, "Can you save me one of those brochures, Peter? I'll be right back."

Outside, Patrick Jefferson hurried down the marbled hallway. Once inside the men's room, he breathed a grateful sigh and noisily relieved himself. As he stood at the porcelain urinal, Hamilton's high-pitched voice projected from the lavatory's overhead speakers.

Standing at the sink, Jefferson detected that Hamilton's tone had grown more strident as he was saying, "At a meeting two years ago in Switzerland, the current members of this PATRI met with a sister organization, the present-day Europe League. The two decided to embark on a concerted course of action, to install a new brand of American leadership. What we have . . ."

Patrick finished washing up and prepared to return to the chamber. When he half-opened the heavy door with its century-old grillwork in the bottom panel, he saw two Representatives come out the chamber's padded exit doors. Suddenly, they were strong-armed by three heavily dressed operatives who hadn't been there minutes before. Although they struggled mightily, the two were forcibly gagged with duct tape and handcuffed with zip cords. Standing in the shadows of the partly opened door, Jefferson was startled to see a company of armed, black-uniformed troopers further down the corridor hurriedly taking up positions outside the other exits to the House Chamber.

He quietly back-pedaled, closed the door softly and entered one of the stalls. The presence of these soldiers quickened his growing dread. Jefferson realized that his colleagues inside the House were not even aware of what was going on out here yet. He wished that he could let them know, but then immediately thought the better of it.

Patrick tried to text John Madison at his office. "Surely, he would have a perspective on what's happening," he imagined. When he turned on his cell phone, the screen lit for a moment before going blank. "That figures," he realized. "We're all trapped."

Frightened, Jefferson locked the stall's door and clambered up unsteadily onto the toilet seat. He hoped that none of the soldiers in the corridor had seen him. If the troopers did enter the lavatory, he prayed that they would only make a cursory search. Fortunately, he was quick to realize that a locked stall door simply wouldn't do, would be too suspicious. The stall had to appear empty. He bent down and unlocked the stall's door, then opened it a crack and repositioned himself, angling behind the door.

60

January 26, 2021 9:30 PM EST

Inside the chamber, Evan Hamilton's tone of voice sounded even more harsh. "Many PATRI members are here tonight. They already know most of what I am about to say."

On the House floor, many members of Congress suspiciously eyed one another. Minutes before, the new President's chief-of-staff had merely seemed loose-at-the-hinges; now he appeared to be fully unhinged. Pockets of respected Senators began to angrily voice their protests. The lawmakers felt somewhat comforted knowing that their opposition was being faithfully transmitted live via television and the Internet throughout America.

Hamilton vainly raised his arms to calm the uproar that his statements had provoked. Vice President Richard Thompson, seated motionless behind him, remained silent but his red face and deep scowl said it all. The Speaker of the House, Julia Minor, stepped forward and pounded the lectern block.

"Please, please, everyone take your seats. Give Mr. Hamilton a chance. After all, there is a First Amendment." As the Democratic leader spoke, piercing catcalls echoed down from the upper reaches of the House. She frowned in their direction and said, "There's no harm in talk. Please be civil."

She then addressed Hamilton standing below her. "At the same time, sir, can you make your comments a little less provocative?" She disliked having to be such a parliamentarian but saw that, besides these unruly interlocutors, her fellow members of Congress had grown testy. Their nerves were frayed by their recent deliberations.

Hamilton wheeled to face Speaker Minor. "For the sake of order, Madam Speaker, I would like to request the Gallery be emptied at this time."

"Precisely why is this needed, Mr. Hamilton?"

"It is necessary to permit the members of the Joint Session of Congress to give their undivided attention to what I will next say. President Winfield himself insists on it." Hamilton gestured back to the seated figure. David gave his own assent with a vacant expression.

Julia Minor was skeptical of Hamilton's reasoning, but nonetheless went ahead and ordered the House of Representative ushers to clear the Gallery.

Within minutes, some two hundred invited guests were escorted out of the House Chamber. Everyone had to leave, including the Winfield family and the PATRI and Europe League invitees. Hamilton knew that the ushers were, in fact, disguised members of Mason's security detail. The guests were directed to go down the side stairs and shortly thereafter, were taken off the premises by coach.

Once he received a thumbs-up from one of the so-called 'ushers,' Evan Hamilton motioned in Gayle Eccles's direction. "Dr. Eccles, would you please join me here at the microphone. Thank you, Madame Speaker, I promise to be more direct." He apologized as Dr. Eccles joined him on the rostrum. "What Dr. Eccles and I have to say will soon make matters clearer. The two of us will now begin to explain the contents of this Caesar Box."

Before the two American Federalist leaders resumed, they requested that the pages pass out the informational binders to each legislator. "This," Hamilton repeated, "will allow each of you members of Congress to follow our expositions more easily. When you get your binder, for instance, you can see a close-up photograph on page 1 of the Caesar Box, present here on the table."

As the first few legislators received their copies, some of them questioned the real objectives of Hamilton and Dr. Eccles. As they sifted through their brochure's contents, the rustling made by the turning pages seemed like the sounds of college students skimming through blue book finals.

"Hear me out, fellow Americans," Hamilton said. "To begin with as the booklets are being distributed, I will describe this, the PACT of 1795." He pulled out a second item from the valet case and said, "This PACT mentions that the Europe League ' . . . will fully assist in the formation of a new Government,' which 'thereby would ensure the state of order in America – order that is so necessary . . .' This is precisely what you have done with your selection of David Winfield."

Hamilton thought it brilliant that Gayle Eccles had told him to not to read the phrase 'a legitimate Monarchy in America' on page 4 of the information booklet. "Too much information at first," she had mentioned. "Tell them *when* they need to hear it."

Paying no heed to the uproar that his words had provoked, Hamilton loudly proclaimed, "The members of PATRI have always known of the existence of this agreement. Now you can see it for yourselves. It provides the means to the restoration of civil order through a proper government.

"The PACT declares that certain royal houses of the Europe League will help PATRI establish a new form of American government for the preservation of America whenever it is deemed to be necessary. The arrangement was intended for the benefit of what is called the 'Pan Atlantic Community.' The big question we must ask ourselves is this: What American could ever have a legitimate, verifiable claim to say that he (or she) is the rightful leader of such a new form of governance? Dr. Eccles and I will try to answer that crucial question by reviewing some items stored within this Caesar Box. They are listed in your brochures, more or less in chronological order."

Generals Mason and Greene were sitting sullenly on the side when a major moved down the aisle and crouched next to them. The officer whispered, "The halls to the chamber are secure. We've put our men into position around the Mall too."

"Thanks, Major – good timing, good work," General Greene said.

Up on the dais, despite the persistent murmurs of protest, Hamilton plowed right ahead and retrieved the testament of a dying Lawrence Washington from the Caesar Box. He then said over the rising din, "You'll find that on page 6 of the booklet." He added, "At the time, George Washington's older brother was the scion of the Washington family. You can see that Lawrence was clearly writing about his baby daughter Sarah's welfare in his testament, dated 1752."

Gayle Eccles stepped forward alongside Hamilton. She read a letter found in the Caesar Box and said, "This personal note of Sally Cary Fairfax is found on page 3."

When she was finished, Gayle looked up and realized that the first lawmakers who received their brochures seemed to be wondering why she had omitted reading the phrase *as an American monarch* that they could see on page 3. To regain the moment, she quickly added, "For those of you who may not know, Mrs. Sally Cary Fairfax and her husband, George William, were extremely close friends with the Washingtons.

"These Virginia aristocrats acted together with George Washington in a scheme to hide the true identity of Sarah Washington, the sole surviving heir of Lawrence Washington after his death. The little girl nearly died at the age of two from a suspected plot against her life. Let me tell you the story of that event," and she did. "To make the relationships more understandable, I refer you to a genealogy in your booklet that is on page 7."

When she had finished, Evan Hamilton repositioned himself at the lectern and continued to reveal what he called "more pieces of the puzzle."

After he droned for another several minutes, Gayle Eccles took a cue from the blank faces of the legislators and moved forward interrupting him.

"Take your time, ladies and gentlemen. I know there's a lot of material. For those watching at home," she said, "the informational brochure that your representatives have in front of them, provides copies of everything we are describing. Now then, what else does this Caesar Box hold that tells us about the true bloodlines of the House of Washington? And more importantly, is this information relevant for us today?"

Suzanne leaned over, and in a haze whispered, "David, I don't think either of us expected anything like this. I think we've been hoodwinked. Getting elected President is one thing, but this?"

Winfield struggled to stand up. As he did, he glanced to his left and saw his friend General Mason sitting rigidly in the front row. He guessed that Phil of all people would understand, but surprisingly Mason looked away.

President Winfield somehow stumbled forward, and interrupting Gayle Eccles, spoke with her and Hamilton off mike. "Evan, Gayle, damn. I'mm Prez'dent, don' forget. I don't want to be a pretender to some sorta throne. I said I'd be a king if, and *only if*, it needs to be that way."

Hamilton stared him down. "Well now, friend, it should be obvious. We think it needs to be that way. So?"

Gayle Eccles patted Winfield's shoulder and gently helped him back to his chair. She then returned to the lectern and said, "Now, Madame Speaker, let me turn to the 'necessary proof,' of which Mrs. Sally Fairfax writes, that pertains to our one, true American royal family. The real questions before us should be: 'Is there any necessary proof?' And if so, 'What is it?' "

Six Representatives who had heard too much already suddenly bolted from their chairs. From what Hamilton and Eccles were now saying, they felt that it amounted to sheer fantasy, or worse, treason.

Seeing this, General Ronald Greene flipped his hand as if he were shooing a fly. Unbeknownst to the members in the chamber, the NSA and DOSECOF scrambled the television and audio feed from the Joint Session of Congress. The signal went dead.

Janet Melone, watching from her Manor Media studio, was stunned. The evening had started out strangely enough earlier when she had seen Hugh Rochan sitting in the Gallery. And now this?

Usually an important network-pooled coverage had a backup with fail-safe technologies, but her studio engineer had just given her a thumb-down signal. As if by habit, Janet continued to speak into her microphone.

"No one can hear ya, Jan," a sound technician yelled. "No use."

"What the hell's going on?" she asked. It was as if someone had pulled a plug.

Shouts continued to echo in the House Chamber as, unbeknownst to them, the NSA-orchestrated blackout took hold. A few Senators and Representatives tried to contact their families or assistants on their mobile phones, but they quickly discovered that their connections were jammed.

During the shutdown, Evan Hamilton and Gayle Eccles continued to shock the Joint Session with even more preposterous-sounding 'divulgences.' He finally concluded his rambling diatribe, saying, "You didn't elect and we didn't inaugurate a President today, my friends. You, in fact, have chosen a king!" Hamilton spun around with a flourish and gestured towards President Winfield.

Gayle Eccles knew that General Greene's promised blackout was now fully activated. She was pleased that no person outside the hall could see or hear any of this, since General Mason had warned that it might turn ugly before the night was out.

A flock of Secret Service personnel clambered to get close to the seated, remarkably unemotional President and his wife. They clustered about in a programmed, protective cordon, and as they did, fell to the carpet one by one, all victims of curare-coated projectiles. DOSECOF marksmen swiftly immobilized the other dozen Secret Service men positioned throughout the Gallery. Secret Service backups, standing outside, had already been taken down, bound and detained by two DOSECOF battalions who had suddenly emerged from the tunnels running beneath the surrounding plaza.

General Mason's son, Colonel Ken Mason, was the commander of the third DOSECOF battalion. He clambered onto the podium and signaled to the side. Instantly, twelve steel-faced members of his elite strike-force formed their own protective semicircle around David and Suzanne Winfield. The troops carried fully loaded semiautomatics, and each man had multiple clips of ammunition on his belt.

Two medics joined them on the crowded rostrum and carefully checked on the Winfields' conditions. The remaining cowed legislators were thankful that at least the President appeared to be unharmed in the troopers' midst. Only a few ventured to guess what might come next.

David tried to reassure Suzanne, but his words were garbled. "Phil Mason said it might come to this . . . we've got to follow his lead. To be honest, it's like we're caught in a crossfire but right now I don't know. I can't think straight. Everything's a blur."

As the six firebrand legislators tried to push down the crowded aisle, a dozen newly arrived DOSECOF troopers muscled towards them from the other direction. The soldiers brought out their three-foot-long anti-riot clubs and struck the six on their necks and shoulders. Converting to horizontal swipes, they smashed their truncheons into the Representatives' torsos with sickening thuds. Two female lawmakers desperately struck out and clawed the troopers' faces before they were roughly restrained with chokeholds.

Mayhem broke out as all sorts of materials and papers sitting on the legislators' desks were hurled in the direction of these rogue forces. A separate phalanx of another group of Congressmen tried to work its way across to assist their colleagues. As they did, scores of fresh DOSECOF troops rushed in from all directions, thrusting their way through the rioting members, brutalizing the outliers.

A thuggish warrant officer grabbed a rudely gesticulating man and hauled him roughly from his seat. "You can't do that! I am an elected member of this hallowed House!" the Congressman yelled in protest. The pudgy Representative from Missouri went pale and toppled to the floor when his protests were met by a hand chop to his neck and a kick to his groin. Blood streamed from the corner of his mouth as he bent over retching. Elsewhere in the chamber, DOSECOF medics attended to other badly beaten members of Congress.

"Try to keep calm, everyone," Speaker of the House Minor called out. She had already pushed the alert-button hidden on the side of her chair many times, to no avail. The device was used in the case of any disruption in the chamber to urgently summon the Capitol Police. She realized that tonight no such response would be forthcoming. Instead it was these cruel men in black shirts with their heavy riot gear who were maintaining their own special brand of order.

Patrick Jefferson remained frozen in place standing on the toilet seat. Several times over the past half-hour, the washroom's door squeaked open and after a cursory check, whoever had come in quickly left, leaving the Illinois Congressman alone. Over the wall speakers, he could barely understand Evan

Hamilton and Gayle Eccles's rants – something about having a king. Their high-pitched voices reverberated in the chilly lavatory. Hearing the furor, Jefferson was convinced that he too would be harshly dealt with if he stepped back into the hallway. He did not dare to get down and open the door to see the situation firsthand.

Jefferson tried to keep his emotions in check. If he didn't do something soon, the soldiers would surely discover him when they made a more thorough sweep of all the rooms along the hallway. He remained perched on the toilet seat, peering over the top of the stall to scope out his surroundings. Then he became aware of a faint draft of cold air coming into the stall from a nearby frosted window. "Thank goodness," he thought, "the last person in here must have opened it a crack. It looks like it might work . . . let's see."

He climbed off the toilet seat, edged himself out of the stall and lifted the sash nearly a foot. The freezing night air rushed in and prickled his forehead like needles. "Drat," he thought, "the window can't go any higher. There's a governor-lock."

In the background Patrick heard muffled voices in the hallway. "Hold them all – especially the young ones," a gruff voice called out. "We need more zip cords. Watch that old guy sitting down, Hank. He's turning blue. Don't let him keel over."

Jefferson feared that it was even worse than he thought. Something incredibly bad was going on. Even though it would be risky, he knew that somehow he had to get out of there.

Looking over his shoulder at the still-closed door, he quickly assessed whether there was a possible escape route. He stared outside the window and concluded that this was his only option. The Capitol's usually glaring floodlights were turned off and the surrounding area was unnaturally dark. He could see the District was blacked out too, all the way up past Bethesda.

He studied the dimensions of the half-open lavatory window and figured that he might be able to barely crawl through the ten-inch space without getting stuck. Patrick estimated he was a story or so above the Capitol's piazza. He didn't know if he would be forced to leap once he got through the window . . . and if he did, whether he would survive.

Jefferson gingerly tiptoed as he carried a waste can to the sidewall and carefully lined it up under the window. He pulled several long runs of toilet paper and put them on the tile floor to soften any scraping noise from the overturned can. He had to take off his sport coat and sweater to slip through the tight window opening. Concerned that his escape might be quickly detected if any clothes were left behind, he threw them out the window, hoping he could retrieve them once he got below. Even though security cameras would likely record his escape, he figured that he had to take the risk.

Jefferson cautiously stepped onto the bottom of the trash can and pulled himself up beneath the wooden windowsill. He first put one shoulder and his head through the small opening. The ground looked more than twenty feet down. Patrick half-turned in the window to sort out his options and was relieved to see a thick cast-iron downspout on the outside wall of the building, just six inches away. It seemed strong enough, he guessed, grabbing the ice-cold metal.

Pulling himself back into the room, he reasoned he had to climb out feet first and face down. Once he was dangling by his arms from the sill, he could transfer himself over to the pipe. He just hoped that he remembered some of his high school gymnastics. Patrick slowly eased himself up in order to sit fully on the window ledge, first with one, then both legs dangling out. With a quick, twisting scissor kick, he pronated his lower legs and came about.

Representative Patrick Jefferson went out into the night.

61

January 26, 2021 10PM EST

Gayle Eccles knew that the House Chamber was like an island in America. The radio, television and Internet transmissions were blocked. All of the legislators still in the chamber had either been restrained or were sitting stonily in front of her. Members of the DOSECOF units strode menacingly up and down the aisles, while many of the elderly Senators wept in angry disbelief. Their hallowed institution was being defiled. David and Suzanne Winfield remained seated on the rostrum with strangely plasticine expressions. House minority leader Moore sat disconsolately, wondering why everything that had seemed so good only that morning had suddenly turned out so bad.

"Hear me out, hear me out," Eccles said loudly. "You must now hear the evidence that establishes that David Winfield has a legitimate claim to lead a New Order." She lifted Anne Washington's porcelain urn out of the Caesar Box and commented, "This repository contained hair from two adults and three infants as shown on page 11 of your brochures. In addition, there was a similar locket found inside a jewelry box presently owned by Mrs. Winfield. This is pictured on page 12."

A Senator on a side aisle rose to challenge her nonsense but was immediately silenced, his blood spattering colleagues nearby.

"We had DNA from these six hair samples," Eccles continued without hesitation, "as well as present day samples from David and Suzanne Winfield analyzed by three prestigious medical laboratories." She held up the medical report folders. "These, ladies and gentlemen, are the results. The scientific details are on page 13 in your booklets. The summary from the three labs is as written:

"We conclude that the DNA analysis irrefutably establishes a blood-relationship with all save Mrs. Suzanne Winfield, date of birth 7/14/1981. "

Evan Hamilton returned to her side and spoke out perfunctorily. "It is said that George Washington often referred to a saying during the Revolutionary War, 'Desperate disease doth desperate remedy make.' My friends, we live in our own desperate times. If you accept, then, the premise that George Washington and others constructed this far-sighted contingency plan of instituting an American monarchy to be used only if the situation warranted it, then it seems logical that he would also provide us with a roadmap to identify a worthy heir.

"I am sure we would all agree that only a Washington could legitimately ascend such a throne. What these scientific experts are telling us is simply this: *Our elected President David Winfield is a Washington*. His direct bloodlines are summarized on page 14 of your brochure." Hamilton cocked his eyebrow and seemed to snarl. It was as if he were a pit bull challenging anyone in the chamber to confront him.

The Speaker of the House leapt to her feet. No longer connected to a sound system, she screamed, "This is absolutely bizarre, sir. Sit down now! You have totally misread the Constitution, and force me to direct Congress to begin hearings tomorrow for the impeachment of President Winfield."

Hamilton cackled and held his arms out to silence her. "Madame Speaker, he is still the President!" His gesture was a directive to the back of the chamber. Five platoons of heavily armed Defense Forces, all wearing black combat uniforms and bearing semiautomatic weapons, stormed through the eight closed leather doors and took up positions around the semicircular room. Two of them scrambled up and physically restrained Speaker Minor and Vice President Thompson as they tried to flee.

General Ronald Greene had an aide transmit word to Hamilton and Eccles on the rostrum that the NSA had just then reopened the television feed from the House Chamber as per the plans. General Greene had also scrawled a note: *Now is the time, Evan . . . Tell everyone . . .*

Sometime during the past half-hour, the television coverage of the inauguration had again suddenly frozen in the *Washington Post* copy room. This time, there was no picture on the screen as well.

John Madison was annoyed that the glitch was happening just when it seemed that the proceedings over at the Capitol were starting to heat up.

He yelled out in frustration, "Washington – Winfield, Mount Vernon – Woodlawn Mills . . . Dammit! What's happening?"

He and his coworkers had been intently listening to the speeches of Evan Hamilton and Dean Gayle Eccles. The journalist could clearly recall when he had first met them together at Bowdoin College two years earlier, and here they were together again. When the audio had gone out earlier that night, the interruption had lasted only a minute or two, but not this second time. Madison was puzzled by the prolonged delay and tried to check the Internet. The monitor showed: *SERVER NOT FOUND.*

Hurriedly, he tried to reboot his computer. Instead a static image flashed onto the screen. Madison thought it strange that a picture of Independence Hall in Philadelphia was shown while some martial music played. He got up and joined five coworkers over at the pressroom windows.

"That's weird," an assistant noticed, "the floodlights are off at the Capitol. I haven't seen that around here since the week of 9/11."

"How about that?" a layout specialist observed pointing westward. "Right now there are no lights around the Mall, either."

"Let me try my cell phone . . . see if I . . . No, I get nothing."

A young copy editor was amazed at what had happened to the office's bank of screens and computers. Everything was shut down. "When I started at the paper, you always told me, Mr. Madison, that if I stayed in Washington long enough, I'd see plenty of history in the making."

"I guess you're seeing plenty tonight, Jake."

"It sure makes for an interesting dilemma, Mr. Madison. Here we are sitting in the middle of D.C., but with all these systems down, we're not able to see or hear any history, even with a capital 'H'. I have a hunch there's a lot going on all around us and we don't even know. We're not even a part of it. I just can't believe, or maybe I don't want to, that Winfield and his crowd are turning out to be some new breed of tyrants."

"For those in our profession, it goes without saying," Madison said. "Tyrants and despots have always risen to power by first controlling information, through whatever means at their disposal, whether by censoring news or producing propaganda. Hamilton and his ilk look like they are quite aware of this. Whether these PATRI characters are true despots or not remains to be seen, but we've got to be concerned. Time will tell."

As Madison spoke, he heard a familiar 'twing.' Somehow his iPhone was working again. He had just received a tweet from Maureen Nightbird-Reynolds: *IM SORRY JOHN THEY WOULD HAV KILLED US BOTH. BE SAFE, LOVMO.*

As he pondered her message, the TV monitors inexplicably flashed back to life. The television screen in the newsroom revealed that Evan

Hamilton was still speaking to the Joint Session of Congress. "Madame Speaker, members of Congress, people at home. Do not let this show of force frighten you.

"President David Winfield, Gayle Eccles and I . . ."

In the chamber of the House of Representatives, Evan Hamilton testily spoke out after reading the message that General Greene had just given him, *Now is the time, Evan . . . Tell everyone else in America and throughout the world*. Once he had Greene's assurance, Hamilton knew that the proceedings were fully back on the broadcasts and the Internet.

"President Winfield, Gayle Eccles and I have introduced you to PATRI, the Europe League and the PACT," Hamilton shouted above the din, "What now? Tonight, you have witnessed that the PACT is starting to take hold. Tomorrow, we will distribute even more written material about the New Order in the form of citizen-pamphlets. They will explain all that matters, my fellow citizens.

"Here, for instance, is the Second Constitution of the United States still resting in this unopened glass cylinder that I am holding." He recognized he had to be careful not to appear too maniacal – he was now being aired again. "It was written and signed by the sixteen original members of PATRI in 1797. The responsibility of storing it has always been tasked to my Hamilton family through the years."

He held it high and demonstrated it to those legislators still inside the chamber and to the viewers following on TV. "This document was drafted for just the kind of circumstance that we find ourselves in today." He hesitated a moment before darkly pointing out, "The future America that the original PATRI was intent on protecting is no longer far off. That 'future America' is now. It remains our solemn duty to protect our nation and America's traditional values." Hamilton paused to set his jaw and stare directly at the camera.

He finally added, "The members of Congress have no voice in the matter. Rather than merely swearing in a President tonight, we will be crowning a king soon after this Second Constitution is read tomorrow. It will also be published in Citizen-Pamphlet No. 3 and distributed to all our fellow-citizens."

Once again, Evan Hamilton lifted the large, glass closed-cylinder and yelled into the clamor, which had risen like a brush fire swirling through dry grass, "This new document paves the way for a new system of government – a

New Order. Be ready, America. We will read it to the Congress whenever order is again fully restored. It has been a long day," he concluded abruptly. "We all need to get some rest."

He turned and asked President Winfield off mike, "Do you have anything else to say, David? Remember what we talked about."

David Winfield nodded and managed to slowly step forward. He seemed wooden as he approached the lectern. Tightly holding onto the microphone, he haltingly read a note that General Greene had just given him. "As of an hour ago, I have imposed martial law in the District of Columbia and in the surrounding counties of Maryland and Virginia. The rest of the United States is on Condition Imminent alert. I have also ordered various other strike forces to move into the District and several other cities throughout the country. Lastly, General Greene's NSA-command has taken control of all national cyber- and communication systems."

As he spoke, the live feed from the Capitol went dead. The proceedings were once again cut off. David Winfield wearily stepped back after announcing, "Evan Hamilton has some brief logistical items to go over with you."

Hamilton came forward, wiped his heavily perspiring face, and sternly commanded, "Everyone here will be required to wear an electronic ankle bracelet. General Mason's tactical forces have made arrangements for you to stay overnight here in the Capitol. Your safety and security will be guaranteed, but you are required to remain in these accommodations. Now, good night."

He, Gayle Eccles, David and Suzanne Winfield, and the two attendant medics joined Generals Mason and Greene. Without a word, they went out a rear door. A serious-looking DOSECOF lieutenant came forward, picked up the glass cylinder holding the Second Constitution of the United States, and led several soldiers carrying the other objects off the rostrum.

Glancing back at the dispirited members of Congress and the Supreme Court Justices huddled with various military chiefs-of-staff, General Ronald Greene tightly smiled and said, "Well, Phil, it's done."

General Mason quietly reflected, "No, I'm afraid it's only begun."

62

Georgetown Washington, D.C.
January 27, 2021

Holly Rhyne woke with a start. Her heart pounded as she groggily peered at the illuminated clock on her bed stand. It read 1:15AM. The downstairs security buzzer went off once more. She nearly tripped over her bedspread and shuffled toward the door. Her condo's co-owner, Cary McAllister, was out of town. Holly guessed it was likely one of her besotted suitors, another 'lost puppy,' as Cary called them.

Holly turned on the outside visual monitor. She gave a gasp, frightened by the sight of a bedraggled man huddled in a blanket. His teeth were chattering so loudly that she could barely understand him. "Holly, it's m-m-me – Patrick. Sorry it-it-it's s-s-so late."

"Patrick, I hardly recognize you! What's going on?"

"Shi-shi-sssh. We've got to-to-talk 'bou'-'bout . . .'"

Holly rang him in. On her monitor, she saw Patrick Jefferson open the outer door to her 8-unit building along the C&O Canal. She hurriedly put on her fluffy cotton bathrobe and as she stood in her hallway, could feel her heart racing. Something menacing seemed to be going on. Shortly, there was a soft knock on her door.

"Shissh, Holly." Jefferson put a finger against her lips after she opened the door. "I daun' know if I'v benn follow'erd. I'm scared." He halted in the hallway and said, "I better leave this blanket out here – might haf' lice."

Holly Rhyne was fully awake – adrenaline surged through her body. She eyed his distress with alarm. "You'll be alright, Patrick. You're here, OK?" She couldn't think what else to say. Seeing him shivering, she asked, "Where's your coat?"

"I didn't have un; I even hadda leave my sport jack' and sweater somewhere . . . threw 'em out a window. I gave a guy on d' street twent' bucks for this rag."

When he entered Holly's condo, she led him through her bedroom straight into the bathroom. "I obviously don't have the faintest idea what you've been up to but you need to get into hot water, Pat, and fast. I'll fill the tub."

"I'm so cold . . . soo-oh c-c-cold, Holly. I can't think straight." He seemed to be disoriented as he tried to move in the cramped space.

"Sit on that towel, Patrick," she directed, and took him by the shoulders to the covered toilet seat.

She turned on the bath water full-force and the bathroom soon got comfortably steamy. As he sat, Jefferson attempted to clear his head by rubbing his face. There was an awkward pause before she suggested, "I know you're independent but let me help you get undressed, Pat."

When he didn't protest, the matter was decided. Holly purposefully took charge. Patrick was content to passively lean back and let her do all the work.

She first pulled off his wet shoes and socks. Then she eased off his tie and shirt and put them on a chair. "Get your trousers off yourself, but don't try to get in the tub by yourself. You need help. I'll give you a hand when you're ready."

The spigot's splashing sounds gurgled as the water level rose. Holly put her hand in to stir it around. "Come on, fella, get going. Don't mind me. Remember, Pat, I've already seen you before."

It had been a long night – he finally felt safe. Jefferson clumsily pushed himself off the toilet lid in order to lower his pants. "Good 'ding you isdt home, Holly. I was in no sh-sh-shape to walk en-ee fur-der." His jaw clenched uncontrollably. "I could n'a gone to my place – they wou'da foun' me. I was wor'ri you wou'dn be here."

Holly knelt on a towel and tested the hot water. Without looking back, she heard Jefferson dump his pants and belt on the tiled floor.

"Get over here, Hol' – I need help," he muttered. "Let me hol' onto your-your shou-shoulder a sec'." As he got in, he blurted, "Ouch, oh 'eee – it's hot!"

"Oh sit down, you big baby." Holly Rhyne handed him a washcloth as he sat down in the tub and said, "I hope my pink soap is not too girly for you. It's from a spa in Sedona, Arizona. My mother always sends me some for Christmas."

"You seem like a good mother yourselve righ' now, Holly," Patrick said weakly. He knew he was acting scatter-brained as he leaned forward in the tub.

She moved behind him, lathered his back with the washcloth, and then squeezed rinse water on his blue-mottled shoulders. Holly then eased herself up and said, "After you do your front, Pat, I think you'll be ready for my father's proven remedy, some Johnny Walker."

He felt partly revived by the thought. "Great idea, Holly," he said, moving the sudsy washcloth on his own. As she left, cold air streamed into the steamy bathroom and he shuddered. "Quick, close the door, will you?" He lay back to submerge his belly and as he did, his folded legs and knees stuck out accordion-like in the soapy water. A minute later, Jefferson's reverie was interrupted.

"Two hot toddies coming up," Holly announced and sat with their glasses next to the tub. "I'll hold your glass for you between sips. Stay in the water, though, Pat. You were freezing. Here, take a good slug. Dad always says it works."

She leaned over the edge of the tub and gave him his whiskey. "I couldn't find Johnny Walker, but there was a bottle of Wild Turkey. It'll do."

As Jefferson took a deep gulp of her home concoction, Holly couldn't help glancing down at his soft body hair. She appreciated that he had preserved his own sense of modesty, partially covering himself with the washcloth while she was in the kitchen.

Patrick smiled. "Wow, that's some toddy, Holly. I have to say I'm not feeling nearly as frozen as I was. Something must be working." He took another swallow of the bourbon and brandy mix, and handed his nearly empty glass back.

As he continued to sit in the tub, Holly finally asked, "Before I get you another one of these Rhyne specials maybe you can tell me what is going on, Patrick?"

For the next ten minutes, as he sat soaking, Jefferson told her what he knew – the historic nighttime inauguration, the speeches, the strange-looking soldiers and, finally, the tale of his escape from the men's lavatory. He said that he didn't even know how the Joint Session ended. Jefferson was almost afraid to ask, but did nonetheless. "Did you see anything like this on TV, Holly?"

"I couldn't make any sense out of it, Patrick. I was here by myself and it seemed so disconnected. Shortly after David Winfield's speech, my television's audio briefly went off.

"Right after the audio resumed, Evan Hamilton and Gayle Eccles went onto the rostrum. Thereafter, the two of them completely took over from President Winfield. It was weird. Every time the TV showed Winfield's face, he looked like a zombie. Meanwhile, Hamilton gave a rambling discourse about a PACT or something like that. Then Dr. Eccles proceeded to have the

Congressional pages give out some sort of information booklet. Did you get one? No? That's right, you were hiding by then. Do you want to keep listening to any more of this while I make you another hot toddy?"

"I know that this Wild Turkey must be helping so sure, keep going Holly."

She got up and went back to the kitchen. From there, she continued her account. "At times, I felt like this Eccles-Hamilton twosome were acting like attorneys presenting a brief, trying to prove something. Whatever. In the course of what I thought were their rather pointless and meandering remarks, something they said seemed to provoke a near-riot on the floor of the House. A few of your fellow Representatives appeared to rush the podium but I couldn't be sure, because my TV suddenly went blank. No, that's not completely correct. The live picture was replaced by an image of Independence Hall in Philadelphia, coupled with some martial-sounding music."

Still sitting in the tub, Jefferson had a hard time following her disjointed narrative. He couldn't be sure whether it was his problem or the story itself.

"I turned on my radio," Holly remarked, "and all the stations were playing the same kind of music. No talk, just dirges. I attempted to get on the Internet, but it was down. Then I tried phoning a few friends . . . no luck, either. The lines were dead. With that, I remembered what my mother used to say. 'If you are confused about something, sleep on it and check back tomorrow.' So with her back-home advice, I went to bed early. And here I am, or was, until you showed up."

At last Holly came back from the kitchen and sat on the closed toilet lid. Patrick took a deep quaff from his refreshed tumbler. "Whew, I don't know, Holly."

"Don't know what, friend?" She lazily rubbed some bath oil on his neck and kneaded his muscles.

"Oh right, I left out some details. When I first opened the lavatory door, I saw two Congressmen being hog-tied by soldiers in the hallway. Judging by the commotion I heard coming from the House chamber, it sounded like many others were being subdued in there too. It was frightening."

Holly frowned and said, "Let me go recheck the TV — I'll see if anything's on."

It was only a moment before Holly came back with her half-finished drink in hand. "It's still the same type of funereal music," she reported.

"I probably should get out of the water now, Holly. My fingertips are getting crinkly but I guess that's probably a good sign."

"How so?"

"Must be getting my circulation back," Jefferson said. After drying himself off, he wrapped the towel around himself like a sarong and asked, "What now, friend?"

"What do you mean Patrick? Oh – that. You could use Cary's room, but I'm kinda chilled myself thinking how frozen you were, and probably still are in a way."

"And? . . . . . ."

"Why not lie together," Holly suggested. "That way, I can make sure you stay warm. I hear it works, Patrick. Trust me, but no shenanigans. Don't worry about it . . ." She reached over to turn out the overhead lights and led him purposefully to her bed.

The bedside lantern cast shadows on her rumpled sheets and covers. One pillow still held her head's mark. "You remember. That side is mine, it's taken," she yawned.

"Do you have some regular men's pajamas, Holly?" Jefferson stood next to her in the semi-darkness with only the towel around his waist.

"Heavens no," she said feigning shock. "Why would I have men's clothes in my dresser? Here, wear my bathrobe." Before he could protest, she took off her plush garment and handed it to him. She then moved past him wearing a loosely fitting Orioles nightshirt.

"Holly, you are amazing," Jefferson said as he dropped his towel and fit himself comfortably into her warm terrycloth robe.

"Now, let's see if we can keep your temperature up, Pat." With that she scrambled over to her side of the bed. Patrick followed her lead and climbed in on the near side.

In the dark, she reassured him again. "It's alright, Patrick. You're exhausted and need the sleep more than anything."

Soon, very soon, they lay hard against each other, fast asleep.

Patrick Jefferson was aware that Holly was up. He squinted at the bright light coming under the bathroom door. Lying in her bed, he thought he could hear a shower splashing somewhere. A clock radio glowed – 6:15 AM. The tussled cotton sheets on her side of the bed were still warm and Jefferson decided to stay horizontal.

Holly turned the shower off and started to lazily dry herself. As she did, she came out of the steamy bathroom and noiselessly plowed through her dresser. Jefferson moaned and by turning on his pillow caught a glimpse of her trim profile.

"Are you peeking, young man?" she coyly asked when she saw that he had stirred.

"Uh huh," he answered as he ducked under the pillow, "maybe just a little."

"A 'little' can give you lots more than you bargain for. You know a guy can get blinded even if he only takes a little peek at the sun." She laughed as she sat down to put on a lacey bra and underpants. "You've got to get lots more sleep, Patrick." She came over to his side of the bed and gave him a light kiss.

While she continued to dress, Patrick wondered aloud, "Anything happen between us last night, Holly?"

"Nothing could happen," she giggled. "You were exhausted. At least you got warmed up." She glanced at him over her shoulder as she adjusted her bra in front of her mirror.

"Well then, how about . . . ?"

"Heavens no. I've got to get to work."

"But, Holly . . ." As he looked at her, he knew he was starting to get aroused.

"Tonight, young Mr. Jefferson, perhaps later tonight. And then only maybe."

She put on a woolen skirt and loosely tucked in a cotton shirt as she walked back into the bathroom." I hope you don't mind but I've got to blow dry my hair."

While she did, Jefferson buried his head under his pillow and tried to shut off the whirring noise. After what seemed like hours, Holly shut off the hair dryer. The condo unit mercifully became quiet again.

"Do you want some coffee, Patrick?" she whispered. "I put on the brewer."

"No thanks, I don't want to get up for another few hours. I ache all over." Lying there, he relaxed in the feel and smell of her bathrobe. This new level of familiarity was making him feel comfortable. "But Holly, do see if the TV or radio is getting a signal yet, will you?"

Holly walked past him into the kitchen and called back, "No – just static now."

"Try getting on the Internet," he suggested.

"I tried to reboot it before I took my shower. I didn't tell you but there is still just a blank screen. No luck, Pat."

"I'll try to work on your P.C. later. Give me your password and PIN."

She carried a large cup of steaming coffee back into her bedroom. The light from the bathroom coming through the partly closed door illuminated their faces as she sat next to him on her queen-size bed. Holly jotted down

'Elves42' and her four digit PIN. Sitting on the mattress, she spoke softly, "I assume I can get to work. If I can't, I'll be back. If that's the case, I suppose the two of us will just have to take the day off together."

"While you're gone, try to find out what's going on out there, Holly. Will you?" Patrick squeezed her hand. "I'm afraid of being recognized if I go out."

Holly took a last gulp of coffee and washed down her half-eaten bran muffin. "I'll see you later. I'm glad to see you're feeling better, Pat."

"Thanks to you, dear friend. I promise not to answer the doorbell unless I see that it's you on your security monitor."

"Don't even bother. You forget – I have a key." She leaned over and gave him a warm kiss on his forehead and tousled his hair. "Now go back to sleep before I get back in order to be good for . . . whatever," she said teasingly. "Right now, it looks like the two of us might be having plenty of time to spend with each other, so be sure to rest well, Patrick."

She brightly called back as she opened her condo's door, "There's juice and cereal when you do decide to wake up. See ya later."

Holly Rhyne grabbed a heavy overcoat and left to go to work.

63

Washington, D.C.

Wednesday, January 27, 2021 8AM EST

Generals Philip Mason and Ronald Greene stood in front of a projection-screen; the day was about to start at the DOSECOF headquarters. Morning report meant exactly that, the same timeworn procedure he had known since his West Point days.

"What's our status this morning, Paul?" he asked the outgoing officer-of-the-day. He had been posted all night at the Capitol and was more than ready to be relieved of duty. During his recent half-year at the War College in Carlisle, Lt. Colonel Paul Schroeder could never have conceived of his current assignment.

"Paul . . . How's the President?" Philip Mason asked. He was first and foremost concerned about David Winfield's status that morning. He had last seen his friend as he and Suzanne were being loaded into an unmarked ambulance.

"Word from the White House is that the Winfields are still being treated with supportive measures at their home and appear to be responding."

"Thank heavens for that. What does that mean specifically?"

"The staff doctors and medics say that although there are good preliminary signs, sir, it'll take three to four more days for a full recovery. Evan Hamilton said that they, and their family, would have to remain under watch at Woodlawn Mills, no matter what, until they've got things fully under control."

General Mason's face reddened and he barked, "What the hell do Evan Hamilton and Gayle Eccles mean when they say 'they've got things under control?' Are they the ones in charge? I think not! Seems to me that we're under the direction of President Winfield, Schroeder. He's the President, after all, at least for the moment."

"Let's not quibble, Phil, I think you're overreacting," General Greene cut in. "David Winfield hasn't fully regained his faculties yet. Moving on, Colonel Schroeder, what about the Europeans who attended the Inauguration, the special guests?"

"We lifted the air-restrictions and they flew out of Reagan at 2400 hours on Philippe Rouen's Lear jet. I understand that they arrived in France sometime within the past two hours."

Ronald Greene and Mason next inquired about the situation over at the Capitol.

Lt. Colonel Schroeder pointed to a Power Point graphic in his reply. "We have a pretty thorough head count, sir. In all, we've detained more than four hundred Representatives and ninety-seven Senators. The nine Supreme Court Justices and the military service chiefs are in private holding rooms." The lieutenant colonel went on. "There were six Congress members ill at home or already in hospitals with assorted medical problems. We've got them under guard, too."

"And the casualties?"

Schroeder projected a second chart and said, "That's always bothersome, the collateral damage, sir. Despite our precise field operation, three Representatives died during the mission, one from a skull fracture, one from asphyxiation, and a ninety-year- old Congressman had an apparent heart attack. So far, some twenty-odd members of Congress have been taken to the George Washington Hospital for various injuries, but most should recover, sir. Two have already been released and brought back to the infirmary at the Capitol. The others remain hospitalized under guard."

"That's it?"

"Afraid not, sir. One Representative is still unaccounted for, a Congressman Patrick Jefferson of Illinois." Several photographs of the red-haired Jefferson came up on the screen. "As of this morning, we're working on a few leads. We should bring him in shortly."

General Ronald Greene turned to the incoming duty officer-of-the-day and said with a scowl, "Did you hear that, Captain Blackwell? Don't tell us when – just get him."

Georgetown –

Later that day, Patrick Jefferson sat upright as he heard the snap of a moving deadbolt. He had been in a deep sleep, dreaming about childhood fishing holidays at Lake Okoboji in Iowa. Seeing the bright daylight outside, he was totally confused as Holly whispered, "Shssh, it's only ten, Pat. I'm home early. My office is closed."

Jefferson wrapped himself in her bed sheets and tried to get oriented. He vaguely guessed that Holly had left only a few hours ago. Suddenly, he was fearful to hear why she was back so soon. "Did you find anything out this morning, Holly?"

"Not much, but whatever is going on seems pretty spooky." She turned the TV on. David Winfield's image filled the screen. A crawl-message repeatedly read: 'Due to conditions in the District all Government offices are closed until further notice.'

"It's really bizarre, Patrick – it's so silent. The streets and the buses are nearly empty. When I got to work, martial law decrees were posted on the outer doors of the Rayburn building and the doors were chain-locked. On my way back, I saw posters of David Winfield everywhere. Besides that, there are funny-looking pamphlets being freely given out at all the newsstands instead of the regular newspapers. To show you what I mean, I brought two of them from Ralph's SmokeShop up on Wisconsin."

Jefferson spread out the crudely produced street sheet on the bed.

Holly went on, "On my way from the bus, I read one of these pamphlets. What does it mean, 'The Second Constitution of the United States,' Patrick?"

"I have no idea. Let's look at these together, Holly. The smaller one here says that a new national Constitution is to be read to the Congress. The full text will be contained in another pamphlet." Jefferson paused and put the first pamphlet aside.

"Maybe that's what Evan Hamilton and Dr. Eccles were leading up to last night," he wondered aloud, "but it says here that it will be presented 'only after order is fully restored.' Why the need to restore anything, Holly, and maybe just as important, how will this so-called restoration take place? I'm sick about everything that's going on. It's certain that a coup of some sort occurred in the Capitol last night, but now this? Oh my," he fretted, "what does this second pamphlet say?"

The two looked over the other cheap-looking newssheet that was titled *Citizen Pamphlet No. 3*. On the front page, there was a grainy photograph of David and Suzanne Winfield waving from the podium.

The written piece began: *The Second Constitution of . . .*

A little further down, the article described the rationale for the new manifesto: *The people will henceforth be ruled by our legitimately authorized first family, which will become the basis of an American royal dynasty . . .*

The Second Constitution was reprinted in full on the middle pages. The two friends read in amazement that among other things, the new Constitution specified that there would be a legislature and court system that would be totally responsible to the king and his Privy Council and court ministers.
We all are in alliance with the Houses of the Europe League . . .
The article quoted Evan Hamilton: *The signatories on this Second Constitution of the United States are the original sixteen PATRI members. All these patriots had signed their agreement to this Second Constitution following their initial meeting in Philadelphia on February 22, 1797.*
The pamphlet's account went on: *The original Constitution of the United States ratified in 1787-89 is now made null and void. No such state ratifications are necessary for the new Second Constitution.*
Patrick Jefferson looked steadily at Holly. "I can't believe President Winfield is a part of this, I really can't. Besides Hamilton, I don't know who else is involved but I have suspicions. I've got to try reaching John Madison again. He always seems to be in the know."

After several attempts, Jefferson thought it fortunate that he was finally able to reach the newsman on his secure phone line. He anxiously reminded Madison that the NSA was probably listening in, but said that he felt he had to contact him nonetheless and quickly cut to the chase. "What's happening, John?"

"I should be asking you the same question, Patrick. You're the first person that I've spoken to who was in the Capitol last night. What the hell did you and your friends think when Evan Hamilton said there was absolute proof linking David Winfield to George Washington . . . and because of that, he was a legitimate king for America?"

"What?" Jefferson gasped, "I missed that completely, John. In fact, I consider myself lucky to be here at all."

"Well then, how about the issue regarding a Second Constitution?" Madison inquired. "Did you miss what Hamilton had to say about that, too? . . . Really? After seeing these so-called 'Citizen Pamphlets' this morning, I can't figure out if they're the real deal or smoke screens. Do you have any idea, Pat?"

"Not a clue. I've only just now seen these pamphlets myself." Jefferson felt drained and added, "I obviously don't have a clue or I wouldn't have called. I thought you, if anyone, would have the dirt on all this by now. John, you can tell I'm quite frightened about what's happening and what else might come down the pike. I'd like to get together as soon as possible. What do you say?"

Madison suggested a possible meeting place. "Across the street from where we first met for lunch two years ago. Remember? And don't bring your cell . . . In fact, as of now, you should probably leave it in some sort of trash bin, if you know what I mean."

"Why's that, John. I may need to call . . ."

"Pat – figure it out. It's the new world. General Greene and his NSA operatives will trace your movements like bloodhounds, even if you don't use your phone. I have another one, though, that we can use if we need to. It has a false owner ID. Only a few people know how to get me."

"Okay John, point well made. Can you meet about three, then, this afternoon? I'll be coming with a close friend."

"Sounds good, Patrick. I'll come alone. Best cover your own trail. I presume that whoever might want to know your whereabouts hasn't latched onto you yet, but watch out."

In the mid-afternoon, Patrick Jefferson and Holly Rhyne walked hand in hand into a nearly empty Fox's Glen tavern on the edge of Rock Creek Park. John Madison saw them enter. He hardly recognized Jefferson, his hair was shades darker. Madison motioned them over to a dimly lit table in the corner.

Jefferson introduced Madison to Holly. After various tonics and light appetizers were served, Madison leaned forward and spoke in a conspiratorial tone. "Since your call, I managed to find out some more information, Patrick. I suppose I should say *lack* of information. There's some sort of a military directive severely restricting activities here in the District and surrounding counties. With that, it's not too surprising that communication systems up and down the East coast and west to Chicago are down. As a consequence, it's impossible for me to sort things out."

Madison took a deep swallow of his lemon seltzer before saying, "I'm amazed that you were able to even contact me earlier. My regular cell service has been totally shut down ever since. I do know this, though. You are the only person from Congress that's been heard from, Pat."

"I was afraid you'd say that."

"Patrick, bottom-line, what do you think you're going to do?"

"Get away from here as soon as possible, that's for sure. I can't sit around here like a sitting duck." Jefferson described in painful detail the physical abuses he had been witness to at the Capitol. The Congressman was sure that he was now a prime target.

"Specifically, you asked, what am I going to do? Let me tell you, John." Jefferson sketched out a plan to John Madison. "Holly and I have been debating what are my limited options. She has a new car with dealer plates still pasted on the back window. Her car is a nondescript sedan, and I think it will be relatively unnoticed on the open highway. So, in that sense, we've caught a lucky break. We're thinking of leaving town this evening – all the while avoiding toll roads, busy gas stations and rest stops as we go. Wanna' join us? It could be quite a story."

Madison took an even deeper swallow of his tonic and asked, "Where to?"

"Illinois . . . I have friends there."

"Sounds interesting," John Madison decided. "I'll share the driving."

Five days later, on February first, the second American Revolution began in East St. Louis, Illinois.

Informational Booklet

For: U.S. Senators and Representatives
Attending the Joint Session of Congress

January 26, 2021

1. *Caesar Box*

Made in Austria 1796
Presented to George Washington & Alexander Hamilton by
      George Washington du Motier, son of Gilbert du Motier
      from the House of Lafayette

Ebony; steel-reinforced; gold-plated etchings on sides
      opened by two different, Bastille keys

      (as pictured)

2. "The King's Promise

Sent to George Washington in Philadelphia during July 1787

The King's Promise

To: George Washington, Esq.

Being that you are reading this, sir, I surmise that you recognize at this time that you need my assistance in restoring civility and order to my former colonies of America. Lord Fairfax of my Privy Council and his nephew, George William Fairfax recently of Virginia, assure me of your good nature and noble character. As with the Roman general, Cincinnatus, you can assuredly lead honorable men once again.

On reading this, please allow that I intend not to be meddlesome but rather to be merely of service to you and your aims. Please communicate the manner of assistance that you might require directly to the Crown. All manner of support is at your disposal.

His Highness, George III of England
Attested by Lord Fairfax   May 1787

3. Sally Cary Fairfax letter to King George III

My dear Royal Highness, Your Excellency, King George

You had raised several questions when last I saw you at Windsor. No doubt you were confused by my news and I trust by this explanation, it will be clearer to you.

I have certain irrefutable knowledge that George Washington, Esquire, former General and the owner of Mount Vernon, Virginia, though childless himself, has a previously unknown direct descendent for his House of Washington.

His niece, Sarah Washington, is the sole surviving daughter of his deceased brother, Lawrence. My dearly departed friend, Anne Fairfax Washington Lee, is her mother.

For important reasons for her personal safety, this Sarah Washington was raised under a pseudonym as Priscilla Farris-Fairfax. She is now known as Priscilla Winfield, the wife of Jonathan Winfield of the Northern Neck in Virginia.

As you asked me recently, kind sir, this should serve to legitimize the person and her family line such that she or her heirs could rightfully serve as an American monarch for your plans.

This is my response to your concerns about whether any such person exists though not by itself a necessary proof.

Your most humble subject,
Sally Cary Fairfax

Attested by Lord Aplington;   Sir Reginald Farrington
Somerset May 1787

4. Pan Atlantic Community Treaty – PACT – of 1795

PAN ATLANTIC COMMUNITY TREATY

Wherein there is a natural and common bond of our peoples across the Atlantic waters and whereas there are clear and present internal dangers roiling all of our Nations positioned along both shores and whereas there is a recognized need for a common, civilized approach to quell those insurrections in any or all of our sovereign States and Kingdoms, we hereby make this treaty of Alliance and mutual Assistance.

The peace and tranquility of America now and in future years is necessary for the Welfare of the entire Atlantic community.

Should this experiment politic of the new American Confederation fail, now or at any time in the future, we of the Europe League pledge to fully assist in the formation of a new Government, a legitimate Monarchy in America.

This PACT thereby will ensure future order in America – order that is so necessary for all of our civilized Nations.

Europe League	*January 1795*
Attested hereby	*Lord Aplington*

George III of England	*House of Hanover*
Louis Charles, dauphin of France and Navarre represented with M. Jean Laurent	*the House of Bourbon*
Catherine of Russia	*the family Romanov*
Francis II of Austria and Tuscany	*the House of Habsburg*
Gustav IV Adolph of Sweden represented with Regent Charles, duke of Sodermanland	*House of Holstein-Gottorp*
Frederick William II of Prussia	*House of Hohenzollern*

5. *Original PATRI Roster –* *As signed in Philadelphia* *February 1797*

George Washington

Philip Schuyler

John Marshall

John Jay

Frederick Reynolds – of Franklin Family

John Adams

Justin Laurens – of Laurens Family

Nathan Greene – of Greene Family

Alexander Hamilton

William Shippen

Robert Morris

Gouverneur Morris

Governor Henry Lee

Henry Knox

William North – in lieu of

Pierre L'Enfant

Baron von Steuben

6. *Lawrence Washington Testament* — *1752*

This is my last testament as dictated for my brother, George Was'.

. . . . . statements of wishes followed by his conclusion . . . .

Finally, I direct my wife Anne her family and my brother, George, to be forever mindful of my only living child, my Sarah.

I go, soon, to join the ages.

When my time comes, Sarah's inheritance must be sure, nearby to our home of Mount Vernon.

Most importantly, she will have my good name, a Washington, too.

Lawrence Washington   May, 1752

7. Selected Genealogy of Sarah Washington

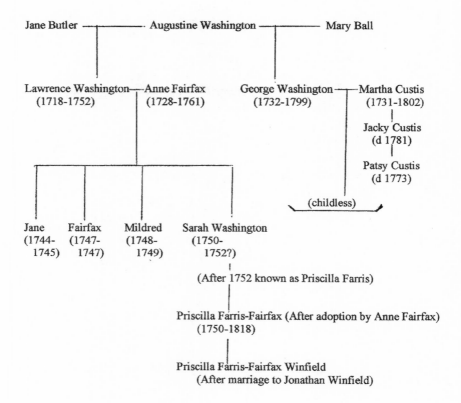

Jane Butler —————— Augustine Washington —————— Mary Ball

Lawrence Washington——Anne Fairfax   George Washington ——Martha Custis
(1718-1752)   (1728-1761)   (1732-1799)   (1731-1802)

Jacky Custis
(d 1781)

Patsy Custis
(d 1773)

(childless)

Jane   Fairfax   Mildred   Sarah Washington
(1744-   (1747-   (1748-   (1750-
1745)   1747)   1749)   1752?)

(After 1752 known as Priscilla Farris)

Priscilla Farris-Fairfax (After adoption by Anne Fairfax)
(1750-1818)

Priscilla Farris-Fairfax Winfield
(After marriage to Jonathan Winfield)

8. George Washington's Letter for the Ages – 1797

I have decided to include herein a copy of the Woodlawn transfer agreement to the Winfields in case there is future dispute . . .

. . . . based on the experience gained as the first President of the United States, I now favor a larger requirement for a strong national executive . . .

. . . . regarding PATRI . . . because of the fractious winds of rebellion seen all around us, I am pleased that such a group (sic PATRI) is now firmly in place . . .

. . . . Should there ever arise circumstances wherein PATRI and the Europe League agree together that the PACT and a transition to an American monarchy is required, Mr. Alexander Hamilton and I have also left in the Caesar Box the necessary proof of Mrs. Priscilla Winfield's legitimacy for the royal house of Washington.

Signed

G Washington   April 1797

9. *Deeds to Mount Vernon* and *Woodlawn/Woodlawn Mills Transfer*

1746 Deed of Mount Vernon

(Originally known as Epsewasson)

This renamed home and lands about belong to

Lawrence Washington, his wife Anne,

And their future survivors (sic).

This new deed shall supersede all others.

May Providence continue to bless this house.

July 1, anno domino 1746

Lawrence Washington

Transfer Settlement at Mount Vernon
Woodlawn Mills   -   Subdivision

As of this date, 22 hectares will be transferred from part of
the property of Mount Vernon to the adjoining Woodlawn estate
which will henceforth be known as Woodlawn Mills.

G Was'	Jonathan Winfield
Martha Washington	Priscilla Winfield
Of Mount Vernon	Of Woodlawn
	June 30, anno domino 1785

10. Maps of Land-Holdings Mount Vernon & Woodlawn Mills thru Years

(10-A)   1754

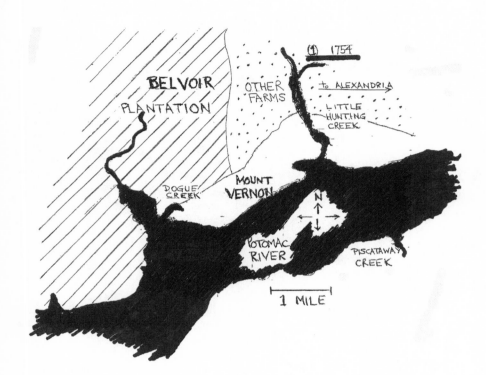

(10-B)   *1754-1760*

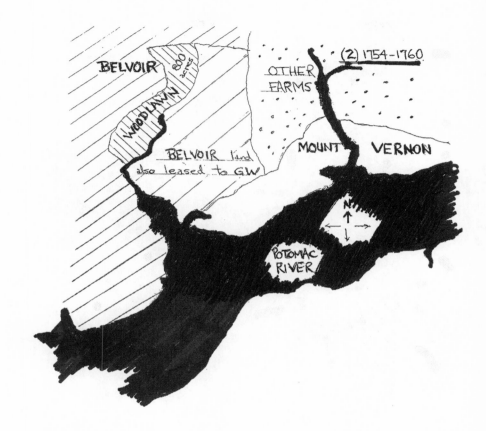

(10-C) 1761-1773

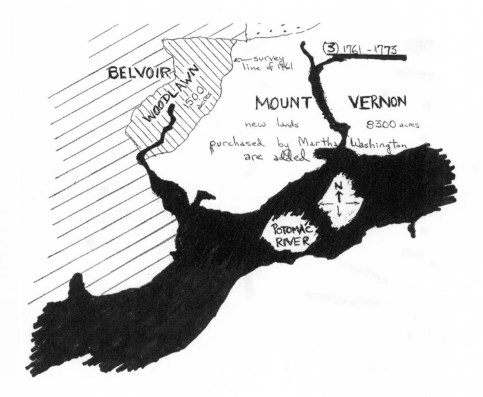

(10-D) 1785-Present

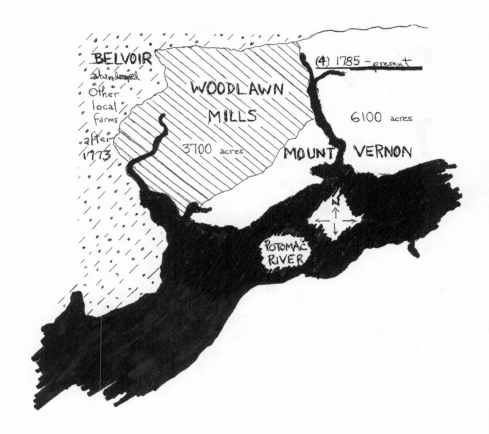

11. *Chinese Porcelain Urn*

With double-fluted, octagonal key

(as pictured)

With three lockets   *1746-1750*

(as pictured)

LW & AW	LW & AW	LW & AW
JW 1744	FW 1747	MW 1748

With hair-wreath   *1746*

(as pictured)

12. *Lacquer Jewelry Box*   *currently owned by Mrs.*
                               Suzanne Winfield

(maintained at Woodlawn Mills)

With double-fluted, octagonal key

(as pictured)

With single locket — 1750/1752

(as pictured)

Front	*Back*
AF	*lw & aw*
1750-PFF-1752	*sw 1750*

13. *DNA Analysis of Washington/Winfield Family-Connection*

(Six tested specimens, results as a graphical printout)

Conclusion: We conclude that the DNA analysis irrefutably establishes a blood-relationship with all six save for Mrs. Suzanne Winfield, date of birth 7/14/77.

As recorded from:
Volker Institute of Zurich; Zurich, Switzerland
Institute of Pasteur; Paris, France
Cell Gen; Silver Springs, Maryland
Date of testing: March 2019

14. Direct Lineage from George Washington to David Winfield

(Extraneous Persons Not Included)

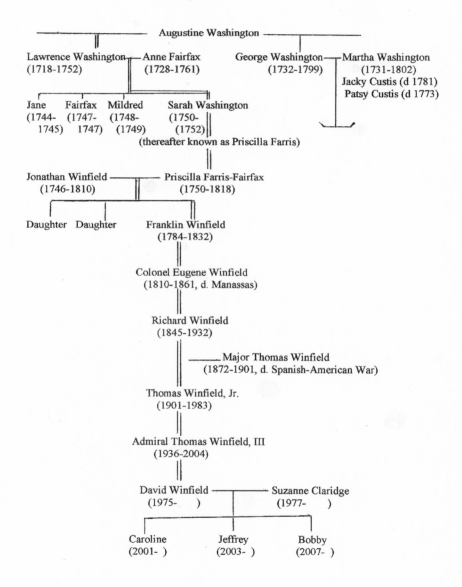

APPENDIX A

PATRI *Membership*   *Past & Present*

1797   *2021*

1797	2021
George Washington	David Winfield
Alexander Hamilton	Evan Hamilton
John Adams	Gayle Eccles
Henry Lee	Philip Lee Mason
Philip Schuyler	Denise Donasti
Frederick Reynolds	Maureen Nightbird-Reynolds
(of the Franklin family)	
John Jay	Karen York
Gouverneur Morris	Leone Gutierrez
William North	Gerald Schubert
(in lieu of Baron von Steuben)	
Robert Morris	Diane Fleming-James
John Marshall	Connie Marshall-Rubin
Henry Knox	Edward Finch
Nathan Greene	Ronald Putney Greene
(of the Nathaniel Greene family)	
Justin Laurens	Robert Laurens
(of the John Laurens family)	
Pierre L'Enfant	Katherine Blitz
Nicholas Shippen	William Shippen

APPENDIX B

Europe League Membership	*Past & Present*
1795	*2021*
George III of England & Lord Aplington (of the Privy Council)	Sir Ronald Farrington, the 14th Lord of Aplington – Kent
Lord Fairfax	Hugh Rochan – London; Dubai
Gilbert du Motier (M. de Lafayette)	Francis du Motier – Aix
M. Talleyrand	Philippe Rouen – Lausanne
Louis Charles – dauphin of France & Navarre	Catherine Bonard – Versailles Maria dela Caves – Barcelona
Catherine of Russia	Elina Romanov-Pederson – St. Petersburg
Francis II of Austria & Tuscany	Marcello Bonapiento – Milan
Frederick William II	Eric Stahlen - Hamburg
Gustav IV Adolph	Olga Frederickson – Stockholm

THE SECOND CONSTITUTION OF THE UNITED STATES

We, the Undersigned members of PATRI, in order to preserve our Country, do ordain this Second Constitution for the United States of America.

Article . I.

The (original) Constitution of the United States, written in 1787 and ratified in 1789, and all current and future Amendments contained therein is and are declared null and void. No such state ratifications are necessary for this succeeding Second Constitution.

Article . II.

The American government consists of the following entities:

Section . 1. The executive power shall be vested in a Monarch who must be a lineage-member of the House of Washington.

The King (or Queen) shall be Commander-in-Chief of the Royal Army and Royal Navy of the United States.

All current Militias of the several States are herein disbanded or placed under Royal discretion.

The King (or Queen) shall ensure that the Pan Atlantic Community Treaty is upheld and that the Alliance with Europe is maintained.

Section . 2. The executive will maintain a Royal Privy Council comprised of all Descendants of the original PATRI as constituted in 1797. The King (or Queen) and Privy Council will determine all Matters of State.

Section . 3. All present democratically chosen Legislative Bodies are herein terminated. Thereupon, any succeeding Elections for all local State and National Representation will be nullified.

Future selection to any Administrative Post will be made only by a grant of the Royal Executive and His (or Her) Privy Council.

Section . 4. All present appointments to the Judiciary are herein terminated. Thereupon, future Justices and other Members of the Courts will be solely appointed by the Supreme Royal Court under the granted approval of the Royal Executive.

Article . III.

Section . 1. The Royal Executive will be Commander-in-Chief of the entire Royal Military.

Section . 2. The term 'Royal' will be used as an adjunctive phrase to any and all United States Military Organizations.

Section . 3. The purpose of the Royal Military will be to ensure domestic tranquility and provide for the Common Defence. The Royal Army and Navy will be commanded by a senior Royal Officer Corps officers of which must be of direct lineage from the Military members of PATRI.

Section . 4. The Royal Privy Council will administer the Royal Military Academies at the interest of the Royal Executive.

Section . 5. There will be separate Departments composed of military task forces, a civil police bureau and a national intelligence administration. A member of the Royal Privy Council will administer each Department.

Article . IV.

Section . 1. The Royal Executive will give an Annual Message to his subjects, the Persons of the United States.

Section . 2. The Second Constitution of the United States requires no ratification by the various States. The Royal Executive acting on the advice of His (or Her) Privy Council will be the sole guarantor of any future Amendments to this Constitution.

It is written and presented on the 25th day of February in the Year of our Lord one thousand seven hundred and Ninety seven and of the Independence of the United States of America the Twenty First. In witness thereof We have hereunto subscribed our Names.

George Washington   Alexander Hamilton

John Jay   Philip Schuyler

Henry Lee   Gouv Morris   John Adams

Signed February 26th, 1797

Robt Morris   Frederick Reynolds

William Shippen   Wm North

J Marshall   Pierre L'Enfant

Henry Knox   Justin Laurens   N. Greene

Signed February 27th, 1797

Newtown PA

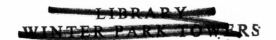
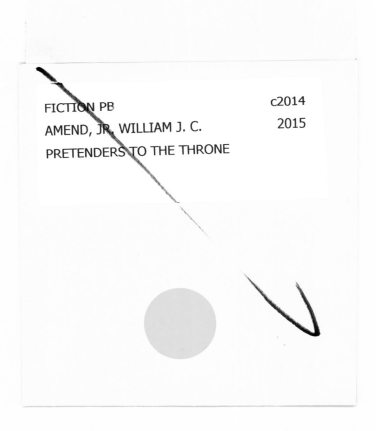

Edwards Brothers Malloy
Oxnard, CA USA
December 23, 2014